EVERY SHADE of HAPPY

T0017717

PHYLLIDA SHRIMPTON

EVERY SHADE of HAPPY

An Aria Book

First published in the UK in 2022 by Head of Zeus
This paperback edition first published in 2023 by Head of Zeus,
part of Bloomsbury Publishing Plc

9 7 5 3 1 2 4 6 8

A CIP catalogue record for this book is
available from the British Library.

ISBN (PB): 9781803281377
ISBN (E): 9781803281346

Typeset by Divaddict Publishing Solutions Ltd
Cover design: Leah Jacobs-Gordon

Printed and bound in Great Britain by
CPI Group (UK) Ltd, Croydon CR0 4YY

Head of Zeus
5–8 Hardwick Street
London EC1R 4RG

WWW.HEADOFZEUS.COM

For my sister Pam
For being the wind beneath my wings

In memory of Peter and Shirley Shrimpton

Thank you to fabulous H,
(the late Helene Dendy Frostick), for lending
me your name. I hope it made you smile.

You were a wonderful lady who touched everyone's
heart and brought happiness to so many people.

PROLOGUE

1929

ALGERNON

Algernon's feet, constricted by brand-new leather shoes, dangled a good two inches above a bare wooden floor where he sat. The narrow bed, metal-framed and identical in every way to all the others in the dormitory, sagged wearily beneath him, and a coarse woollen over-blanket made the back of his legs itch. A single pillow, where he was to lay his head that night, whispered to him of other schoolboys' nightmares still caught inside its cotton slip.

Algernon's bony knees, poking out from black flannel shorts, sported ruddy brown grazes which peppered their way over the bulge of his kneecaps before disappearing into the carefully folded cuffs of his new grey socks. Dragging a nail along the skin of his right leg he gathered a line of pinprick scabby crusts, which, when bringing his finger up close to his face, he was able to examine closely. Each one, he thought, was a beautiful relic of the life he'd left behind. He flicked the debris from his nail onto the floor and watched how a single tear of blood trickled down his shin before rather satisfyingly staining the cuff of his new grey socks. His knees told of a very recent and daringly triumphant act of bravery and for a brief, liberating moment Algernon indulged himself in the memory of it.

His fingers curled tightly around the railings of his village school and his face pressed against the cold, black iron. He was on the outside looking in. A ball, accidentally kicked onto the roof of the school, had wedged itself in the dip between the gables and the chimney and his friends were all looking up at it, defeated by the problem. Being the most adventurous of boys Algernon had, quick as a flash, climbed over the railings and scaled the side wall knowing every inch of it as he did. Having officially left the little school only the day before, he was trespassing now of course but finding himself back on the right side of the railings once again a delicious sense of familiar belonging lifted his heavy heart. In his mind he was shinning up the drainpipe, the rough brick catching his hands until he reached the chimney stack and clung to it.

Two boys staged a fight to distract the schoolmaster while a gathering of upturned faces waited for the ball. He tossed it down to them. Still clinging to the chimney stack he tilted his face until he could feel the fresh wind against his cheeks. From his vantage point he could see past the village and out across an expanse of glorious fields, each patchworking their way towards the shores of the River Fal and an overwhelming need to fly gripped his soul.

Algernon stared at his knees, at the evidence of his ungraceful dismount from the roof into a surprisingly deep puddle where he was treated like a hero by his friends. The story they told belonged to yesterday. Yesterday he had said goodbye. Yesterday he was free to run wild in the green fields of Cornwall. Yesterday he was a child. Today, according to his parents and the sign above the entrance to his new private boarding school, Algernon Edward Maybury, aged seven years, was now a young Catholic gentleman.

God, Algernon had noticed, was in the very architecture of his new school, resplendent in arches and glorious through stained glass windows and His only son hung flogged and bleeding from a cross on seemingly every wall. God, however, felt entirely different in this place where his heart now quivered inside his skinny chest. Algernon's God was in his church back in Cornwall where every Sunday a congregation of familiar faces coughed and rustled through hymns and the Divine Liturgy. Algernon's God asked that everyone wore their best clothes to church and greeted each other with a smile on the way in. At Algernon's church the priest always had a precarious dewdrop on the end of his nose and Mrs Dyer, the organist, had an enormous bottom that always made him and his friends laugh behind their hymn books when they weren't having their wrists slapped for being more interested in the contents of their nose than the word of Our Lord. Crying babies were jiggled in their mothers' arms and the air smelt of incense and the promise of Sunday luncheon.

This new God was different. The air in this building, this school where Algernon now sat on the narrow bed, was heavy with a thousand secrets all spiralling silently among the dust motes and hiding behind the eyes of the Brothers who held the futures of all one hundred and sixteen schoolboys in their care. Algernon knew that despite God or because of God, he wasn't sure which, this place was not a happy place.

He also understood that from now on he could no longer expect to be called Algernon. He would, as his father informed him in the brief minutes between decanting his son from his Austin motorcar and hauling his huge school trunk from the boot of the car onto the drive, now be addressed by his surname 'Maybury'. His father also informed him that he would excel in class, be victorious in the sports field, and take it on the chin when a likely drubbing were to come his way. Algernon had nodded sombrely and wordlessly while his mother had simply smiled encouragingly, her earlobes stretched and wobbling from the huge pearls that hung heavily from them. His parents then climbed back inside their car offering final stiff-upper-lipped farewells and casting promises through the open window to see him in a few weeks' time.

Algernon clenched his fingers tightly until his knuckles turned white and he craned his head towards the open leaded windows of the dormitory. If he willed them hard enough his parents might change their minds and return for him. The long drive outside, which led all the way to the huge iron gates, remained heart-breakingly empty. The overwhelming desire to fly away filled him to the brim and he wished with all his heart that he could climb onto the windowsill, grow wings and soar high into the clouds.

Echoes of the voices of other boys bounced across the dorm, along cold corridors and out from shadows. They told of pecking orders and alarming rites of passage that made Algernon... rather *Maybury* feel so terribly small. He didn't cry, not then at least, but cast his gaze down towards his own, unpacked trunk and breathed in air that smelt of fear. When at last he understood that his parents most definitely would not be returning for him, he squeezed his small hands tightly together and prayed to his God back home that the school holidays would come quickly so that he could leave this place and return to the fields, the rivers and the beautiful craggy coastline of Cornwall where he belonged.

1

And Then There Were Three

2019

ALGERNON

Algernon glanced at his carriage clock. The steady tick of its mechanism nudged its delicate gold hands to 5.28pm, telling him that it was nearly time for his ready meal and another cup of tea, virtually the highlight of his whole day. That hideous thing had marked time ever since the day of his retirement when it was handed over with a handshake and a smattering of applause, followed by cheap filter coffee, a plate of fondant fancies and a hasty escape by everyone attending. He'd hated it then and he hated it now but he just couldn't bring himself to throw it away. It would be like throwing away each of the thirty-nine years he'd worked for the Corporation. He had kept it, punishing himself daily with the fact that the sum total of his worth was a gaudy mechanical device, encased in glass, which told him with audible regularity that he had one less second to live.

A shard of evening sunlight sliced across the room, highlighting dust motes that circled aimlessly outside his field of vision before landing in a golden stripe upon the empty armchair opposite him. He bruised himself further by forcing his gaze to rest in the light where it pooled upon the tartan fabric. Cat sauntered into the room and wound his way round Algernon's legs, pressing a warm cheek against his shin and giving a sharp 'eck' to get his attention. Tearing his gaze away from the empty chair Algernon gave both the animal and his clock a cursory glance, never ceasing to be amazed by the accuracy of the cat's inner clock. It was now exactly 5.30pm.

'Cupboard love,' he grumbled, fumbling for his stick and heaving himself out of his chair, knees creaking and hot pains shooting across his shoulders and down his arms. Cat trotted towards the door turning to give another insistent 'eck' as Algernon straightened into an upright position and headed towards the kitchen to make their mutual evening meals. By 6pm they were both ingesting something vaguely unappealing but nutritionally robust if nothing else.

Then Algernon's phone rang. Algernon's phone never rang.

ANNA

For Anna, losing everything was a sudden thing. It had happened the moment her mother's partner, Harry, made a declaration of genuinely surprising and apparently insuppressible love for the man who fixed the coffee machine at his place of work. Harry, at the age of fifty-three, had finally found someone who could make his life complete but, in doing so, he'd managed to scatter the entire contents of both Anna's and her mother's comfortable lives in one swift, highly emotional confession.

They'd been watching *The Great British Bake Off* when it happened. Apparently, the perfect moment to destroy their lives was the final stage of the biscuit Show Stopper and it couldn't even wait until the end of the show. Anna's mother Helene had been horrified by what she was hearing, swinging between unrestrained anger and total disbelief. 'I thought it was just the male menopause,' she'd sniffed, wiping the flats of her hands across her damp eyes and cheeks once her initial outburst had abated. 'You know… why you're always so… *bland*… in the bedroom department. Lights off, unenthusiastic and quite frankly, unrewarding fumbling…'

Anna, who'd been curled in a large tan leather armchair, her face already flushed with the shock of Harry's announcement and the ensuing row, had made a show of blocking her ears. '*Overshare*!' she'd complained, forcing the grisly details of her mother's sex life out of her mind.

Shooting a red-eyed glance at her, Helene had jerked her head in the direction of Harry. 'I'm sorry, Anna, but we've been together for *six* years and now he's running off into the sunset with a man called *Derek*! I've a right to be pissed off, don't you think?' Harry had passed round a box of tissues and all of them, including Harry, had taken one, each dabbing at their tear-stained faces and blowing their noses, their hearts pounding in their throats over what should happen next. The stark reality of exactly what was about to happen next had hit Anna in the very next moment, when she'd realised with awful certainty that the ground beneath her was about to fall entirely away.

'Technically speaking *I'm* not doing the running.' Harry had sniffed offering a genuinely apologetic glance at Anna, rushing his words under his breath in a failed effort to make them less wounding. 'Derek will be moving in with me. This...' He'd cleared his throat and paused with discomfort '... is *my* house.' Regardless of Harry's efforts at empathetic delivery, his words had plopped like cow shit into the centre of the room splashing in the faces of both Anna and her mother.

'So how is your application for the Diplomatic Corps coming along?' Helene had growled at him. 'You could have given us at least five minutes to process the boyfriend thing before landing us with eviction!' She'd reached for the box of tissues again, snatching at several more before throwing the half-empty box at Harry who'd let it bounce off his head with barely a flinch. Knowing her mother all too well and that she would shortly be searching for more missiles to throw, Anna had uncurled herself from the armchair, removed the fruit bowl from the table in front of them, placed it on the sideboard and quietly left the room.

Lying on a spray of stars printed on a black cotton duvet cover she'd pushed her earphones into each ear to drown out the sound of the continuing one-sided argument going on downstairs. She'd heard enough. Her mother declaring that she barely earned enough on her own to rent even the smallest flat in the area and how they'd both starve now and why the *fuck* didn't he know he wanted to bat for the other side six years ago before they first got together?

Wiping at the hot tears that ran down her cheeks, Anna had tried desperately to cope with the idea that her mother and Harry were about to part ways. Harry was pretty decent as people go and his cooking was amazing, but it wasn't like he was her father or anything. She'd never known who her father was because her mother, as it happened, hadn't known either. Her conception sixteen years ago was just her mother's hazy recollection of a wild night out ending in Jägerbombs and a one-night stand. Anna had always generously insisted that not knowing her father was OK by her, as she'd reasoned how can you miss what you never had? When the security of her life was eroding rapidly away, however, she'd found herself to be unexpectedly angry about it. A father, she was sure, wouldn't so easily have cast her adrift as Harry was about to do.

Her bedroom, her own space, her own place since they'd moved in with Harry six years ago, had suddenly become frighteningly temporary. She'd imagined what her room might look like when it was empty of all her belongings. Empty of everything except for the huge mural she'd painted on the opposite wall. Harry had once given her carte blanche to express herself artistically in whatever way she chose and as a result the entire wall had been taken up by a huge silhouette of herself sitting in the crescent of a silver moon, holding the string of a bright red kite. She'd painted the ceiling black and pressed glow-in-the-dark stars and planets into the black-paint sky until her bedroom transformed into a beautiful, private universe. Her universe. That night though, Anna had stared at her painting for a very long time until, sleepy with silent tears, she'd imagined herself letting go of the bright red kite and tumbling from her moon into a dark unknown abyss below.

ALGERNON

Algernon wasn't sure how he felt about the telephone call. He'd spent years inside a tidy box created by his own mind. It was neither awful nor lovely in there. It was just where he happened to be. Each day was like the last, governed by a need to wash, to dress, to eat and to feed Cat, who he'd never invited to live with him in the first place and yet had sauntered in unannounced three years prior making himself a permanent guest.

Each day Algernon walked to the shop for his newspaper, listened to the news on the radio, then made a valiant attempt at completing *The Times* crossword which, to his intense but private shame, he managed less often these days. He would always have an afternoon nap and later, after a supper prepared at exactly 5.30pm, he would watch the news probably followed by a detective series on television. Each activity was marked or perhaps dictated by the carriage clock on his mantelpiece and that was just the way it was. If he were to hold a conversation with himself, Algernon might admit to having been more than skilled in the art of creating tidy boxes in which to place the various stages of his life. He was unlikely, however, to hold a conversation with himself. He was unlikely to hold a conversation with anyone, being a man of so few words as he was.

Until the phone call, Algernon had been pretty sure that each tomorrow would be like each of his todays and the yesterdays before that until he passed off this mortal coil. Now, however, he found that he was to be expecting guests and his head jangled with anticipation over the very thought of them coming to stay in his house.

His house, as it happened, was rather unusual for the area in which he lived. It had two small bedrooms upstairs, one double, one single and two very large rooms downstairs plus a small kitchen. There were three chairs in the small kitchen, six chairs around the dining room table and two armchairs in the sitting room either side of the chimney breast where an electric bar fire burned a patch of red lace on his legs on cold winter evenings. Nothing had changed in his house since Evie had died and Helene had left, except for the fact that some time back he'd got rid of a large old sofa, which was surplus to requirements, and that Cat had knocked an ornament off the mantelpiece causing it to break upon the hearth. The ornament, a porcelain basket brimming with tiny porcelain flowers had been carefully repaired by Algernon, the fine lines of glue hardly visible, a wad of Blu-Tack now holding it securely back in place. The rest of the house was orderly to the point of fastidiousness and that was how he wished it to stay.

ANNA

When, during the original row with Harry, Helene had complained that she couldn't afford to rent a flat in the area, Anna hadn't appreciated the true extent as to exactly what that would mean in terms of her own situation. Not only did it mean that she had to leave her private painted universe behind in her bedroom, it meant she would also have to leave her school, her city and all her friends. The stability of her life cruelly unravelled around her, the shreds of it catching on the wind, flying too wildly for her to gather back in.

In the end Harry had given them five weeks to sort out somewhere to live, an offer he'd believed to be entirely generous yet in reality had simply not been long enough for them to find any kind of suitable alternative. As a result, Anna now sat in the passenger seat of her mother's car, full to the brim with their belongings, while she attempted to prepare herself for a three-hundred-mile journey to another life. Those five weeks had been way too brief and too painfully precious, each event with her friends ultimately becoming her last. The last time they went to the cinema together, the last time they hung out in the park or at each other's houses and then, finally, the last time they hugged each other goodbye. The familiarity of her city, its buildings, houses, parks and shopping centres were sadly soon to be far behind her.

Now, the only tangible friend in Anna's world, if you could call it that, was Gary, her cactus, whose pot she now clutched on her lap for want of any other space in the car to put him. Harry had given him to her as a leaving present, along with a soft blue blanket and an extensive collection of make-up. He'd presented the blanket first, the heavy hint of apology in his eyes. 'Your comfort blanket. Soft as an evening cloud,' he'd said, wrapping it round her shoulders, while her mother had tutted audibly and rolled her eyes.

Next, from behind the sofa, he'd produced a large cactus. 'I got you this because I know they're a *thing* these days. It's a fine example of a *Parodia magnifica*… the hot air balloon of cacti.' He'd proudly held it towards her and she'd reached for it, causing the blanket to slide off her shoulders into a heap on the floor. The cactus, planted in a glazed pot of similar green, was made up of segments, like a chocolate orange, each segment edged with prickles. Anna had decided instantly that it was a botanical representation of the way she felt, and she'd reached to touch it with the pad of her index finger. Harry had picked the blanket up from the floor where it had landed and proceeded to fold it again. 'Careful of the spines though, sweetheart – they cause irritation if they come into contact with you.'

'Then we understand each other,' Anna had replied.

'These things are just gift-wrapped sticking plasters,' Helene had objected. 'They're hardly going to make up for you wrecking her entire life.'

'I shall call him Gary,' Anna had said.

Harry hadn't reacted to Helene but had calmly placed the blanket on the sofa. 'Gary it is then… and now put him down for the moment, because here…' He'd beamed at Anna while Helene had given another exaggerated eye roll, showing the whites of her eyes for so long that Anna had thought they might have got stuck there '… I have the pièce de résistance of sticking plasters.' He'd winked at Anna and reaching behind the sofa again, had brought out a large package wrapped in beautiful multicoloured paper, tied with a multicoloured ribbon.

Offering no reaction to his conspiratorial wink Anna had ripped open the package without the ceremony he may have hoped for. As the paper dropped to the floor, she'd found herself trying hard not to show her genuine pleasure at what she'd held in her hands. Inside a beautiful silver case were palettes and pots of make-up plus an array of brushes, all from a particular brand that she knew was massively expensive. There was also a box of the special body-art pens she'd coveted for a very long time having had to resort to biro or felt pen to create delicate artwork on her skin. She'd stared silently at her wonderful gift while both love and anger had raged inside her. Placing a hand on each of her shoulders Harry had stooped to look her in the eye, speaking softly as he did so. 'I got you this last gift so that you can truly express how very unique you are.'

'You can't be *very* unique. You're either unique or you aren't,' Helene sniped. She'd then left the room in a display of annoyance, leaving Harry to hug Anna tightly for the very last time.

'Go be who *you* are,' he'd urged as he rested his chin on the top of her head. During that hug she'd felt the last seconds of life with Harry melt away making her push the flats of her hands against him, as she fought the urge to beat his chest with her fists.

'Stop being so *nice* when I want to hate you!' she'd said, her words gurgling through the tears in her throat. He was not her father, he was just her mother's ex-boyfriend but she'd known, in that moment, she had loved him all the same.

ALGERNON

Algernon knew he hadn't been an ideal father in the eyes of his small family. In fact, he knew with certainty that his view of parenthood had been at total loggerheads with theirs and so, unable to find a mutually agreeable line of action for raising a child in a modern era, he'd admitted defeat. When Helene was just a young child, he'd willingly handed the primary role of raising her over to Evie and breathed an inner sigh of relief. He only had one template for raising a child and that was the one his parents had used on him, a template that consisted of strict boundaries and rigid rules that Algernon had been unable to transgress.

Evie and Helene were able to see life in an entirely different way from anything he was used to. They had always skipped and twirled their way through each day as if nothing he'd been taught in his own upbringing could be of any consequence to them. Life to them was something light and frivolous, which should not be taken too seriously. As a result of his letting go of the parenting strings, however, he had subsequently spent many of Helene's formative years believing that his stricter ideas of raising a child may have been sadly correct. Life, as it happened, did have consequences. Helene, whose mind was as sharp as anyone's, if not sharper as far as he was concerned, did not excel at school. She gave up learning the piano, much to his disappointment, and Evie had simply let her.

'If she doesn't get on with it, Algernon, she shouldn't be forced into it,' Evie had said. 'Our child isn't a natural musician,' she'd added, when after the piano the idea of learning the violin was enthusiastically embraced by Helene yet abandoned after only a few short weeks. Algernon had not been quite so disappointed about his daughter's disregard for the violin as he had over the piano, having suffered many an evening listening to a sound akin to that of a cat being strangled. 'She hates long-distance running... as did I,' Evie had defended when Helene was reported by the school to be strolling in at the last and having a leisurely chat with the other stragglers as she did so. 'She's at *that* age,' Evie indulged, when Helene was discovered playing truant in town.

So it went on. Helene drifted and weaved her way uncertainly across the years, through university, in and out of multiple jobs, plunging headfirst into various relationships, leaving home and always returning again when everything went awry. Then sixteen years ago Helene had delivered her final crushing blow as she stood in front of himself and Evie and announced the fact that she was pregnant. No husband, no boyfriend, no future. Algernon had thrown up his arms in dismay as years of suppressed frustration bubbled over and released itself, gushing out from inside with such force as a whale spouts water. Evie had cried, Helene had cried, and Algernon had ranted until the air that circled around inside the little house grew heavy with wasted opportunities.

ANNA

As they now reversed out of the drive for the last time, the air cloudy and blue with the early dawn light, Anna stared up at the house they were leaving behind. *Go be who you are,* Harry had said. She supposed that was what he had done. He'd gone to be who he wanted to be and although she knew she shouldn't blame him for that she couldn't forgive him for it either. He was on solid ground while she and her mother now trod a precariously flimsy path.

Harry had most probably heard them leave yet he hadn't come to the door, or even to an upstairs window. His goodbyes belonged to yesterday; *he* belonged to yesterday. Her family had been built on straw, blown too easily away in a single breeze. *And then there were two,* she thought sadly. In her head she imagined getting her mother to stop the car so that she could run back to Harry and demand of him, *How can you be who you are when you don't even know where you're going?*

ALGERNON

Algernon searched his mind for anything in there that might be out of place, anything that might jar or jangle his thought processes more than they already were. The last five weeks had been difficult to say the least and he was exhausted by all the goings-on and the upheaval of his usual routine. Having discovered, at the age of seven, that it was possible to put lids on things that were difficult to tackle, he now found himself facing another such situation. He'd always been rather proud of himself for discovering and honing his mental survival tactic and was not pleased when Evie had challenged him, in the early days of their relationship, saying that his ability to distance himself from sensitive matters wasn't at all healthy. She'd told him that it was as if he looked at life through his fingers. The organisation of his mind was the only matter in which Evie had trespassed and Algernon made it sternly clear to her that his psychological make-up would never be a subject for discussion.

Five weeks ago, however, the lid on the box he'd long since put his daughter in had come off and without Evie to deal with it, he knew he had to cope alone. Having survived into his nineties in his own way Algernon knew that he wasn't at all skilled at revisiting his past.

ANNA

Anna had been silent for most of the journey, allowing the humming of the car on the seemingly endless motorways to lull her into a temporary sense of calm. She'd rammed her earphones in almost as soon as they set off, her playlist filling her mind, the rhythmical beat and story behind the lyrics nursing the ache of sadness inside her. Her phone had vibrated with messages first thing that morning, her entire friendship group offering wishes and sympathies. As the journey grew longer, she'd imagined them disappearing from view, like people on films who stand on the shore waving as the ship carrying their loved ones sails over the horizon. Everyone was making promises to keep in touch, to come for the weekend or spend holidays together but she'd feared that such promises were all too desperately fragile, the distance too great to make them a reality.

After a brief breakfast stop and then a horribly uncomfortable sleep where the strap of the seatbelt carved a deep groove into her cheek, she stirred and stretched, pausing her playlist when a sign ahead of them told her they were near their destination. A flock of jitters took flight in her chest, the tiny wings of them brushing against her ribs. 'That sign says we're only ten miles away.' She pulled out her earphones and looked at the scenery that belonged to their new destination. Scenery that seemed far too wide and sparse and nothing like the dense urban skyline of home. She'd felt at home in the city, hugged by its vibrancy and by the closeness of everything. Here the scanty landscape that stretched endlessly before her made her feel vulnerable and exposed.

'Yes,' Helene answered, her tone one of glum resignation as they broke away from the motorway and turned left off a roundabout.

'Tell me he doesn't live right in the middle of all this nothing?' Anna moodily took in the tedious canvas of farm fields, which were now the only things that lay between them and their destination.

'He lives in a very small town… only a few shops, no leisure centre… part-time cinema, that kind of thing. On the plus side, it's surrounded by all this beautiful *nothing* rather than the urban jungle we're used to.'

'Boring then!' Anna said, feeling quietly irked that her own appreciation of city life should be so readily dismissed. She didn't want a new life, the old one in the urban jungle had been just fine.

'It will be what you make it,' Helene replied. 'Try to approach this with a positive attitude.'

'Like you are?' Anna managed to surprise even herself with the barely veiled aggression that had suddenly issued forth from her mouth. The meltdown Helene had displayed back at home when she'd finally admitted there were no options left to them other than to contact her father, Anna's grandfather, was still a frighteningly vivid memory.

'I've had to go cap-in-bloody-hand back to my dad at my age and it's all *your* shitting fault!' Helene had spat each word accusingly, jabbing the phone angrily in Harry's direction as he put on his coat and picked up his keys to make his hasty escape. Harry hated confrontation. Stunned at what she was hearing Anna had turned from his apologetic expression to her mother's angry red face.

'Your *dad*?' Anna had been extremely surprised to hear that her mother had contacted the grandfather she'd never seen. 'I thought we... *I* wasn't to have anything to do with him?'

'You weren't. You will now though, thanks to *him*.' Helene had jabbed the phone in Harry's direction again as he quietly shut the door behind himself.

'But... you said you fell out when you got pregnant with me... *because* you got pregnant with me. You said he didn't want to know about me...' Anna's heart had raced at what her mother was suggesting and she'd begun to feel slightly nauseous at the idea of it.

'I did say that, yes.' Helene had placed the phone quietly

down on the table and sighed, looking back at her daughter with a look of sad defeat clear upon her face. 'But we have no option I'm afraid.'

'And he's *suddenly* all right with this, is he?' Anna had asked.

'Well, it's hard to tell from the limited conversation we had but I'd say he sounds exactly the same as he always did about everything.' Helene's answer had been ambiguous and Anna had felt confused.

'Which is?' She'd waited expectantly, watching a downturned smile curl its way towards Helene's chin.

'Cold!' Hardly had the word left her lips though, when Helene had raised her eyebrows, her bitter defeat suddenly switching to decided positivity. 'But, amazingly, he agreed that we could *both* move in with him until we can find a more suitable alternative, so that's good, isn't it?'

'Whoopee,' Anna had said flatly. 'When do we go... I can hardly wait?'

The car slowed at another roundabout where they waited for a gap in the traffic and Anna found that, now they were so close, she was becoming even more agitated by the uncertainty of new beginnings and the stirrings of hidden truths. Suddenly, the few old family photos her mother had dug out showing a severe-looking old man whose moustache dominated his face, a pleasant-looking grandmother and Helene looking much younger, wasn't enough. The town where he lived and the age that he was, wasn't enough. 'I want to know more about him, this man who wasn't interested in his own grandchild.' Anna turned to her mother, noticing a deep crease appearing on her brow as she scanned the road for an opportunity to pull out. Helene waited for a van to pass then put her foot down on the accelerator and pulled out, indicating to take the first exit.

'He's old and he's called Algernon,' she replied unhelpfully, checking her rear-view mirror.

'I know that already. If anyone asked me what my mum was like I'd have plenty more to tell them than you're old and you're called Helene.' Anna's frustration was palpable, caught as she was in the tangled yarn of her own family history.

'*H*.' Her mother glanced at her briefly before looking again at the road ahead. 'The only person who ever called me Helene was my dad. So, if you're going to tell anyone about me you can tell them I'm called *H*.'

'OK, I'll tell them you're old and you're called "H". And what do I call Algernon? Shall I call him A or Alg?' Anna watched how the expression on her mother's face transformed to one of horror and it made her grin.

'Good God no you can't do that! He'd go mad. You'll have to call him Grandfather or Grandad I suppose... to be honest I don't know what you should call him when he was so unreasonably opinionated about how you came into the world... but definitely don't call him "A". He's got a limited sense of humour and it will really rattle his cage.'

'I was joking.' Anna sighed, the grin sliding from her lips.

'We're doing all right for time. I told him we'd be there for half past eleven and I think we will and it's just as well because he always was, and probably still is, a stickler for time. We'll only start off by annoying him if we're late.' Helene was becoming noticeably taut, biting down on her lip and nervously checking the clock on the dashboard. Anna turned her attention back to the world outside the car where a field of bright yellow had appeared in amongst the nothing. Surprised by the unexpected intensity of colour in the middle of all the browns and greens she fantasised about falling into it, absorbing its brightness into the dark and scary crevices of her mind. As they left the field behind, a large cottage appeared to the left, set back off the road, little dark windows peeking out from under the overhang of heavy grey thatch and a gathering of chickens appeared pecking at the ground from behind a muddy tractor and an old caravan blooming with moss. 'Go on then, what else would you tell people about me?' Helene asked.

'I'd tell them *H* wanted to know good things about herself yet couldn't be bothered to tell me much about my own grandfather before forcing me to live with him.' She lifted her phone to her face and took a fed-up-face selfie, posting it forward to her friendship group. The outside world came and went for another two miles before Helene eventually spoke again.

'You're right, I'm not being fair, except… to tell you the truth, I don't know much about him myself. He is not a talker, as you will probably find out, and he rarely shared anything about himself so I can only guess that there isn't much to tell. I only know snippets, really.'

'And the snippets are…?' Anna focused on the world outside the car window while she waited patiently to hear anything that might help her build up a picture of him.

'So… your grandfather was a manager in a big company where he'd worked for absolutely ever. He liked to play chess, do crosswords and other similarly mind-numbingly boring pastimes. He and my mum worked a lot in the garden, rarely went out or on holiday and what they saw in each other I'll never know. They were different in every way.' Anna spotted another farmhouse where a collection of old black barns rose like rotten and broken teeth in the land beside it. A child's swing and slide set was in the garden and a dog roamed aimlessly between the barns. *Apocalyptic,* she thought silently.

'My mum was a great cook; she was funny and warm and gentle and…' Anna groaned loudly, stopping her in mid-flow. She was quite sure that her grandma had been wonderful and wished more than anything that it was her and not her grandfather who was going to greet her shortly, but sadly that wasn't the case.

'*Mum*! Can you stick to telling me about the grandparent who's still alive please… the one I'm going to meet any minute *now*?'

Helene flicked the indicator and waited for traffic to pass so she could turn right. 'OK, I'm trying! It's not easy though. It was so hard growing up with my dad and his strict ideals. He was, still is I assume, old-fashioned with his principles. He's the no-sex-before-marriage type… which is why we ended up arguing about you in the first place. He likes to dress formally; he demands good manners, disapproves of swearing… unless he's the one doing it, doesn't drink much other than a good whisky, and on top of all that he probably votes Conservative. Otherwise, he's basically a monosyllabic old man whose only claim to fame is that he's managed to make it into his tenth decade without dying.'

'He sounds awesome and more than old-fashioned… positively prehistoric and… *burger and fries*!' A giant sign came into view at the side of the road and Anna pointed hopefully at it, feeling a sense of dismay as Helene shook her head and glanced pointedly at the clock on the dashboard again.

'You ate enough crap when we stopped at the services earlier and talking of your grandfather being a "stickler for time" we'll end up being late if we stop again.'

'What does it matter if we're late?' Anna said, wistfully pressing her finger against the glass. 'We're already fifteen years too late.' They looked at each other then, a world of silent reasoning taking place behind their eyes.

'Oh, sod it!' Helene yanked the steering wheel sharply round to the left, pulled into the drive-thru and came to a halt at a speaker system next to a menu board. Then she grinned at Anna as if such a simple action might now be full of mischievous daring. The bag of food, when it came, smelt of grease and salt and borrowed time. 'My parents had me obscenely late in life,' Helene continued, mid-mouthful of a jammy apple pie. 'I apparently surprised them way after they'd given up trying.' She paused momentarily before she took another bite, seemingly juggling private thoughts inside her mind. 'I was their one and only child. The sole focus of their divided attention. My mum indulged me, and my dad... well, he didn't. I grew up in an era he didn't understand. Even though I had my own flat by the time I got pregnant with you, he said I was "a floozy and an embarrassment to the family".' Anna gave a sudden burst of laughter at the thought of her mother being a *floozy*, and Helene joined in. 'I was in my thirties for God's sake. I'd been a floozy and an embarrassment for years before you came along.'

'I don't suppose not having a clue who my dad was helped your cause though?' Anna lifted the top half of her burger bun and placed fries on top of a lifeless slice of waxy cheese.

'Well, yes. It wasn't my finest hour to be honest. My biggest regret in life though, isn't that I got pregnant with you... never that... but that my mum died before she could meet you. It's all so unfair. Then because my dad was such an arse over it all, he never got to meet you either. He never got to see how lovely you are... *most* of the time.' She pulled a wry smile, trying to inject a little humour into the conversation but, reminded of her grandfather's old-fashioned principles, Anna's sense of humour had slipped back down her throat where it landed in her half-digested food.

'What if he hates me?' she said. 'Nothing has changed since you told him about being pregnant with me. As far as he's concerned I'm still... you know...'

'A bastard?' Helene raised an amused eyebrow.

'Funny. I was going to say illegitimate.' On any other day Anna would have laughed but today was not the day for such jokes. Her mother, serious now, reached out and took her chin gently in her hand, turning her face until they were looking at each other.

'He won't hate you, Anna. You are funny and kind and beautiful. No one could hate you.'

ALGERNON

Algernon fidgeted with his tie, the fancy green one with the red spots, received countless years ago as a Christmas tree present from his daughter. Having anticipated, for most of the morning, the sound of the heavy brass knocker against the peeling varnish of his oak front door, he was unsettled to the point of rattling his dentures. Threaded through the teeth of his comb were several white hairs from his preparatory grooming and the carriage clock was telling him with steady inevitability that it was nearly time.

At 11.29am he swept a rheumy gaze around his house, at its absolute orderliness, its comfortable familiarity, then he sighed heavily as the ghosts of his past stepped aside to make way for his imminent future. It had been a while since Helene had last phoned to check up on him, the atmosphere between them having been seemingly irreparably fractured. Once, a long time ago, she had brought the child with her and left her still strapped in a child's car seat in the back of her car. He'd caught a glimpse of a woollen hat and a chubby hand but that was all. His own stupidity had lassoed him, holding him back from any kind of moral surrender, tethering him to his own awkwardness. Helene had never repeated this peace offering, and Algernon had never relented.

The anticipated knock, however, did not happen at 11.30am. Nor did it happen at 11.31am or 11.32am and by 11.52am, a full twenty-two minutes after their proposed agreement, Algernon had become quite discombobulated.

ANNA

'I suppose the days of listening to loud music in my bedroom are gone then?' Anna made a cloud of her own breath on the window and drew a sad face in the steam. Helene looked at the time on the car dash, jumped a little and screwed up the apple-pie wrapper before pressing it into the pocket of the car door.

'*Shit*, there's late and then there's really late!' She turned the ignition on and released the handbrake. 'And you don't have a bedroom don't forget. We're sharing my old bedroom and to be honest I have no idea what we will or won't be able to do.' She shot out of the parking space then immediately stepped on the brake pedal so hard that last-minute loose bits rammed precariously in the car shunted forwards. Gary toppled over, his spines prickling Anna's fingers as she caught him in her lap. 'Imbecile!' Helene gave two angry fingers to the heedless driver who drove past in his van, a double cheeseburger pressed halfway into his open mouth. Anna brushed her lap with the flat of her hand, sending a spray of soil and a stray chip onto the floor of the car.

'Calm down, Mum,' she begged, instinctively feeling how the atmosphere in the car had abruptly changed, swelling until it felt as if it were squeezing her from the outside in. 'Why are you so worried about a few minutes?'

'I'm worried because he's a stickler for time and we've just stolen some of it from him.' Helene roared out of the services car park and down the road while the nerves jiggled in Anna's stomach and churned amongst her food. When a miserable-looking high street came into view, they silently appraised each building that came and went as they drove slowly by: a convenience store, a betting shop, a hairdresser, three charity shops, a greasy spoon café, an Indian restaurant and two pubs.

'It hasn't changed much, the old hometown,' Helene commented, while Anna wished with renewed intensity that Harry had never met Derek and that her world had never changed. *There's nothing here,* she thought, panic and disappointment squeezing her eyes shut, forcing unbidden tears to bead upon her lashes.

'We'll have a new start when I get a job. Just you and me, hey?' Helene, sensitive to her daughter's disappointment, reached out again and squeezed her arm while Anna drew the pad of her thumb across her eyes, attempting to collect her tears before they fell.

Promise? she wanted to say, but the request was stuck in her throat. Perhaps, she thought hopefully, they *would* get a flat of their own soon and they would leave this awful place, maybe move back closer to home so she could still see her friends. Maybe something of her life could be salvaged from the wreckage of it. She stared out of the window, her heart breaking just a little more until the entire miserable little town had swallowed her all up.

'I know I'm going on about it but I wish you could have met your grandma,' Helene suddenly said. 'She was always the glue in our family, the mediator, able to understand modern progress and embrace change in a way that my dad never could. She could always take a bad situation and make everything right again. I... I miss her... and how *bloody* brilliant she was at holding us all together. Without her my dad and I just broke in two and fell apart...' As she spoke, a crack appeared in her voice and Anna realised then, that she had never fully accounted for her mother's own feelings, so carried away was she with her own. 'I have to confess, I'm also pretty scared about this.' Anna reached her own hand out and placed it briefly on the steering wheel over the top of her mother's hand. 'All these years later, we've got to somehow find a way to live together again... without her.' Helene's voice was barely a whisper.

'It will be OK, Mum,' Anna said, with a false kind of cheer.

'We will *make* it OK,' Helene replied, with an identical false cheer as she turned the car down a no-through road lined on each edge with modern houses and neat front gardens. 'Oh *blimey*, this is all new!' She gasped and turned her head from left to right as she drove slowly down the road, her mouth gaping open in the process. 'They've gone and built an entire new development around our house. This all used to be grassland… I can hardly believe it. He would have absolutely hated this happening all around him, poor old sod!' Anna's attention, however, was diverted by the fact that they were aiming for the driveway of a very strange old house, totally out of keeping with every other house in the road.

'Tell me it's not that one?' she said, pointing at it, a further wave of dismay threatening to overwhelm her.

'It certainly is. Brace yourself – we're here. My old home.' Helene drove up the drop kerb and halted the car in front of a narrow old garage with wooden doors badly in need of a lick of paint. She sucked at the air, making rapid breaths as if she was about to give birth and appraised the upstairs section of the house where two small windows with scalloped gables poked their way out of the roof. 'I told you didn't I… that it's crazy small upstairs and we'll have to sleep in my old bedroom together because there's only the two bedrooms?'

'Yes, you said…' Anna wrinkled her brow at how tiny the upstairs windows were compared to the big windows downstairs. The house had wide concrete steps leading up to a large and solid wooden door, which was also in need of a lick of paint, and a huge chimney graced the roof at the side. Right at the top, balanced upon the ridge, perched a little bell tower sporting a rusty weathervane that was pointing east. 'What *is* this place?' she asked, nervously grasping Gary's pot and crinkling her nose as they climbed the steps. She took a photo and sent it to her friends with the caption: *Ultra cute or ultra creepy?* The replies came back from all her friends confirming that *ultra creepy* had won the vote.

'I was born up there.' Helene stood with her face tilted upwards, her words floating nostalgically upon her breath before her gaze ran slowly over the house she once knew so well. 'Oh look, here are the pots my mum planted bulbs in every year... They're empty.' She sighed sadly as they both turned their attention to a series of big old pots lining the brickwork next to the steps. 'They were always full of something welcoming and pretty... winter pansies, daffodils, sometimes bright red begonias... but now...'

She looked so crestfallen that Anna felt unable to think of a single thing to say. The lifeless terracotta husks stood devoid of anything other than dust and memories.

'My mum and dad bought this as their first house when they got married and they loved it so much they never moved out.' She reached towards a heavy brass knocker, now tarnished and dull, which hung in the centre of the large front door, then she banged it hard three times and grimaced as if she were summoning the grim reaper. 'Here we go...'

They both stood in silence, shuffling from foot to foot until after a full two minutes Helene reached for the knocker and banged it three times again. 'Fuck's sake. What's taking him so long?' She stooped in order to peer through the letterbox but the sound of a bolt being opened, just as her hand touched the letterbox flap, caused both of them to stand immediately to attention like two frightened hare.

ALGERNON

Algernon opened the front door, appraising his guests swiftly and wordlessly. It had taken him a goodly while to navigate the distance between his chair and the front door and the effort of it caused him to puff. The preparations required for this moment had taxed him and his fingers trembled as they clung to his walking stick. He'd never felt more tired.

Creased at the corners by an enormous and perfectly forced smile, once familiar turquoise eyes looked back at him. He pushed down on his walking stick in an effort to stand as tall as when his daughter had last seen him but the spongy bit between his vertebrae had let him down several years back. Even standing as upright as his arthritic body would allow, he was reduced forever by a good few inches in stature. Three generations of Maybury, all hurtling through life's inevitable stages, now stood at exactly the same height.

'Dad,' the forced smile said.

'Helene,' Algernon replied, giving a single cursory nod of his head.

'This is Anna. My daughter... your granddaughter.' Algernon detected the slight defiant tilt of his daughter's chin that he knew so well, before they both turned their heads in the direction of the child who stood beside her on his doorstep. The last time they were all in such close proximity the child was nothing more than a defiant announcement, a jellybean of a thing tucked in his daughter's swollen belly. Now, sixteen years after the very argument that set them apart, all fatherless and basically destitute, the end product of his daughter's swollen belly was now standing on his doorstep carrying a cactus.

He peered at the child with unashamed scrutiny. Young brown eyes confronted him, nervously assessing him back with equally cautious suspicion and, Algernon thought, the same defiant tilt to her chin. The child was dressed as if she'd chosen her clothes at a blindfold charity sale and her feet, in a pair of chunky lace-up ankle boots, seemed enormous at the end of her legs. Despite that, he silently caught his own breath as the image of Evie appeared to linger upon her face. Same high curve to the cheek, same upturned tip to her slender nose.

Algernon turned and shuffled back inside, leaving the front door open behind him. He used to have an opinion but now no longer knew what it was his business to say, so took it upon himself to say absolutely nothing. The values implicit in his very being had long ago pooled into an oily puddle at his feet.

2

A Shed at the Bottom of the Garden

ANNA

Anna couldn't quite get over how enormous her grandfather's eyebrows were, like two long-haired hamsters glued to his face. He had the same colour eyes as her mother, like the sea on a holiday postcard, only the whites of his were all yellow and veiny and his nose, protruding through a tangle of facial hair, was cratered by giant pores. He didn't look much like the man in the photograph Helene had shown her. This man's moustache was now white and had merged with a full white beard so, combined with his wayward eyebrows, she could hardly see his face.

He'd said nothing when he opened the door but then, to be fair, nor had her mother and nor had she, all three of them struck dumb by the moment. Even to her inexperienced mind though there was no mistaking the fact that there was something very sad about the density of the air between her grandfather and her mother, as if it were filled with things they were never going to be able to say to each other. He'd stared at Anna for a long time, examining her as if he'd never seen a teenager before and managing to put the fear of God into her as he did it. Despite her nerves, though, she'd proudly held her own against his scrutiny, feeling confident that she looked her absolute best for him with her carefully chosen clothes and hairstyle.

The minute he turned his back to shuffle inside, however, she dropped her serene expression and turned to Helene with her mouth aghast, pointing to her own forehead to indicate the enormity of his eyebrows. They both ineffectually suppressed a nervous laugh until Helene pushed a finger to her lips to shhh themselves before he heard them. As they entered his house, awkward and uncomfortable in the wake of his shuffle, Anna noticed a cumbersome set of hearing aids wedged behind each of his ears and how a sour smell of old skin clung to the air.

The old man halted in his step once they all entered a room that had very high ceilings and was situated just along the hallway. It was a large room and, so Anna thought, horribly old-fashioned with a carpet that swirled with gloomy browns and long russet drapes that hung heavy with brocade and dust. The whole room was dominated by a muddy-coloured painting of a country scene that hung on the wall against faded rosebud wallpaper. A little gold clock on the mantelshelf above the fireplace ticked loudly with each depressing second.

Anna could just glimpse a narrow staircase off to the right and through another door she could see a very small kitchen with brown cupboard doors and a little table with three chairs. She couldn't help but compare it all to Harry's beautiful house with its white shutter-blinds and cotton-coloured walls. Harry's kitchen had a shiny range oven and a breakfast bar and double doors that opened out to a sunny terrace. Harry's house had lots of lovely things in it that this house didn't.

She finished her unhappy surveillance of the place she was condemned to stay in and became uncomfortably aware that the old man was looking her up and down. His turquoise eyes were washing their way from the top of her head all the way down to her bright red DMs. That morning she'd wound her hair into twin donuts on her head, tying them in bright blue ribbon and she'd chosen her yellow and black spotted oversized jumper to wear over black skinny jeans. She'd wanted to look bright and welcoming for her new grandfather, yet his expression seemed to be one of disapproval. She suddenly felt like an intrusion of colour in a black and white movie, so very obvious and so very out of place.

ALGERNON

It felt to Algernon as if time had glitched and rushed him across the years in a matter of only seconds. The cause of his anger all those years ago was now here in the flesh, yet he was no longer that man who'd blasted Helene out of the very same room they were all in now. Life's latter years could take a lot from a man – he knew that – shrinking him like old fruit in size and height, dulling his mind and filling it with regrets. He tried to read the expression on his daughter's face and was pretty certain it was shock as if she was thinking: *Where has my father gone?* He sniffed at nothing, sensing that the space around Helene was still most definitely brittle, something he understood very much. His own had been brittle for decades.

'Thank you for this. For… you know… taking us both in.' Helene played with her hair, twisting a lock of it around in her fingers as she used to do if she was nervous as a child and he nodded by way of acknowledgement, his own conscience blistering inside him. The child, tall for her age and wide-eyed, was gazing around his room, up towards the high ceiling and across to the big window that looked out over his garden. He saw a frown form on her face and a wrinkle appear on her nose, and he tried not to let it ruffle him. Perhaps his house was not modern enough for her taste, but he liked it like that. He often felt as if he and his little house were the only relics left from a bygone time, like living ghosts in a modern era.

A previously undisturbed layer of phlegm vibrated in his throat as he began to speak. 'This house was a school once upon a time before "*development*" – if you can call it that – ravaged the entire village and turned it into a town. It's almost unrecognisable now as the village it was.' The irascible tone of his words was punctuated by a series of loud blasts forcefully issued to clear his throat, followed by a sharp cough and then the removal of a large white hanky from his pocket in which he proceeded to blow his nose. He hadn't spoken to anyone since getting his newspaper from the shop that morning and as a result his voice box had taken a moment to catch up with his thoughts. He'd intended to inform the child about the unique nature of his house and yet somehow the information he wished to impart had come out as an accusation.

'The grassland outside has disappeared, I see.' Helene walked across the room and ran her hand slowly along the back of the empty armchair where once her mother had sat. Algernon watched her carefully, recalling that as a youngster she and her friends had played in the grassland building dens and hunting for creatures in the hedgerow. He was quite sure she was searching, and possibly failing, to find any feeling of 'home' she may once have had. She'd been born upstairs in the bedroom he now occupied alone, in the early hours of the morning to the sound of Evie's agonised yelling and the midwife's enthusiastic encouragement. The whole, long ordeal had been horrendous as far as he'd been concerned from his standing point at the bottom of the stairs and he'd been hopeful that it was not something either of them should have to go through again.

'Dad?' Algernon shook himself out of his reverie at the sound of her voice, realising that he'd temporarily lost himself.

'Like I said, *development*!' He harrumphed disparagingly and felt a twinge in the pit of his stomach as he tried not to think too deeply about the loss of land they'd all once enjoyed around their home. 'They managed to cram thirty-two houses in that space, all of them on top of each other. Ironically they call the estate "Meadow Fields". Imagine. They take away something beautiful, turn it into something ugly then give it a beautiful name to convince people it's still beautiful.' He shook his head and sniffed loudly.

'I thought you'd be hating it. I said that to Anna when we drove through it just now.' Helene gave a wry smile then went over to the window to look out at the garden. The room fell silent as they all stood, an awkward trio. Algernon wished for the umpteenth time that day, and with the whole of his increasingly dodgy heart, that Evie was here to deal with the situation. Evie had always been so much better with affairs of the heart but Evie had left them sixteen years ago when she died on New Year's Eve to the sound of fireworks exploding at midnight. Evie could no longer help to prevent the rounded curves of the little schoolhouse from becoming jagged with the charged atmosphere of both his and Helene's combined misgivings.

ANNA

As all three of them stood in the high-ceilinged sitting room, Anna wondered if she was about to take part in a game of musical chairs. Two old-fashioned tartan armchairs were placed either side of a fireplace where an electric fire was now housed and that, apart from an old television and an old stereo unit, was basically all the room had to offer. One of the armchairs, she guessed, belonged to her grandfather as it had a little side table next to it with a folded newspaper, glasses and pen while the chair opposite had probably belonged to her grandma. She'd noticed how Helene had stroked the white cotton cloth that was placed upon its high back, a lace trim around the edge and embroidered white flowers in the corner. Regardless of who the chairs belonged to Anna could not ignore the fact that there was no third chair. If they were ever going to be invited to sit down, she could tell that someone wasn't going to be successful. Unless she wrestled her mother or the old man to the floor, she was pretty sure who that person was supposed to be.

She felt like she was growing in size, a huge, illegitimate elephant in the room and she suddenly wished she could think of something funny to say to break the moment. Instead, she held tightly to Gary's pot, waiting desperately for someone else to do or say something.

'I'll show Anna up to the bedroom then hey?' Helene waved a hand in the general direction of the ceiling above them and Anna almost swooned with gratitude. Not waiting for an answer, they both rushed for the stairs as if they'd just been given starters orders to race to the top. Then, all gruff and croaky, as if he still found the process of communicating a very difficult thing, the old man called above the furore.

'The child will be sleeping outside!' he announced. Anna stopped in her tracks, having got to the stairs first, while her mother shunted into the back of her with the speed of their desperate escape.

'*The child*?' Anna repeated, her head spinning on its axis to gawp in disbelief at Helene. She thought she could hear the mutual panicked beating of their hearts as they stood stock-still, pressed together against the newel post. 'He's joking, right?' she said, making no attempt to say it quietly, hearing aids or not.

'From personal experience he's no comedian,' Helene answered through gritted teeth as a teary sheen came into Anna's frightened eyes.

'You can't share a bed,' her grandfather now called from the kitchen where he was making his painfully slow way towards the back door.

'*Mum*?' Anna shot her mother a desperate look, begging for protection, fear gushing straight through the walls of her chest and into her extremities so that even her toes and fingers started to prickle.

'Stay there, Anna!' Helene showed the flat of her hand before striding past her towards her grandfather. 'The *child*, as you call her, has a name, which is Anna and *Anna* is not going to sleep outside. The only thing out there is the shed that's been there for as long as I can remember and she's not sleeping in that. You're being ridiculous, Dad. We *can* share a bed, even if we have to sleep top to toe. Tomorrow I'll sort something else out and we'll be out of your hair... before you can say Alzheimer's.'

ALGERNON

Algernon acted as if he hadn't heard their pleas. Taking a large brass key out of his pocket, he opened the glass-panelled door to the back garden and lowered himself carefully down the step, catching his foot on the lip of the threshold, which made him 'tut' loudly. He *had* heard their pleas, however, his hearing aids picking up the referral to Alzheimer's with wounding clarity. There was not a lot wrong with his brain, just his old body which, these days, was sorely letting him down. Helene and the child followed his slow progress, as he knew they would out of curiosity if nothing else, as he made his way along a stepping-stone path that ran through the centre of his lawn. The sound of his stick tapping plus the soles of his slippers scuffing on the ground peeved him. Once, not so long ago even, he could pick his feet up and enjoy a comparatively brisk stride, yet of late his knees and ankles seemed to have given up such fanciful ideas.

Algernon could see how the child scowled moodily, her feet in those big red clown boots of hers flattening the grass where she chose to walk, instead of placing her feet upon the stepping stones for which they were intended. The lavender, which had once grown in abundance along the flower beds was now suffering from unsightly rotting, while the white climbing rose, still clinging to the boundary fence, had grown woody and shapeless. Everything else appeared to have been attacked by a prolific growth of weeds apart from a froth of forget-me-nots and, miraculously, some peonies which, undaunted by neglect, were bursting forth with orange blooms.

Facing the three of them, flanked by a mass of yellow- and green-flecked laurel hedges, was his garden shed. 'Mum? Can we go? Sleep in the car or something? Anywhere but here?' She was whining now, and Helene had thrown an arm around her shoulders in a sign of solidarity but Algernon steadfastly inserted the big brass key into the lock of the shed door and turned it with a weighty-sounding clunk. A tremor played along his fingers as he pointed to a wooden sign nailed above the doors where in bright blue paint the words 'Little Argel' greeted them.

'What's that? Little *Ar... gel*?' Helene read the words carefully and Algernon wondered how his daughter would know what was new around the old homestead, given that she hadn't visited in a very long time.

'Ar-gel! It means retreat or secluded place in Cornish... It's my project room.'

Helene gave him a pointed look. 'I'll say it's secluded – it's down the bottom of your bloody garden, Dad. And project room? What for? Practising taxidermy on murdered relatives?' Her last words were lowered, a crass joke supposedly for her own ears, yet thanks, or perhaps *no thanks*, to the new batteries in his hearing aids they had managed to reach his own. 'Whatever you call it, it's still our old shed. What were you thinking? This is not OK.' Algernon closed his eyes and took a slow meditative breath as she continued. 'And do you really think she's going to creep around in the middle of the night to use *that* toilet?' She indicated the outside loo, the door of which was now painted in the same blue paint as the sign.

Algernon remained silent; he simply opened the door to the shed to let them inside.

ANNA

Anna slipped into the shed behind her mother and stood by the safety of the door, swallowing the agony of her disappointment. She hugged herself as if it were cold inside but in truth the temperature within the thick wooden walls was kindly benign. It's a bit like the Tardis in *Dr Who*, she thought, bigger on the inside or smaller on the outside. Regardless of its size and whether it had been his project room or not, it was most definitely just a shed.

'He's cleaned it out at least... sort of.' Helene ran a hand along a row of empty shelves and rubbed the pads of her finger and thumb together to remove the residue of dust. 'And there's two plug sockets, *and...*' She tugged at a cord near the door. 'There's a light!' A bulb glowed yellow under a small cream lampshade before she pulled the cord and turned it back off. The back wall, which was about two and a half metres wide, was lined with low-level cupboards built underneath her father's old workbench and an odd-looking wooden frame had been built onto it. 'That's new.' She pointed to the wooden frame then up at the roof. 'So is that.' They all looked up towards the ceiling where a large Velux window had been recently installed and a moody sky could clearly be seen above them.

Anna placed Gary on one of the shelves then she looked

42

carefully around her, unsure how she was feeling. Her choice was to sleep inside the house under the same roof as a man she'd decided was no grandfather of hers and who apparently didn't want her inside anyway, or she could sleep alone in his garden shed.

'Was this to do with your project?' she asked, placing a hand near her mother's on the old planks of wood that formed the frame on top of the cupboards.

The old man sniffed at nothing again and gave another sharp cough. 'It was, and now it will serve as a perfectly decent bed,' he said.

'Good God, no it won't! It's like a coffin!' Helene was almost screeching and the sound of it made Anna flinch. She noticed that it made the old man flinch slightly, too.

'There's a mattress in the cupboard upstairs, if you care to get it down. Despite its age it's rolled up and protected from dust. Should fit perfectly all right in that space,' he said, ignoring the reaction from his daughter.

Anna ran her hands along the dark wood and tried to imagine climbing up onto the workbench and sleeping there. She could feel a distinct age and curve to the shape of it and thought it looked like the same wood that had been used to make the 'Little Argel' sign.

Helene, however, suddenly yanked at her arm, pulling her hand away from it while glaring in the direction of the old man. 'If you've still got that old mattress then *I'll* sleep on it, even though it's probably got mice living in it by now. Anna can have my bed and I'll sleep on the floor. There's absolutely no need for this... this *pantomime*!' She threw an arm around Anna's shoulder again and Anna could feel her shaking through the wool of her yellow jumper. Two angry red splotches were burning on her mother's cheeks as she began to push Anna determinedly towards the door. Anna, however, used the hardy soles of her red DM boots to plant herself firmly on the wooden floor. The harsh truth was they had nowhere else to go until her mother got a job and she didn't want to stay inside a house that smelt of old things and where bitterness and shadows lay in every corner.

She tipped her face up towards the skylight again and hoped she could be brave enough to sleep in the shed at the bottom of the garden of a creepy old house belonging to the most frightening man she'd ever met. 'You can close your mouth,' her grandfather snapped, and, embarrassed, she immediately did so.

'You're not actually contemplating sleeping out here are you?' Helene hissed in her ear. 'What about the toilet? It's *outside*!'

Anna shrugged. 'According to... to...' As she tried to speak, she couldn't quite bring herself to call the old man Grandfather, so she avoided calling him anything. 'Well anyway, apparently this is where I'm required to stay. I won't be giving it many stars on Tripadvisor but I'm not going to lie, I think I'll prefer to be out here than... *in there*.' She pointed in the direction of the house and as she did so she knew she'd made the right decision. She gave the shed and the skylight one more defiant appraisal and squared her shoulders. She'd show him that he couldn't hurt her. 'I *like* it out here. It will suit me fine!' She spun round to throw the old man her most confident smile but he didn't see... he'd already turned away and had begun to make his way back down the stepping-stone path.

★★★

ALGERNON

Algernon stepped back inside his house and stood by the kitchen window in order to study everything from his vantage point. Resting his gnarled hands on the windowsill he leant forward to afford a better view through the yellowing net curtains. Sooty black mould was flourishing in the corners of the cracking paintwork and Algernon felt a pang of disappointment in himself for not noticing it before. Forcing his attention away from the evidence of his own failing and, squinting now, he turned his mind to more imminent matters. His daughter had aged since he last saw her, her pale hair now dyed with brighter blonde streaks to hide the grey and she had a roll of extra weight clinging to her belly and hips. The child, however, was an anomaly. 'Good, sweet Jesus in heaven,' he muttered aloud as he pondered, with no small amount of confusion, as to why she'd tied her hair into two buns instead of one and why she was wearing a garish jumper of such enormous proportions it could quite possibly fit all three of them in.

He watched how the two of them stopped on their way back to the house to peer at the outside toilet as if they were expecting to find something other than an outside toilet. Helene pulled the sour face he remembered only too well as she opened the door to the cubicle, yet his mouth twitched as she looked inside. She'd always been afraid of the outside lavvy, convincing herself there were armies of spiders in there just waiting to drop on the heads of anyone who went in. Algernon tried to read the body language of his guests as they leant forward, their heads inside the cubicle, but he was never good at that sort of thing. He was, however, surprised by how the two of them appeared to simultaneously laugh at something and he recalled how both Helene and Evie could also find humour in even the smallest of things. It was an outside toilet for God's sake! What on earth could be funny about that?

They pushed the toilet door shut and clicked the iron latch into place and made to come back inside the house whereupon Algernon turned quickly away from the window to poke his head into a nearby cupboard. *Would they like custard creams?* he wondered. He had enough orange squash and bread and cheese for everyone, but should they eat at the kitchen table or should they sit in the dining room, a now barely used space? He gave a heavy sigh at the uncertainty of it all, becoming suddenly even more tired and wishing mightily that he could take a much-needed nap.

'I love it!' The child smiled brazenly, looking him directly in the eye as she followed Helene inside, stepping lightly through the back door and bringing with her a rush of false enthusiasm and spring air. Algernon found this sudden burst of energy into his little kitchen quite jarring, made more so by the slamming of the door behind them and he instantly formed the decision to take the lunch things into the dining room. An unfamiliar and awkward state of affairs deserved a formal setting, he decided.

ANNA

Anna could only describe lunch as something *endured* and nothing short of crippling. Fortunately, thanks to her partially eaten burger and fries she wasn't that hungry but her mother, only out of politeness she was sure, was earnestly eating brown bread sandwiches followed by slightly stale biscuits.

The room smelt of museums. It was another large room but depressingly dark, lacking in natural light due to an overgrown vine plant of some sort hanging directly over the large window that blocked any kind of view of the garden. Two matching antique cabinets stood either side of the window, their tall mirrors now covered in dust and doing little to reflect any of the meagre daylight back into the room. Anna found herself becoming genuinely eager to get away from the room and back out to the shed as she fidgeted in her chair with the uncustomary formality of it all. She picked at something encrusted on her plate that resembled old gravy missed in the washing-up process and at the same time Helene looked her in the eye and surreptitiously pointed to the teacup she was about to drink from. A sliver of dried green vegetable was clinging to the china. They gave each other a secretive wince.

'It could do with being lighter in here,' Helene announced, placing the teacup back in its saucer and appraising the vine-choked window. Her demeanour was still unyielding after coming in from the garden and Anna, though too nervous to comment, silently agreed, feeling thoroughly stifled by the gloom. The old man carefully finished chewing a mouthful of his sandwich and swallowed loudly and Anna thought she could see his upper false teeth temporarily come away from his gums. It made her stomach turn. 'It's still painted this awful red,' Helene added, screwing her nose up as she looked at the dark shadowy walls she obviously remembered so well.

'Period red,' the old man declared, before taking another bite of his food.

'He means in keeping with the period... Victorian red,' Helene hastily clarified as Anna felt herself go pink with a nervous need to laugh out loud. 'And the sitting room still has the original—'

'Yes. It still has the original wallpaper,' he interrupted testily. 'Your mother was going to make changes. To paint the house in modern colours. She was going to choose something suitable after the New Year celebrations. Something *summery*, I recall. But, well... you know the rest.' Anna shot a look at her mother to see what else it was that she was supposed to know but saw that her expression had darkened and how, as if injured, she dropped her unfinished biscuit onto her plate.

What? Anna mouthed the question at her but Helene rolled her eyes and shook her head in a *leave it be* kind of way. She took an educated guess that her grandma had never got to choose the new summery colours because she hadn't lived long enough to do so. How different, she thought, the house might have been had she lived, not just in terms of decoration but in atmosphere too. The air in the room had become so spiky and uncomfortable that she wondered what her grandma might be thinking if she could see her family now, a silent observer of the mess she'd left behind. Blame over her death, the person her grandfather and her mother had each loved most in all the world still clearly jostled for attention between them. Anna pushed her miserable leftovers of food aside and an overwhelming need to escape forced her to stand abruptly up from her chair.

'I'll go and get the mattress. Where's the upstairs cupboard, Grandad?' She immediately bit down on her lip and wished mightily that she hadn't called him 'Grandad', but the word had come out before she knew it. Grandad was a far too friendly and intimate term for a mean old man with fearsome eyebrows and she desperately wanted to snatch it back out of the air. She left the room without waiting for his reply.

ALGERNON

Grandad? Algernon mused. A child he had never met until today had just called him *Grandad*, and he wasn't at all sure he knew what to do with this new title. He felt strange upon hearing it, as if he'd just put on a coat tailored for somebody else.

With a certain amount of relief, he found that the child's question had hastened the completion of the dining process and enabled him to send them on their way to retrieve the mattress. It also provided the lever he needed to decline Helene's insistent offers that they help with the luncheon dishes. He was satisfied that they had manners at least but was more than happy to divert them away before they messed up the orderliness of his existence any more than they already had. Each of his kitchen items had a specific place and he would be rattled if he couldn't find anything after they'd been at it. Once alone in his kitchen he set about the task of scraping unfinished food into the bin. He clucked his tongue against the roof of his mouth at the waste of bread and cheese from the child's unfinished sandwiches but was at least able to salvage two untouched custard creams, which he put back in his biscuit tin. When finally everything was washed up and put away, he made his way back to his armchair and eased himself carefully into it.

The momentary pleasure experienced at the relief his chair

gave to his back and shoulders was soon ruined, however, by the chaos of the moving-in activity. The whole process proved itself to be a virtual jamboree and the sound of the front door slamming every time the two of them came in from the car with their belongings rocketed through his hearing aids. All the busying about toing and froing between car and house, garden and upstairs bedroom, made him utterly tense. His house and indeed his world was far too small for such goings-on. The last time he and Helene had been in close proximity in the house had been Evie's funeral, and he was sure that the significance of this was not lost on Helene either. Their mutual grief had forced a canyon between them, as grief so often does, trapping blame and guilt and anger in its bitter net, and now they had to face each other again.

'I'm afraid this is only the start,' Helene confessed, popping her head round the sitting room door after what seemed like a monumental number of belongings had finally been reassigned to their various places. 'I'm supposed to be having a few boxes delivered by van tomorrow but I'll have them put in the dining room against the wall. They'll be mostly out of your way until we can find somewhere else to stay.'

He offered her a perfunctory nod, knowing he had no further choice in the invasion of his territory, or indeed, a choice as to how long they stayed. That detail, he decided, was in the lap of the gods – or at the very least it was in the lap of the rental and employment market.

'Thanks again, Dad. It's… you know… *helpful*.'

He offered her another nod and wondered just how many boxes would be arriving tomorrow. Helene, to his mind, had always been a bit of a dreamer and it was highly likely that those dreams for a swift solution to her current status could well be dashed yet again.

Eventually, to his relief, when his guests were at last otherwise occupied in their respective locations doing whatever they needed to do, a familiar but brief stillness came back to his home once more. He took a deep lungful of air, held on to it for as long as his respiratory system would allow, then exhaled it back out with measured control. Once all the particles of frustration and tension had released themselves on the outward flow of his breath he allowed his weary body to sag and mould into the shape of his chair. As he did so, the carriage clock seemed to tick even louder than before in the ensuing hush. It was as if the clock was reminding him that time played cruel tricks. That time would move either too fast or too slow and always at the opposite speed from that which was desired. As he thought about this, he let his gaze rest sadly upon the empty chair until the day finally relaxed its hold upon him and gave permission for his weary eyes to close.

ANNA

It might be unconventional to find yourself about to spend the night in a shed at the bottom of a garden but as far as Anna was concerned it was definitely better than the alternative. She peered at the back of her grandfather's house through the shed window and felt sorry that her mother didn't have the same option. Her mother would be sleeping in her old bedroom, trapped by her father's strict regime as if she were still a child and Anna shivered at the thought of it. The two old-fashioned armchairs in his big old sitting room made it obvious to her that she was not expected to spend time inside the house other than for meals. The shed, she knew, despite being the better of the two options was basically just a fancy dog kennel for an unwanted, illegitimate grand-daughter, somewhere to hide the embarrassment of her out of plain sight.

She'd spent the rest of the afternoon carefully placing some of the things she'd brought with her from her own bedroom. The mattress, after a brief airing on the lawn, was now on the ledge above the cupboards and her own duvet and pillows were on top of that. The blanket that Harry had given her was placed at the opposite end to the pillows, and Gary was still on one of the shelves supervising the process.

She breathed in the wood-scented air as she lay within the unfamiliar frame of her makeshift bed, scrolling through a string of missed messages on her phone. Her gut twisted with a new kind of agony when, there, on the screen of her phone, she saw a photo of her friends huddling in a group outside the cinema. *Missing you,* the caption said. 'They're going out after school, Gary... to the cinema... without me.' She pictured her friends side by side in their seats, faces tipped up towards the screen, then spilling out at the end of the film to hang out in the park or the shopping centre until it was time to go home. 'They get popcorn and surround sound and we get cobwebs and YouTube.' She thumped her phone down on the bed, as if the phone itself was the traitor, just as her mother knocked on the door and stepped inside.

'It's me,' she whispered loudly as she shut the door behind her.

'Why are you whispering?' Anna asked, using the same whispery tone.

'I don't know.' Helene grinned stupidly but, even so, she glanced through the glass doors towards the house before speaking normally again. 'I just wanted to see if you're all right and have a moment together before I have to brave your grandfather again. I'm going to show willing... make him a nice cup of tea or something.'

To Anna, this comment sounded desperate somehow and almost fearful. It reinforced the nightmarish reality of their situation and she suddenly felt weighed down by it. She closed her eyes and felt another wave of total despair come over her. 'I'm all right, Mum... providing we don't have to stay here for long. I couldn't bear that.' As she spoke the last words, her own self-pity jabbed at her and she wiped at wet cheeks, a rush of tears spilling down them. Helene gave a gasp of dismay and stepped over the unpacked suitcases until she was next to the bed, unbridled sympathy now glistening in her own tears from the guilt of her parental failure.

'Look at me! I've messed up my life and now I'm messing up yours.' She drew the back of her hand across her eyes and sent smears of mascara across her skin as she impulsively climbed over the wonky frame of the bed to join her daughter. Anna budged over until they were sitting side by side, the whole day bulging with a raw emotion that neither of them knew what to do about. Entwining their fingers together they simultaneously squeezed, remaining in silence like this for a long time, their miserable faces tipped up towards the skylight, searching for answers in the clouds.

★ ★ ★

ALGERNON

Algernon's usual after luncheon nap had taken up much of the afternoon, which was unusual for him. When he eventually awoke he was surprised not only by the time on the carriage clock but also by the fact that Evie was in the armchair opposite, quietly crocheting in companionable silence. The sight of her caused him such a rush of pleasure that he fumbled for his distance glasses in order to quickly put her into focus. 'Hello again,' he said, battling to put his glasses into place.

Evie did not look up. 'Fuck!' she replied, her head still bowed, her fingers still working on her crocheting. Her expletive, the likes of which Algernon had never in his life heard her utter, forced the air from his lungs and a disappointed 'Oh!' to travel out on his breath. As he pushed his glasses up his nose, however, and his sensibility realigned itself, he realised it was not Evie of course; it was Helene. She was back and was sitting in the chair opposite, her concentration focused not on crochet but on a mobile phone she held in her hand. Helene was squashing the space that belonged to Evie and Algernon experienced an unexpected wave of grief so great it threatened to suffocate him.

'There are hardly any jobs round here,' Helene said, looking up at him without a word of apology for her language. She waved her phone at him then as if the phone might somehow have a say in what the employment situation was in the area. 'And the rental prices aren't as low as I'd hoped either. I'm beginning to think we'll be here way longer than I thought.' She pulled a pained expression for his benefit, but Algernon had no answer for her. He tried not to think too deeply about how successful or not she may be in the current climate. She'd tried so many jobs in the past, flitting from one thing to the other within a matter of months, never quite managing to stay at anything for any length of time. The same, he believed, was very likely about to happen again.

'I'll get you the local *Chronicle* tomorrow when I get my newspaper. There may be something in the classifieds.' He took a little leather-bound notebook from his side table and jotted a note to remind him to do so, but as he placed it back on the table he realised that Helene was looking at him as if he'd said something outlandish.

'Thank you for offering, Dad, but I don't need the paper, I've got this. Google!' Algernon had no idea what a Google was and decided he was probably better off not knowing, although he did pick up his little notebook again and firmly crossed out the note to remind him to get the *Chronicle*. Helene groaned aloud again and, staring at her phone, pulled another face. 'I was hoping not to have to go too far,' she complained. 'I don't want to add much travel on top of a working day... not until we're in our own place and Anna is settled.' She looked up at him again as if appealing for an answer to her predicament, her frustration plain upon her face and he looked back at her, unsure as to what she thought he could do about it.

'Cup of tea?' He was thinking that due to his extended nap it was now a good forty minutes past his afternoon refreshment and in the case of a crisis what better solution than a good old cup of tea? Just as he was beginning the laborious process of getting out of his chair, however, Helene placed her phone down on the arm of the chair and leapt up with the kind of speed a whirling dervish would be proud of.

'I'll make it! I was going to make you one anyway but you were asleep.' She offered an insistent palm of her hand in his direction and made her way into his kitchen. When she returned, she was carrying one of his bone china teacups in one hand and a huge yellow mug with a black smiley face in the other. 'I like a proper cup of builder's tea, so I've dug out my own mug,' she said, as she placed his cup on the table beside him before collapsing in an ungainly fashion rather than lowering herself into the armchair opposite. With her legs curled underneath herself, she wrapped both hands round the huge mug and looked at him through the steam that arose from it. The mug was so unnecessarily large that Algernon thought her entire head might be able to disappear inside.

It was the first time someone else had made him a beverage in a very long time yet, as he reached for his cup, rather than it being a luxury, it instead made him feel somewhat redundant. The process of making his way to the kitchen each afternoon, boiling the kettle, brewing his tea for exactly four minutes, then getting back to his chair again without spilling any liquid into the saucer, had been a physical activity for him if nothing else. Each and every day was marked by certain events which, apart from being functional and comparatively difficult these days, let him know at least that he was still alive. In fact, now that he thought about it, it was those such events that were possibly what kept him alive. He looked down at his cup and tried not to mind that his tea was not the colour he liked.

For a full, awkward fifteen minutes the room was silent as he sipped at his over-milky and under-sweetened tea and endeavoured to work on his crossword, but his mind was all over the place. His daughter being back in his sitting room obsessing over her telephone and a child being in his shed was a distraction of such proportions that he wasn't at all sure he could concentrate on anything that required a degree of sense. 'It is a question of parentage!' he suddenly announced, tapping his pen on his newspaper as he looked across at Helene.

'It certainly is,' she answered.

'It's a clue,' Algernon said, addressing her from behind his brows. 'It is a question of parentage, four, four and six.' He continued to tap his pen, frustrated at his inability to think straight. He missed Evie immensely at times like this. Between them they would dissect the question, ponder over each word and then at some point the solution would inevitably come to one of them. It was always a moment of triumph, a very satisfying eureka moment, when the answer was found.

'Mind over matter?' Helene suggested half-heartedly.

'How does that fit with the question?' Algernon asked, frowning at the printed clue and wondering how to tackle the cryptic element of it.

'Trust me, it does,' Helene answered, as she stood up and reached for his now empty cup. 'You stay there, Dad. Have a rest. I'll wash up.' Algernon had prepared to rise from his chair but yet again she'd offered the palm of her hand as a suggestion that he sit back down. 'It's the least I can do.'

'I've had a rest thank you,' he grumbled, fumbling for his stick. 'And now *I'm* going to do the washing up!' He was so damn slow these days. His body was on a mission to work against whatever he wanted his mind to do and it made him utterly furious. Helene was already out of the room and in the kitchen carrying both cups before he was even halfway through the conquest of standing up.

'No need, I've got it. Stay where you are,' she called cheerily.

Algernon replaced his stick but with an element of frustration he picked up his pen and proceeded with his crossword again. From where he sat, he could hear the sound of water running and crockery chinking for so long that he wondered if she might be washing up the entire contents of his kitchen.

ANNA

'Oh my word! I've just had to wash up the entire contents of his kitchen.' Helene opened the door to the shed and stepped inside looking slightly frazzled. 'I don't think he can see to wash up properly anymore and I can't eat and drink out of crockery that's likely to give us botulism.'

'We're not staying though are we?' Anna eyed her mother with suspicion as Helene wandered hesitantly across the shed floor, exuding guilt in her wake. She ran the palm of her hand over the soft blue blanket folded at the end of the duvet.

'Look, Anna...' she began. Anna found that with those words, in the pit of her stomach began the stirrings of a horrible feeling. She focused intently on the place where the evening light was casting a rose-gold hue through the side window and wanted to lose herself in the glow of it. 'I promise I'll get us out of here as soon as I possibly can, *really* I will, but I've already had a quick Google on my phone for what sort of jobs are available in this area and... well, it's dismal.' Anna continued to stare hard at the rose-gold hue but her soul felt as if it were being sucked further away from it and far into the shadowy corners of the shed.

'How many days?' she murmured, her voice sounding to her own ears as if it were coming from the end of a tunnel. When a dull silence was the only answer forthcoming, she felt her heart start to hammer. 'Not *weeks*? Tell me we won't be here for weeks?' She forced her gaze over to her mother in time to see her offer a listless shrug.

'I'll go to the job centre, plus all the agencies and I'm sure there'll be something for this thrill-seeking single mum with a low-level Geology degree and minimal experience in, well, just about *anything*.' She grinned at Anna, trying to make her laugh a little but Anna, still caught in the grips of the shed's dark shadows, simply couldn't find anything amusing about the situation. She was trapped.

'It's year ten Mum. You expect me to study for my end of year exams in here?' She cast a critical gaze around the bare walls, the bare floor and the empty shelves and yearned again for her bedroom at Harry's.

'It's actually not as bad as I thought.' Helene followed Anna's gaze around the shed as if now seeing it in an entirely different light from earlier. 'And you're bright, you'll rock those exams. You'll be OK in here, Anna.'

'I'll have to be.' Anna managed to sound as if she didn't care, but she did care. She cared so much it hurt to breathe.

'Come on! Let's make something of it.' Helene bent down full of inspired enthusiasm and without asking opened up the first of Anna's three suitcases. Crammed into the two sides of the suitcase were contents of what had once been her normal life. Socks that had belonged in a sock drawer, sweatshirts that had hung in her wardrobe, toiletries that had lived in the bathroom cupboard, now all in a hectic mixed-up pile. 'Chocolate?' Helene held up a bag.

'Snacks. I raided the cupboard before we left home.' Anna took the bag and placed it beside her pillow for later. She didn't want her mother going through her things, nor did she want to make the shed her home, but regardless of what she wanted, within an hour, all the cases were emptied and her clothes were neatly folded into the two cupboards underneath the bed. Her school books were stacked in a tower, DMs, all six pairs of them, were lined along the lowest of the wall shelves and her many sunglasses, all the same design, with their pink, blue, green or yellow, perfectly round lenses, formed neat lines on the shelf above. Art things, her jewellery stand, mirror and the new make-up collection given by Harry, decorated the whole of the top shelf. Candles, which were housed in little glass holders, were lit and placed on a stool Helene had brought in from the house and covered with Anna's beach sarong. Gary was retrieved from the shelf and given centre place on the stool, now makeshift table. Her dream catcher hung from a nail in the wall and her fairy lights were now strung across the ceiling glowing like tiny shining stars in the failing evening light.

ALGERNON

Algernon knew that his daughter had furtively left the house to make her way down his garden. He wondered what Evie would think of him making the child sleep outside. Helene and the child both thought him cruel, but he was the one who had to make the decisions now and this was the decision he had made. It was true that he hadn't offered any alternative choice in where the child should sleep but he believed it to be an entirely appropriate place for her now. Spring was well underway and the days were getting longer so she would be adequately housed for the current season and as far as he was concerned she should be grateful. A hot water bottle at night and she'd be positively in the land of luxury.

He leant heavily on his stick looking at Little Argel through the large sash windows of his sitting room. The child, he believed, was lucky. His own experience of leaving home had been so entirely different. He shivered at the memory of it. His own first night had been spent curled into a tight ball under the itchy over-blanket on the narrow, metal bed. The dormitory had been freezing cold, the leaded windows remaining open to the elements. The Brothers had informed the boys that their moral and physical development would be achieved through adversity and discipline and this had left them in no doubt that their journey to become young gentlemen had begun.

Grief for his own bed and his own home had wormed its way inside Algernon, rasping through his veins and writhing in his stomach. He'd tried to imagine it as a beast, a dragon that must be fought. He was a warrior wearing armour and drawing his sword ready for battle. His mother had not stolen her way back to the school to comfort him as Helene had just done for the child. His mother had not cast a protective arm around his shoulders and hugged him tight. His mother had not saved him. The little boy had pulled the itchy blanket tightly over his head and tried so hard to be brave but the beast could not be slayed.

Algernon looked down his garden at the painted blue sign above the door to his garden shed and thought how on his first night away from home he would have given his eye teeth to have had such a space of his own. Maybe then he wouldn't have had to cry so silently into his pillow each night.

★ ★ ★

ANNA

Anna surveyed their work on the shed and surprised herself with the tingle of pleasure she felt over how it all looked. Little Argel it seemed, might actually turn out to be what it said on the sign... a little retreat, a solid place to hide away in an unstable world controlled by unreliable adults. *We can do this,* she thought, giving her cactus a brave thumbs up. Gary sat, round and silent, on the makeshift table surrounded by her candles, their flames casting a golden light upon him. 'It's not bad... for a kennel!' she announced, as Helene made her way inside the shed, giving it an approving look.

'It's not a kennel.' She laughed. 'He probably thought it would be OK for you to sleep here because there's not much room in my old bedroom. That's all.' Helene gave Anna a quick motherly squeeze then moved over to the window to look out at the garden. 'Shall we spend money we don't really have on a takeaway? We can eat saturated fats until we're fit to burst.'

'Can we eat in here?' Anna asked. 'It's so horrible in there... so *old*.' She gave a little shiver, the smell of the old man's house still lingering up her nose.

'He's really let some things go, that's for sure. There's dust everywhere, and the garden... it's so overgrown.' Helene placed a hand against the glass of one of the doors as if reaching out to touch the view and her voice was an ache of sadness. 'Mum would hate to see it now. Especially the garden – it used to be her *thing*. Her joy. He's let it all go. To be honest, I didn't think I'd ever say this but I feel quite sorry for the poor old boy. It shocked me this morning when he opened the door to us. He's half the man I knew.'

'With twice the eyebrows!' Anna walked over to the window

where her mother stood and gave her a cheering shoulder bump and thin smile, which slipped from her face when they saw the back door to the house open and the old man step out. He was making his way down the garden towards them, leaning precariously on his stick. Anna studied the stooped, white-haired figure as he scoured the ground, gingerly placing each foot in front of the other, his bottom lip hanging slack in his effort, and she couldn't imagine what he might have looked like before he was old. As far as she was concerned, he could never have been young. 'What do you think he wants?' she asked as they watched his slow progress towards Little Argel.

Helene gave a mirthless laugh. 'Maybe he's going to do an inspection. Stand by your beds!'

Anna didn't laugh. 'I think he's ashamed of me. He can hardly bear to clap eyes on me.' That she might be something to be ashamed of was a concept that had never entered her mind before now and, to her dismay, she realised her chin was wobbling. Suddenly her mother's arms were around her in a fierce embrace, and she pressed a damp cheek against her shoulder. Helene swept a lock of hair from Anna's face and kissed her ear, shushing her softly and stroking her hair while the ominous sound of the tapping stick got closer.

'Anna,' her mother said, collectedly, 'it's not *you* he's ashamed of. It's *me*.'

ALGERNON

When he knocked on the door of Little Argel, Algernon guessed he might not be so welcome, judging by the expressions on their faces.

Cat, who'd been keeping a low profile all day, had been 'ecking and purring' around his ankles again. It was time, of course, for three ready meals and three cups of tea – or should it be two cups of tea and an orange squash? Children, he assumed, did not drink tea, not even in this day and age. Had he told them that he and Cat prepared supper at 5.30pm and ate at 6pm sharp? He must have done... *would* have done, surely? Regardless, he had placed the three ready meals in the oven and popped an unopened sachet of salmon and tuna succulents on the work surface, ready to empty out in thirty minutes' time. For the next half an hour he'd waited, fingers tapping on the kitchen work surface, eyes darting to the view of the garden through the window. He'd hoped they would have come inside because the thought of having to dig them out made him feel almost as if he'd become an intruder in his own home.

In the end, the ready meals were already cooling on the plates and Cat had finished his salmon and tuna succulents before he found it in himself to venture down there. Twice in one day they had knocked his routine quite out of kilter, and he wasn't at all sure he could deal with the anxiety it raised in him. He'd tried to ignore the unwieldy flutter in his chest as he knocked on the door, yet immediately knew he'd been right to feel trepidatious.

The child opened the door looking none too pleased to see him and although she stepped aside to afford him a view of her transformation of Little Argel he reasoned that this was not an invitation to come inside, more a polite viewing, extended to him but not desired as such. 'How's your father?' he said, looking past the child and over at Helene.

'What?' Helene looked confused and pulled what he thought was quite an ugly expression.

'The answer to the clue. "*It's a question of parentage.*" How's your father?' Helene looked only marginally enlightened by his revelation and nowhere near as pleased about it as he knew Evie would have been. She would have raised her hands in delight. He shrugged his neck into his shoulders and gave two dry sniffs up his nose. Not one to force himself upon others, he didn't step inside even though the child continued to hold the door open but managed to see everything from where he stood. There were a number of brightly coloured boots lined on one of the shelves, similar to the monstrosities she'd been wearing on her feet earlier. He could also see colour and light and dangling things and that the frame on top of the cupboards now looked satisfactorily like a bed. He could also see a gathering of flaming candles, which ought not to be left burning unsupervised. 'Supper's been ready for ten minutes... and blow them out before you come inside,' he muttered. 'Don't want the place burning down.'

ANNA

Supper wasn't takeaway. Supper was beige gloop, straight out of an oven-ready container, masquerading as chicken stew and dumplings. The gloomy dining room and old plates with a brown and orange geometric design made the food seem even more unappetising if that were possible. Unsurprisingly her grandfather had been grouchy and rude when he came knocking on the door of the shed, prompting Anna and Helene to follow him back into the house like two scolded dogs. 'Sorry, sweetheart,' Helene apologised lamely. 'When we go to get your new school uniform tomorrow we'll eat out then. Make an afternoon of it.' Anna, however, found that the mention of her new school uniform set off the jitters in her stomach again and her appetite for anything instantly evaporated.

The beige gloop oozing across her plate tasted OK as gloop goes but, like the sandwich earlier, she struggled to swallow it, the ache of sadness in her chest being far too big. Like the two armchairs, there were only two cups of tea placed on the table as if she wasn't part of the equation at all. She sipped at a watery-looking orange squash, her tongue searching the liquid for some sort of flavour. Not that long ago, in a time before Derek, Harry would have handed her a Coke and asked her about her day. He or her mother would be getting something freshly prepared and deliciously edible ready for dinner, and they'd have all chatted round the table, or taken their food on a lap tray into the sitting room. Anna wasn't back there though, she was here, in a dingy dining room, labouring at a meal that apparently would be taking place every evening at 6pm with military precision from now on.

'She's actually managed to make that old shed quite habitable,' Helene piped up between mouthfuls. Anna ran her tongue across the roof of her mouth in an effort to remove a large wad of dumpling that was stuck there. Her grandfather gave a single silent dip of his head. 'She's got fairy lights in there and everything – haven't you, Anna?' Anna nodded.

'And candles,' her grandfather added.

'She blew them out. Don't panic she won't burn the place down.' Helene shot to defend her daughter but the spikes that had appeared in the atmosphere at lunch were already returning. Anna fidgeted in her seat and wished she was back at home eating supper with Harry. Her real life was still almost touchable. Only last night she'd slept in her own bed. Harry and her mother might have been mismatched when it came to pheromones but at least life with him had been good. Derek would now be enjoying the good life that she'd enjoyed. Perhaps Derek was right at this moment eating supper with Harry in the light, bright dining room oblivious to the fact that the sparkle of their new life had snuffed the light completely out of hers.

Only the unexpected arrival of a large grey cat with yellow eyes, which sashayed into the dining room during a dessert of tinned fruit salad, caused Anna to smile. She'd somehow not expected a man like her grandfather to be interested in caring for a pet and the idea of there being an animal to fuss over was the only good thing to come out of her being there.

'Hello,' she whispered as she stooped down from her chair to greet it.

'He doesn't like strangers,' her grandfather warned as she ran her fingers over the cat's side and felt the rhythmic vibration of his pleasure through his dense velvet fur. *Then we will become not-strangers you and I,* she thought, curling her fingers around the nudging fuzzy grey head, drawing the gift of his velvety welcome into the cup of her hand.

ALGERNON

Algernon didn't enjoy having his meals in the dining room. He missed sitting at the kitchen table under the welcome glare of the overhead strip-light where at least he could see what he was eating. The gloom caused by the untamed wisteria growing over the window bothered him, reminding him of tasks he'd long since forgotten to pay attention to. It prompted him to question himself as to when he had begun to let such things slip. He didn't like that one bit. His critical appraisals of self were always uncomfortably harsh and the older he got the more he despised himself.

Cat had come into the room during dessert and the child had seemed pleased. Algernon could tell by her look of surprise that she'd not suspected him to be a 'cat' sort of person and she would be right. He'd always believed that the aloof animal had only remained a resident in his house in order to be fed. Apart from the brushing of furry body against trousered leg each day at 5.30pm sharp, he and Cat had always much preferred their own company to each other's. Feeling the need to explain the situation to the contrary he'd coughed sharply to clear his throat. 'He doesn't like strangers,' he'd said, noting immediately how Cat proceeded to prove him wrong by pushing his head into her cupped hand.

When Cat had first appeared through an open window several summers back, Algernon had shooed the creature back out through the front door. This event had been repeated for thirteen full days in a row until Algernon had finally given in, buying three matching bowls, one for water, one for crunchies and one for meat. From that day on the meat bowl was filled every evening at exactly 5.30pm when he prepared his own meal. The meat bowl was then placed on the floor at exactly 6pm, the same time as he placed his own meal on the kitchen table. He'd also purchased a small basket for the animal to sleep in which, as it happened, it never did. Cat preferred instead to lie on Algernon's bed, or the spare bed, or occasionally on an old battered green suitcase on the top of his wardrobe. 'He's not mine as such. Walked in one day... never left.' Algernon spooned the last chunk of peach and the remainder of the juice from his tinned fruit salad into his mouth, keeping one eye on the bonding of animal and child occurring in front of him.

'They choose their human,' the child had said, rubbing at Cat's cheeks then stroking him down the length of his back to the tip of his grey tail.

'Apparently so!' he sniffed.

'What's his name?' Algernon saw that the child was far more interested in the animal than in the meal that he had prepared and it peeved him a little.

'Cat!' he said, reaching to collect everyone's bowls. 'Because he's a cat.'

3

Wings to Fly

ANNA

At some point, when the harsh light of morning forced her eyelids open, Anna realised she'd managed to survive her first night sleeping in a shed three hundred miles from home. She woke to a cold sky that hung over the window in the ceiling, her ears filling with the chorus of garden birds as she lay drowning in the song of them. How she ached for her own bedroom and for the sound of the city awakening. Here the sounds were different, muted and distant beyond the garden as if she was alone in the world, Anna Maybury, all snagged up in a void somewhere between real life and an uncertain future. Finding her phone under her now lukewarm hot water bottle she saw that she'd received a string of unread messages from her friends plus one from her mother.

> Morning. I had your grandfather's teeth grinning at me from a glass in the bathroom while I used the loo! Did you survive?

Anna tried not to think too hard about how her grandfather

might look without his teeth, his lips collapsing into the hole in his face caused by absent dentures. She screwed up a Twix wrapper and brushed the debris of crisp crumbs from her duvet then sent a text declaring that she had, indeed, survived the night.

Last night after supper she'd crept down the dark garden with her mother, using only the torches on their phones to light the way. Helene had gripped her arm. 'I don't like it, Anna. Now that it's dark it doesn't feel right that you're out here. Are you *sure* you'll be OK?' Anna, now that they were picking their way across the damp grass, wasn't at all sure but she wasn't going to admit it. Weary and hurting she'd just needed to escape the house and crawl into bed.

'Yes, Mum, I'm *sure* I'll be OK. I'll be just as OK as I was going to be when you asked me two minutes ago and two minutes before that.' A sudden burst of light from an external security lamp, however, had startled them both into a statue-like pose.

'Let there be light!' Helene cried. 'If nothing else it means if you get taken short in the night you'll be able to find your way to the loo. You know... a dodgy oven-ready meal is all it takes...' She nudged Anna and laughed but Anna wasn't finding anything remotely funny by then. Her heart, which had all day been feeling as if it were suspended from the string of a yo-yo, dropped into her boots as she eyed the dark outlines of the surrounding houses against the evening sky and the path that led to the outside loo.

The inside of the outside loo, much to Helene's amazement, had turned out to be a relatively pleasant surprise. Apparently, when she'd lived at home it had housed an old, cracked toilet pan with a rotten wooden seat, several garden tools and a million spiders. Now it was painted blue, had a new loo and new wooden seat and only the one solitary representative of the arachnid community, a huge bulbous European garden spider whom Anna named Spud. She'd restrained her mother from plotting the immediate assassination of Spud, thereby managing to secure him a lifetime guarantee... so long as he kept to his side of the bargain and didn't start moving about or inviting members of his community to join him. Spud, Anna believed, should be allowed to continue happily dangling and doing whatever spiders do in their spider lives.

'So, I give a floodlit announcement to the world every time I need to use the toilet?' Anna groaned.

'Maybe but you'll be able to see Spud before he leaps on you.' Helene tickled the top of Anna's head with a clawed hand, making her duck abruptly out of the way.

'For someone who's worried about me being out here alone, you're not helping.' She took the brass key from her pocket and turned the lock to the shed.

'I'll go back then. Watch a bit of television with him! Are you sure I can't persuade you to join in? I still don't understand why you have to come out here so early.' Anna resisted the urge to lose her cool and instead took a very deep and very patient breath. Pushing her mother gently away, she stepped inside the shed and began to shut the door, grinning a toothy goodbye at her through the ever-decreasing gap. She hadn't mentioned that, apart from it being the very last thing she wanted to do that day, there was also the matter of the very obvious two armchairs instead of three. She hadn't mentioned it because to do so would hurt even more than it already did. Despite everything, when the door clicked shut and she turned around and leant against it, she had to admit that the shed, Little Argel, looked almost welcoming. It could perhaps, while her mother hunted for a job, really be a little retreat, somewhere to go, or to hide... or be hidden.

She'd slipped into her onesie, said goodnight to Gary and climbed into the creaky old structure that was now her bed. Rain fell on the roof above her and rapped loudly against the skylight while a crescent moon in a jet-black sky was disappointingly hidden by clouds. Even so, she'd known it was there, high in the sky, hanging above her new world. She'd fallen asleep imagining that she was flying through the inky air until she was sitting upon the curl of it, the red kite still dancing out of reach of her outstretched hand.

She took a photo of her morning skylight view, where a grey cloud puffed out its chest, outlined perfectly by the wood of the frame. She posted it to her friendship group back home and immediately received one back of a lampshade, a dead fly clearly dangling from one of the tassels. This triggered a series of bedroom ceiling photos from various members of the group, a fabulous red chandelier, a single bulb hanging from a flex, a yellow glow through a wicker shade, a ceiling hand-papered with sheets of music. Tears of ever-present raw emotion beaded in the corners of Anna's eyes and her throat constricted as she remembered she was no longer part of it all. Could no longer spend evenings or sleepovers in these rooms she knew so well. Her new school and the prospect of all that it may or may not bring was happening tomorrow and she was dreading it more than anything she'd ever dreaded in her entire life. Making a whole new friendship group when she already had one was far too hard to contemplate.

'Tell me what's going to be good about my new school, Gary, because right now I can't think of a single thing? I won't know a soul and the uniform is a hideous grey.' She pulled an expression of agony and rolled over in bed to confront her cactus, wise and succulent, on the little table beside her. 'A new best friend you say? How unrealistically hopeful of you, oh prickled one. I'm not convinced there will be any takers for that position in year ten because everyone will probably already have someone.' The flock of jitters that yesterday had taken up residence inside her chest took off again, irritating her insides in their flight. She tried to imagine what her first day would be like but her imagination failed her.

Breakfast is served. Be prepared, it's porridge! x

Another text from her mother lit up the screen of her phone and Anna pulled a face. 'Glue in a bowl, Gary, glue in a bowl. Pray for me and if that doesn't work, come to my funeral and think fond thoughts of me.' She then levered herself over the curved wooden frame of her bed, jumped onto the floor and made her way barefoot through the cool, rain-soaked grass, still in her onesie, her long brown hair now released from the confines of the twin buns on her head.

ALGERNON

Although much of the light from the window was almost completely choked by the wisteria, Algernon could see at breakfast that morning, that the child looked like a proper child. All that black eyeliner she'd been wearing on her arrival had gone, her skin now fresh and clean and her hair all loose and long. He couldn't help but be slightly rattled again, however, about the fact that she had nothing on her feet and was wearing something even more unusual than yesterday, a bright green all-in-one romper-suit item with yellow printed bows. Her head resting in one hand at the table while she pushed her porridge round her bowl added to Algernon's chagrin. She was whining again and he heard every word.

'It's... it's like... wallpaper paste,' she moaned, placing a small spoonful in her mouth.

'She said it's not got a lot of taste, Dad.' Helene gave a warning shot to the child and slid the sugar bowl across the table. 'It's good... *healthy* mmm yum!' Algernon raised an eyebrow at Helene's attempts to cover for her daughter's rudeness then watched with surprise as the child proceeded to ladle large amounts of sugar onto her porridge. He didn't need to be patronised and hadn't missed the looks that frequently passed between them both, like a secret game of minds that he wasn't party to.

'It doesn't need sugar – it's made the traditional Scottish way. Water and salt... no milk,' he said, noticing how the child's face slipped quicker than his disc had done several years back. He felt his neck begin to pulsate when they shared another look between themselves. It was as if they believed he might have committed some sort of food preparation crime.

'*Water* and *salt*?' The child spoke as if the words themselves tasted bad, then to add insult to injury, Algernon witnessed her poke her tongue out as far as it would go.

'Anna! Roll it back in!' Helene spoke in a theatrical whisper but then spoke loudly afterwards to deflect his attention. 'We can't keep eating your food, Dad. Anna and I will go shopping today. I could make us some homemade meals, you know, something fresh – lasagne, Bolognese, Chicken Kiev

– that sort of thing? Something *not* out of a tin perhaps or a packet?'

Algernon could barely disguise his alarm at the thought of all that over-flavoured food and felt the need to say so. 'Sounds positively cosmopolitan! I only eat plain food and I don't like spice and I certainly don't like chilli.'

'Well, they're hardly…' Helene began.

'Or garlic,' he interrupted. It annoyed him that Helene looked put out by the fact that he might have an input into his own dietary wishes, but he had to speak now or not at all.

'Well, I could…'

'Or anything too tough. It's my teeth.'

'What about…'

'I do like a sausage,' he said, 'certainly a roast chicken… definitely a crumble.' He and Evie had always liked their meals plain and simple. Anything more than that did particularly unnecessary things to his insides. The more he thought about the kind of food he hadn't eaten in so long he became quite excited as to whether Helene might indeed be able to rustle up something palatable. 'I'm rather partial to a jam roly-poly,' he added.

'If I could finish a bloody sentence perhaps we could actually discuss a menu that agrees with us all,' Helene snapped. Algernon cleared his throat loudly over the fact that she'd used an expletive where there was absolutely no justification for one but Helene didn't seem to care. 'I'll get some shopping in, start with something bland… I mean *simple*, and we'll take it from there OK?' Algernon nodded his agreement and rested his spoon in his now empty porridge bowl. As appealing as a homemade meal might be, he tried not to think too deeply about the chaos the proposed shopping trip and subsequent culinary activities might cause to his kitchen. Helene reached for his bowl and made to leave the room.

'Remember the teeth!' he called out. He thought he saw her roll her eyes just before she disappeared through the door.

'Like I'll ever forget,' she called back.

ANNA

Anna finished putting tiny yellow dots in the middle of a row of white daisies and studied her reflection in the mirror. She checked the image on the tutorial video on her phone, feeling satisfied she'd got it just right. Five little flowers now formed a chain under the arch of her eyebrow, resting on a swirl of eyeshadow that incorporated all the colours of a peacock's tail. Emerald green and cobalt blue with sparkles of copper blended their way from the inside corner of her eye, across her lid, eventually ending in a sweeping curl at the thin end of her brow. She turned her face again this way and that in front of the mirror and smiled. Three daisies, white with yellow centres, also paraded on the shell of one ear and she toyed with the idea of growing the flowers down her neck into a mini meadow on her shoulder. *Go be who you are*, Harry had said when he'd given her his gift. She took a photo of herself and liked what she saw. It was her, only much better.

The world, according to Anna, was always in need of more colour so she took it upon herself to provide it where possible, dressing like a rainbow for every occasion and leaving a generous wake of pigment with every step she took. She even used colour where colour was least expected in her school artwork: a pencil portrait with metallic green lips, charcoal people with multicoloured shadows, a single eye depicting a jet-black iris but with a multicoloured pupil.

She glowed with pleasure when she posted her photo to her friendship group and their positive replies came streaming back. Next she pulled on a green T-shirt, which perfectly highlighted the peacock colours of her eye make-up, a pair of brown and white cow-print shorts, black tights and purple DMs to finish the look. After taking one more full-length photo for her Instagram album she made her way out of the shed blowing a kiss to her cactus. 'See you later, Gary. We're going shopping for my school uniform!'

'That's... *amazing*!' Helene said, peering in closely to get a better look at her daughter's face as she entered the sitting room. 'It looks like something straight out of *Vogue*.' Anna felt an instant thrill of delight fizzing inside her at the idea that her creativity might ever reach such fanciful heights. She turned her phone camera on again and indulged herself with another moment of pleasure at how perfect the daisies were.

'Looks more like you're straight out of the circus,' her grandfather called from over the top of his newspaper, swapped his reading glasses for his regular ones and raised his overzealous eyebrows in her direction. There was no humour in his eyes, just a kind of disgust or disapproval, which made the colour of his irises turn a cooler shade of seawater. His comment stung Anna hard and her confidence seemed to freeze solid in her chest before dropping down into the pit of her stomach. Her initial pride became unexpectedly tainted with a mixture of hurt and embarrassment and in silence she stared back at him until his face blurred into a watery blob. She wiped hurriedly at her eyes before he could see her tears until all her hard work became nothing more than ruined smears upon her cheeks.

'It doesn't at all! It's *brilliant*, Anna.' Helene stepped forward and pressed the palms of her hands against her daughter's cheeks sympathetically. 'Well, it *was* brilliant,' she added, almost growling in the direction of her father as a dog might growl to protect its young. 'Don't let *anyone* tell you differently.'

For Anna, her mother's protection was too late. The words had been said and could not be unsaid. She turned tail and ran back to her shed to erase what was left of her make-up daisies.

'Don't let him get to you like that, Anna.' Helene opened the shed door and slid inside, reaching her arms out to embrace her daughter in a sympathetic hug. 'He's an old fossil and because of that he can't understand that you're different from what he's used to, that's all.' She squeezed extra tightly. 'You're my *Moonchild* don't forget.'

Anna secretly loved her mother's pet name for her, like she belonged to an inky sky in a galaxy of shimmering stars, unconditionally loved for being Anna. 'Quirky!' was the way Helene had always described her. 'You're a free spirit all full up with imagination and specialness,' she'd say when Anna was little and would come out of school covered with pictures she'd drawn on her skin, or with glitter she'd poured on her hair, or coloured tissue paper stapled to her school skirt. She'd climb the trees that were out of bounds on the edge of the school field and for every non-uniform charity day would go one step further and spray her hair a vibrant blue.

Helene was nearly always met at the gates by a frustrated teacher who wanted to complain about something her daughter had done; slipping her shoes off under the desk or kicking them off in the playground, preferring to run around in bare feet like a woodland imp. When Anna would ask why the teachers always got so mad with her and why she had to conform to stupid rules that didn't make sense her mother would always reply, 'Because you see the world in a different light from them. You're my Moonchild and you shine with all things lovely.'

She never grew out of decorating her skin with her own artwork and liked to think she was becoming successfully alternative when it came to fashion. She'd grown comfortable with herself… until the crashing moment when one comment from a mean old man had somehow sent her confidence into a spiral. 'What if he's right and everyone thinks I look like I'm out of a circus?' Anna sniffed juicily and itched her jaw where a dangling tear was tickling it. 'Maybe I've never realised how stupid I look. Maybe you can't see it because you're my mum and you'd probably say I looked great in a bin bag.'

The awakening of self-doubt began to grow in the pit of her stomach. It mixed with her new vulnerability and in that moment Anna began to question who she was. A cold fear was taking root and growing like a magical vine along every inch of her body until it was tight around her neck and icy down her spine. 'What if no one at the new school gets me either?' She searched her mother's eyes for an answer but a fresh round of tears prevented her from seeing one. Pulling a tissue from her pocket, Helene handed it over and pressed it into her hand.

'They will "*get*" you. It will be fine.' Anna blew her nose into the tissue, surprised at just how much there was to blow, then searched amongst the crumples for a dry corner to blow into again.

'But what if it's not *fine*?' She hated the word *fine*. It was always such a flimsy word, a fob-off... a veiled lie. She handed the tissue back to her mother and Helene wrinkled her nose a little before dropping it in the bin. Then she circled her arms back around her daughter and hugged her like only a mother can hug. It was as if she thought she could draw the pain straight out of her child's body and into her own. Anna, however, knew differently.

'It *will* be fine. Trust me,' she crooned into the top of Anna's head, her breath warm on her scalp. 'Anyway, you can't wear make-up at school so don't stress about it – you'll look exactly the same as everyone else.' This may have seemed a simple thing, to look the same as everyone else, but for Anna this had always been an issue. For Anna, expression of self was just as important as nurturing a talent or honing a skill. At her old school she always weaved blue ribbons into her dark hair, braiding it into thick vibrant plaits because it was as near as she could get to having coloured hair without actually dyeing it. The uniform at her old school had been blue whereas now it was to be grey. She felt herself sag, held up only by the strength of her mother's embrace when she realised that this too was a thing of the past.

'I feel like I'm leaving myself behind,' she sniffed, 'that the person I've always been doesn't belong in this place.'

ALGERNON

Algernon initially felt distinct relief when the child appeared the next morning wearing her new, and very smart, school uniform, a neat pleated grey skirt with a grey blazer over a crisp white shirt and striped grey and gold tie. Unfortunately, as his eyes travelled up towards her hair, he experienced entirely the opposite feeling. The child's head was blue! She'd braided her long hair into two plaits and had somehow wound a ridiculous quantity of ribbon through each. Blue strands appeared somewhere near the crown of her head and ended in a silken fray, which was even longer than the length of her hair.

Last night Helene had fractured the air in the room like a cracked nut after they'd both retired to the sitting room for the evening. 'You would love her if only you knew her,' Helene had suddenly said, and Algernon had found that he'd needed to manage his composure, so taken aback was he at being required to enter into a conversation at such an hour. He'd reached for a TV magazine and proceeded to fold it carefully on the television column for that day, trying to defuse the situation by quizzing her from over the top of his glasses.

'*Morse*?' He suggested. 'Or I have a recording of *Midsomer Murders*?'

'She's your grandchild,' Helene had added. She'd slipped off her shoes and tucked her feet comfortably under herself in the armchair opposite. For two evenings now he'd struggled to put himself in check with the fact that it was she, not Evie, sitting there. Evie had died in that chair and yet it always felt to him as if the essence of her still rested there, a part of her always lingering within the tartan threads. Algernon had dropped his eyes away from the glare of Helene's and had steadfastly continued to examine his magazine, his head bobbing up and down as he scanned the viewing choices in front of him. He was tired and knew that to speak now would be to begin a verbal autopsy on their situation. Pointing the remote control at the television he selected an episode of *Inspector Morse* that he hoped he hadn't seen before. Two hours followed where they both suffered his favourite detective programme, the plot of which he now had absolutely no recollection of.

You would love her if only you knew her. Helene's words bounced around in his head as the child now stood before him. 'I really don't think your new school will let you get away with that,' Helene commented.

'Ridiculous!' Algernon added, hunting for his distance glasses, to afford him a clearer look. 'You look like a ruddy maypole!' He'd spoken out loud again before consulting his own self as to whether it was appropriate to do so and Evie would have shushed him harshly, he was sure. Promising himself to remain silent without any further input he clenched his false teeth together while Helene shot a look at him. The child, who remained rooted to the spot, cocked her blue head.

'I don't know what a maypole is,' she said, twiddling the ends of each plait in her fingers. Finding his distance glasses on his head rather than on the table, Algernon put them on and noticed how a flush had bloomed across the child's cheeks. *How can a child not know what a maypole is?* he thought. Helene forced a smile and then pierced him with it as she rose to the child's defence.

'It's to do with a beautiful event where a tall pole with lots of ribbons is used in a day of celebration for the arrival of spring,' she said.

'Oh.' The child shrugged. 'That's nice... I *think*.' Algernon kept his promise to himself and managed not to enter into a corrective discussion about decorated trees and the goddess Flora but he really wanted to.

'Yes! A maypole is a *lovely* comparison.' Helene was smiling widely, her lips barely moving as she spoke through her teeth, then to Algernon's relief she added, 'But you should save the hair thing for when you get home. I hear that this new school is very keen regarding appearance.' *Hallelujah!* Algernon thought, but then the child tilted her chin and squared her shoulders in a manner he recognised only too well from both Evie and Helene. He realised that the discussion was not yet over.

'*I'm* keen regarding *my* appearance and there isn't, as far as I know, a school rule against wearing ribbons in your hair... so I'm keeping them in.' She nodded sharply as if to punctuate her point just as Helene glanced at the carriage clock and gasped at the time.

'Shit,' she breathed, fumbling for her keys in her handbag. 'Come on, Anna, we need to go... on your head be it.' She laughed a little at her own joke and ushered the child down the hallway towards the front door. Algernon's glasses slipped down his nose as he struggled to get out of his chair. He needed his daily newspaper and hoped that a walk and some fresh air might help to put his world to rights again. *Blue plaits indeed!* Helene was standing by the open front door where she pointed her key fob at her car, which emitted a beep that allowed the child to climb inside. She hurriedly did the zip up on her coat as Algernon reached for his own. 'I'll get your paper for you while I'm out, Dad. Save you the trip.' She had already made her way down the steps before Algernon managed to get one stiff shoulder far enough back to slip his arm in the sleeve. The effort of it distressed him.

'I'm not dead yet,' he grumbled after her, issuing a breathy huff when at last he shook his coat on. He'd made his trip to the corner shop almost every single day for a good many years and he wasn't prepared to stop now. It was part of his routine and he believed that it was quite possibly the only thing that had kept his heart beating adequately enough to stop him perishing. He appraised the child's profile in the car as she waited for Helene and bristled at the fact that she was to be charioted a meagre half a mile instead of walking herself. 'Why are you driving her anyway? It's not exactly a hike,' he called, gripping hold of a handrail and gingerly placing his foot on the top step.

'Because it's her first day and I'm nice like that!' Helene called back as she got in the car and shut the door behind her.

As he watched them drive away, Algernon experienced an unwelcome feeling that stirred up an old image. Helene's car, as it disappeared down the road of new houses, became an old Austin leaving a cloud of dust and a small boy on the road behind it. The Austin wouldn't return the small boy to his home in a few hours' time as Helene would for her child; it would be weeks before he saw it again. He hunched his painful shoulders to shake off the past, which had cruelly reached out to him and brushed his skin with icy tendrils. He was no longer a small child; he was no longer that boy. He was a very old man who needed to take the first of his many slow steps to the shop.

When Helene brought the child back to his house later that day with her hair tousled and loose and the ribbons nowhere to be seen, he felt quite triumphant. She looked like a proper schoolgirl now, with regular hair and wearing a regular school uniform. The normality of her appearance made him feel more settled inside and it pleased him to know that the monstrously big school that had replaced the little school he now lived in still held fast to traditional values. At least that aspect of modern living hadn't changed.

★ ★ ★

ANNA

'It's bad, really *really* bad.' Anna sat on the bed in Little Argel wearing only her underwear, holding a handful of blue ribbons, yet another dribble of tears on her cheeks. Her uniform was on the floor in the various stages it had taken her to strip off the second she came through the door. 'They told me to take the ribbons out of my hair… in *front* of *everyone*.'

'Who are you talking to?' Helene asked, opening the door to the shed and stepping inside.

'Gary,' she answered, wiping at her damp face with the back of her hand.

'It's a cactus, Anna!' Helene said, closing the door behind her and bending to scoop up the uniform that was strewn across the floor.

'Yes, well he's the only friend I'm going to make in this shitty place,' Anna said.

'That bad?' Helene asked, taking the green onesie off the bottom of the bed and handing it to her daughter. 'And don't say "*shitty*".'

'You say it all the time,' Anna accused, sniffing a gurgle of snot up her nose as she slipped into her onesie and zipped it up. 'You said my first day would be just "*fine*" but it wasn't *fine*.' Despite the early hour she climbed onto her bed and pulled Harry's soft blue blanket over her head, the wood of the frame creaking beneath her.

'Can I guess they didn't like the hair?' Helene bunched the ribbons together and placed them in a wicker basket that contained an abundance of colourful hair accessories.

'It's *uniform policy* apparently. No "*silly*" hairstyles! Everyone laughed at me.' Anna tapped angrily at her phone from under the blanket, offloading the misery of her new life to her faraway friends back home.

'I don't suppose they did.' Helene slid the blanket off Anna's head and her hair crackled and lifted into a static halo.

'I don't suppose *you* were there?' Anna snapped. 'At my old school no one ever said anything.' She could hear a long sigh travelling outwardly on her mother's breath and wanted to grab it out of the air, screw it into a ball and throw it on the ground.

'Kids would get bullied if there wasn't a uniform policy. Some would come in wearing designer labels and some wouldn't have the money.' Helene rubbed Anna's back and spoke words that didn't make sense. It was such a stupidly *adult* thing to say. Why, she wondered, didn't teachers wear a uniform if they were so keen on representing the school?

'Kids get bullied anyway.' If school taught her anything it taught her that kids could be cruel. It taught her that body weight or lack of money or physical clumsiness, or culture, or looks or thick glasses or *absolutely anything* could get you bullied if a bully wants to bully. What stopped you getting bullied was confidence in self and she had just lost that confidence in self. Helene smoothed Anna's hair down then she reached for her hand and squeezed it tightly. Anna did not return the squeeze.

Pitching up halfway through year ten with no good reason for the school transfer other than your mum's boyfriend left you both in abject poverty and now you have to live with some ancient relative with false teeth and massive eyebrows that you'd never met before in your life, took some effort to style out. Anna knew with a horrible certainty that she had *not* managed to style it out. Without warning, the person who she thought she was had got sucked so deep inside herself that she was in danger of disappearing, leaving nothing but an awkward Anna-shaped shell behind. The last thing her mother had said to her that morning was: *You're my Moonchild don't forget. It's OK to be you,* yet for the first time, Anna wondered if perhaps it wasn't OK to be her.

'Give it time, Anna.' Helene squeezed again at the limp hand within her own. 'When they get to know you like I know you, they will love you too.'

'And Grandad? Will he want to get to know me… or love me too?'

Helene gave a long sigh at this and Anna imagined Little Argel filling up with their mutual sighs all lingering sadly in the air. 'I don't know about your grandad. I sometimes think that your grandma was the only person he knew how to love and who knew how to love him back.'

Anna lay on her back and stared through the skylight, picturing the old man in his armchair, inside his house, hunched and alone. 'Maybe…' she began. 'Maybe he's got an invisible uniform on and he can't find a way to take it off and be who he is? Maybe no one other than Grandma could see the real him?'

At this, her mother leant over and kissed the top of her head several times in a row. 'You know, you're so very much like your grandma. Perhaps that's exactly what's happened to Grandad.'

* * *

ALGERNON

That evening, surrounded by gloom and boxes, the three of them sat down to a meal that Algernon instinctively knew, just by the look of it, he wasn't going to appreciate. He valiantly attempted the task of eating what had been put in front of him but whichever way he looked at it, the first food anyone had cooked for him since Evie had died was more of a challenge than a joy.

'It's like trying to eat something that's still alive,' he grumbled. 'Totally pointless! I don't understand why we should battle with our food when there's a perfectly good potato to be had!' He noticed, as he was complaining, how Helene shared another of her not-so-secret eye rolls with the child. He stabbed his fork into a mound of spaghetti and muttered under his breath as he twizzled and scooped, totally unable to keep the stuff on his fork for any fruitful length of time. Finally, lowering his face towards his plate, he managed to get some of the strands into his mouth but they were so long the ends hung down his chin before he could bite them in half.

'Oh cut it up then,' Helene snapped. 'Anna, get a knife for him, although I can't believe he's never eaten spaghetti before. *Everyone's* eaten spaghetti!'

Algernon made no comment. He took the knife from the child when she returned from the kitchen but he offered no gratitude. Why, he thought, should he be thankful for needing a knife instead of a spoon and fork he would never know. Slippery food was always going to use up far more energy to consume than it provided and energy was something he was sorely lacking these days.

He had, of course, eaten spaghetti. He'd also eaten linguine, fettuccine, tortellini and several other types of pasta, but it didn't mean he welcomed it now. He'd been introduced to pasta when he was stationed in Italy after the war, a heart-breaking lifetime ago. His fork rattled against his plate as his hands began to tremble more than they normally did and he realised that it was happening again. More memories were threatening to burst through the tidy boxes inside his mind. Memories that had stayed dormant for so long were stirring again and disturbing the equipoise of his mind. He could almost smell the strong Italian coffee he had drunk in Italy, and almost feel the blistering sun on his face, his skin sweating under the cloth of his Royal Air Force uniform.

Ever since he'd climbed onto the roof of his village school to retrieve the ball, he'd dreamt of flying, of growing wings and soaring up into the clouds to escape his fate. Night after miserable night he'd imagined climbing onto the windowsill in his boarding school dormitory and flying away. When World War Two broke out the RAF had offered him a chance to go to America to gain his pilot 'wings', he'd grabbed it with both hands. By the time the war was in full swing, not only was he entitled to wear the badge of a pilot, but he could finally take control of his own destiny. Algernon at last had wings to fly.

He twirled his spaghetti around his fork, then watched it slide limply back off onto his plate. Italy, although war-torn in parts by 1947 when he was stationed there, had been a beautiful country. He could still picture the splendour of the Italian landscape below him as he flew over it on Air Force duties that would lead him over Europe, across the deserts of Africa and finally to Egypt. The war had been over for a while, the loose ends of it still being gathered and tied, yet for

Algernon, the RAF was his job for life. He remembered how, during this mission in Italy, he had turned to salute each of his pilot buddies whose aircraft flanked his, their disembodied voices coming through the radio. As the twin engines of his aeroplane vibrated through his soul he had known that there was no other feeling in all the world like flying.

'I guess you're not enjoying it then?' The sound of Helene's voice brought him harshly back to the present and she was clearly annoyed that he wasn't eating his food. It took him a second or two to gather his bearings and to ground himself. His reverie had been so vivid, so *yesterday*, so part of a time when he still had dreams.

'How was the new school?' he asked the child, trying to shake off the aching sadness that his memory had left him with. The child groaned loudly into her plate of food.

'It was rubbish,' she said, sucking on a string of spaghetti that slipped into her mouth and left a blob of orange sauce on her lips.

'What does that mean, *rubbish*?' He retrieved his large, white hanky from his pocket and wiped at his white beard which, he was fairly sure, was now spattered with the same orange sauce. Algernon scrutinised her from under his eyebrows and noted how Cat circled the child's legs, hoping for some attention from his new friend. The defiance and bolshiness he'd detected only that morning from her had thankfully gone but rather than compliance he was detecting something else. He didn't enjoy guesswork when it came to the human psyche yet if he were to give it a go, he'd say the child was unhappy. 'Didn't you make any friends?' he asked, immediately understanding that life, as he well knew, was not that simple.

The child swirled another tangle of spaghetti around her fork, successfully piling it inside her mouth and talking through it.

'No! Apart from the fact that they made me look stupid in front of everyone, they tried to buddy me up with two girls who as soon as we had break time all they talked about was sex and smoking. They weren't my kind of friends.'

Algernon choked on the small amount of food he'd successfully scooped into his own mouth and as he coughed he felt his dentures come partially away from their moorings. He'd long ago given up trying to anchor them in place. '*Sex* and *smoking* – for God's sake you're fifteen!' he cried, having chomped his dentures back into place. He turned to Helene for desperate moral backup but Helene frustratingly appeared to be on the verge of laughing, her annoyance over his lack of appetite seemingly forgotten.

'Calm down, Dad. Like Anna said, sex and smoking are not her thing.'

'I should hope not!' he spluttered.

'At least, not at the same time.' Helene laughed coarsely at her own joke while Algernon tutted and continued to peer at the child from under his eyebrows. The air of melancholy surrounding her caused him to privately acknowledge that he might have been wrong to ask about the events of the day. Although uncomfortable about this fact, Algernon was entirely used to putting his foot in things so instead, clearing his throat, he decided that it was a pertinent moment to change the subject.

'I have a delivery coming tomorrow,' he announced. 'Apparently if I had something called text message or the online they'd be able to tell me what time my delivery is due to arrive. As it is I can't even leave the house to get my newspaper for fear of it arriving at the very moment I'm not here.' He was rather proud of himself for having organised his delivery and found himself to be quite bucked up at the idea of sharing the news. Helene scraped her fork along her plate, an irritating sound that pierced through his hearing aids as she turned to look at the child with something akin to eagerness.

'Why don't you get Wi-Fi then? You could join the *real* world, Dad. You wouldn't have to wait in all day for your deliveries...'

'Delivery... *singular*,' Algernon interrupted.

'... and Anna and I could stop using up all our phone data.' Algernon had absolutely no idea what Helene was talking about regarding data and he didn't need the Wi-Fi thing. He was quite content to remain old-fashioned and to keep things simple. 'Anyway, if you were online you could have received an email notifying you of the time slot for your delivery... *singular*.'

'Is the world so full of imbeciles that no one can pick up a telephone anymore to communicate... like real human beings?' He jabbed at his plate, no longer able to make any effort with food that tasted of the bitter regret of his past. 'I don't know what you mean by data or the Wi-Fi but if it's something to do with the online business then I don't want it!' He saw the child suddenly bow her head, allowing her hair to fall forward into her plate. Then he believed he heard her issue a snort. So *this* she finds entertaining, he thought and his embarrassment over being made to feel inconsequential poked a painful dent in his pride.

'Yes it is something to do with being online, Dad. It's

broadband! The internet! The World Wide Web! It's almost impossible to get by in this day and age without it. You need it for communicating, googling, basically *everything*...' Helene pushed an unwieldy forkful into her mouth in a manner that he found quite off-putting and which prompted him to place his knife and fork down on his plate and push the lot away. He'd get himself some bread and jam when this fiasco was over. He didn't want technology in his house... or spaghetti!

'Everything?' he echoed, certain that it was indeed *not* required for everything.

At this, the child sat up straight, flung her hair back over her shoulders and looked the most animated he'd seen since she'd arrived. 'Everything! Just *everything*. Snapchat, Instagram, music, books, maps, games, TikTok, YouTube, shopping...' Strange words issued from her mouth with a rapidity that made Algernon wonder what on earth had happened to the English language. He studied them both and their avidity was baffling him.

'I have a shelf of books, a cupboard of games, a wireless, and an atlas... and I don't need to know what this snapping insistagram thing is. I get by perfectly well without all that twaddle.' He felt a vein pulsing in his temples and did his best to calm himself down despite the fact that the child was squashing her mouth together in clear amusement of him.

'For God's sake, Dad,' Helene groaned. 'You make it sound as if progress is a bad thing. You'll just have to wait in all day until your thing arrives. I'm going to the job centre so make sure you've got your hearing aids in to listen out for when they knock on the door. What are you having delivered anyway?'

Algernon pushed himself up from his seat in order to go

and make himself something more palatable to eat. 'I've ordered another armchair,' he said.

ANNA

There wasn't much that was different about Anna... on the outside. On the outside she now looked the same as everyone else at school. On the outside she was grey, shackled by the school uniform, swept along in a grey sea, drowning slowly and silently amongst a grey crowd. On the *inside*, however, she was a riot of colour and imagination. Today would have been a floral DMs kind of day, the black ones painted with multicoloured flowers on the leather. Today would have been a yellow skirt and a rainbow-striped top kind of day and her hair a vibrant cascade of ultramarine. Her ears would have sparkled with a row of silver hoops and her make-up would have been a work of art. Perhaps today she would have created a seascape on her eyelids, palm trees spreading their greenness into her brows, a sprinkle of golden starfish across her cheeks.

As far as Anna was concerned, only the confident kids who possessed brains or beauty or personality... sometimes all three, could shine through the *sameness* of a uniform. Anna, stripped of all that was Anna, could not shine. The way she dressed on the outside reflected how she felt on the inside. It was her strength, a personification of her emotion, an expression of her energy. Her blue hair was her statement... her *Anna*. Adults, she thought frustratedly, could decide whether the day was going to be a white shirt kind of day, or a blue jumper kind of day, a pink shoes, green skirt or a purple jacket kind of day. They could change the colour of their hair or the beads on their jewellery or the colour of their nail varnish… all depending on what mood they were in. No one, she was sure, had ever considered what it felt like to be lost in the way that Anna Maybury was lost.

She pressed her forehead against the warm body of Cat who'd taken to following her down the stepping-stone path into Little Argel. 'I wish I was a cat,' she murmured into his fur. 'I wish I was anyone other than me.'

Today was another school day that had to be endured, painfully, sadly and so very, very alone. She'd tried, she really had, but the first two girls she'd been buddied up with at the beginning were now whispering about her and they'd gathered other whisperers to join them. Heads had begun to turn when she walked into the classroom, and the rock-solid friendship groups that gathered at break times were impenetrable. She was stiff and awkward in her own body and the possibility of smiling at people she didn't know, or randomly walking over to them, or chipping in to their conversations was impossible. It was as if she had become a nervous actress in a play about herself.

There was another whole year of awful days ahead of her before she could leave school forever. Would she ever be able to find the Anna Maybury she used to be before she had to move, the Anna Maybury who laughed at funny things until her belly hurt, or took up a dare, or drew flowers on her skin, or danced at parties?

'I've become a fairground sideshow, guys.' She looked miserably between Cat and Gary as if they might offer her some sympathy. Some of the kids in her new history class had invented a game that day. A missile, which hit her head without the teacher noticing who threw it, scored a full ten points! An apple, thrown by a boy called Adam, won him a further bonus of five points because it bounced off her head and landed in her school bag. When she accidentally yelled loud enough to create a stir, there was nothing visible to incriminate him. She was becoming the easy target for any bored kids who were partial to the sport of bullying and there was nothing she could do about it. If she told her mother, she'd demand they go to the school to sort things out and that would only make things much worse. Everyone would find out that the new kid was a baby who had to get her mummy to fight her battles for her and that might as well, thought Anna, be the end of her life.

'Don't say anything either of you,' she said, pointing a finger at Cat and then at Gary before placing it against her lips. 'It will only make things worse. No one can help me now.' She fingered the blue ribbons tied around her wrist, carefully braided and tied with a fast knot. However hard they tried they would not erase her completely.

4

Square Pegs

ALGERNON

Every now and again the three of them, like now, found themselves sitting in Algernon's sitting room together in a moment of forced familial bonding. He could see that Helene had, to give her her due, been trying to get employment but, as yet, had been entirely unsuccessful. The three generations of Maybury now sat, with the television on, trying to convince themselves that it was perfectly pleasant to be sharing their time in this way and that they were all there of their own accord. Algernon tried to ignore his certainty that Helene had probably dragged the child out of Little Argel to show her face and a bit of respect, such was the air of melancholy that surrounded her. There were edges and angles to the atmosphere in his house when they were all three together and he knew that each and every one of them felt it.

He was rattled again. The child was occupying the new armchair, sprawled across it with her legs hooked over the arms, in a very unladylike manner and wearing another odd outfit of strawberry pink and lemon yellow. She looked like one of those chewy sweets that got stuck to the roof of children's mouths. Helene was occupying the empty chair opposite him which, however hard he tried to overcome it, still rattled him more than anything. It was as if she was squashing the space that belonged to Evie. As if she was actually sitting on the ghost of her. He'd never shared with Helene the full details of when Evie had last sat in that very chair. How Evie's face had become slack, turning a ghastly shade of waxy yellow, her glass of sherry, ready to toast in the new year, slipping from her hand. How he'd knelt on the carpet by her feet repeatedly assuring her that she would be just fine... until the paramedics arrived to confirm what he already knew. How he'd held her lifeless hand until they'd prised him away, severing her from him forever.

'Have you visited the museum yet?' he asked, shaking off the image and hoping to inspire a modicum of enthusiasm from them to go out and do something other than lie like lizards on his furniture. They were both staring at those infernal phones of theirs and not even watching the programme that was on. He might as well be alone for all the company they were.

'Yes,' Helene said, without looking up.

'The town gardens?'

'Yes,' she said, still not looking up.

'The library.'

'Yes we've been to the library too.' Her words flowed out on the tide of a single sigh and he knew he was grating on her nerves but the fact that they were motionless, save for their fingers swiping at the screens of their phones, was something that grated on his own nerves. The programme on current affairs that was on was interesting albeit somewhat alarming, yet they seemed to be totally disengaged with the real world.

'Wasn't like this in my day,' he said, referring to the story and trying to extricate some kind of reaction in the hope of intelligent conversation.

'Unless you died without telling me, I think you'll find this *is* still your day.' Helene looked briefly up at him. 'Every day is everyone's day until we bugger off to buffalo... I mean *shuffle* off to buffalo.' Algernon turned down the volume on the television, relieved to see that she had the decency to look mildly apologetic regarding the *buggering off* comment. He reached for his stick and used it to poke the child on the shoulder, making her jump out of her skin. Pulling one of her earphones out, she looked quizzically at him to see what he wanted.

'What are you doing? You haven't stopped staring at that thing for over an hour.' He waved his stick in the general direction of the child's phone.

'You could have someone's eye out with that thing,' Helene intervened as he placed his stick back against the corner of the fireplace. 'This is what they do now, Dad. They socialise in the virtual world with their phones... smartphones they're called.'

'In my day...' He coughed, then corrected himself for her benefit. 'When I was young we used to do this thing called *talking* to people.'

'Two baked bean tins at each end of three hundred miles of string are not going to cut it, no matter how many times you try to sell to her what you did when you were young.' Helene sounded as if she were cross with him and he couldn't for the life of him work out what he'd done this time. Did people not pick up the telephone to speak anymore? Was humanity destined to lose the power of conversation as well as everything else the political world was tossing up and refashioning? The child was eyeing him with a sullen expression on her face, and he found himself feeling further rattled by the notion that he somehow may have put his foot in things again.

'Well whatever's going on in that smartphone thing it's not healthy if you ask me. Head bowed, staring at it all day long.' Algernon sniffed but continued to watch her tapping away at her phone.

'All the people I know are miles away now... I can't just go and see them even if I wanted to.' As the child spoke he saw that her sullen expression was not sullenness at all but sadness and he shrugged his shoulders, wincing a little at the pain.

'Why don't you write to them then? It's an activity that would pass the time nicely,' he suggested. Writing newsy letters to friends and family across the miles had always been a satisfying form of correspondence to his mind. The anticipation of return mail was not only thrilling but the wait for it was deeply rewarding. He himself still had an abundance of letters that he and Evie had saved from their earlier years. Letters that spanned years, continents even, bound with ribbons and still stored neatly inside an old hatbox under his bed.

The child held her phone up to him as if he should understand its capabilities. 'We don't need to write letters. We're on a group chat! We can all message each other and see everything we're doing even though we're not in the same room... or county even.'

Algernon really didn't understand. How could there be a gathering of youngsters inside the technology of such a tiny thing? Processing the idea of it made him fidget and he wished again that the chair opposite him was not occupied by Helene. He wanted to picture Evie sitting in her chair handling the situation for him, being everything that he could not be for their family... like she always used to. She would have been able to ask all sorts of questions of the child with an ease that he just didn't possess. Even so, to please Evie, were there the possibility that she was still close by him, he took a deep breath, knowing that he was about to venture into uncharted territory.

'Tell me how that tiny scrap of metal or plastic or whatever it's made of can enable you to do all this?' He waggled a finger in the direction of the child's phone, feeling a degree of surprise when she obediently proceeded to unhook her bare feet from the arm of the chair and lifted Cat off her stomach to plonk him on the floor. She made her way over to him and knelt on the carpet next to his chair and held her phone towards him. The way she casually instigated their close proximity, caused him to catch himself with the unfamiliarity of it.

'Here, this is how I talk to my friends. See? This last message was from Amy and this...' she tapped at the screen using the pad of her thumbs '... is my reply. It's instant!' She pushed the screen of her phone towards him where, if he peered close enough, he could see a string of letters and picture symbols.

Algernon felt his heart quicken, being unable to make a blind bit of sense out of anything in front of him. He'd been an intelligent man once upon a time and it pained him to think that he'd lost his grip. He'd been a flight lieutenant in the RAF for crying out loud, had another position of responsibility within the Corporation for years after that, yet he couldn't fathom a modern mobile phone.

'What is all this gobbledygook?' he asked.

'It's just text. It's like code I suppose but we all know what we're saying.' The child aimed her phone at her feet and Algernon hardly dare ask what on earth she was doing. Between her toes and across the top of one foot he noticed that she'd drawn an intricate trail of tiny, coloured flowers. The toenails on both feet were painted in alternating shades of red, yellow and orange as if she hadn't been able to make her mind up as to which colour to use. She pressed her finger on the screen and seemed pleased about it. 'There! I've just sent a picture of my feet to my friendship group.'

Algernon stared in wonder, becoming extremely perplexed and more than a little confused about what was happening. 'Oh really? And why would anyone want to see your feet?' he enquired.

'I'm showing them my artwork and also how I've painted my toes,' she answered.

He peered even closer, imagining a world of the totally unfathomable going on with the youngsters of the day. 'And people want to see that do they?' Even Evie and her keenness to embrace change might have been befuddled by this one surely? 'Do you think they would want to see *my* feet?' He felt unexpectedly quite tickled by what he'd just said but the child studied him briefly and not detecting any humour said nothing.

'My friends used to like the things I did,' she said, a wistful tone in her voice. 'See, here are some photos of my artwork and my doodles.' She ran her finger swiftly over the screen of the phone where a series of colourful hand-drawn pictures whizzed past Algernon's inspection. In amongst the strange and the beautiful, her photographs clearly depicted aspects of the life she had before coming to his house. He thought he saw a picture of a silvery moon and a child holding a bright red kite.

'Look!' she said, as her finger stopped scrolling and on the screen now was a photograph of several young people. 'These are my friends. That's Amy and that's Kieran, Joshua, Gracie, Imogen and Ava. Obviously that's me in the middle.'

'Obviously,' he echoed, taking the phone from her and studying the scene where, in the middle of a huddle of laughing teenagers was the child, wearing a pair of light blue flares and a rainbow-striped top, her hair parted into two blue-ribboned plaits. She was smiling. A smile the likes of which he hadn't witnessed since their arrival, not one single time. Caught in the creases of her smiling face was Evie. He'd seen the likeness when he first opened the door to them, and he could see it again now. It brought about an unwelcome tremor to his hands, which prompted him to hand the thing back to her.

'I don't have any friends here. Everyone at school thinks I'm weird.' She got up from the carpet and went back to her chair, flopping herself into it in that graceless fashion of hers; then pushing her earphones back into her ears she curled into the chair with her back to him. Cat leapt onto the arm of the chair and across the child's body until he made himself comfortable, his grey body draped across her shoulders.

Algernon found himself dwelling over the intimacy of their mutual encounter and pondering this most unusual child. He thought about the colours she wore and the seemingly mismatched clothes, the theatrical use of make-up and the bright nail varnish she frequently applied. He thought about her first day at school and how she'd left, utterly defiant, with bright blue plaits in her hair and yet had come home, utterly furious, without them. He couldn't understand her at all and, apart from the traces of Evie that lay upon her features, she was certainly like no person he had ever met in his lifetime.

Lifting his stick he tapped her and once again she pulled out her earphones to see what he wanted. 'You've only been there five minutes,' he heard himself say, immediately dismayed at the accusatory tone that had come out of his throat. It was as if his own voice box always disobeyed his brain's orders to show a degree of pleasant exchange. She glanced at him derisively.

'I've been there for ages and it's never going to change. Square pegs don't fit into round holes!' They held each other's gaze for a short while after that as unfurling inside himself were distant memories that knocked upon the door he'd closed against them decades ago. Before looking away and returning to his programme on the television he offered her a single nod of his head. He knew this statement to be true: square pegs don't fit into round holes... not even when you tried to force them to.

ANNA

A huge butterfly with silver-tipped wings landed on Anna's exercise book, each of its six delicate feet treading in the ink of her handwriting before casting kisses of blue across the page in butterfly footprints. Mr Beacham said at the beginning of his ramblings from *The Biological World*, that butterflies taste with their feet and they smell with their antennae. She'd been inspired to create the masterpiece of butterfly doodles, complete with little mouths on the feet and tiny noses on the antennae, and with extra big, shiny eyes. Now she was in the satisfying process of detailing each minuscule scale layered upon its wings with a silver-inked pen. When she'd finished she'd send the photo to her friends back home who, she was sure, would love this latest creation.

'Am I boring you, Anna?' Mr Beacham had, at some point, halted his walkabout of the classroom and stopped at the desk where she now ineffectually spread her hands across the page to hide her artwork. 'Am I? Boring you?' He brushed her hands away from her work, exposing her crime and jabbing at the open pages of her exercise book with a tobacco-stained nail. Her intricate and daringly large drawing covered the entire open pages of her book, beneath the only sentence she'd written since the beginning of class: *Butterflies have compound eyes made up of thousands of ommatidia – a cluster of light receptor cells...*

'I covered *ommatidia* several insects ago!' He continued to jab at the butterfly with his yellowed finger. 'What is all this? *And...* BACK IN YOUR SEATS!' Seemingly everyone in the class was craning their necks and shoving their chairs back to stand up and get a better look.

'I... I... was drawing a diagram?' She knew it was a lame excuse and the barely suppressed laughter that rippled through the classroom made her want to completely disappear. She balled her hands into angry fists under the desk while Mr Beacham kept his finger pressed on her work, the stench of stale smoke making its way up her nose.

'I don't know about teachers at your other school but here we prefer it if students actually bother to stick to the given subject. I kind of like my students to do *science* in my lessons. Know what I mean?'

'Yes,' she replied, breathing slowly out through her nose to prevent his odour from invading her lungs. Who she was *inside* was all she had, and Mr Beacham could not be allowed to trespass.

'Not interested in passing your GCSEs? Is that it?' he said.

'No,' she replied.

'What? Not interested in passing your GCSEs?'

'No... I mean yes.' She knew she'd gone bright red. This teacher was tying her in knots and she really wished she could throw him a clever line, make everyone laugh *because* of her rather than *at* her. *Where was she? Where was Anna Maybury, the girl who wasn't afraid to be herself?*

'This is not an art class do you hear?'

'I hear,' she said, her words whispering out of her mouth as if they too were scared to be heard. Her amazing doodles were almost iconic at her other school, yet here they were something to be ridiculed.

Mr Beacham turned on his heels and walked back to his desk, shouting to the class, 'FUN'S OVER. Pick up your pens.'

Anna unballed her fists and wiped her hot palms along her school skirt before picking up her pen with shaking fingers, then she sucked in the same stale air as the thirty other students who were crammed in that room but, unlike the others, she was suffocated by it. This place was a prison, a concrete nightmare full of people who didn't understand her. She imagined the butterfly she'd drawn spreading its wings, growing large enough to let her climb onto its back, its silver-tipped wings flying her through the open window and out of that school, forever.

★★★

ALGERNON

Algernon wiped the steam off his glasses then emptied the washing-up bowl of soapy water before refilling it with clean water. His underpants and hankies lay in white twisted mounds on the draining board next to a row of dark twisted socks. He began the process of dunking each item into the clear warm water to rinse off the soap while trying to ignore everything that was churning inside his head.

The child had somehow found her way into the orderliness of his mind and was disturbing things that really should remain laid to rest. The quiet submissiveness that had started to come over her was harder for him to deal with than any display of teenage overconfidence might have been. Her loneliness was reflecting itself in his own loneliness and despite knowing nothing about the child, or the modern world she lived in, he did understand this much about her – her life had changed and she was not dealing well with it. Finding himself as a child in boarding school fresh from the security of a little village school he'd been ill-equipped to cope and had not dealt well with it either.

He plunged his smalls in and out of the water, wringing them out again as tightly as his arthritic knuckles would allow, then he carried them out to the washing line in the garden. Boarding school had left him with an insecurity that had plagued him all his life and Evie had been the only person who could understand him. She not only could put up with him but she could also handle the matters in which he floundered... and he was floundering now. He thought he could hear her these recent weeks, *shushing* him when he became rattled by the child. *Let her be,* he could hear her say when the child lay upside down on the armchair, painted her skin with patterns and flowers, ate sandwiches stuffed with crisps or dressed as if she were doing it for a bet. *Talk to her,* she urged when they were together in the same room. *Help her,* she whispered. The stark reality though was that whatever he imagined Evie to be saying, she wasn't here in the flesh to deal with it herself. Instead, he was trying to manage alone and as a result the tidy compartments inside his head were beginning to spill their contents.

He placed his bowl of washing on the garden table near the washing line and pegged each sock by the toe and each pair of underpants by the waistband before tackling his hankies. From where he stood he could see Little Argel and wondered how the child was getting on in there, as neither she nor Helene had said much about it. Helene, as far as he could see, was a good mother, gentle in her ways and very much as Evie had been with her as a child, but she was a believer that everything turns out fine in the end. Algernon knew differently. *Square pegs don't fit into round holes,* the child had said and now her words simply would not leave his head. Sometimes things did not turn out fine. His own education had come at a cost and his compliance obtained through fear, the young boy thrashed and suffocated out of him within weeks of arriving.

His own parents hadn't understood him, his fellow school peers had scared him and God... well, God had quite frankly let him down. Like the child it would seem, his homesickness made him weak and his weakness made him a target. The gorse bushes were where the older boys threw him, the sports field was where they tripped him and the shadows... they were still too dark for him to even think about. When twenty minutes later, seven pairs of underpants, seven large white hankies and seven pairs of socks hung neatly on the line Algernon took a last look at Little Argel before making his way back inside his house.

They shared something, the child and him, and he was pretty sure it wasn't a good thing.

5

Of Letters and Lamenting

ANNA

A little boy dressed in a doctor's outfit, with a stethoscope, sticky-up hair and chocolate around his mouth, knocked on the front door while Anna was upstairs finishing blow-drying her mother's hair for a job interview. To her annoyance, her grandfather clearly wasn't going to drag himself to the door when someone else was there to do it for him and her mother was justifiably otherwise occupied. 'Are you the girl in the shed?' the boy asked, holding a letter with *Girl in the Shed* written untidily on the envelope in black ink.

'I also go by *Anna*,' she'd said, taking it off him, her heart thumping in her ears as she looked him over. 'What is it?' she asked.

The boy looked at her as if it was obvious. 'A letter!'

'Did *you* write it?' She'd turned it over in her hand, her fear increasing over who might know she lived in a shed.

'Get lost,' the boy scoffed. 'I'm just the messenger. I got paid in chocolate.'

'I can see,' she said, eyeing his chocolatey face. 'Who told you to give this to me?' She anxiously scanned the area around the front of the house her heart pounding and her fingers trembling. There was no one to be seen other than the squirt in front of her who had turned on his heels and was running away. The road outside, dulled by a dirty grey sky, contained only parked cars and the scent of damp concrete. Back in Little Argel, having run down the stepping-stone path, dodging all the huge white underpants hanging on the line, her stomach churned as she studied the letter.

'I thought this was a dying art?' she said to Gary as she sat cross-legged on her bed holding a handwritten letter. Gary didn't answer her but that was OK, he didn't have to; no one should ask more of their best friend than they are able to give. She turned the letter round in her hands, slightly crumpled along an edge and with a curved stain on one corner like the partial ring of a drink can. 'I don't like this, Gary, I don't know anyone round here.' She showed him the writing, black ink and sketchy, high dots over the i's. Ripping the envelope open, she found that inside was a page torn from a lined exercise book. It was written with the same black ink as the envelope.

To the girl in the shed. I'm Jacob. I'm curious about what sort of person dresses like an explosion in a paint factory and lives in a shack at the bottom of Mr Maybury's garden. In case you're wondering, NO I'm not a pervert spying on you. I'm 17 and in year 12 at the same school. I just happen to be able to see his shack from my bedroom window, seeing as it's only yards away. And no, I can't actually see inside, not even a little bit, not that I've been trying – don't get all weird over it. There's a permanent glow coming out of it so I thought maybe, weed factory?

Jacob, Number 5
PS: I didn't send the letter myself in case you slammed the door in my face so I sent my little brother so you could slam the door in his face instead.

With her pounding heart still doing somersaults, and with the letter in her hand, Anna climbed onto her bed, stood on her duvet and looked out of the skylight towards the houses whose gardens ran adjacent to her grandfather's property. The upstairs back windows of the house directly to the left of Little Argel had a prime view of her grandfather's garden. Whoever this Jacob was, even if he couldn't actually see inside her shed, he'd just managed to trespass and trample all over her private space. People at school already laughed at her and talked about her behind their hands. Was this boy next door going to start spreading rumours about her too?

Until she'd moved, she'd always thought that anxiety was what you got when you went to the dentist, or were waiting your turn to go on stage, or were stressing over exams. She hadn't understood that anxiety was nausea. That anxiety stole your breath. That it burnt your skin and squeezed your heart and made you sweat. That anxiety was everyone you met and every face you saw. Halfway through a term at her new school Anna understood exactly what anxiety was.

She appraised her surroundings, her DMs, her make-up collection, Gary and the canopy of fairy lights that were glowing across the ceiling. Until her mother got a job, Little Argel was all she had. It was her sanctuary, the only place left to be 'Anna' and now some... *Jacob* from her school, who happened to live next door, had just invaded it. 'You've ruined everything, Jacob from number five,' she sobbed, screwing the letter up and throwing it into the bin.

ALGERNON

Algernon heard the knock on the door and had been disinclined to open it. The child had been in the bedroom with Helene but had eventually run down the stairs wearing the green all-in-one thing again with the yellow ribbon detail. He noticed that she wore the green all-in-one item quite a lot these days, almost as if he was living with a giant emperor moth caterpillar. When she came home from school the item was back on again quick as a flash, as if she found donning the fabric of her uniform completely intolerable. She rarely wore those mismatched colourful clothes of hers, choosing instead to creep caterpillar-like around the house or to go to bed early in Little Argel. He'd also noted that she didn't go out after school or on the weekends for that matter as Helene had done at this age.

He'd had to call out for the child to answer his front door and afterwards she'd only briefly hovered in the doorway of the sitting room holding a letter in her hand. 'It's for me,' she'd said, sounding not only surprised but also unexpectedly fed up about it.

Helene had come clattering down the stairs at that point, briefly kissed the child's cheek then raised both hands showing tightly crossed fingers. 'Wish me luck. Tell me about your letter when I get home, Anna. I'll be a couple of hours, Dad.' Then she'd rushed out, wearing a pair of black training shoes but carrying a pair of blue high-heeled shoes in her hand. As far as

Algernon understood, the position was something to do with administration in the council offices. No doubt poorly paid, he'd reasoned. Her degree in Geology had been a pointless exercise, a three-year-long, disproportionally expensive party, followed by a year of backpacking, then a series of unfulfilling jobs. She'd floated through life untethered and without boundaries until life had bitten her on the backside.

Helene had banged the front door behind her and Algernon winced at the sound it made. 'Does she have to bang that thing?' he'd grumbled to the child as she stood clutching her letter, an ugly scowl on her face. It made him disgruntled to think how this new generation understood little of the simple pleasures handwritten correspondence could bring.

'We always wrote letters to each other back in the old days. None of this virtual rubbish.' His mind had wandered back to the letters under his bed, which if opened again would reveal, once more, snippets of news both good and bad from family and friends who apart from himself were sadly no longer alive. The thought of them, however, caused a crack to appear in his concrete heart and Algernon did not like it one bit.

Pushing the memories away to where they belonged, to the far corners of his mind, he'd forced himself back to the present. By the time he had done so, the child had disappeared back to Little Argel with her own letter.

ANNA

Jacob from number five's letter had been silently making a racket from the inside of her rubbish bin for some time. Anna had listened to fifteen music tracks played at volume and yet she could still hear it like it was saying: *I can see you. I know you're strange. I'm going to make your life hell.*

She picked her armour carefully. It had felt like weeks since she'd had reason to wear her clothes and, although this reason was a rotten one, it was still important to find just the right thing... just the right *Anna*. Wearing black tights and her silver DMs, she pulled on a purple sleeved top and stepped into a black, layered, netted tutu skirt. Finally, with a glitter of pink and tiny purple stars highlighting her eyes, she braided her long hair into one thick blue-ribboned braid.

When she was completely satisfied, she made a tight twist of the now retrieved letter and waved it in the air. 'Ready, Gary? We're going to have a cremation!' Next she ramped up the volume of her music through her compact speaker, took the lid from a metal biscuit tin, stepped out into the garden and dropped it so that it clattered loudly on one of the stepping stones. Stealing a glance at the upstairs window of the house next door she was disappointed to see only the reflection of a bright sky against the glass, but even so, she offered Jacob her most special wave. One middle finger pointing at the sky.

'I hope you're there, Jacob, so you can watch your words burn,' she said quietly, squeezing each syllable through clenched teeth. 'I don't *care* what you and all the other freaks in that stupid place think about me.' After setting fire to the letter, she placed it onto the biscuit tin lid and watched the satisfying flare with a huge smile on her face. Then she went back inside Little Argel and cried silent tears of loneliness.

★★★

ALGERNON

Algernon watched the goings-on in his garden from his sitting room, the large sash windows of what was once the original classroom of the old village school affording an excellent view. The child had emerged from Little Argel, looking, as far as he could tell with his failing eyesight, like an ethereal creature from a fantasy story. He also wondered if he'd just been witness to her giving an extremely rude hand gesture towards next door. She then set about igniting something papery, which he surmised was the letter she'd received earlier. This could only mean one thing, that the contents of it had not pleased her. He shook his head slowly and tutted. That would never do.

What could have been written that would ignite such fury? he wondered. He frowned and rapped hard on the window with his knuckles to gain her attention but the child couldn't hear him through that awful racket she called music. She didn't know what music was. Music was, to his mind, the perfect harmony of entire orchestras or lone violin players, of opera singers or, at a push, jazz but the catastrophic arrangement of sounds she seemed to prefer had no right to be put in the same category. He rapped harder but she turned and went back inside Little Argel leaving the evidence of her pyromaniacal activities on the stepping stone behind her.

Algernon imagined that a frisky wind might blow the ash across the grass, or lift the tin lid and hurl it into the plants. He fretted over how Evie would be quite disheartened to know her garden was being misused like that and became consumed with determination to have words with the child about the reason she had chosen to behave in such a way.

The moment he placed his slippered foot on the step outside, however, he stopped short, catching his breath, which rasped harshly through exertion. The lobelia and alyssum, antirrhinum and coreopsis where the offending tin might have landed had that frisky wind blown, had, of course, long gone, choked and destroyed by his lack of attention. Ivy, undisciplined and destructive, now snaked its way aggressively along the borders and in and out of unchecked suckers from an overenthusiastic bay tree. The badly rotting lavender, the peonies, forget-me-nots, the lawn and its stepping stones were the only thing that now maintained the façade that was once his and Evie's garden.

Without approaching the child about the burning of the letter Algernon turned his back on the garden and shuffled slowly back inside to the embrace of his old armchair. Catching sight of himself in the heavy mirror that hung, as it always had, on the wall by the sitting room door, he properly appraised his appearance for the first time in years. His head jutted forward where his back had begun to curve and his face, apart from his cheeks and nose, was almost unrecognisable behind the dense follicle accumulation. He sighed so deeply at his own reflection he was in danger of never reinflating.

ANNA

Anna twitched a curtain at the front window of her grandfather's house and wrinkled her nose a little. His white net curtains had long since faded to cream and now smelt of age and dust as she peeped through them hoping to catch a glimpse of the person who could be Jacob from number five.

If she were able to identify him first it would mean that she would be better prepared to defend herself against him. Since she'd received the letter a couple of days ago, every boy in the sixth form at school had become her potential enemy, making her head spin and her heart jump with each sighting. The walk to and from school had become filled with dread and the echoey corridors and hectic classrooms made her even more edgy. Worst of all, the thing that made her insides constrict with panic was that she expected by now for the whole school to know she had to sleep in a shed and use an outside toilet.

She placed a hand against the cool glass, feeling the roughness of the net between the window and her skin. The street was empty save for a lady getting out of her car and two men walking a very small dog. There was a world outside her grandfather's house that she didn't have a place in, nowhere to go and no one to go with even if there was. Cat was circling her ankles, supper had been eaten, and her mother and grandfather were ensconced in the sitting room watching something incredibly boring on television. It was the demise of another day and the air was turning a soft yellow where the sun was sinking behind a blanket of cloud.

Stepping away from the window she made her way back to join the others, flopping despondently onto her new armchair and joined swiftly by Cat. The purchase of the new armchair by her grandfather meant he hadn't expected her to stay put outside after all and now, with her legs dangling over the arm of the chair she attempted to lose herself in the virtual world of her phone while the ticking clock on the mantelpiece brought the end to another day.

She still didn't know what Jacob looked like and the thought of it tormented her. It had been two painful days since she'd received the letter and another awful tomorrow was already looming. For Anna, Sunday evenings were the worst time of the week, Friday evenings were the best, and everything in between was just pure survival.

ALGERNON

Algernon rubbed his hands across his mouth and chin where his beard used to be. He assessed the barber's handiwork, unsure of how he felt about the fresh nakedness of his face. A trip to the barber had, for many years, been a pointless expedition involving a hazardous walk, five stops on the number 42a bus, fifteen minutes of mindless conversation and a return home, £9.70 lighter in the pocket. Since Evie's passing, Algernon hadn't exactly cultivated the kind of social life that may have required some semblance of order regarding appearance, so had taken it upon himself to keep his hair more or less at bay with a pair of Evie's sewing scissors. It had been an age since he'd seen his own jawline. This morning, when appraising his own reflection in the mirror, he was momentarily inspired to think that a radical haircut, professionally undertaken, might be a timely thing. Appraising his reflection in the mirror again he met his own self for the first time in years.

'Where did you go, Algernon?' he said, trying not to give way to a despair that threatened to cause his shoulders to droop more than they did already. The tell-tale folds of skin that had, at some point, cascaded so much further down his face than he remembered, told him he was, indeed, a very old man. He'd been young and strong and able once. In his mind's eye he was still that man... until the mirror told him differently that is. When he looked closer, however, past the cruel ravages of time, he could most definitely see that, although the child possessed a strong resemblance to Evie and Helene within her features, there was something about him in the shape of her face too.

ANNA

Somebody knocked at the door when they were all having supper one evening, but Anna refused to budge to answer it. 'Why are you being all funny about it? Just go will you,' Helene flashed. Anna groaned inwardly and had to steel herself to open the door. Her mother didn't, *couldn't*, understand that, for Anna, being confronted by people had become a terrifying thing. She slowly pushed her chair back and left the table, her heart sinking all the way down and out through her toes, the varnish now chipped, the drawing of flowers long gone. She fiddled with the little braid of blue ribbon tied round her wrist and tried to find strength in it.

'Girl in the shed?' The little boy with sticky-up hair was back again, this time dressed as a firefighter with a yellow plastic helmet on his head and red wellington boots on his feet. He carried another half-eaten bar of chocolate and spoke in a vaguely bored kind of way, shoving another envelope at her.

Anna grabbed the letter and hurriedly folded it up, shoving it inside her sleeve before shutting the door and returning to the table. 'Wrong house,' she lied as she slipped back into her chair, trying to ignore the jitters that the hidden letter was causing.

'Not easy to get this house wrong when it's the only one like it in the area.' Her grandfather looked suspiciously at her and she tried to avoid his gaze in case he could tell she was lying. It was hard not to look at him, though, when he'd appeared at the table looking so completely different. He'd kept his moustache – he'd apparently always had a moustache – but his wayward beard had gone and so had a large percentage of his eyebrows, which were now trimmed into some kind of spiky semi-normality. She was able to see what he actually looked like for the first time since she'd met him. He was very wrinkly indeed. The skin under his jaw wobbled like the loose bit on a turkey neck and his lips were pale and slack but there, with all the evidence now on show, was the shape of her own face within the angular lines of his. Although she shared her mother's high cheekbones and tilt to her nose, which apparently they both got from her grandmother, there was no denying where the rest of her came from. She was a Maybury for sure, which was just as well because no one had a clue who had provided her paternal genes.

'You look an awful lot better like that, Dad,' her mother complimented. 'Doesn't he, Anna?'

'Yes,' she replied meekly, playing with the food on her plate while the letter burnt a hole in her arm. She wasn't sure if he actually did look better or was just as scary in a slightly less hairy but more wrinkly kind of way. Whatever the answer, she could hardly wait until supper was over.

'He's persistent,' she said, shakily waving the second letter at Gary and beginning to read out loud.

So, girl in the shed. Thank you for your arsonistic display with my previous letter in the garden the other day. I also saw your special one-fingered message for me and I think it means that you want to be friends. What do you think?
Jacob, number 5

She reread the words carefully to Gary twice, looking for something she may have missed. Something unkind or threatening which, although she couldn't see it written in the actual words, she knew must be there. Jacob was playing games with her and she just couldn't put her finger on what angle he was coming from.

The pile of ash in the biscuit tin lid was now dark and damp but still offering its *back off, Jacob* message in full view of the upstairs window of his house. He hadn't backed off though, he had advanced. Dressed again in her *Anna* armour; red flared jeans plus a crop top worn over a blue mesh long-sleeved top, her hair in a ponytail of multicoloured ribbons, she performed the same ceremony as last time. This time she tore pages from a school textbook to give impetus to the flames and waited until it was dark in order to offer Jacob a floodlit show.

Spud, and his occasional uninvited friends, was not the downside to having an outside toilet, nor was the possibility of rain or even the evening chill, or anything relatively uncomplicated like that. No, it was because the security light continued to burst into action, regardless of how creative she was at dodging its beam, skirting the edge of the garden or ducking down low. Jacob from number five would never be in any doubt as to where she was going or for how long.

Now, with the security light flooding her garden, she

thought she could see the outline of a boy peering down from the upstairs window of the house next door. She gave him another special one-fingered wave and shut the door to Little Argel firmly behind her.

ALGERNON

Helene was going for yet another job interview. Her fifth in as many weeks. Algernon could sense her desperation this time as she stood in the doorway of his sitting room wearing a suit and trainers and again, carrying her heels. 'What is this one for?' he asked, not altogether liking the scarlet lipstick she'd recently applied. In his opinion, it didn't suit her and she didn't need it. Her youth was still there, nestled within the contours of her face and the colour she'd picked was too harsh.

'Office assistant in a college. Lots of holidays, which is good for Anna. Not so good for income. Beggars can't be choosers though,' she replied lightly. 'I know you think it's beneath me but, trust me, there isn't a lot out there for someone like me who's out of the loop.'

'Did I say it was beneath you?' Algernon asked, having been thinking exactly that.

'No, but I *know* you were thinking it,' she said. 'You used to tell me all the time that my degree was pointless and now here I am going for another job that also doesn't require a dissertation on tidal marsh sedimentation.' She was right: he *had* always told her she was aiming too low. He'd had high hopes for her once upon a time, hopes that she might find her niche in the world, do something of value, yet he'd always found her flighty and inconsistent whenever it came to employment.

'If I recall, your degree was not an essential qualification to work as an assistant in a veterinary practice either, or a car showroom, a market stall… *potato* factory?' Unsurprisingly his daughter rolled her eyes heavenward as he unnecessarily recalled her rather long list of failures.

'Yes *thanks*, Dad!' She gave a sarcastic smile then did a quick about-turn before he could haul up any more treasures from her past. 'I'm off. I'll be back when I've wowed them, if not with my employable skills, then with my wit and charm.'

It had come forth… the potato factory comment. Issued from his mouth without a moment's hesitation. Algernon rested his forehead in his hand before running the palm of it over his now short white hair. The potato factory had been where Helene had resorted to working, having been 'let go' from an almost promising position. It was at this point that her behaviour had sunk from bad to worse, ending in rows, disappointments and the unplanned arrival of the child. He reproached himself for alluding to a time that he'd promised himself he would let go of. He knew that Evie would be reproaching him too. 'You wouldn't have done that would you?' he said to the empty chair. 'You would have thought que sera sera. You would have simply said good luck with your job interview.'

Algernon was weary. He was tired of life. Tired of all the conflicts it brought him, the frowning faces and hurt feelings he precipitated without intention. He was tired of the carriage clock that ticked so cruelly and how the chair opposite had been empty for too long. The arrival of Helene and the child had stirred up his past, reminding him that he had not and did not deal well with life and all that it offered. He wiped at a smear of moisture in his eye, tipped his head back and rested it on the antimacassar, never taking his eyes off the chair. 'My dear,' he said, 'I'm a lost old fool without you.'

ANNA

It had been a hot day and Anna lay on Harry's soft blue blanket on her bed, wearing nothing but her underwear and a vest top, reading her book. Saturdays, fragile as a dandelion puff, were glorious. They were a time when the whole weekend was ahead of her, lazy and long and blissfully free of school. Cool air breezed its way pleasantly through the open skylight across her skin, and a fly buzzed backwards and forwards, busying itself with a discarded jam sandwich.

When a sherbet lemon, still in its clear wrapping, fell through the open skylight and landed on her stomach before rolling off onto the bed Anna dropped her book and hurriedly pulled on her green onesie to cover herself. Two more sherbet lemons came down as if from the sky, one of them hitting her on the arm and the other falling onto the bed next to the first.

'Peace offering?' a deep voice called from outside, causing her breath to catch in her throat and her heart to quicken. She stood on the bed and poked her head through the skylight to see a teenage boy standing in his garden. He was tall with brown hair and was holding a bag of sherbet lemons and Anna could only assume that this was Jacob.

'Go away,' she shouted, pulling the skylight window down and locking it back into place. 'I don't like being pelted with boiled sweets!' A clattering sound followed by footsteps on the roof made her guess that he'd somehow managed to climb on top of Little Argel and was currently walking across her ceiling. Her heart pounded, releasing adrenalin into her system so rapidly she thought she was going to be sick.

'Are you going to let me in?' he asked, kneeling down and putting his face right up against the skylight until his nose was squashed against the glass. Anna pulled her blanket over her head and held tightly on to it.

'No!' she shouted.

'I guess we could chat like this then?' he called, tapping on the glass.

'You're trespassing... GO AWAY!' she shouted, fear and anger rising in her chest.

'Sure you're not up for a chat?' He tapped on the window again but Anna stayed, covered and mute, until eventually there was more clattering as the sound of his footsteps retreated to the edge of the roof. There was a thud as he landed on the ground and then it all went quiet. Pulling the blanket off herself she looked up at the empty skylight and allowed herself to breathe with relief until she turned towards the open door. There, with a huge grin on his face, was Jacob from number five... on her territory.

Anna had never felt more vulnerable in her entire life. First she lost her home, then she lost her friends, now she'd lost the only place in which she could feel safe. The palms of her hands became sweaty and her lips tightened across her teeth and she was very aware that she was now wearing her stupid onesie. Perhaps if she was wearing something more 'Anna' she would be better armed. Defeat ached in her throat and tears pricked at her eyes as she gave up the fight. 'Go on then.

Have a good look inside. Take pictures if you like. I'm sure everyone at school will love the fact that I wear a green onesie and my best friend is a cactus.'

'Your *best friend* is a *cactus*?' Jacob whistled a high-pitched note through his teeth. 'And I thought having a fish was lame.' Anna instantly kicked herself for not keeping her mouth shut and could feel her anxiety burning, her blood rushing round her body.

'Fish?' she asked lamely, waiting expectantly for whatever joke he was going to throw at her.

'I have a fish! He's called Sheep Head… Sheepy for short. It's an oranda goldfish. Here…' He appeared totally oblivious to the fact that he'd upset her and stretched his arm through the door of Little Argel, shoving the screen of his phone towards her face where *Sheepy*, a goldfish with a huge bubbly head, stared boggle-eyed at her.

'Are you for real?' she asked, certain that Jacob was leading her into a cruel trap and that very shortly he was going to do something genuinely horrible.

'Very real. *And* very harmless. I go to your school and I'm doing A levels in Psychology, Maths and PE because I want to do Sport Science at uni. I have a pet fish and my garden backs on to the garden of someone who lives in a shed… with a cactus for a best friend!' He grinned down at her again and Anna was at a complete loss over how to respond. He had a nice face and an open smile but she felt as if she should be defending herself, even though she didn't know exactly what she should be defending herself against. He was correct, she lived in a shed and her best friend was a cactus. Apart from intruding and then stating the obvious, Jacob hadn't said anything unkind.

'How come you've stopped sending your messenger boy round?' Anna asked, sulkily.

'My little brother? Because he was costing me a lot in chocolate. Plus, I feared for his life: he didn't have fancy dress riot gear for the delivery of a further letter.' He stepped past her and entered Little Argel without an invitation and it made her smart.

'Come in,' she said.

'I have,' Jacob parried. He looked slowly around at everything, whistling through his teeth for a second time. 'I must say I'm *impressed*! My bedroom is very boring by comparison.' He went and stood next to Gary and looked down at him with an air of expectation on his face. 'Introduce me, then.'

'Gary,' Anna mumbled, reluctant to trust him with such precious information.

'Hey, Gary!' Jacob greeted her cactus as casually as if he were greeting a person, but then he looked rapidly between Gary and the green and yellow onesie she was wearing. 'You guys share the same dress sense!' He grinned again and hoisted himself over the wonky wooden frame and onto her bed in one easy move, popping a sherbet lemon into his mouth as he did so. Anna melted with embarrassment and felt horribly silly.

'Make yourself at home, why don't you?' she snapped.

'Thanks, I am,' he replied, sucking loudly on his sherbet lemon while Anna fought to calm herself. She needed to pull herself together, to appear as if she could handle him being there better than she was. She slipped down to the floor and hugged her knees tightly to her chest and rested her chin on top of them.

'Why are you here anyway?' she asked, thinking all the time *this is a huge mistake* and wishing he would just leave. He threw her a sherbet lemon, which she unwrapped as casually as she could muster then put it in her mouth.

'I told you in my letter... you know, the one you set fire to? I thought we could be friends... plus I'm curious about you. I've been wondering how you're getting on out here and what sort of person inspired old Mr Maybury to get all busy in his garden.'

'What do you mean *get all busy*?' She frowned deeply, finding it hard to imagine her frail old grandfather getting all busy over anything.

'Just before you and your mum arrived he got someone in to run a cable from the house, under the flower bed and into his shed. He also got them to knock a hole in the roof to put the skylight window in. This wood, though—' he tapped the frame of Anna's bed '—is the wood he was outside sawing and varnishing and huffing over for days. I thought he was going to drop down dead in the process.' He threw her another sweet and took one more for himself.

'But...' Anna was totally stuck for words. Her eyes wide, she rolled her eyes towards the bed, up to the skylight and then back down to the plug sockets in the wall.

'Are you in control of those eyeballs?' Jacob asked, forcing Anna to blink and return her gaze back to him.

'He did all that?'

'Yup!'

Anna studied the wood where Jacob now sat. She had no idea why her grandfather, who had hardly said a kind word to her since she arrived, would spend so long exerting the kind of energy that could well have killed him off.

'I think it looks like a baby's cot and my mum thinks it looks like a coffin!' She tugged her lips into a downturn grin.

'Or... how about, he just thought it would look cosier like this? Or safer... so you don't roll straight off the cupboards in your sleep.' He slapped a hand against the wood and patted it like a dog. 'It's not straight though, is it? More curved, like it used to be something else.' Anna thought about this and nodded slowly. She had a lot of unanswered questions about Little Argel.

'I've been convinced that this shed is my grandfather's version of a human kennel.' She offered him another downward grin, an expression of resignation rather than humour.

'Really?' Jacob sucked the sherbet thoughtfully through the hole in the centre of his sweet then crunched down on it. 'How many dog kennels have you seen with a skylight? A large skylight at that. And why did he clear everything out and bust a gut to varnish the wood rather than leaving it all rotten?' He patted the frame again as if to reinforce his point. 'If he just wanted you out of the way he could have given you a torch, a sleeping bag... a dog bowl if you were really lucky... and told you to hunker down on the floor! Oh, and a packet of poop bags instead of bothering to have the outside loo all done up!'

As he spoke her brain whirred. 'I suppose,' she said uncertainly, casting her mind back to the first day when her mother had said the outside loo used to be unusable. The bed was unnecessarily *over*-framed though... she wasn't a baby, but if he'd gone to the effort of making the rest of the shed habitable just for her, he'd never said. He'd never even bothered to come properly inside to see how she'd made it look.

'I know, I've had a great idea,' Jacob suddenly said, with an air of theatrical mockery. 'Call me controversial… but why don't you *ask* him?' He tossed a sherbet lemon into the air and caught it in his mouth before looking at her with his eyebrows raised in sarcastic expectation.

'I don't want to ask him. He's not a chatty kind of guy,' she defended.

'Nor is a cactus, to be fair, and that hasn't stopped you.' This time Jacob raised a single derisive eyebrow at her and gave a wry smile.

'And *Sheepy* has a whole lot to say does he?' Despite herself, as she said this, she found herself battling with a tiny smile that threatened to grow into a laugh. The idea that, out of all the company either of them should keep, she should have a cactus and the boy next door should have a fish was actually quite funny!

'At least he's a living thing. With big googly eyes,' Jacob said, holding his phone towards her again with Sheepy's photo on the screen. 'Look at those eyes! And he likes me to stroke him, which I'm guessing isn't the same with Gary… him not being a tactile kind of fella.' He unwrapped yet another sweet, barely finishing the last.

'You can't stroke a *fish*!' Anna said, losing her battle against her smile as it spread reluctantly into her cheeks.

'You can, and I do. Sheepy likes it. Google it… "*how to train your goldfish*". Trust me, he can go through hoops and everything. His tank is by my window. That's how I see so much going on in your garden… not because I'm stalking the Maybury clan or anything weird like that.'

'I'm not sure which is weirder… the idea of you looking out of your window at us, or the idea that you're only at your window because you're *stroking* a goldfish.' Anna actually laughed then, a quiet and hesitant laugh but a laugh all the same and it felt good.

'Are you mocking me, Anna Maybury? If you don't believe me you'll have to meet him.'

She eyed him with suspicion. 'How do you know my name is Anna?'

'Because your grandfather told me,' he answered.

'He speaks to *you*, then.' So it was just *her* that her grandfather struggled to communicate with.

'He told me you were coming, that's all. He's a man of few words.'

'You're telling me,' she replied just as her mother shouted from the back door of her grandfather's house.

'ANNA! It's nearly six o'clock!' Anna got up from the floor, resigned but obedient, unenthused by the thought of another stilted meal with her grandfather.

'Supper time,' she groaned. 'We have to eat at exactly six otherwise we all turn into pumpkins.' Jacob took his cue and got up from her bed and placed his half-empty bag of sweets on the coffee table next to Gary.

'I'll leave these. Maybe we can feast on them another time? Maybe you'll even offer me a drink next time or do something vaguely hospitable like that?' He stepped through the open door of Little Argel and made his way towards the boundary fence. 'I'll look out for you at school on Monday hey?' Anna followed him, her heart instantly racing at the thought of school, wondering if she was even more vulnerable now that Jacob knew so much about her or whether he would be able to keep her secret.

'Don't tell anyone else... about me, will you?'

He stopped, one foot on the bottom of a branch of laurel and the other on a higher branch ready to leap over the dividing fence and he turned and squinted at her, the sun in his eyes. 'Why? Doesn't anyone know you exist?'

'The opposite. *Everyone* knows I exist. I'm not exactly popular. If they find out about... you know...' She pointed to her onesie then at the shed, drawing her hand across her neck as if she would be dead if rumour were to spread. He looked down from his position on the fence and drew a serious hand across his lips as if zipping them together. Heaving his body over the fence to the sound of rustling laurel leaves he dropped down onto the ground on his own side. She waited for a moment, unsure as to whether to call 'goodbye' or not but suddenly his head popped back up through a gap in the leaves.

'See you around, then?' he called.

She wanted to grin and say 'yes' but instead she disguised her fragile pleasure at the idea that he may want to see her again by uselessly checking the time on her phone. 'I've got to go. My grandad is a stickler for timing, like he used to be in the army or something.'

'Air Force, actually,' Jacob replied. 'I don't know much about him, but I know that.' Then he stepped off whatever it was that he'd been standing on and she heard the sound of him jogging away down his own garden.

For a while Anna stared at the point by the fence where the laurel grew and where Jacob's face could no longer be seen. Two things had just happened: one, she might possibly have just made a friend and two, was the realisation that there was obviously a lot more to her grandfather than she had realised.

* * *

ALGERNON

Inspired by the child receiving her letter, Algernon had spent much of the morning with his old hatbox of letters, now retrieved from under the bed and open in front of him on the floral counterpane. At the top was a clear pouch containing a photograph of him with Helene, taken by Evie, on Helene's university graduation day, plus all the Father's Day cards she had ever sent him. He had kept every one. Handmade cards, stuck with sequins and drawn with pen, betrayed a time when father and daughter trod a lighter path. A remorseful sigh came from within him as he placed the pouch on his bed and sorted through the contents of the box. In amongst letters written in the hand of various family and friends now long gone were little treasures from the past. Brooches and trinkets, certificates and cards all with memories attached, packed inside the hatbox just waiting to tell their stories again.

A small wooden chess set given to him as a leaving present by his father when he joined the Air Force still had its monogrammed leather case. *This little box has travelled to almost as many places as I have,* he thought. As he re-examined the little pieces, he imagined he could still hear the chat and laughter of his fellow RAF crew as they played, the air thick with their cigarette smoke and heady with the scent of beer. Next he examined his old silver cigarette box, checking the engraving of his initials on the plaque at the front. It had been a Christmas present from Evie, complete with a packet of cigarettes inside, even though she had hated the habit. His pipe was there too, an old locket, a watch, several brooches, and his RAF badge snipped from the left breast of his uniform. He ran his fingers wistfully across the embroidered wings of the badge, feeling within the silken threads the long-forgotten sensation of true happiness that flying had given him.

An unbidden tear meandered its way down the side of his nose and as it disappeared into his moustache, he whispered a silent apology to Evie that the man he had been back then had become so tragically lost in the past. Picking up a tiny jeweller's box that held her engagement ring, he opened the lid and studied the ruby stone held within its gold setting. It shone with the same colour red as Evie's lipstick had been on the day he'd given it to her. Dressed for a dance in a green satin dress with a ribbon in her hair, she had smiled so widely as he slipped the ruby on her finger that the image of it was imprinted on his mind forever. He knew without a doubt that Evie would want the ring to be passed to Helene one day, but he closed the lid and held the box tight in his fist. 'I'm not ready to let you go,' he said.

Putting everything back, he came across a letter containing several sheets of blue paper decorated with sprigs of pressed larkspur, the delicate petals now hardly more than a mere breath. Algernon closed his eyes and inhaled deeply. 'Lily of the Valley,' he said to himself, experiencing the memory of the scent rather than the smell itself. He read softly as he walked over to his bedroom window to look down at the garden he'd allowed to go to seed. *It is such a dear little house, Algernon, and when we are married it will be so completely perfect to grow a beautiful garden and raise a beautiful child.*

Evie had written with such passion about the little schoolhouse, such hope and positivity for a future that was so different from the future he'd originally envisioned for them that even now he found it hard to read. Evie, being

Evie, had always made the best of things and this letter was no different. She'd been his rock through thick and thin yet as he looked down at the tangle that was the 'beautiful garden' she had wanted to grow, he knew that even now he was still letting her down. With a pang of guilt and a renewed sense of determination, he pushed the box back under his bed and made his way outside before he could change his mind.

The potting shed, once the boys' toilet when their house was still a school, was now packed to the rafters with everything that had once been stored in Little Argel and Algernon wondered if he were in danger of being defeated before he'd even begun. By the time he finally unearthed and freed up a pair of unwilling clippers, he needed to go back inside the house to take a rest and a drink of water.

Although, strictly speaking, it was not the correct time of year to prune a wisteria, it tumbled with such a profusion of lilac fronds that he believed it should be the first place to start. If they were all going to continue to eat in the dining room together he believed it had reached the point where a degree of daylight should be allowed to aid them in doing so. Not entirely sure he could balance on the step stool and snip away at the overhang without courting a nasty accident, his stubbornness got the better of him and he decided to do it anyway.

In retrospect he'd been a little overenthusiastic to think that Evie's garden basket would accommodate all of the wisteria cuttings and subsequently the patio was now splashed with an abundance of green and lilac. Revealed once more, however, were the rather dusty sash windows of his now lighter, brighter dining room. Stepping down from his precarious task, thankfully alive to tell the tale, Algernon felt satisfied that he had, at least, accomplished this task. 'Now, you sweep up and then we'll have a nice cup of tea,' he heard Evie say in his ear. 'We'll drink it together while we sit on our bench and look upon our garden.'

6

Old and Wonky

ANNA

'Grandad?' Anna poked her head round the sitting room door, her uncertainty painfully obvious in the sing-song way she sounded his name. Her grandfather was sitting in silence with his eyes shut and she wasn't sure if he was awake or asleep, even though his crossword was on his lap and his pen was still grasped in his hand. Sometimes her grandfather spent hours sitting quietly like this, alone, without even the television on and it always amazed her how he could be so content doing absolutely nothing.

'Grandad,' she whispered loudly, already thinking that perhaps she should wait for another time to approach him but then he opened his eyes, looked across at her and gave silent approval for her to ask the rest of her question. Her heart fluttered with trepidation and she wondered if this was going to be one of those sorts of questions that would annoy him. 'Um…' she began nervously, taking the risk and plunging in. 'Why is the wood in Little Argel, the wood that is… er…

my bed now... different from all the other wood in the shed? You know... kind of old and wonky?'

She didn't move from the doorway while she waited for an answer, the flutter beginning to quicken and pound when her grandfather just continued to look silently in her direction. A heavy silence stretched between them in which she mentally kicked Jacob for being the one to suggest she try to talk to him. She began to fidget and unbidden tears pooled in her eyes. Turning slowly on her heels she prepared to run back to Little Argel. 'It's OK. It doesn't matter,' she said.

'*River Pisky*!' His words grabbed at her from across the room, coming out of his mouth with such force that phlegm caught in his throat and it made him cough. Anna turned back to face him. 'The old and er... wonky wood... your bed now... belonged to a boat called *River Pisky*.'

Anna carefully pressed her sleeve to her eyes to remove any evidence of her teary weakness before she turned round to face him. 'What's a... river *pixie*?' she asked from the doorway, unsure now as to whether she even cared about how the old wood had come about.

'Not a pixie... a *pisky*. It's a sort of Cornish fairy, a mischievous creature. It was the name I called my sailing boat when I was a child.'

Despite her upset, Anna found herself leaving the safety of the doorframe, instantly mesmerised by the idea that her grandfather had once been a child... never mind the fact that he'd had a sailing boat.

'You used to sail?' she asked, bravely looking into his faded turquoise eyes while she waited interminably for him to elaborate. She was almost ready to give up again when he lifted his old, speckled hand and waved a finger in the direction of the dining room.

'Go to the cabinet with my wedding photograph on it. Open the drawer of the cabinet and bring me the photograph that's inside.' He didn't say please but then she supposed she didn't expect him to. She just speedily went to do as she was asked in case he changed his mind before she could get back. As she entered the dining room, however, she stopped short. The long yellow fingers of afternoon sun were now reaching brightly into every corner of the room, lighting it up in all its antique glory. Apart from a visible layer of dust and the huge pile of their packing boxes still stacked up against the wall, she could see that the room with its big dining table and two antique mirrored cabinets was actually rather grand. Removing a silver frame from the drawer of the cabinet she stole another appreciative glance at the room before she took the photograph back to her grandfather.

A teenage boy in a black and white photograph was leaning casually against the furled sail and mast of a small wooden boat. He was wearing shorts and a vest top, his fair hair pushed away from his tanned face and in his hands he held a packet of cigarettes. Behind him was a wide river with a cottage nestled in the backdrop of trees and next to him a cluster of boats were moored to a jetty. 'Is this *River Pisky*?' she asked, pointing to the boat as she carefully placed the frame in his hands and sunk to her knees on the carpet beside him. He nodded his head wordlessly as was his way and studied it closely. 'And who's this?' She spoke hesitantly as the boy in the photograph was smiling, which was something she'd never seen her grandfather do. 'Is... is it you?'

'Was,' her grandfather answered. Anna looked between

him and the photograph, searching for any resemblance between the two Algernons in front of her but struggled to find any. The boy in the photograph was handsome, the sun was on his cheeks and he was smiling. The Algernon who was sitting next to her was frail and crooked and so terribly old that she simply couldn't compare the two. She noticed that there were lilac petals caught in his hair but couldn't bring herself to brush them away.

'You used to smoke?' she asked, pointing to the packet of cigarettes in his hand, having seen no evidence of the habit since they arrived.

'It was fashionable back then. I smoked like a chimney in those days. Wrecked my lungs. They say now that it will knock years off my life.' A pair of veiny solemn eyes looked over the picture frame at her and Anna wondered if he may have been making a joke. She thought about laughing but managed not to just in case he wasn't trying to be funny.

'How old were you?' she asked.

'I can't remember. Your age maybe... possibly older.' He placed his index finger on the photograph and ran it along the hull of the boat. 'As you can see she had a single sail. When there wasn't enough wind I'd furl the sail and use the oars to row down the river. Sometimes I towed my little sister Isobel behind me in an even smaller boat called... called...' Anna waited, hardly daring to utter a sound in case she popped the unseen bubble surrounding this unbelievable moment. 'Oh blow it. What was that little boat called?' He looked at her in anguish as if she might be the one to know the answer but Anna just tentatively shrugged.

'Anyway, mostly when I came home from school in the holidays I was alone and I would often stay out on the water for as long as possible... even after dark sometimes, tying a torch to the front of her so that I could find my way back. I'd tie her to a buoy, lie in her and look at the stars and the constellations for hours and hours, listening to the creak of the wood and the ripple of the water around me. The night of a full moon was the best.' The silence once again stretched between them, the picture quivering in her grandfather's hands as he desperately fought with his memories. 'I found her all bashed up and half submerged,' he said eventually. 'Gone in the flash of a Cornish storm. That's how she came to be just a pile of wood instead of a boat. I think it wasn't long after that photo was taken that I found her.'

'That's really sad.' Anna pulled a sad face and her grandfather nodded gravely.

'It *was* sad. Terrible in fact. I spent several cold and wet hours gathering the bones of her to take home and I vowed to restore her one day... rebuild her or make something of her. And now I have.'

'Gosh, Grandad, that's amazing. To think that my bed is made out of... *River Pisky*!' She pronounced the word *Pisky* very carefully as it was such an unusual word.

'*Peanut*!' He stabbed at the photo with his finger, an excited flush spreading over the otherwise grey pallor of his cheeks. 'That's what the other little boat was called. I remember. *Peanut*! Once or twice, in the early days, I'd agree to tow Isobel in *Peanut* over to Smith's Island, and we'd light a fire and bury potatoes beneath the embers until they were cooked. Then we'd eat them hot and blackened with ash for our supper. Or sometimes I'd make us cheese sandwiches, take a bottle of pressed apple juice out of the store, cut slices of cake from the tin in the pantry and we'd have a picnic over there.' Once he'd started, Anna wondered if her grandfather was ever going to stop and it was as if the boy he had once been was coming to life in her imagination, grinning at her from underneath a flop of sandy hair. She felt as if she could listen to him for hours.

'What's Smith's Island?' she asked.

'It was a place on the river that we named after the old farrier who lived on the estate where we lived.'

'And what's a furry... a fairy...?'

'A farrier. In simple terms, a smith, someone who puts shoes on horses. He taught me everything I know about horses.'

'Wow!' Anna sat back on her heels in surprise. 'So, did you ride horses as well then?'

'Put it back now and make me a cup of tea.' Her grandfather abruptly shoved the photo into her hands and, feeling very confused, she realised that for whatever reason story time was over. Dutifully, but sadly, she made her way back to the cabinet in the dining room to replace the photo. Then, instead of placing the frame back inside the drawer, she made the impulsive decision to hide it down the front of her top. She wanted to study it in her own time, to bring the boy back to life again and so she pressed the frame and all its unanswered secrets next to her body and went to make his cup of tea.

'Look after it,' he said, when she placed the cup of tea on his little table and she shot him a look as she grew horribly hot with guilt. 'The photograph... the one you've secreted down the front of your top... at least, this time, it's a proper garment and not that awful green thing you wear.' He waved his hands in the direction of her stomach where the four corners of the frame were forming a rather obvious rectangular shape beneath the thin material of a magenta and white striped top. She suddenly didn't know why she hadn't just done the honest thing and asked him if she could keep it for a while and she hung her head in shame.

'I'm sorry,' she muttered.

'You've got the decency to go red,' he approved, as she pulled the frame out from its hiding place and made to return it to the cabinet in the dining room. 'It's all right, you can keep it,' he called. She stopped and looked back at him, embarrassment still pulsating in her veins. 'She's been waiting a long time you know.'

Anna frowned. 'Who's been waiting a long time?'

'*River Pisky...*' he said. 'She's been waiting a long time.'

'For what?' Anna asked.

'For someone to lie in her and look at the stars again,' he said.

ALGERNON

Algernon sat in ponderous silence for some time after his conversation with the child. He'd faced the past head on and it hadn't been without a significant degree of difficulty on his part. Although he'd always known that the topic of the unusual bed frame had been a likely conversation starter, he was unprepared for it when it came. He'd found himself unable to speak when she'd asked the question, as if he had to brush away many layers of debris first in order to find the words and he hadn't been in the mood to do so. Cutting back the wisteria had taken such an amount of energy that he'd really have preferred to be left to nap instead of having a conversation. Stirring up the past was a very tricky thing for someone like Algernon, determined as he was to maintain the equilibrium of his state of mind, yet ultimately the gathering of tears in the child's eyes had jolted him into shape. He'd thought he could hear Evie from the empty chair, urging him again, *Speak to the child, Algernon. Let her in...* and so he had. Certainly he hadn't expected his own uncharacteristically descriptive response once he'd started.

His little sailing boat and his beautiful horse had been the only constants in his tumultuous early life yet when the child had quizzed him about his horse he'd harshly sent her away. Firefly, a chestnut gelding had been the most magnificent of beasts and the sudden pain of his memory had caught Algernon squarely in the solar plexus. Every school holiday as a boy he would find Firefly in his stable, stamping a hoof and whinnying loudly when he heard his name being called. His horse would stand patiently being groomed while Algernon confided in him of everything that haunted the darkest corners of his mind. His sister and his friends from the village school were growing up, their lives being moulded by experiences and memories that he could not be a part of but his horse, his Firefly, had been his friend and Algernon mourned his passing still.

Making his way to bed later that night Algernon found himself to be more tired than he could ever remember being. His hand, still a little green from his gardening activity, gripped the banister rail tightly as he leant heavily on it, the stairs creaking beneath his slow progress. He used the bathroom, wrung out his flannel and placed his teeth in a glass of Steradent on the shelf. His dentures, he realised, had probably smiled on his behalf for years.

Yawning wearily, he lifted his neatly folded pyjamas from

the embroidered floral counterpane but, in doing so, revealed to his surprise, a package underneath. It was wrapped in paper, hand-painted with yellow sunflowers and tied with blue ribbon. Algernon, as he held it in his hands, experienced a rare feeling of pleasurable interest growing inside his belly. He hadn't received such a gift for countless years. Sitting carefully on the edge of his bed he pulled at the end of the ribbon and allowed the silky bow to come apart.

'What a day,' he said out loud to himself as there, inside the wrapping, was a photograph frame with eighteen identical sections cut out. Fifteen of the sections were filled with a series of photographs labelled 'Anna' with the year and the event each was taken written in pen underneath. Anna as a baby on her first birthday. Anna as a toddler, aged two years old. Anna on her way to nursery school at three years old. Anna on her way to big school... and so on. There was a photograph for every year of her growing up that he had missed. He turned the frame round to find a label stuck to the back, and written in swirling letters of black and silver, was the word 'Swapsies'.

Algernon held the frame in both his liver-spotted hands inspecting each photograph for a very long time. From downy-haired baby, to rosy-cheeked child and finally to spindly teenager, the child was growing up before his eyes. 'Well I never,' he said, as he pushed a faded box of tissues and a dusty bowl of potpourri aside on his chest of drawers and propped the photo frame where he could see it from his bed. Next he tied the ribbon in as careful a bow as his clumsy old hands would allow and placed it alongside the frame. 'A little bit of blue, a little bit of you,' he said tapping the frame lightly.

Later, as he lay on his side of the bed, carefully preserving the side that was Evie's, he knew that something fundamental had changed. The crack that had recently formed in his concrete heart had allowed its contents to leak out and the child herself was finding a way in.

7

A Little Bit of Blue, a Little Bit of You

ANNA

Anna walked through the front door of her grandfather's house barely an hour after she'd left for school that morning and, as she expected, her mother was waiting for her. 'Let's have a look?' she said, placing a hand on her daughter's shoulder, turning her round.

'Blue,' Algernon said.

'Blue,' Anna confirmed.

'Definitely blue,' Helene rasped. 'What were you *thinking*?'

Anna walked to the mirror and looked at her newly dyed hair. 'I was thinking that I might add some purple.'

'Don't get flippant with me, Anna Maybury. You knew this would get you sent home from school so why on earth did you do it?' Helene placed her hands on her hips, her chin jutting forward, two angry spots staining the apples of her cheeks. She was right of course – Anna did know that she would get sent home from school and was about as pleased as it was possible to get about it. She mused over how long she could stay suspended if she refused to dye it back to brown.

She hadn't seen Jacob once since his surprise visit with the lemon sherbets. For days before she took the drastic action to dye her hair, her head had been on a constant swivel at school in an effort to catch sight of one friendly face in the sea of grey. 'See you around,' he'd said, before he'd disappeared over the fence between their gardens, and those three words had allowed her to dare to hope ever since that she would actually *see him around*. It had become apparent, though, as the days rolled on that he hadn't meant it and that her desperate hopes for the lifeline he'd offered were dashed. In addition, some girls had taken to intimidation as their bullying tactic at school. They hadn't touched her, just gathered far too close for comfort during breaks, forming an intimidating fence of *beautiful* people around her. They talked about a nameless *someone* who was 'too good for them' or 'high and mighty' all the while flicking their hair over their shoulders or placing confident hands on their hips. They made audible social plans for sixteenth birthday parties or shopping trips or just about anything they could think of that sounded exclusively fun. Life at school had gone from bad, to worse, to unbearable.

'It's actually ultramarine. It means "*from beyond the sea*".' She admired herself in the mirror and caressed the blue ends of her hair. The previous night she'd locked herself in her grandfather's bathroom, bleached her hair from the shoulders downward, then dip-dyed it with ultramarine dye. She'd trembled at her own reflection as she emerged positively shining with the blueness of it. 'Ultramarine!' she'd breathed, astonished at her own daring, and in that moment she felt as if Anna Maybury had at last returned. Hiding her crime by scraping her hair into a ponytail, she'd tucked the ends of it behind the hood of a sweatshirt and once dressed in her school uniform, she'd managed to get out through the house without anyone realising.

'That won't do,' her grandfather said, now.

'No, it won't do,' Helene snapped again, siding, Anna noticed, with her grandfather for once.

'I like it!' Anna made a show of admiring herself in the mirror, pulling the collar of her school shirt away to reveal a chain of matching blue flowers painted on her neck as if they were falling from her hair and onto her skin. 'It's *empowering*!'

'It's an abomination,' her grandfather said.

'Yes, it is,' Helene confirmed.

'I know!' Anna agreed.

'And now you've been suspended from school.' Helene was sounding angrier by the minute.

'You make it sound like that's a bad thing,' Anna retorted, holding her ground even though her heart fluttered like a caged wild bird behind her ribs. Despite everything, she was enjoying how the atmosphere around her was charged. It was as if all the anger and shock she was causing was rising up into the room like an invisible, glorious phoenix and it felt fantastic! For a while she was almost high on it and she wanted the feeling to last.

It didn't last though. The pointlessness of her actions was already dawning on her. She knew she'd be forced to correct the error of her judgement and that the moment she had to walk back into school would be torturous but, as she turned tail and went off to Little Argel, she still hugged herself tightly with secret pleasure. If nothing else, she had two whole days away from that school before she had to go back.

* * *

ALGERNON

'She's like you were.' Algernon and Helene sat glumly facing each other after Anna had made her exit. Helene shrugged her shoulders and breathed a puff of air through both nostrils as if she might also be mad at him, but for the life of him he couldn't think why. 'She *is*,' he repeated.

'You always have to go for the jugular, don't you?' Helene retorted. 'I didn't pull a crazy stunt like that when I was fifteen did I? Not—' she added hesitantly '—that you particularly noticed what I was like at that age.' Algernon held her gaze remembering exactly what she was like, possibly, he thought, more accurately than Helene herself. He could still recall the blue eyeshadow and copious hairspray, the secretive smoking and the endless show of boys like bees round a honey pot. He could also recall the many times she was caught playing truant. His daughter had transformed in front of him from a blonde-haired little girl with chubby cheeks to a striking teenager with determined independence and inner strength. Algernon might be old, but he had not forgotten everything.

'I think that Anna being like me is a good thing!' Helene threw her words at him as she got up from the armchair opposite and followed her daughter down the garden to Little Argel.

'I think it's a good thing too,' Algernon said, but no one was left to hear.

* * *

ANNA

'I'm not going back,' Anna said steadily, when Helene appeared at the door to Little Argel and stepped inside. Cat trotted in after her and leapt up onto the bed.

'You have to, Anna. You can't stay home without a good reason. And before you say it, this—' Helene waved a hand in the direction of Anna's hair '—is *not* a good reason. What do you expect me to say to the school? That the rules don't apply to Anna Maybury?' Anna didn't reply. 'You're not at primary school anymore, Anna, and I can't make any excuses for you.' Helene snatched a half-eaten packet of Oreos from the duvet and swept the stray crumbs into her cupped hand, her movements jerky with anger. Cat nonchalantly stretched out on the soft blue blanket and licked at his paws. 'I'll book you an appointment at the hairdresser's to get the colour removed and matched with your own colour, which, I hasten to add, is going to cost me a fortune. You had such *beautiful* hair!'

Anna remained slumped, silent, against her pillows, her phone flashing with messages of admiration over her latest photo from her old friends back at home. She didn't want an appointment at the hairdresser's and her fingers found their way to her hair and held tightly to it while Helene stared down at her with an air of angry expectation. 'Everyone laughs at me,' she said, after a period of suffocating silence had filled the shed to bursting point.

'I'm not surprised when you go in looking like that!' Helene's frustration was etched in every one of her frown lines and she tapped her foot on the ground in agitation.

'No, I mean they've *always* laughed at me. Since the first day... they never stopped. They whisper about me, they throw things at me. They don't *like* me.' Her lips began to stiffen, making it almost impossible for her to finish her sentence coherently. Helene took a step closer to the bed, her frown of frustration immediately changing to one of confusion.

'What do you mean, they *throw* things at you?' Anna avoided her gaze and instead focused hard on Gary, hoping he could anchor her down and prevent her from free falling out of control. The whole awful nightmare of school was about to be confessed and she could hardly bear the humiliation of it. 'Go on,' Helene urged.

'They... they have this game... They score points if they hit me when the teacher isn't looking... a pencil, screwed-up paper... once it was an apple.'

'An *apple*?' Helene's voice rose by a full octave and Anna winced at the sound of it. 'But... that's... that's *bullying*.'

'Yes. It's bullying. They are bullies. I am bullied.' She felt her shame burn her cheeks but didn't take her gaze from her cactus as he blurred into a watery shape in his pot.

'But... what? *Why*?' Helene unceremoniously dumped the Oreos wrapper and crumbs on the table next to Gary and climbed up over the frame of Anna's bed. Anna scooted reluctantly to the side and allowed her limp hand to be held while Cat remained beside them in languid oblivion.

'Because I'm new... I don't know... *different*?' she mumbled.

'Quirky. You're colourful and artistic and vibrant... and they're just jealous.' Helene stroked Anna's hand with pity, all previous anger forgotten.

'But that's just it, I'm not *allowed* to be colourful... I have to be grey, and they're not jealous because they don't know anything about me to be jealous of.'

'But... but how could I not have known what was going on?' Helene was clearly horrified and tried to look into Anna's eyes. Anna closed her lids tightly to avoid seeing her mother's pity but instead two tears squeezed out and ran down each cheek.

'Because I didn't want you to know,' she replied.

'Why on earth not?' Helene was offended that such a secret should be kept from her, but Anna knew she wouldn't... *couldn't* understand the awful shame of it all.

'Because you'll go to the school.' Anna knew, as she said this, what was going to come next. Her mother was loving and good fun as mothers go but she was also impulsive and clumsy and she charged into everything without due thought.

'Too right I'm going to the school! I'm going there first thing in the morning!' Helene squeezed Anna's hand with determination but Anna groaned. *There it is,* she thought. In that moment all barriers of her self-preservation fell away and she let go in a way she'd not allowed herself to do since her arrival. She sobbed as if her heart would break. Her pain was noisy and wretched and came out of her in a convulsion of hiccups and gasps that was so frightening in its lack of control that Helene tried to wrap her arms tightly around her daughter in her alarm, feeling at first the frosty rejection of her body until slowly she relaxed against her.

It was a very long time before, exhausted and spent, Anna blew her nose on the slightly crumpled, possibly second-hand, tissue her mother handed her. 'I *hate* it at that place, Mum. I miss home and my friends... and Harry *so much*. I feel like... like I'm actually *dying* inside.' At this, Helene placed both hands either side of her daughter's damp face and kissed the salty water of her child's agony.

'Fucking hell, Anna,' Helene murmured as she squashed Anna in another tight hug. 'I'm so sorry. I've been so blind. I'll think of something. You're suspended for two days anyway, which buys us some time and after that... we'll see. I'll tell the school you're sick for now. Remember... you're my Moonchild and you shine with all things lovely. Don't allow those little *shits* to *ever* let you forget that!'

Anna didn't answer. She'd forgotten that a long time ago.

ALGERNON

Algernon was fully aware that Anna would be spending a few days at home from school after dyeing her hair that outrageous colour. The next day, however, Helene had unexpectedly changed her tune and was no longer cross about it. Helene had appeared in the sitting room after breakfast wearing what looked like a pair of pyjamas and carrying a purple rolled mat under her arm. She immediately began telling him not to mention the *situation* again to the child in case he put his foot in it. 'She's being bullied at school, Dad, and she's got enough on her plate without you adding to her problems.' Algernon knew he had form when it came to disgruntling people but even so, he felt bruised by her accusation.

'You think I set about deliberately trying to add to people's problems?' he asked.

'Whether you deliberately set about to do it or not I really don't know but you manage to give them a hard time regardless. You don't think before you speak and it often makes matters worse.' Helene immediately looked mildly apologetic, as if she'd waited a very long time to tell him a home truth and now regretted it. 'Anyway...' she shrugged '... I'm getting very worried about her. It's like she's losing herself. She's certainly not the carefree girl I raised.' She placed the rolled-up mat on the floor and plonked herself heavily down on the armchair opposite. Algernon winced as he always did.

'What do you plan to do about it?' he asked.

'No idea!' Helene replied, chewing half-heartedly on a fingernail, a pensive expression on her face. As they sat together mulling over the situation Algernon, yet again, found himself willing Evie to come and save them both from their quandary. She would have clucked and smiled and held out her arms, but unable to imagine what she might do with this current problem, he tried desperately to think of something of his own volition.

'It's not going to help matters if she pulls another stunt like this,' he said. As soon as the words were out of his mouth he knew that this was not the advice that Evie would have offered. In his head, as always, it had sounded so very reasonable before it came out in the open.

'I'm aware of that, Dad.' Helene's reply was shirty and Algernon knew that he'd irritated her again. The jagged edges that had first appeared in his house on his daughter's arrival were always there, waiting on the periphery to snag them both if they strayed over enemy lines. They'd always viewed the world differently, each misunderstanding the other in the most unfortunate of ways. Evie had embraced the idea of a grandchild, but his inability to accept Helene's unplanned pregnancy had ultimately broken Evie's heart. He would never forgive himself for that.

'I don't want you wading in and upsetting her with your opinions when you don't know anything about it,' Helene suddenly piped up again, and what she had to say catapulted Algernon back in time over several decades. 'Bullies don't stop bullying just because you ask them to you know.'

So, the child was being bullied. Algernon sat up and cast his eye through the sitting room window in the direction of Little Argel, where the child had been ensconced since being sent home from school. He felt the layers of past debris shift in his gut again and suddenly knew that this was one thing his daughter was quite wrong about. If he understood anything at all about people it was that bullies absolutely don't stop bullying just because you ask them to. He could remember only too well how he'd been the sport for the older boarding-school boys. How they would regularly corner him on the path to the main school and each grab a limb, swinging him backwards and forwards until they could get enough momentum to toss him into the gorse bushes. Or how they would make him stand on their beds so they could use him as target practice while they threw tennis balls at him.

'Are you listening to anything I'm saying?' Helene's raised voice tugged Algernon back to the present and although she might be cross with him for drifting he was mightily relieved that she'd pulled him back into the present. He could thankfully leave his own young self behind in the past, with his skinny knees knocking together in fear, his arms lacerated and bruised, his shorts wet at the front.

ANNA

Anna walked into the sitting room just at the moment her mother appeared to be snapping at her grandfather and she looked between the two of them. Her mother had a scowl on her face and her grandfather appeared to be all of a dither. 'So, what is it that Grandad is supposed to be listening to?' she asked loudly.

'I was saying that it's the school summer holidays soon so maybe we can limp along and hope that you have a fresh start next academic year.' Helene then leapt up from the chair with a bright expression on her face and blew Anna a kiss. 'Anyway, I've got to go. I've joined that yoga class I told you about so I'm off to learn how to bend myself into the shape of a pretzel. Fingers crossed I can get rid of this!' She pinched the roll of fat around her waist then turned to Anna's grandfather. 'Back in an hour or so, Dad.'

Anna felt a wave of disappointment wash through her. *Limp along? A fresh start?* She had hoped for more after their conversation in Little Argel. Much more. She bent to stroke Cat as Helene left the house, slamming the front door behind her, and heard her grandfather's tut of disapproval at the sound of it. 'Always one to assume everything will turn out fine, that one,' he said. Anna nodded. At least she and her grandfather were in agreement over *something*. She'd come into the house intending to forage for a snack or a drink and wanted to get away as soon as possible but he was still looking at her as if he wanted something.

'Could you get me a drink?' He didn't say please but then she didn't expect him to, being the kind of man he was.

'Cup of tea? Coffee, whisky, water... Coke?' Anna noticed that an animated expression lit up his face when she mentioned Coke.

'Do you know what? I haven't had a Coke for years,' he answered, raising his eyebrows up into the furrows of his brow. 'I think I'm jolly well going to have one now.'

Anna opened the fridge and took out two cans of Coke, placed a straw in each, then took them back to the sitting room. 'Here,' she said, handing her grandfather his can.

'I haven't had a drink with a straw in it for years either,' he said, and Anna felt quite touched over just how pleased he seemed about it. She stood awkwardly for a while, wondering whether she should stay or leave when, quite out of the blue, he gave her such a smile that it made his eyes twinkle. Caught off guard, she nearly told him that drinking from a straw makes people burp more but decided to keep her thoughts to herself. Instead, forcing herself to settle down into the new armchair, she decided to keep him company for a while.

ALGERNON

Algernon spent some time sipping at his drink after the child had contorted herself into the new armchair. She was in a semi upside-down position with her legs propped up on the backrest in a way that looked decidedly uncomfortable. Despite the blue hair and being a teenager in the modern world, racing to get to be all grown up, his granddaughter looked, to him, still very much a child. Childhood was purported to be the best time of your life, yet, in his experience, it had been the most difficult of times. He wasn't one for conversation, to say the least, but he felt again that if Evie were with him now she'd be telling him to make an effort to help their granddaughter. So, taking a breath so deep it made him cough, he reached inside himself once more and rummaged through his memories for something to say.

After five minutes had gone past, he found himself struggling. The task of digging up the past in order to appease Evie was not an enjoyable thing. He wanted to do the right thing by both of them yet his thoughts were getting wildly out of control and he hated himself for it. He put his can down on his side table, gave a low grumble under his breath and clenched his fists. 'It's too *bloody* difficult.' He sighed.

'What?' The child looked quizzically at him. 'What's too difficult, Grandad?'

He looked over at her, at her vulnerable dark eyes and absurd blue hair and braced himself. *You can't save a drowning soul unless you're prepared to drown while doing it,* he thought. 'Would you mind turning the right way round? You're making me dizzy like that.' She immediately flipped herself upright and sat properly in the chair, her hair falling like a vibrant silk shawl across her chest. 'I know what it's like when life takes a different turn,' he began.

'You do?' Her eyes opened wide at the notion that he might have another story to tell and she cocked her head to hear more. While the carriage clock counted the seconds – or was it minutes? – one of the tidy boxes inside his mind was rattling, fighting to be opened and to have its contents spilled. He delved into his pocket for his big white hanky and then blew his nose, a stalling tactic that Evie had brought him up on many times in the past. *One thing at a time,* he thought.

'I didn't like my new school either you know,' he began. 'I was sent away from my village school to another school when I was a child. A strict religious boarding school where I didn't have the privilege of coming home at four o'clock each day like you do.'

'Really?' The child sat up, suddenly straighter and more attentive and he found that this pleased him.

'Really. I only ever came home in the holidays, in the seemingly fleeting gap between endless academic terms.' He paused, taking a laboured breath then a sip of his Coke, his eyes scanning the carpet as if searching for something in it.

'Only in the holidays?' she echoed, her face a picture of horror.

'Only the holidays,' he confirmed. 'I was seven years old when I had to leave home!' He had barely got to the end of his sentence when he saw the child's jaw drop.

'Seven?' She peered closer at him, as though doing so might help her believe what he was saying.

'Seven,' he repeated, quietly. 'Stayed until I was eighteen years old... holidays aside.' Then he added, not without bitterness, 'I was a privileged child, apparently.' Not for the first time since the child had arrived, the turmoil of his early years revisited him and stirred an ugly soup in the well of his stomach. For his seventh birthday a small party had taken place. He had been allowed to invite a few friends from the village school for tea. Bobby Passmore, his chum through thick and thin, had stayed overnight for a midnight feast, polishing off Cook's delicacies by torchlight in a makeshift tent in the bedroom. On each visit home Algernon had thought his friends, especially Bobby, had changed and become more distant. It had hurt him greatly. It took him a long time to realise that it was in fact he who had changed. Amongst the letters in the old hatbox under his bed, he'd come across a letter he'd written to his parents when he was nine years old.

Saturday afternoon, October 1931
Dear Mother and Father,

I write with news of my recent achievement in cross-country running. It was with huge pride that today I managed to outrun Legs McBeckwith and Blazer Radworth, both extremely fast chaps. I was covered head to foot in mud by the time I got back to school. I also sustained a cut knee but I didn't know that at the time due to all the mud. It has a bandage on it now so you mustn't worry. Anyway, I came in at first place and received hearty pats on the back by everyone.

I hope that you and little Isobel are in the very best of health. Please hug her for me and tell her that I will be home soon.

Your loving son, Algernon

He'd refolded the thin paper with its childlike handwriting and blatant lies and slotted it back inside the unstamped envelope. The letter had never been posted that Saturday afternoon because Algernon, even back then, had been unable to declare such terrible untruths. That the Brothers used the older boys to rule the younger boys was the real truth, and on this occasion Legs McBeckwith and Blazer Radworth had taken it upon themselves to teach Algernon a lesson. When his foot caught on a tree root in cross-country running they had kicked him while he was down, forcing him to squirm in the mud and slice his leg on a rock. When Algernon had limped back to school other boys had laughed, pushing and jostling him until Brother Savage – savage by name and savage by nature – had caned him for coming in last.

For the entirety of his school life Algernon had rarely

written letters home to his parents due to the fact that news worthy of putting pen to paper had been rather scarce. The reality of his school life, he'd instinctively known, would either not have pleased them or worse, would not have been believed by them. His parents' letters to him had always been consistently and unflinchingly formal, not only during his school years but also into his adult life. Letters that had always been bittersweet, reminding him that he was on the periphery of everything rather than a part of it.

Even now, decades later, trying to explain to the child that she was not alone, his heart ached for home. Remembered resentment bled into his mouth, a familiar and bitter taste of the past. His sister had been allowed to stay at home, as had Bobby Passmore, and all the others from his village school, to be free to live as children with no idea what it was like to be trapped and afraid.

He couldn't bring himself to tell the child all that. It was too much. He pushed his painful thoughts aside and focused on her again. She was looking at him with a slightly bewildered expression, and he wondered how long he'd been lost in his memories. 'So you see,' he continued, 'I know what it's like to feel lost. *River Pisky* and my horse, Firefly, became the most important things in my world.'

'Like my cactus and Cat,' she agreed, nodding her head as if she knew all about important things.

'They weren't just my friends, though. They were my escape.' He watched how a ripple of a frown appeared on her forehead and he knew that he had come to the part where he would have to explain himself.

'Escape from what?' she asked.

'Escape from everything in here.' He tapped his head on

the bald patch circled by his thinning white hair. 'Like I said, I didn't like school. It was a boarding school so there was nowhere to run or hide while I was there and… well, it was no Enid Blyton story I can tell you.' He could almost feel the fabric of his uniform, the cap on his head, the stiffness and weight of his blazer on his skinny shoulders. The dust in his throat as his parents' car disappeared down the long school drive. The endless, endless days ahead until the school holidays.

'You were basically a baby, Grandad.' As the child said this he thought again how very young she looked. She was almost a baby herself and yet when he was her age he was already moulded into the shape of a man. He'd been battered and bruised on the rugger field, frozen solid in his bed during winter nights, thrashed and caned, bullied and tricked and lonely… he'd been so goddamn lonely.

'So, didn't you like school either… just like me?' The child looked at him, her big round eyes shining with her own hurt and vulnerability, and his heart went out to her.

'No. I didn't like school either. Just like you,' he echoed.

'Were you bullied too, then?'

Algernon thought long and hard about how much to share, his gnarly old knuckles whitening over his clenched fists. He wanted to do something to help her but had no idea if sharing his nightmares was the right thing to do or not. Not even Evie had known his darkest secrets: frightened schoolboys, the hell and damnation, and the absolute cruelty of the men who taught them.

The child waited, her dark eyes watching him carefully, fishing for an answer that might offer some solidarity between them. He had meant to show her that she wasn't alone in her dislike of school, yet he couldn't possibly share the whole truth. That even worse than the thrashings he'd received with all the regularity of the Angelus bell were the shadows that he could feel again, pressed up against his unwilling body and the fear that rained down through his chest and into his bladder. Finally, he answered her questioning look. 'Yes. I was bullied too.'

ANNA

'INCOMING!' Anna heard the call, just before something landed on her bed through the open skylight window. She'd been intending to study, bathing in the stream of sun that fell into a glorious warm pool of light on her duvet but instead was piecing together the snippets of information her grandfather had given her regarding his childhood. Clues that were patchy and frayed at the edges about a childhood he'd hinted at that was scarred with fear and loss. 'So, Grandad understands a little of how I feel, Gary,' she said to her cactus. 'Only he got to share his heartache with a sailboat and a horse when he was young.' Gary sat, silent on the little table, fat and round and full of all the secrets she'd told him, as if they shared prickles.

Anna felt as if she'd peeked through the long telescope of years that stood between her and her grandfather and almost as if she'd touched fingertips with the child he'd once been. The photo of him now hung from a nail hammered into the wall and as she looked at it she realised that now she had someone other than a cactus and a cat who understood her, and it was the person she'd least expected in the whole wide world.

She picked up the thing that had been thrown through the skylight and turned it around in her hand, her thoughts about her grandfather sliding away as her upset over not seeing Jacob at school was rekindled. The sound of scraping and thumping told her he was climbing onto the roof again, then his feet appeared, followed by his legs dangling through the open skylight, before he dropped down onto her bed. Cat, who for a full hour, had been lying across her stomach, vibrating with noisy contentment, leapt down onto the floor. Anna watched with dismay as he silently padded his way out through the open door. 'You could always knock on my grandad's front door and come in the polite way, like a normal person,' she complained, struggling to feel pleased about Jacob's casual rooftop entrance after so many days of silence.

'Then it wouldn't be any fun, would it?' Jacob replied. 'What's the point in having a friend who lives in a shed if you can't launch yourself through the roof from time to time?' Against her better judgement Anna felt a thrill ripple through her at his use of the 'friend' word but fought not to let it show. She was far too cross with him for forgetting about her for so long.

'What if I wasn't decent?' she protested, recalling the last time he'd appeared and feeling very grateful for the fact that at least this time she was fully clothed.

'That's the point of lobbing something in first, gives you warning. Look at it then.' He pointed at the item she was still holding in her hands, which Anna could see was basically a piece of reversible cloth. Black with white polka dots on one side and white with black polka dots on the other, tied in a knot for aerodynamic purposes. She untied it and held it out for inspection..

'A bandana?'

'Yep, a bandana! I heard you'd been suspended for dyeing your hair and guessed that everyone would be on your case. As you've only dyed it around the bottom section I thought you could disguise it by tying it in a bun and wrapping a bandana round it.' He looked very pleased with himself and promptly made himself comfortable at the end of her bed, bunching up her blue blanket and using it to lean against the wood. Anna moved obligingly and propped herself up on her pillows at the other end of her bed. She continued to inspect the polka-dot cloth.

'How did you know it was only dip-dyed? I haven't seen you.' She eyed him with suspicion.

'I saw you from my window and the security light in your garden is bright enough to illuminate a premier football match to be fair. Got any snacks?' He reached for the pile of food she had in a shopping bag hanging by the bed. 'This will do,' he said, rummaging through it. 'Mmm pickled onion.' He took two bags of crisps and threw one to Anna.

'Er... thanks?' she said, as the bag hit her in the chest. She felt instantly as if he'd been watching her and yet hadn't made any effort to meet up with her as he'd promised. She pretended not to care and instead scooped her hair into a knot and practised hiding the blue with the polka-dot cloth. Tying the ends of it on top of her head she checked the result on her phone camera. 'Quite retro,' she said, turning her head from side to side so they could both see what it looked like on her. 'It's a cool gift.'

'I know,' he said casually. 'Anyway it does the trick. All you can see is...'

'Gloomy brown?' she interrupted.

'If you say so.' He shrugged.

She pulled a glum face and opened her crisps, the thought of going back to school filling her stomach with ice. 'I don't want to go back to school. It isn't going well... to say the least.' She saw how Jacob raised a single questioning eyebrow and knew he was expecting more.

'Want to share?'

Anna crumpled inwardly at the thought of sharing her shame again and found it impossible to know where to begin. 'Not really,' she replied lamely, already anticipating how Jacob was bound to probe her further.

'You don't like it then I guess?'

'Not much.' She couldn't think of any appropriate adjectives that could adequately describe exactly how '*not much*' she liked school, so she left it at that. He could probe all he liked but she was done with elaborating further.

'I was trying to look out for you like I said I would, but I had a mad week with a sports project. It took up most of my lunch breaks and everything.' He looked apologetic and Anna wanted to forgive him but she couldn't quite manage it. 'Then yesterday there was a major scandal over the new girl in year ten who'd walked through the school gates with bright blue hair.' He raised another eyebrow at her as she silently pressed a thin smile between her lips. 'Way to go, Anna!' he said jokingly, pumping his fist in the air, then he scrunched up the rest of his bag of crisps and tipped all the broken pieces into his mouth in one go. 'You know what? I kind of like it blue.' At least that's what she thought he said through all the crisps in his mouth. 'And you made quite a stir... so I heard, and I thought I'd come to see for myself.' He grinned, a line of crumbs clinging to his lips, then he folded the now empty crisp wrapper, tied it in a tight knot and aimed for her bin. '*Yesss*!' he hissed, the wrapper landing a direct hit.

Anna cringed at the thought of making a 'stir'. It had seemed like such a good idea at the time, a way out of everything in the most spectacular Anna Maybury way she could think of. Now it felt like a self-indulgent, attention-seeking nightmare that was only going to make it so much harder for her to go back. 'Despite my mad week though, I did find the time to put someone on their arse,' Jacob added, licking his lips clean of the stray crumbs.

'What do you mean you put someone on their arse?' Anna held a single crisp suspended between the bag and her own mouth and waited to hear more.

'I *mean*, I overheard some boy in your year going on about the weird new kid who'd dyed her hair. He was bragging about how she'd managed to make an even better target of herself by doing that and that he'd once scored a bonus of five points for hitting her on the head with... What was it? An orange or a melon or something?'

Anna's stomach knotted and she placed the crisp back in the bag. 'An apple,' she mumbled.

'Anyway, whatever it was the next thing he knew he was on the floor and his school bag was on his head!' Jacob grinned then delved into her bag again and pulled out a packet of malted milk biscuits and a can of lemonade.

'For real?' Anna couldn't believe what she was hearing. Had Jacob just told her that he'd got the better of Adam, the bully who'd never stopped giving her a hard time since her very first day at school? His answer was a nod of the head, the hiss of the ring pull, a gulp and an extremely long burp.

'You look a bit like Sheepy,' he said, opening his own mouth and widening his eyes for demonstration purposes. Anna blinked and shut her mouth.

'I... I can't believe you *did* that. Did anyone see?'

'No... Only *everyone*!' Then he laughed out loud in such a way that to Anna it sounded beautiful and reminded her of how it felt to be with her friends back home. 'I didn't hurt him... just dented his misplaced pride. I just wanted to remind him what it feels like to be made to look stupid in front of everyone. When he stood up, he realised I'm a whole lot taller than he is... and so are my friends... actually, most people to be fair. Oh, and I told him in no uncertain terms that it wasn't cool to pick on people... especially my friend with the blue hair.'

Anna suddenly wanted to spontaneously hug him for saying that but knew she never would. 'Everyone laughed at him,' Jacob continued, 'so I don't think he'll do it again. I told him that I and most of the sixth form have their eyes on him now.'

'Thank you for doing that for me,' she said quietly watching him shrug and slurp on his lemonade as if it were no big deal.

'I also heard a girl saying how much she loved your hair. "Awesome" I think she said. She also said you must have balls to walk into school like that and that she thought you were probably all right... if you weren't so... what was it? *Stuck-up*, I think she said. Others agreed with her... about your hair that is... and possibly about the *stuck-up* thing too, I'm not sure.' Anna sat up, her ears positively burning. Was it possible that somewhere in the school there was someone who didn't hate her?

'What did they look like... the person?'

'Dunno.' Jacob twisted the wrapper of what was left of the biscuits and put them back in the bag.

'*Think*, Jacob! Did they have dark hair or fair, long or short?' It became suddenly desperately important to her to know who the girl was, as if by doing so she might be able to see an olive branch floating her way in the sea of grey.

'They definitely had hair. I really don't know. I wasn't doing a survey.' Jacob looked at the time on his phone and stood up on the bed so that his head and shoulders were out of the skylight. 'I've got to go – three minutes exactly till your dinner time! Don't want to upset Mr M.' He levered himself up through the skylight then dipped his head back inside and looked down at her. 'The whole world isn't full of bad guys, Anna. You've just got to look for the good people.' He pointed theatrically to himself when he spoke. 'Like me.'

'That's what my mum said I should do. Only I can't find any... except, yeah, maybe you.' She felt a flush of self-consciousness warm her cheek and Jacob grinned his very wide grin back at her.

'Finally, you admit it! I *knew* your special wave the other day meant you wanted to be friends.' He balled his hand into a fist then slowly pointed his middle finger upwards. Anna looked up at him, raised her own hand and did the same back.

8

Unspoken Thoughts

ALGERNON

'I've got a job!' Helene stood in front of Algernon with an open letter in her hand and read the contents out loud. '*We are pleased to inform you that you have been successful in your application for the post of visitor experience assistant.*' She waved the letter enthusiastically at him, the paper crackling in her hand, her success after weeks of job-hunting shining on her face. 'It's at the nature reserve just outside of town and they need someone to be "*flexible and self-motivated and with a desire to succeed*". That's me! It's only twenty-two hours a week but there are progression opportunities. And I'll have you know that I plan to progress!'

Algernon managed to contain the medley of opinions that queued up in his throat to be voiced as she read details of her new job description. He found himself picturing his daughter out in all weathers in wellington boots and a rain hat instructing groups of unruly school children about the conservation of peat bog and salt marsh habitat. He wondered how she'd managed to persuade the interview panel she was the outdoorsy type when she barely owned a pair of robust flat shoes and drove everywhere at the merest hint of rain. He also wondered whether she thought a couple of yoga sessions constituted being '*flexible*'.

'You're pleased for me then?' Her question, heavily laced with sarcasm, broke through his reverie as she waved the letter impatiently in front of him. 'You could at least say *something*.'

Algernon blinked, realising that he may have let his thoughts stray for too long again and hurriedly lassoed himself back in. This was a significant turning point for his daughter and his granddaughter's future and he wanted to contribute a suitable response. She was, at last, using her degree to good end and he was delighted about that. 'That's very good indeed,' he said. He wondered, though, whether this would trigger the start of her plans to rent her own place and whether moving the child again so soon would actually be a good thing. 'So, will you move out?' he asked. Helene looked at him as if he'd just landed from outer space, then she clucked her tongue on the roof of her mouth and marched out of the room.

'I know you want to get rid of us, Dad, but if you could wait five minutes until we can afford it, it would be helpful,' she called over her shoulder with a mixture of frustration and hurt in her voice. Algernon stayed mute, astonished by his own stupidity. Once again, the right words had come out of his mouth yet the meaning of them had glitched somewhere on the path between his brain and his vocal cords.

★★★

ANNA

Helene exhaled wearily and stirred sugar into her coffee where she and Anna were sitting in the only café in town. 'You have to go back tomorrow. They'll want a doctor's certificate if you stay off any longer and as there's nothing wrong with you I can't justify keeping you at home.' Anna stared despondently into the sparse froth of bubbles floating on top of a watery hot chocolate and suddenly didn't want it, or the teacake she'd ordered. She wasn't visibly sick or physically broken but on the inside she felt as if she were both of these things. Why could no one understand that the invisible parts of her were important too? That it was her inside that held up her outside and that right now it wasn't doing a very good job.

'We can't ignore the problem any longer, can we?' Helene reached a hand across the table, pushed aside the plastic tomato and brown sauce bottles and stretched her fingers out for Anna to take. Anna didn't respond. 'Let's start with a meeting with the head to find out what their policy is on bullying?'

'Let's,' Anna said, her voice flat with condescension. Panic at the very thought of it was crawling along her skin, making her palms grow sweaty and her mouth go all dry. The café was half empty, just a bored-looking man serving behind the counter, an elderly couple in the corner and another man in a wheelchair making a sandwich out of his full cooked breakfast, piling it onto thick slices of buttered white bread. Everyone looked so calm and none of them, she was sure, had hearts that were thumping through the walls of their chests with anxiety like hers was. 'You said you'd think of something,' she accused sulkily. She had believed her mother.

Believed that she would find a way to rescue her and here she was, about to throw her to the lions and she didn't even seem that sorry for it. 'You *said*!' she repeated.

'I did say that yes… and I've been doing my best to think of something but there just isn't another answer. On the plus side, when you tie your hair in a bun and wrap it in that polka-dot cloth thing that Jacob gave you, you can't see any colour, so I won't make you dye it until the end of the summer holidays. How about that?' Anna reached for her hair, caressing the blue of it with her fingers, feeling hugely let down that her mother had offered her such empty promises.

'I can switch schools and start again. If you let me start at a new school I'll talk about sex and smoking *and* drugs like I'm the world's best at it if that's what it takes. I'll even dye my hair back to gloomy brown right now, I *promise*.' She let go of her hair and offered two pleading hands across the table, squeezing them so tightly together they hurt. Her mother had to say yes, she *had* to. 'I'll be grey or black or whatever colour the uniform will be and I'll make sure I'm not noticeable ever again… really I will.' The sympathetic expression that was travelling across Helene's face, however, told Anna that she was unequivocally fighting a losing battle and as Helene reached towards the pleading hands Anna snatched them from her touch.

'There are no other schools in the area, Anna. Besides, don't ever sell your quirky little soul to the devil. Don't change who you are. You've always been noticeable, even when your hair is its natural beautiful colour. *And…*' she pointed a finger at Anna's skin, where a koi carp drawn in fine navy-blue pen swam along her forearm, its feathery tail wrapping around her wrist '… you've always done crazily and beautifully noticeable stuff like painting on your skin, or wearing the wrong colour tights... or rising to the challenge of a *dare*...'

Anna knew that her mother was referring to an incident back at home when she'd been dared by her friends to paint graffiti flowers on the wall at the back of the art block in her previous school. She'd not only completed her dare but she'd made each flower a metre tall with huge colourful petalled heads, winding stalks and curled leaves as if they were growing from the ground. Bravery, fear and pride had coursed through her veins, each one making her feel so gloriously alive. The head, of course, had been furious but then, after fining her with several detentions, had a change of heart, resulting in Anna being issued with the task of overseeing the art group to convert another bare wall into an entire flower garden mural.

'If you're talking about the graffiti flowers, Amy said they're still there. My old school was cool.' She felt another sharp stab of regret that she wouldn't see the flowers again for herself or ever stand in the school playground with her friends. She wanted to go back there so badly, it gnawed holes in her stomach. 'I just want to go home,' she said, a lump forming in her throat that she couldn't swallow down.

'You *are* home,' Helene replied softly, making the lump in Anna's throat grow bigger and her watery hot chocolate to blur in its mug. Why could her mother not understand that this was *not* home?

'Home schooling?' She crossed her fingers under the table and sat forward with renewed hope, but Helene took a sip of her coffee and shook her head over the rim of her mug.

'I can't afford a tutor for you and I'm hardly the right person to take on that task myself, now, am I? I have the attention span of Jacob's goldfish! Plus, you know I've accepted the job I've been offered in the nature reserve, which is the best thing to happen to me for ages. It means we'll be staying put here.' Anna slumped back in her chair and felt like screaming. She knew she was defeated. Her mother ploughed through life like a bowling ball and she, Anna, was a skittle in her path. 'It's nearly the summer break, Anna, and then you and all the other kids will have six weeks away from each other and by the end of that, with the school's help, I'm sure everyone will have forgotten there was ever an issue.'

'It will be *fine*,' Anna responded, adopting the flimsy word her mother used so often.

'That's the spirit,' Helene replied, and Anna wanted to scream again that her mother had completely missed the irony.

Later, back in Little Argel, with her cactus silently watching the proceedings and the soft grey fur of Cat pressed against her thigh, Anna took out her science book and opened the page at her drawing of the butterfly with the silver-tipped wings. The day she'd created it she'd imagined that it could take her on its back and fly her away; now she took her felt-tip pens and drew a large glass jar around its wings then enclosed it with a lid. 'Trapped,' she whispered, tearing the page out of the book and pinning it to the wall.

ALGERNON

'She's going back to school tomorrow!' Helene came into the room carrying a small tray with tea and a slice of cake brought home from the café for Algernon and placed them on his table by his chair. She then took her own cup and cake and sat on the chair opposite.

'This looks very nice.' Algernon inspected a large slice of lemon drizzle before taking a bite out of it. The sharp tang of lemon combined with the stickiness of sugar was a delight and, with his mouth full, he issued a muffled grunt of approval. 'Did you make it?'

'No, I bought it,' Helene answered, taking a bite out of her own slice.

'Why don't you bake your own?' he asked, slipping his reading glasses off and putting his distance glasses on, almost poking himself in the eye with the temple end.

'Why don't you get varifocals?' Helene retaliated.

'I don't need varifocals,' he replied, feeling irked. What did his choice of spectacles have to do with the question of shop-bought over homemade cake?

'And equally...' Helene mirrored his annoyed expression, pointed to her slice of cake and took another bite '... I don't need to bake my own cake!'

'Checkmate,' Algernon replied, wondering how something so benign as having a cup of tea and a slice of cake could so easily become a war between them. 'Anyway, about the child...'

'Anna,' Helene reminded him.

'Yes, Anna,' he confirmed. 'What are we going to do about her problems at school?'

They looked at each other, their mouths full of cake, and he wondered if he could feel the war between them quieten in their need to be on the same side for the sake of the child.

'I'm sure it will all be fine. She doesn't want me to go to the school. She's fifteen now, nearly sixteen, and she's promised me that she can deal with it herself. Apparently, Jacob got involved in some way that might have put a stop to the bullying. We'll see.'

Algernon gave a quiet nod and wondered, not for the first time, how his daughter always believed everything would turn out fine.

'You'd think they'd organise ice-breaker sessions for new kids like her who have to join a new school mid-term. A game, a question-and-answer session, a group puzzle… *something*! I can see now that it must have been hard for her to rock up there and be as confident as she was in her old school.'

Algernon nodded again and took another bite of his lemon drizzle cake while Helene chatted on.

'I'm nervous about my new job and I'm an adult *and* I'm going to get paid! At her old school, when they started the new academic year, they had to play a game called "*get to know me*" where they each had six things, or however many things it was, and they had to tell the others about themselves. You know? Questions like, something you do well, something you like to listen to, something you can't live without. Things like that.'

As Helene continued, her voice faded into the background and Algernon could not help but recall the terrible fear of his own awful experience of starting school. To his unbearable shame he had wet himself that first night, curled tightly beneath the thin bedspread and itchy blanket of his dormitory bed. The ridicule and humiliation had haunted him all his days. 'What do you think?' Helene's voice broke into his thoughts and he tried to snap himself out from where he'd fallen. *What did he think?* Would it have helped him if everyone in *his* school had known that he liked to listen to thunderstorms, that he loved to sail and ride his horse, that he could climb any tree and swim across any river and that, above all, he couldn't live without his Cornwall?

'She might have got a chance to say something positive about herself if they'd done that for her here. That sort of thing could get even the shyest of people talking to each other, couldn't it? They just throw those poor sods in these days and watch them sink or swim.'

As he listened to Helene, Algernon took a sip of tea and tried not to mind that it hadn't been made to his taste again. He knew nothing of schools in the modern day and age other than the fact that children had probably been forced to sink or swim since time began. Some, like himself, had drowned – and now the child was drowning too.

Helene took two large gulps of her tea and swallowed noisily. 'They leave the new kids to find their own way, like they're not as important as the ones who started at the beginning of the year… like they have to be stronger and braver… and some of them, like Anna, they just aren't.'

He shook his head woefully by way of reply.

'I told her I'd give her until the summer holidays, which is only a couple of weeks away, and if she can't convince me that she's finding her way, or can't convince me that there isn't a bullying problem, then I'm booking an appointment with the head before the new academic year.'

'That's probably best,' Algernon said mildly.

'No summer holiday away this year though, I told her. My new job is only part-time at the moment and we need to save our pennies so we can gather the deposit to rent a little flat. You'll be delighted to know that if I save hard, we should be in our own place by autumn.'

Algernon picked up his cup and saucer, china chinking against china thanks to the annoying tremor in his hands and he downed the last of the dregs of his unpleasantly cool tea. As he placed his cup down again Helene abruptly stopped talking, groaned audibly and, getting up from her chair, took his tea things from him. 'Do your hearing aids work?' she asked, talking unnecessarily loudly into his left ear.

'Perfectly well thank you,' he replied, automatically tapping at his hearing aids with his fingers just to check.

'Only I was beginning to wonder if I was talking to myself! You just don't understand, do you?' She exited the room, leaving him to wonder what on earth he could have done to offend her this time. He did understand. He understood only too well.

ANNA

'I can't find my balls!' Anna was sitting on the roof of Little Argel complaining to Jacob who was sitting on the grass of his garden next door.

'You can't?' he answered, grinning and frowning at the same time with amused bafflement. The early evening brought with it a lazy wind that lifted and played with Anna's long hair while a line of birds gathered on an overhead wire. Two pigeons called to each other in a sequence of soft, rhythmical murmurs and she watched Jacob take a photo of them with his phone, their fat feathery bodies outlined by a setting sun.

'That girl you told me about... she said I must have balls to walk into school with blue hair. But I don't. I was just stupid to do it. I've got the brains of those pigeons.' Anna had spent a considerable amount of time over the previous couple of days trying but failing to find the courage that the nameless girl at school had apparently said she had but she just couldn't. She'd always thought that life was so easy, so *fluid*, not something that had such huge hurdles or needed such great courage.

Jacob looked up at her and then back across to the pigeons. 'They're very intelligent, you know... pigeons. One of the most intelligent of bird species in fact.' Anna wrinkled her nose at him. 'They're also excellent navigators and can find their way home from hundreds of miles away.'

'Then I wish I was a pigeon!' she said testily. 'So I could fly back home.'

'You already live in a shed so you're halfway there.' He grinned at his own joke, inspiring Anna to pick a large lump of moss from the roof where she was sitting and throw it at him. She was pleased when it hit him squarely in the chest.

'This isn't my home,' she called as Jacob gave a theatrical gasp just before falling backwards into a heap on the grass. He lay there, pretending to be dead for so long that she had to throw another lump to revive him. Fun came to him so easily, she thought as he deflected the ammunition she threw at him with a huge smile on his face. He lived as if he didn't have a single care in the world, and she was so envious of him for that.

'This could be your home,' he said, when she couldn't find any more moss to throw. 'If you'd stop fighting it, that is.' She looked down at him then and rifled through her brain for something flippant to say, something *funny* perhaps, but she couldn't find anything. She was fighting it – she knew that. 'And your neighbours are *particularly* nice,' he added.

As she continued to look down at him and he up at her, she felt her cheeks go pink. She wondered if he realised just how *particularly* nice she thought he was. He suddenly sat up and grinned at her again. 'Hey, girl in the shed, I'll walk to school tomorrow with you if you like. Just in case you can't find the necessary testicular equipment to brave it alone...'

His offer made her flush with pleasure and she was taken aback for a moment. She searched for the right thing to say that would be cooler than biting his arm off and gushing, *Thank you that would be* fantastic. Hearing herself saying, 'So, Jacob from number five, you think I'm a damsel in distress?' She groaned loudly in her own head. *Why on earth did I go and say that?* she thought crossly.

'That's not what I'm thinking,' he replied seriously.

'So, are you thinking of walking to school with me... like my bodyguard?' She grew hot. She knew she was making it worse and dug her nails so hard into the palms of her hands that she left a row of sickles in her skin. Jacob looked at his watch and gave her a bemused smile as he stood up.

'Not like your bodyguard, Anna Maybury. Like your friend.'

9

Tumbling Through Stars

ALGERNON

The carriage clock had been ticking with such annoying rhythmical accuracy for the past hour that Algernon decided to remove his hearing aids. The result was a rather frustrating kind of bliss, a sort of mixture between peace and isolation. He could now no longer hear his life ticking away yet he now couldn't hear the sound of the garden birds squabbling over the peanuts he'd placed on the old bird table outside either. He felt as if the garden was chastising him for not finishing the job. For making it as glorious as it deserved to be.

He and Evie used to work in the garden together until the puff came right out of them, listening to the music of the birds, their gloves and knee pads caked in soil as they snipped, dug, planted and pruned. Together they had turned the original playground, which belonged to the old school, into a place of beauty, planting flowers and shrubs and scented herbs until the whole area was transformed. On warm, dry days like today they would rest together, side by side on the garden bench, listening to the hum of bees busy with the lavender and watching squirrels play in grasslands beyond.

Due to his triumph over the wisteria, met with great appreciation from the others at the dinner table, Algernon had since been pottering about in the garden, endeavouring to revive it, if not for his sake but for Helene's and the child's. His limited physical fitness these days had proven it to be a lengthy and arduous task, his weariness increasing, his shoulders complaining even more than they normally did. Although he and Evie had demanded perfection in their garden, to the untrained eye it was now acceptable. The honeybees and bumblebees, beetles, lacewings, ladybirds and butterflies could return and breathe life into his and Evie's garden once more. He could almost feel Evie's pleasure that he'd managed to accomplish this formidable task at long last and hoped that wherever she was, she could still smell the perfume of their garden. Algernon, on the other hand, couldn't smell a thing with his ancient nose, his olfactory system having now surrendered its duties along with much of everything else in his deteriorating old body.

Now, however, he was cross with himself. After pruning the wisteria he'd had a whim that if Evie were still here she would have wanted them both to sit in the garden. Unfortunately, he'd realised to his distress that the current shabby condition of the garden bench would have prevented them from doing so. Evie, he knew, would have been most disappointed that he'd neglected it over the years, unable to find it in himself to undertake the annual care and restoration of it as he had every spring since making it. Not when he had to sit alone. Today, it being the kind of June day that promised blue skies and warm breezes, he knew for sure that Evie would be telling him that even if he didn't want to sit on it, Helene and the child might like to. Algernon was weary though. Having to do these tasks around the garden was lately proving to be almost more than his tired old body could cope with.

Now, restless and basically deaf without his hearing aids in, he sat inside, slumped in his armchair, the empty chair and the carriage clock harshly reproaching him for his apathy over the restoration of the bench. With his slippers on, a packet of polo mints at the ready and a particularly hard cryptic clue to solve, he endeavoured to convince himself that it was perfectly reasonable to be lazy at his age.

ANNA

It was the first day back at school since her suspension and the trembles that had coursed through her body the entire evening beforehand and all that morning had left her feeling completely drained. As soon as she woke bile filled her mouth, causing her to run to the outside toilet to spit it out. 'Sorry, Spud,' she croaked, washing her face in the sink. She put her uniform on and tied her hair carefully in a bun, using the bandana that Jacob had given her to hide the coloured ends of it. Her mirror reflected a glum version of herself and her grey jumper hid her anxious heart.

'There you are.' Her mother beamed when she went in for breakfast. Triangles of buttered toast were piled in the centre of the table and little cups holding boiled eggs were placed on each plate. There were three glasses of orange juice, a ramekin of jam and a small vase sporting a spray of garden flowers. 'A nice start to the day to help you put a brave face on everything.' Helene continued to beam as she cut the top off her egg but, pretty as the table was, Anna wasn't sure she could eat much.

Her grandfather simply nodded with approval over the effort she had made to look smart in her uniform, then cutting the top off his own egg, a piece of toast at the ready, he peered inside. 'The yolk isn't soft,' he grumbled.

By the time Jacob called, Anna's attempt at eating breakfast to appease everyone was thankfully over. Helene opened the door and stepped aside as he breezed in. 'Morning, Mr M. Morning, Mrs M.'

'Mr Maybury to you,' her grandfather said.

'Call me H,' her mother said.

Jacob was wearing the casual clothes allowed in the sixth form – jeans and trainers that, combined with a loose shirt, made him look rather nice. She could smell a hint of scent in the air as they left the house, and a flutter of delight rose in her chest over the fact that if she *had* to go to school, he was the one who was walking her there. To Anna though, the grey of her uniform had never seemed more grey by comparison. She tugged at her skirt and smoothed her hair, wishing she too could wear her own clothes. Today was a purple boots and yellow dress kind of day. The kind of colours that would make her feel more able to cope with anything. *Brave face,* her mother mouthed as she turned to wave goodbye.

They were barely past the end of her grandad's road, however, when they were unexpectedly surrounded by several older, taller students. Her anxiety imploded in a jumble of terror and she looked at Jacob with horror. He hadn't mentioned that they were meeting anyone and now she was surrounded by a host of unfamiliar kids, people she didn't know or trust. She instinctively turned to run but Jacob calmly held on to the strap of her bag to prevent her from going anywhere.

'Friends, this is Anna, my neighbour. Anna, my neighbour, these are my friends.' He smiled widely and swept a greeting hand in the space between everyone. Anna, though, thought she was going to be sick again. She was Anna Maybury. The new girl. The one who people laughed at and thought was weird and Jacob had put her in the firing line, right there in the street.

'Have you met the fish yet?' one of the boys asked as he slapped Jacob so hard on the back she was convinced it must have hurt. Jacob simply laughed.

'Don't mock the fish.' Jacob slapped his friend in return. 'Or his owner. Anyone who can train a living thing that has a five-second memory has got stamina, I can tell you.' The conversation that followed was loud and funny and full of friendly banter and Anna forced herself to continue the walk to school putting one foot in front of the other until she could finally dare to believe that Jacob's friends were not going to mock her. She began to ache again for home and for the ease of company she'd always enjoyed with her own friends. They too would laugh like this on the way to school, sharing funny moments or even sad moments with each other. She was on the edge of Jacob's group, wishing that the old Anna Maybury would appear. The Anna Maybury who would have joined in with them all. Who would have said something interesting or perhaps even something funny but, as always seemed to be the case these days, nothing worthy would come to her mind.

The mention of Sheepy had triggered a whole conversation about the pets that everyone else had. Sim had a tortoise called

Clyde, Ash had rescued a gerbil with only half a tail, and Emily had a dog that apparently kept humping everything in sight. Anna imagined confessing to everyone that she had an overweight cactus or, better still, a spider called Spud. It might have made them laugh. The old Anna Maybury would have said that without a second's thought. In the end she heard herself saying, 'I've got a cat... sort of. He's called Cat.' There was a brief silence after she'd spoken where tumbleweed might as well have rolled by and she'd wanted the ground to open up and swallow her. She wasn't interesting. Having a cat wasn't interesting.

'Less unfortunate humping then... but more unfortunate pussy jokes.' The first boy who'd thumped Jacob on the back laughed loudly making everyone else laugh too and Anna had wished beyond wishes that she'd kept her mouth shut. Was he mocking her? Should she run?

Three things happened then. Jacob grabbed hold of the strap of her rucksack almost as if he could read her mind, the boy who'd made the joke winked good-humouredly at her, and a quiet girl smiled conspiratorially and rolled her eyes. *So childish,* she mouthed with a smile. They were small moments of secret confidentiality that were warm and well meaning, and stayed inside her when the group reached the school and they all had to go their separate ways. She carried those moments with her everywhere she went, clutching tightly to them when the day became hard to bear.

Back at Little Argel, Anna stripped off her school uniform where the heat of the day had caused her shirt to stick to her back. Her skirt, rolled several times at the waistband, felt tight and uncomfortable and she dropped it into a heap on the floor while pulling her bandana off her head. She shook out her hair, enjoying how it tumbled down her back in all its vibrancy. She hunted through her own clothes until she found the yellow dress she wished she could have worn that morning and slipped it on. Gathering her body-art pens and sitting cross-legged on her bed next to Cat she proceeded to draw a pair of sandals on her feet. Black felt-pen outlines of petals and leaves grew from between her big toe and second toe then worked their way along the top of her feet in the line of a flip-flop. She then carefully filled in each outline with green, blue and white paint. She hadn't painted any patterns on her skin for a long time but school was over for the day, the sun was out and just for a while she felt like finding the old Anna Maybury again. The intricacy of her work and the concentration required allowed her heart rate to steady and her worries about school to finally settle behind her.

Anna finished the last touches of detail on her feet with their painted nature flip-flops and took a photo of them for her friends back home. Then wearing a pair of blue sunglasses, she and Cat wandered out of Little Argel into the garden where the scent of the coming summer played in swirls upon the warm air.

ALGERNON

'Grandad?' The child stood in the garden, near to where Algernon had prepped his garden bench ready for varnishing. He glanced at her briefly. She looked like a summer sky with a simple yellow dress and a swathe of blue hair, and the vision of her melted the shadows in his soul.

'Blast!' he muttered under his breath, fighting to lever the

lid off an old tin of varnish, his arthritic knuckles bulging
with the effort of it. Recognising the child's hesitant and
questioning tone and her general air of uncertainty made him
brace himself for whatever she was about to ask. He prised
the end of an old spoon under the lip of the tin until the
old varnish cracked and the lid popped off, landing on the
ground. Next he dipped a paintbrush into the golden, syrupy
varnish, carefully wiping the bristles on the edge of the tin to
remove any surplus liquid.

'I made this bench a great many years ago,' he said,
overriding the fact that she'd addressed him first. His hearing
aids back in place, along with his conscience over the state
of the garden, he administered careful sweeps of his brush
along the freshly sanded wood, appreciating how it deepened
in colour to a glossy rose brown. 'With a bit of attention, it'll
be as good as new.' He tried not to let it show how difficult
he was finding it to complete a job he would have managed
relatively easily not so long ago.

The child stepped forward and sat down cross-legged on
the ground next to him. Her sunglasses matched the colour
of her hair, but more surprisingly, he thought, she'd painted a
pair of sandals on her feet. She was a quandary to be sure and
he couldn't help thinking why she couldn't just have worn a
real pair? Cat wandered out of Little Argel and hopped onto
a low wall near them both, stretching languidly along the
brickwork, warming his belly in the sun. The child reached
out for him as he twisted his grey head towards her fingers.
As Cat closed his big yellow eyes with bliss, Algernon realised
he'd never offered any kind of fuss to the animal, merely
living side by side with him since the day he walked in.

'He likes you,' he said, grunting in the direction of Cat and noting how he continued to lie purring and recumbent under the child's gentle hand. It was obvious to him now that his own relationship with the animal had only ever been one of casual acquiescence and a part of him suddenly felt rather sorry about it. The child, stroking Cat's grey fur, simply gave a half-smile and seemingly forgetting her reason for questioning him, continued to watch the varnishing process.

'You must be really clever if you made that bench yourself.' She sounded impressed, offering the kind of praise that Algernon had only ever received from Evie and, despite the bodge he was making of it, he felt a flutter of pride. As she'd offered a statement rather than a question, to Algernon's mind it didn't require an answer, so, in his typical Algernon way, he didn't provide one.

'You young people don't know what it means to look after something these days. You just throw it all away and buy something new.' The child didn't answer him but then he didn't expect her to. He had also offered a statement that required no response. The nervous fiddling of her hair, on the other hand, confirmed to him that she wasn't interested in discussing a throwaway society but still had in mind her question. Algernon didn't like difficult questions.

'I thought you said Little Argel had been your project room?' she began. There it was. Another difficult question that he'd known might come his way but, again, was not wholly prepared for when it did. He paused for a moment, dipped the brush back into the varnish and wiped it on the edge of the tin, his answer forming slowly in his head. The child, he was pleased to see, waited patiently as if she'd learnt that communication didn't always require the rapid exchange of unnecessary words.

'I didn't say it *had* been my project room, I said it *is* my project room.' He'd answered carefully, taking out his hanky to blow his nose and stall for a moment before pushing it back into his pocket and resuming his task. 'You will notice there is a profound difference between the interpretation of auxiliary verbs, one being in the past and the other in the present.' He didn't look at her as he spoke but continued to dip and brush, dip and brush, uncomfortably aware of how utterly pompous he'd just sounded.

'The what?' The child sounded distinctly baffled and Algernon felt annoyed by this.

'Do the schools teach you nothing in this day and age?' he said, remembering the repeated stinging of a cane on his palms if he hadn't learnt his studies. It had seemed so tough at the time, to frighten the boys into competence, and yet, he supposed it had worked. At his school he had at least, and despite everything, been thoroughly and formally educated.

'Not really,' she replied, giving a careless shrug. 'Anyway, about Little Argel. Jacob... from next door, told me you've only just had the skylight put in, and the electricity.' Algernon, his head still lowered to his task, rolled his eyes and tutted to himself.

'He did, did he?'

'Yes, he did... *and* he said you made the bed out of *River Pisky* yourself!' Algernon, having finished the back of the bench moved on to work on the arms of it, slow and methodical in his task, primarily out of a desire for adequate coverage but also out of necessity. His hands hurt terribly, and his eyes burnt from ensuring he wasn't missing anything. He hoped very much that he wasn't doing too bad a job and that if he was, the child perhaps may not notice. Once upon a time he was a perfectionist; now he just had to make do with whatever he could manage.

'Don't you like Little Argel?' he asked, hoping that after plunging so clumsily into his reference regarding a throwaway world, he didn't this time sound so accusatory. The child thought about his question before answering, while silently and ponderously still stroking Cat.

'I do actually,' she confessed.

'And do you like sleeping in *River Pisky*?' he asked.

'Yes, I do… especially now that I know the story behind her,' she said.

'And do you like to look at the stars through the skylight?' The child tipped her face towards the warm late afternoon sun as if, perhaps, imagining that the expanse of blue overhead was now a night sky above her.

'I *really* like that bit… and sometimes I can see the moon when it's in the right place.' She expressed an enthusiasm that pleased Algernon so much he laid down his brush for a while to face her. He squinted, partly due to a combination of the sun catching his eyes and partly due to the fact that his back and shoulders were killing him.

'Can you see mighty Jupiter?'

'Er… I think so.' She frowned a little but sounded, to him, wholly uncertain about whether she could or not.

'You *think* so? Mighty Jupiter, king of the gods. He granted…' Algernon realised he couldn't remember the name of the god he was thinking of and the agony of it caused him to purse his lips and fight not to swear in front of the child.

'He granted what, Grandad?' The child was waiting, frowning at him, and he wished she wouldn't. He scanned his memory banks rapidly, searching for the elusive god until, at last, he found him.

'Neptune! He granted Neptune dominion over the sea. Did you know that?'

'No,' she replied.

'You can't see Neptune with the naked eye or Pluto come to that. Jupiter gave Pluto dominion over the underworld of course.' Algernon breathed a sigh of relief. His knowledge of mythology had not failed him after all.

'Of course.' The child sounded dubious but then became suddenly animated as if she'd thought of something. 'I can download an app on my phone that will tell me which stars are which. I'll look tonight when it's dark and try to work out what's what up there.'

Algernon had no idea what an *app* was but guessed that the smartphone and the Wi-Fi had something to do with it. That an *app* could educate her on the constellations though was news to him.

'They aren't *just* stars, you know. They're stories of gods and wars and love. Your app won't be able to tell you about the different myths and legends associated with them all. You'll need to go to the library for that.' The child abandoned her fussing of Cat and folded her legs into her arms until she was resting her chin on her knees. He thought he could detect a smothered laugh but couldn't think what could be funny about what he'd just said.

'At Harry's,' she began, and Algernon thought he could see the humour slip away from her face, 'I had my own universe in my bedroom. I painted a mural of myself sitting on the moon... but then I had to leave it behind.' Algernon listened politely to what she had to say but then he'd known this of course, ever since the lad next door enlightened him before his daughter and his granddaughter had even moved in. He'd sought the lad's help when he'd confessed to knowing nothing about the child who was coming to live with him. Somehow, in a flash, the lad had managed to find a photo of Anna Maybury's universe posted on the online or wherever it was he'd found it. As far as Algernon was concerned it had been nothing short of modern magic, and magic that had ultimately prompted the construction of a skylight. The boy had also helped him with the work on *River Pisky* but all these things, it would seem, had remained their secret.

'Do you know that Selene is the goddess of the moon and that the ancient Greeks believed she drove the white chariot of the moon across the night sky?' The child shook her head again and he felt further dismayed by her lack of knowledge on even the most basic of myths. 'If you like the stars you really should get better acquainted with them,' he insisted.

'Sometimes when I'm in bed I imagine that I'm floating up into the night until I'm lying on the moon, like in my mural... far away from all this... from everything.' She tipped her face towards the sky again as if imagining she were floating upwards.

'You don't like it here?' Algernon asked, unsure this time as to whether he was asking a question or making a statement.

'Oh, I didn't mean that. Well, I *did* mean that, but I didn't mean... Oh I don't really know what I mean.'

'I know what you mean,' he said softly, and he did. He knew very well what it meant to yearn to be somewhere else.

'You do?' The child looked hopeful for a moment as if maybe they were sharing something special together. 'Like you understand the bullying thing?'

'Yes, like I understand the bullying thing.'

They both fell into a contemplative silence after that, the child still hugging her knees, Cat by her side, both of them watching him working with the bench again until at last he finished. Wrapping the brush in a rag and pushing the lid back on the tin he started the almost impossible task of getting to his feet. The problem with sitting in one position for so long at his age was that he was in danger of not being able to straighten his legs again without a good degree of fuss.

The child leapt to her feet and did her best to support him until, with a lot of screwing up of eyes and grunting with the pain of it, he was, at last, upright again. She helped him put his things away in the store cupboard, and to find the white spirit on a shelf right at the back until, when he was as steady as he was ever going to be, they made to go their separate ways. He, towards his house and she, towards Little Argel. Algernon was torn. The arrival of the child in his life was forcing him to dig up his past whether he wanted to or not, and he had no idea if sharing it with her was a good thing.

'Grandad?' The child stopped halfway down the stepping-stone path and called out to him. He managed to turn without losing his balance and waited to hear what she wanted to say. 'The fact that I can see the stars through the skylight in Little Argel while I'm lying in *River Pisky* is *really* cool.' Then she smiled a bright and, so Algernon thought, rather beautiful smile that shone a light of happiness on his doubts.

'*Cool* hey?' he repeated, a rare smile playing on his own lips. 'Then from everything you've told me, I'd say my project is complete.'

★ ★ ★

ANNA

The idea that she had been the 'project' in her grandfather's project room before they'd even arrived, wormed its way inside her head. She might have been pushed off her moon by Selene but her grandfather had been rebuilding Little Argel and *River Pisky* as a safe place for her to land. The next few days for Anna were what she could only describe as sufferable. She was surviving, but only barely, and if it wasn't for Little Argel, her *safe place*, she felt she might have lost herself completely. Her friends from home were cramming and therefore texting less frequently and Jacob and his friends couldn't always walk to school with her. The end of year exams were upon them all, but for Anna they were invading her head and sapping her strength. Everything she'd learnt in her lessons had got all tangled up in her mind and was proving impossible to recall. On the days she'd walked alone to school, she'd had to summon up the courage to just keep going, just to make it inside the school buildings instead of giving up and running all the way back to her Little Argel.

'Little Argel was never a kennel, it was a sanctuary,' she told her mother one evening. 'Grandad made it for me.' Saying the words out loud made her feel unexpectedly warm inside, as if daring to believe that some part of herself might belong somewhere at last. The idea of it pleased her. Helene, she noticed, forced a smile that she seemed unable to maintain. To Anna's mind, she looked a little put out.

'He could have said something at the time then. What was he thinking? He left us both believing he wanted you out in the garden. Daft sod!'

For the first time since her arrival Anna felt herself become defensive of her grandfather. 'I think we both know by now that working out what Grandad is thinking is like deciphering an impossible code. One minute he's grouchy and rude and the next minute he's full of surprises. I would have thought you'd have known that about him.'

'Yes, you'd have thought so,' Helene mumbled. She went over to the black and white photograph that hung from a nail on the wall and studied the smiling image of her father.

'It's hard to imagine that it was him isn't it?' Anna commented. 'He looked happy there.'

Helene took the photo frame from its nail and studied it closely. 'Gosh I remember seeing this years ago. Where did you find it?'

'He let me have it... and he made my bed.' Anna tapped her hand on the wonky bed frame. 'It's made from that same boat. It was called *River Pisky* and she got wrecked a long time ago. She's been a bunch of old wood that he kept for years until he brought it back to life... for me.' Helene looked between the photograph and the bed that Anna was sitting on and Anna saw that two roses had stained Helene's cheeks as if she were trying not to cry.

'He did all that... for you?'

'For me,' Anna repeated quietly, realising in that moment that the things her grandfather had chosen to share with her, he had obviously not shared with his own daughter. She felt the atmosphere grow warm with the sadness of wasted opportunities, with deep hurt and threads of jealousy.

'I don't know much about my own father at all, do I?' Helene said thickly. 'And yet *you* do.'

Anna didn't know what to say to this. It sounded almost accusatory, as if she and her grandfather had embarked on a journey and left her mother behind. She remembered how in the car, on the way to her grandfather's house that first day, her mother had described him as a monosyllabic old man whose only claim to fame was that he'd managed to make it into his tenth decade without dying. She wondered how it was possible to get someone so terribly wrong. She understood nothing herself of having a father and how difficult or easy it might be. All she knew right then was maybe, for her mother, it might have been easier to live without one than to live with one who'd been impossible to understand.

10

The Scent of Summer

ALGERNON

Algernon had noticed a difference in Helene of late. She'd been spending her evenings researching all things that related to nature and wildlife in preparation for her new job. 'I'd forgotten how fascinating this stuff is,' she'd declared the previous night in the middle of his *Inspector Morse* programme. He'd had to turn the sound down and ended up missing who'd done it by the time she'd finished going on about everything she'd just learnt. 'Did you know,' she'd said, 'that peat bog contains layers of historical data? We can tell what the landscape used to be like, the animals that existed and even the weather through analysing peat. It can tell us information all the way back to the Stone Age and beyond.'

Algernon had felt quite fed up that she kept asking if they knew all these facts yet wouldn't pause for breath long enough to find out whether they did or didn't. For a good week now, he and the child had been bombarded with facts to the detriment of the daily news, the evening television programmes and all their meals. Quite frankly he and the child were both going a little doolally over it.

He was mid-way through his porridge one Saturday morning, the child not yet emerged from a lie-in, when Helene announced she had plans. 'I'm just going down the garden to dig Anna out of bed then I'm taking you both to the nature reserve. You can both be my practice run for my new job. No excuses.' Within the hour Algernon and his yawning granddaughter were hauling themselves out of Helene's car and across the nature reserve car park.

A light drizzle, the kind that seeps unnoticed through clothing and into bones, billowed in the breeze and he pressed his cap onto his head and tucked his chin into the collar of his jacket. Helene and the child walked beside him, each wearing brightly coloured waterproof jackets. As he hadn't been out for anything other than his haircut or a newspaper for a very long time, he'd initially felt he ought to dress for the occasion and had been about to change into a white shirt and his green tie with the red spots on when Helene had stopped him. She had deemed such an outfit unnecessary, given the location and the weather, and he was now extremely grateful for that.

Making his way gingerly across the gravel towards the main building, despite his walking stick, he felt unsteady on his feet and fearful that he may trip over. Pausing for breath, he wiped the rain spots off his glasses with his hanky, before putting them back on to scan the environment stretching out before him. The prospect of venturing around the uneven terrain was going to be a challenge and, although sorely wanting to bail out and go home, he struggled on. 'I don't know about the peat bog, but I feel like it's me who's from the Stone Age and possibly beyond,' he grumbled. A smattering of laughter from Helene and the child made him realise he'd just told a joke, which quite bucked up his spirits, and when the child then offered her arm for him to cling on to, he was touched.

'Come on, Grandad,' she murmured conspiratorially into his hearing aids, 'let's get it done.' He linked his gnarly old hand through her sturdy young arm and for the first time in a long time he happily admitted defeat over his own frailty.

'Don't panic about the rain, everyone, it should ease up by around eleven. My weather app says so.' Helene examined her phone whilst wiping the rain off the screen and Algernon gave a derisive huff.

'I grew up with a trusty barometer and a lot of weatherly surprise. I won't be panicking!'

Two hours later, several bench seat breathers, two toilet stops and the reluctant need to rent a visitor wheelchair, Algernon finally finished Helene's 'visitor experience' practice run. Tussling with the packaging of a small packet containing two shortcake biscuits in the Centre Café he sat exhausted, the steam of a hot chocolate with extra whipped cream rising in misty swirls under his nose. 'Confound it,' he muttered crossly as he tried to bite the package open with his uncooperative false teeth.

'Well... what do you think?' Helene plonked a bunch of leaflets about the reserve onto the table and spread them out in front of them all.

'I think they should serve food that isn't part of a *Krypton Factor* challenge,' Algernon grumbled, regretfully handing the package over to Anna's outstretched hand.

'There you go, Grandad,' she said, ripping open the packet easily and placing the two biscuits onto his plate.

'Is that it?' Helene looked crestfallen and she fiddled nervously with a loose lock of her hair. 'Is that all you both have to say? This job is our future, mine and Anna's.' She looked between them and waited for their replies, the shine gradually dimming from her face.

'It's good, Mum,' the child offered.

'You know quite a lot already, it would seem,' Algernon added, noticing how the child had grown quiet.

'I really feel as if when I start here I'll have found my vocation in life.' Helene's voice was fired with purpose. 'I think I'm going to love being outside and I'm going to take any training they give me so that I can work my way up.' She picked up a leaflet showing smiling school children peering at beetles and fungi in an old tree, waving the leaflet at them as if it were the most exciting thing. 'I'm determined that in a few months' time, I'll have the money to rent somewhere. We can get all the packing boxes out of your dining room and Anna and I will be gone before you know it.' Algernon watched, however, how Helene reached for the child's hand and patted it positively yet how the child responded with a vague frown and a sad, distracted smile.

That night Algernon lay on his side of the bed, mulling over recent events. Helene's confidence for her new role and her promises to be out of his house as soon as possible circled around and around in his mind and, gradually, the distracted smile the child had offered Helene back at the nature reserve began to make sense. *We'll be gone before you know it.* Helene's words echoed in his head, and they worried him.

Taking the frame of photographs that the child had given him he cogitated over each one, stopping to tap a finger at the photograph of nine-year-old Anna. Helene had lived with Harry for only six years so the child would have been around nine when they'd moved in with him. Goodness knows how many times she had moved before then. Helene was planning to move the child yet again, and he knew that each time it happened the child would leave a piece of herself behind. '*She's losing herself.*' That's what Helene had once said. The child who had arrived at his house wearing multicoloured clothes and carrying a cactus had been disappearing in front of their very eyes, and it was about to happen again.

Algernon, of course, knew very well what it was to disappear and how impossibly hard it then was to reappear. He himself had disappeared twice. The happy child he'd once been before he was sent to boarding school had gone forever, as had the confident pilot who then could no longer fly. The Algernon who remained had been only a shade of himself ever since.

He placed the frame back on the chest of drawers and said goodnight to Evie, the bones of an idea formulating in his mind.

ANNA

'It's very nice.' Anna ran her hands over the paintwork of a white car in the driveway of Jacob's house. 'When did you pass your test?' She peered inside at the black cloth seats and the little smiley-faced air freshener hanging from the indicator stick, which filled the car with the scent of vanilla.

'I passed six months ago,' Jacob replied proudly, pointing the key remote at the car so that Anna could climb inside.

'I've been using my mum's car, and now I've got my own.' He tapped the bonnet proudly. 'The mileage is high, but other than that it's great.'

'So, where are we going?' Anna felt a thrill over the fact that Jacob had offered to take her out in his car and was pleased that she'd taken time over getting dressed up that morning. She felt for the first time in a long while a little bit like her old self again. The end of the school year was now in sight. Her exams were almost over, the terrible weight of them lessening with each completed paper, plus it was Saturday, her favourite day. She climbed inside the car onto the driver's seat side and with a pang of envy, wished she was old enough to have her own car. For weeks she'd hardly been anywhere since her mother had got the job at the reserve and was looking forward to an adventure.

'It's a surprise,' Jacob replied, making the thrill in Anna's chest vibrate with excitement. 'I'll go and get Mr M and we'll take him out as well.'

She poked her head back out of the car from where she sat, unable to keep the sudden bitter disappointment from sounding in her voice. 'Why would you want to take him out as well?'

He shrugged casually. 'Why not? I just thought it would be nice for him… get him out. You know how it is. He's old and can't do much.' He jogged off around the corner in the direction of her grandfather's house and she slumped back in the driver seat trying not to mind.

'I didn't know it was a Saga holiday,' she grumbled unkindly, pulling the door shut. *I thought it was going to be just us.* She ran her hands over the steering wheel as if she were about to drive away, as if she could turn on the engine and just keep going until the petrol ran out. If she had a car she could be free to go where *she* wanted to go.

A few minutes later Jacob appeared, her grandfather tottering along beside him holding on to his arm, and she was instantly suspicious. Gone were the comfortable brown trousers and hand-knitted brown cardigan with the brown toggle buttons. He was wearing his smart beige trousers and over-jacket as if the arrangement had been agreed beforehand and he'd had time to prepare and she wondered why the desire to wear colour should fade as life itself faded away.

Jacob drove carefully, the air from the car's vents fanning his hair, while the scent of vanilla emanating from the smiley-face air freshener competed with the scent of *old* that clung to her grandfather. It was the kind of day where white, pot-bellied clouds lumbered across a blue sky casting intermittent shadows between long gaps of sunshine. She took her round, pink sunglasses off her head and put them on, silently watching a pink world go by. When Jacob pulled the car to a halt in the car park of the nature reserve, however, she inwardly groaned.

'I said we *knew* enough to get a job here Jacob, I didn't say we *wanted* a job here.' Jacob simply grinned at her in the rear-view mirror then turned the engine off and got out of the car. He opened the rear door for Anna and playfully dragged her from her seat.

'It's a warm day so I thought we could take your grandad for an ice cream in the café. It's nice here.' He looked around him and breathed in deeply as if the landscape were his life source.

'But we could have gone anywhere. Somewhere different.

The coast… the zoo… anywhere.' Her disappointment was palpable and she busily scuffed at the ground with her silver boot in an effort not to cry.

'Well, er… we could have done… but H asked me if I'd bring you both here now that I have a car. I think she wanted to show off doing her *nature* thing.'

Her mother had turned her back on their years in the city and thrown herself into a rural life, expecting her to do the same without a backwards glance. She'd now even hijacked her outing with Jacob. She looked directly at Jacob and let a moment of spite overtake her. 'We've already done the nature thing when she took us here before she started the job. *H* has become a total nature bore.' It felt good to get the jagged shards of her feelings out into the open but now that she had she felt embarrassed that Jacob could hear it.

'This is different. She's working here and she's part of all this now.' He glanced around at the view and offered Anna a kind smile. 'We're at the nature reserve, Mr M,' he called loudly, going around to her grandfather's side of the car and opening the door for him.

'I'm not deaf! No need to shout. I know perfectly well where we are… and it's Mr Maybury to you.' Her grandfather held his arm out for Anna to help him and she stepped forward to oblige.

'Pleasant as ever,' she said under her breath, as she let her grandfather loop his arm through hers again and they set off in the direction of the café.

'I heard that! I *said* I'm not deaf and I'm not getting into one of those wheelchairs again either.' He scowled and halted to gasp for some air. 'Adagio, child!' he chastised. 'It means slow pace… in music terms. In other words, not so *fast* please.'

Anna slowed down her pace and thought about asking him what *tortuously* slow pace was in music terms.

After they'd been greeted by Helene who'd shown them around the staff rooms and teaching rooms, and introduced them to the people she now worked with, she treated them to drinks in the café. 'What do you think, Dad? I've passed my trial and I'm a fully fledged member of staff.' Anna noticed that she'd asked this question last time they were here and that she was fidgeting with her fingers, as if she were nervous or something, as if it were terribly important to her what he thought.

'Very good,' he replied. It was a simple answer and one that Anna could instinctively sense spoke volumes between them. She could see Helene swell a little in front of him, as if she were still a young child trying to seek approval from her parent, and felt a sudden wave of tenderness for her mother.

'It's brilliant, Mum,' she said, kindly.

'It is isn't it?' Helene almost jiggled with pleasure as she stood up from her seat and addressed her father directly. 'Thank you. You know, for coming. I… I just wanted to show you.' Anna watched her blush in her need to impress and suddenly understood why they all had to come again. 'I have to go. A group of children are booked in for a birthday party and we're building shelters and learning about survival.' Helene left them then, in a whirl of importance, asking another member of staff if she wouldn't mind offering them ice creams.

Now, from where they sat, they could see Helene striding in and out of a thicket of trees, a band of small visitors in tow. Her blonde hair was piled into a messy knot on her head and she was wearing wellies, shorts and the nature reserve standard green polo shirt. 'H seems like she's really enjoying this new job,' Jacob remarked, his tongue lapping at his ice cream. Anna studied her mother's body language, her brisk walk, her arms gesticulating wildly at the surroundings and couldn't help realising that she'd never seen her look quite so happy in anything she'd ever done before. She tried hard to push away the envy she felt over the success of her mother's new life at the cost of her own.

'Mum's getting a suntan,' she said.

'And she's not nearly so fat,' her grandfather added.

ALGERNON

The germ of his idea had not only grown but taken flower, leading him to a decision he no longer felt able to go back on. Remembering that he once used to have a sense of adventure, Algernon had reasoned that there was no time like the present.

His plan had necessitated Helene's reluctant approval plus, as a degree of travel was involved, the funds for a loan on a suitable car had been transferred to Jacob's account. The lad had been delighted. Now that a car had been purchased, Algernon was confident that his plan was taking shape. The lad was a careful driver as young men these days went, and with the assurances of his mother, he and Helene were confident that he could deliver them safely.

The sash windows in his sitting room were open, letting in a stream of sunlight and a breeze that offered a pleasant caress on his skin. Birds had now found their way back to his garden and the soft beat of butterfly wings breathed life into the purple buddleia again. Helene had mown the lawn and

Anna and Jacob were deep in conversation lying with their backs on the grass. Cat lay on his side near the youngsters, his fat grey body sprawled on a warm stepping stone, one lazy paw flopped over his contented head.

Algernon's carriage clock ticked its way steadily onwards and the dust motes spiralled in a shard of sunlight that came through the windows. He finished making a list in his little leather notebook of everything that he needed to do then, with his bones creaking and his muscles complaining, he went to get the telephone in order to book a hotel.

ANNA

The last days of school before the holidays were upon them and Anna was virtually counting the minutes. 'I got my exam results. My predicted grades,' she said to Jacob as they lay on their backs on the grass outside Little Argel.

'Any good?' he asked.

'Not as good as I wanted but not as bad as I feared,' she replied. She'd been surprised. The months of disruption and anxiety had taken its toll but somewhere, in amongst it all, she'd found a way through.

He turned to her and grinned. 'See! You did it. You survived. I knew you had it in you. And they're just the mocks.' Anna gave a half-smile. It wasn't a victory as such but it was behind her now and she could hardly believe the joy of it.

'Two more days of year ten and I'm done.' She sucked a deep lungful of air through her nostrils and blew slowly back out. 'You can smell it can't you?'

'Sorry, it was the curry my mum made last night.' Jacob

laughed but gave a mock yell of pain as Anna kicked him with her bare foot.

'Don't ruin the moment. Breathe in... It's the smell of summer. Of warm air and cut grass and lazy days and everything that isn't school for six whole weeks.' They took simultaneous deep breaths then let the air slowly out at the same time, squinting at the canopy of blue sky and clouds above them. Cat who'd been asleep nearby stirred and began to dart about, trying to keep up with the erratic flight of a yellow butterfly and Anna rolled over to watch them. 'Did you know yellow is the colour of happiness?' she asked.

'It is?' Jacob replied.

'Yes. I like to think that yellow butterflies carry happiness around with them and sprinkle it over you with the dust from their wings.' She reached her arm out to stop Cat from getting too close to it and he let her stroke him until a nesting dove caught his attention instead.

'Let's hope this particular butterfly flies over you and does its magic then. You never seem that happy to me, Anna Maybury.' Anna jolted at his stinging accusation. He hadn't meant it unkindly she was sure, but even so he'd shone a harsh light on her raw emotions and she didn't know how to respond.

'I was happy... once,' she said cautiously. 'Before I moved here. And I will be in two more days when the bell finally rings for the end of the year and I can escape school for six whole weeks. No school, no more end of year exams, no grey uniform... I can't wait!' Jacob picked at the grass with his thumb and forefinger, releasing a sweet scent that was laced with the promise of summer. 'What will you be doing for the holidays?' She asked the question tentatively, barely daring to hope that he may be around to keep her company.

'I've got a job,' he answered. He propped himself up on one elbow and shielded his eyes from the sun with his hand.

'Doing what?' Anna asked, pretending to be distracted by Cat who was inching his way towards the dove. It wouldn't do for him to know she was disappointed.

'It's only for a few days. I've just got to drive around,' he replied. 'I guess you'd say I was a delivery driver.'

'Driving what?' Anna asked, her disappointment giving way to hope that he wouldn't be busy for long. She watched the yellow butterfly land on a lavender flower head and another flitter around a bunch of pink clover nestled in the grass that had survived the blades of the mower.

'Just *stuff*,' he answered, not meeting her eye.

ALGERNON

'To be honest, Dad, I'm still unsure about this. It's all come a bit out of left field. A trip to Cornwall with two teenagers when you've hardly left the house since Mum died is quite an adventure at your age, you have to admit.' Helene had the ironing board out in the sitting room and was making a neat pile of ironed clothes out of a messy pile of clean laundry.

'You think I don't know how to have an adventure?' Algernon challenged.

Helene gave him a look that said that she clearly didn't know how to answer his question truthfully, and it made him feel rather sad. It was true; she probably didn't know that an adventurous Algernon had even ever existed.

'Anyway, I've washed most of your clothes, Dad. They were a bit... you know... in *need*.' Algernon shrugged with disdain. He'd managed perfectly well before Helene took over everything, washing his smalls in the sink and putting things in his washing machine if they needed to be put in his washing machine. To his mind, Helene made a pastime out of washing, so much so that the darn washing machine whirred away in his kitchen almost every day.

'I think you wash everything too often,' he sniffed.

'I don't think you wash things enough,' she sniffed back. 'Take it from me, it was time.' She pulled several pairs of his underpants out of the basket, shook them a bit and then folded them into neat quarters. Next, she took a shirt and spread it over the ironing board while he watched a jet of steam discharge noisily from the iron.

Algernon rifled through his memory for the last time he'd washed his heavier garments but to his dismay, he really couldn't remember when that might have been. He harrumphed and wished that the help she offered didn't highlight his impotency.

'You came down yesterday with three baked beans stuck to your jumper like a brooch, Dad. We haven't had baked beans for three weeks!' She proceeded to fold the now ironed shirt before pulling another from the basket. 'Just because you can't see it... or...' she added delicately, '*smell* it for that matter, doesn't mean it isn't there. Anyway it's all clean now, and when I finish the ironing you'll be good to start packing.' Algernon remained silent. 'I'm still really worried about all this though,' Helene added, twisting her lips into an uneasy knot. 'Springing all this on Anna with no notice at all is... well, it's likely to go tits up!'

'Eloquent,' Algernon replied.

'I'm sorry but we… you, me… *one* of us at least, should warn her about the plan. I just feel a bit uneasy about it.'

Algernon fidgeted and sighed loudly, wishing that Helene would stop going on about it and that she would just accept his wish to give the child some excitement in her life. His trip, he believed, was better managed without too much advanced warning.

'No!' Algernon tapped his knees agitatedly with his outstretched fingers. 'I want to surprise her.'

'Whatever!' Helene acquiesced. 'I'll take a break and get us a cuppa. I've bought chocolate biscuits.' He watched her leave the sitting room, his shirts and underpants folded neatly, Evie's laundry basket half full of garments still waiting to be pressed. He glanced at the carriage clock and felt his heart quicken. The child would finish school in a few hours but thanks to Helene, he would be ready. For the first time in years he was going to do something daring.

ANNA

When the school bell chimed for the last time in the academic year, Anna thought her body was in mortal danger of totally deflating with the huge rush of her outward breath. Her relief made her feel weightless, the empty weeks stretching ahead of her being a totally joyous thing. September was forever away, the school gates were behind her and even if she wouldn't see her friends in the summer, she wouldn't see her enemies either.

She tried not to care that her friends back home were racing out of school to meet by the river for a celebratory picnic.

She tried not to care that soon they'd be in the corner shop buying snacks before going to the river to kick off their shoes and mess about in the water. Or that they'd sunbathe on the grassy bank sipping cider smuggled from home in their bags and playing their music too loud. She tried not to care that she was no longer a solid part of the group and had become just someone they used to know. She tried not to care about anything because at long, long last she was free.

It came as some surprise to her then, when she walked into her grandfather's house on that last day of school term and that first day of the summer holiday, to find him in his armchair in his sitting room with an enormous green suitcase by his side.

11

A Mission

ALGERNON

'I've got a surprise,' Algernon announced, as the child stood in the doorway of his living room pointing questioningly to his large and somewhat battered suitcase. 'We're going to make a trip to Cornwall. I've left something there and I think it's about time I went to retrieve it.'

He tried to smile at her but his declaration caused a fizzing sensation behind his sternum which in turn made his chest heave several times before he could catch his breath. The child continued to stand in the doorframe only her mouth now hung open as if he'd said something outrageous. He had, of course, said something outrageous. He, Algernon Maybury was going to take her on an adventure. He had no idea if the item he'd left in Cornwall was even there anymore, if the earth it was buried in had remained untouched since the day he'd patted it flat with the palm of his young hand, yet they were going to hunt for it anyway.

She didn't look grateful and Helene's warning came crashing in on him. 'Close your mouth, you'll catch a fly!'

he said, scowling defensively. The child shut her mouth so quickly her teeth banged together. 'Young lad next door is driving us and I've cleared it with your mother. We'll be off first thing in the morning.' He gave one more heave of his chest followed by a couple of dry coughs, then he rested his head on the back of his chair, closing his eyes as if the whole suggestion had sucked him dry of energy.

'You mean "we" as in me and Mum?' The child tentatively entered the sitting room and perched on the edge of the new armchair.

'Just you,' he said, opening his eyes again. 'And the lad next door of course.'

'Just me?' The child seemed very confused and not at all pleased about the idea. Dismay welled inside him, acrid and suffocating.

'Like a holiday?' she queried.

'No, not like a holiday. More like a mission. We're going for four days… three nights.' Despite his careful planning, he found himself beginning to flounder.

'What sort of mission?' Now she was trying to winkle-pick information out of him that he wasn't ready to give and it caused him to agitatedly drum his fingers on his knees. His idea as to how to help the child had seemed like such a good one up until now but faced with such a question he was unable to answer it in simple terms. He needed to show not tell. He needed to take her to the place where he'd buried his own heart, the place where the concrete inside his chest had set, heavy and very nearly impenetrable. His quest was to save her from doing the same with her own heart even though he was picking at his scabs to do so. The nervous fizzing continued with such force behind his sternum that he wondered if perhaps his heart was going to give out. It couldn't. Mustn't. Not yet. He was going back to Cornwall, she was coming with him, and that was the end of it.

'I told you!' he snapped. He hadn't meant to snap and hearing his words out loud he attempted a softer delivery. 'I want you to help me find something that I left behind in the place where I used to live.'

'On the housing estate, or the council estate or whatever it was?' As she queried where he used to live, Algernon found his eyes widening a little. How strange, he thought, that memories which were so vivid in his head and which he'd attempted to share with her back then, could land so completely altered upon her ears. He stared hard at her, struggling with her lack of understanding. She was a modern child whose modern life had been so utterly different from his own.

'On the estate,' he confirmed, seeing the place where he had grown up materialise so clearly in his mind's eye.

'What was it... the thing?' As Anna asked the question her smartphone made a high-pitched beep and her attention immediately diverted to it. Algernon smarted. He wasn't prepared to battle for her attention over a sliver of technology and if he were honest with himself, he had hoped for a little more enthusiasm from the child. Undertaking a quest such as this was no mean feat for someone of his age. He was worn out from packing the clothes that Helene had washed and ironed, and from his constant vigorous checking that all his plans were in place. He needed to be left alone for a while to lick his wounds and before Cat made himself and his cupboard love known at 5.30pm.

'Enough with all the questions, leave me now. Go and pack your things,' he ordered, picking up his newspaper and pretending to read. When she'd gone, closing the back door to the kitchen unnecessarily loudly behind her, he sighed deeply and placed his newspaper back down. 'Clumsy old fool,' he said out loud, cross with himself for handling the matter so badly. Of course the child wanted to know what it was he'd left behind, of course she wanted answers. Helene had been so right. Why on earth had he thought it was a good idea to spring a surprise on a child who was already battling with all the decisions that the adults in her life had made?

When Evie touched his hand, her fingers gossamer light upon his, he did his best to calm himself down for her sake. He'd tried to take matters into his own hands and now he had no idea as to whether it was a good idea or not. He heaved himself up from his chair and made his way over to his old stereo unit and taking a record out of its sleeve he placed it on the deck. A rhythmic crackle and opening notes filled the room as, when back in his chair, eyes closed, he allowed the music to replace all that was jangling in his head.

He mouthed the words, *We'll gather lilacs in the spring again and walk together down an English lane...* while Evie joined in, singing along beside him. In his mind's eye she was wearing a cotton dress of pink and green, her voice was tuneful and clear, and her hazel eyes were smiling. As the music played and took him back in time he knew he was being fanciful but he needed to know that she was still the wind beneath his wings.

As the record came to its end and all became quiet, he feared that the room belonged only to his foolish old self, the battered green suitcase and the ticking clock. Even Cat, it would appear, had left him for Little Argel and the welcoming embrace of the child.

★ ★ ★

ANNA

'I think he thought it was going to be a nice surprise and he asked me not to say anything.' Jacob's head was hanging through the skylight but, this time, he made no attempt to drop down onto the bed. 'My word is my bond,' he added, with the accent of a foreign spy. 'Forgive me for assuming you Mayburys might actually be communicating more efficiently by now and that the old fella might have handled the situation better.' Anna didn't look up but kept the back of her head to him as she fought with the zip of a bright red suitcase.

'Well, you assumed wrong! Communication with him always has to be on his terms. He's so... so *difficult*.' She noticed a thread of black cotton caught between the teeth of the zip and picked at it with her nails. 'And I'm pissed off with you for keeping it a secret and I'm even more pissed off at my mum for making all my decisions for me.' She growled as she pulled at the stuck zip.

'I think they thought you'd be at a loose end?' Jacob made the statement sound like it was a question and it made Anna prickle. She may not have friends, but she had plans. She was being pushed in a different direction to the one she thought she was taking at the start of her longed-for holiday. No one had considered that the *secret* or the *surprise* or whatever they wanted to call it might not be easy for her to process.

'So what if I was? Perhaps I wanted to be at a loose end!' She thought about the conversation they'd had in the garden a couple of days ago, and gasped. 'We're the *stuff* you're driving, aren't we?' She wanted to punch him. The very people she thought she could rely on had let her down.

'I told you, he didn't want me to say anything. Let it go, Anna. Look on the bright side, you get to spend the next few days with me.' She felt a wave of self-consciousness come over her and hoped that he couldn't tell that this, in fact, was the only bright side of the whole thing. She pulled again at the zip but it wouldn't budge. 'I'd help, but…'

'But what?' She stole a glance up at him, his head still hanging through the skylight, was turning slightly purple as the blood rushed to it.

'But I don't fancy getting tangled up in all your scanties.' She looked around her and could hear him sniggering as her heart crashed through the floor and her cheeks went crimson. She yanked the zip free and grabbed at her underwear, shoving it inside the suitcase as fast as she could. All the time he'd been up there he'd seen everything, even her most ancient and tatty knickers… gusset side up.

She had such a muddle going on in her head that she hardly knew what to do with herself. Her feelings were spiralling out of control, filling her up and clawing at her and she couldn't make it all go away. Her day had become something so different from what she thought it was going to be, so *bent out of shape*. Less than two hours ago she'd rushed home from school on a jet stream of joy, closed the front door behind her with glorious relief and yet in the blink of an eye everything had changed. Her grandfather sitting with his suitcase beside him had surprised her, taking her off guard with his proposal to do something so utterly random for him.

When her phone had buzzed with a video message from her friends – Amy and Kieran, Joshua, Gracie, Imogen and

Ava – who were already by the river, sunglasses on, music playing, beginning their summer without her, he'd suddenly got all cross. 'We miss you,' they'd chanted into the phone camera just as her grandfather ordered her to go and pack her things.

'He just dismissed me from the house without telling me anything.' She aimlessly lifted some garments then dropped them defeatedly back down. 'What am I supposed to pack for a not-holiday to a city, to find something that I don't even know what? I don't even know where we're staying.'

'It's somewhere around Truro, which is the capital city of Cornwall, and that's all I know. Promise. Cross my heart and hope to die.' Even though she couldn't look at him yet, she could hear the casual shrug in his voice. He was always so casual, always so easily pleased.

'What are you taking?'

He gave an upside-down shrug. 'Don't know. Stuff. Shorts, T-shirts that kind of thing. It's summer so you probably won't need the onesie.' Anna crossly grabbed at her green and yellow onesie from the end of the bed and tucked it under her pillow out of his sight.

'Go away. I'm not in a good mood,' she moaned, and gave him her special one-fingered wave.

'No *shit*, Sherlock! I'd never have noticed,' he replied.

'Why would you even agree to this, Jacob? Why would you agree to drive us around on a mission that isn't a holiday?' She took a pair of shorts and folded them badly before sliding them into the suitcase on top of her underwear.

'Because he's paying me. And possibly... definitely... because he bought my car...' Jacob answered so cagily that she shot him a look, searching for the joke that she felt must surely be there. Jacob pulled a wide grin that was more like an apologetic grimace.

'He's paying you *and* he bought you a car?' Her grandfather had got him the car and they had all known about it for ages and yet not let her into their secret.

'Loaned me the money for a car,' Jacob clarified. 'I was saving up for one of my own. I've been driving my mum's and I've been looking for a summer job but your grandad needed a driver. So Bob's your aunty and all that.' Her disappointment bit hard at her insides. *Was he only going on the trip because he had to? Not because he wanted to spend time with her?*

'It's Bob's your uncle,' she corrected moodily.

'Not in my family.' Jacob laughed. 'Anyway, like I said, I'll be paying him back, every penny.'

'He hasn't said anything about paying *me*.' Anna dumped an orange dress with white polka dots into the suitcase and searched for an accessory to go with it.

'Perhaps he's not, then,' he replied, 'but if you're looking for sympathy, you'll find it in the dictionary somewhere between shit and syphilis!' Anna stopped what she was doing and looked up at him again. His face, rufescent from dangling through the skylight for so long, was all screwed up in his attempt at holding back a laugh. As she continued to stare at him in disbelief, she realised that the Anna Maybury who never used to take herself too seriously would have laughed at that comment. That Anna Maybury wasn't here though. That Anna Maybury had been left behind at Harry's.

'How *much* is he giving you?' she demanded.

'Mind your own beeswax. I'm off to pack my own stuff.' Jacob got to his feet, calling cheerily as she heard his footsteps on the roof of Little Argel. Then he hesitated for a moment before reappearing at the skylight. 'See you in the morning at seven. We're leaving early because Mum's insisting that I drive slowly and take lots of breaks. Oh... and stop being a spoilt brat! It's a road trip, not an endurance test.' After a lot of clattering, she heard him jump back down into his garden followed by the thud of footsteps that got fainter until she heard the back door to his house shut behind him. Left alone with a heavy silence and a messy pile of clothes, Anna allowed her shoulders to slump and, curling into a ball, she let the tears plop over the bridge of her nose and land in her hair.

She recalled her grandfather telling her about *River Pisky* and Smith's Island and the place where he used to live. She thought back to all the conversations they'd had over the months and knew how difficult he found it to express himself. Jacob was right: she'd behaved like a spoilt brat. She sniffed. 'I feel rubbish, Gary, and I don't know how to make it go away.' Gary, typical of a cactus, said nothing. He simply listened to her woes, absorbed all her problems into his green plumpness and glistened with sympathetic prickles.

ALGERNON

'I think she just got a bit pissed off, Dad. I did warn you. And now she's pissed off with me because of it!' Helene sat opposite Algernon at the dining room table, looking irritated. She drank a cold beer straight from the bottle, still wearing her uniform and with a leaf caught in her hair. She was eating with far more gusto than he possessed right now and took a large bite out of a particularly fat sausage harpooned on the end of her fork, and then talked through it. 'She rang me at work after your conversation with her and I don't know exactly how you told her about this trip of yours but she sounded pretty upset about it, and I'm not surprised. You've got to admit, dashing off to Cornwall with two teenagers is out of the ordinary for you?'

Algernon had to admit that it was indeed extremely out of the ordinary and obviously the child hadn't welcomed it. He carved his way into the food on his plate, relieved at least that it was recognisable for what it was and didn't involve chickpeas, lentils or other such oddities that Helene was prone to messing around with. The gravy was good and thick too and the mashed potato just how he liked it but, for all that it was, today his stomach was not a willing participant. The child hadn't joined them for their meal and he found that he missed her presence. 'She shouldn't be missing meals,' he said grumpily.

'One meal is hardly going to matter, Dad. Not today. I gave her the choice and she chose not to come.' Helene frowned irritably as she piled a dollop of mashed potato on the last part of her sausage and pushed it through the dregs of gravy on her plate. 'Working outside makes me hungry,' she said, as she swallowed her mouthful and cleansed her mouth with a swig from her beer bottle before reaching over and spearing the sausage he'd left on his plate.

'I was saving that sausage for later,' he grumbled, sipping his own drink and shuddering over the lack of manners that he and Evie had once so painstakingly drummed into their daughter. 'And you shouldn't have given her the choice.' He knew he was being argumentative but he was used to the child being there, so vibrant and youthful, and he wondered how he'd ever endured so many years dining alone in his kitchen before she arrived.

'Then perhaps that's the problem, Dad.' Helene pointed her fork at him as if to prove a point. 'She wasn't given the choice about this trip and now look what's happened. She could have been involved in the plan in some way but you had to go all secret squirrel over it and lump it on her.'

He knew she was right. He'd buggered up the whole execution of his plan and now the atmosphere in the room was horribly lumpy. 'The child hasn't been given much of a choice in anything has she?' he voiced. He felt the pain of his past misgivings stirring and grazing his insides. Had he behaved more graciously when Helene first announced she was with child, everything could have been so very different for all of them. He held Helene's gaze and wondered what he was seeing in her cool turquoise eyes.

'You're blaming me?' she retorted, a hard edge to her tone. A recognisable tightness thinned Helene's lips and a flush crept up her neck. Not for the first time in his life, Algernon was surprised by the reactions he provoked in others. He fancied he could hear the ticking of the carriage clock from the sitting room and that it was marking all the time that had escaped between him and his daughter over the years. 'I did what I had to do,' she said measuredly.

Algernon wanted to say so many things then. He wanted to tell her what an old fool he'd been, and how, as a result, he'd missed out on so much with his family. He wanted to say that he was proud of her for being the mother she'd become. He wanted to thank her for the granddaughter who had brought all the colours into his life that had been missing for so long. He wanted to say that he could see how all the wonderful qualities of Evie lived on in them both. He wanted to say these things, but he couldn't.

'I know,' he replied. Two words, said in two seconds. Two insufficient words that should have spilled into thousands because they spanned a lifetime. 'I know,' he repeated softly.

ANNA

When her mother came into Little Argel later that evening with fifty pounds and a new packet of ultramarine hair dye – gifts that she could hardly afford to give – Anna felt her whole body rush with apprehension.

'Peace offering! You can stay blue till the end of the summer and not a day longer. Deal?' Helene smiled and tried to hand the things over, plus a sausage sandwich that she'd salvaged from dinner. Anna didn't take the gifts, or the sausage sandwich. Instead her eyes glistened and her fingers twisted around the wool of the hat on her head. 'Bit hot for a hat, isn't it?' Helene asked, a frown replacing her smile. 'Anna?' Anna's eyes travelled over to the bin on the floor and Helene's did the same. There, stuffed to the brim, was an abundance of blue hair. Helene gasped then slapped a hand across her mouth in disbelief, and she placed everything slowly down on the table where a pair of scissors lay next to Gary. 'Oh, Anna!' she sighed, bending to pick up a lock of faded blue hair from the bin.

'The trouble with blue is that its vibrancy soon washes away, leaving a miserable trace of what it should've been.' Anna looked at her mother through a pool of unshed tears and tried to speak through wavering lips. 'A bit like *me*,' she added, her voice trailing into a squeak. Helene pulled the hat from her head where Anna's hair, less than an hour ago, had hung halfway down her back. She ran her fingers over the blunt ends that now stopped at her daughter's shoulders.

'What have you done?' she asked, pressing the hand to her lips that held the lock of blue hair.

'I got rid of it. That's what everyone wanted. That's what *you* wanted, isn't it?' She raised her chin and tried to brazen it out, even though the sight of her hair in her mother's hands threatened a fresh round of tears.

'You could have just dyed it back—'

'Shut up!' Anna rammed her hands on her ears to shut out the sound of what she *could* have done, tears spilling in rivulets down her face as she screwed her eyes shut. She thought everyone would be pleased. She thought that maybe cutting it off would save her mother paying for a hairdresser... that maybe it would make her look acceptable in her grandfather's eyes. That it would stop her looking like a spoilt brat. Helene pulled Anna's hands away from her ears and wrapped her arms around her head, pulling her close.

'Get off!' Anna tried to push her away, but her mother's embrace was fierce.

'Oh, my Moonchild,' she crooned, kissing the crown of her hair.

'You don't know who I am anymore,' Anna whispered.

'You're Anna Maybury, you're my Moonchild and you shine—'

'Don't say it, Mum!' She cut Helene off and tried again to pull away from her embrace. Anna Maybury was no longer all the things her mother said she was. She no longer shined at all.

★ ★ ★

ALGERNON

Algernon washed up after supper then sat alone in the sitting room as he had done every day for sixteen years before the arrival of Helene and the child. Cat was nowhere to be seen and the empty chair opposite was still empty. The big green suitcase sat waiting by his side, a wedding gift from himself and Evie to each other. A promise to travel to countries far and wide and yet now just a sore reminder of the fact that they had never in truth travelled anywhere together further than their own shores. The suitcase was battered only by time and dust, and Cat who would jump on top of the wardrobe to sleep on it. The carriage clock chipped away at his time, telling him that soon he would be taking the suitcase on a quest that had already gone wrong.

'Why did I do it?' he asked the empty chair. 'Why did I think I could help?'

There were no answers for him that night, no Evie telling him that everything would work out fine. Just his own uncertainty, a large and battered suitcase and a carriage clock that filled the room with its relentless rhythmic cruelty.

ANNA

'You'll need these.' Helene picked up a pair of flip-flops studded with coloured gems and Anna took them off her. Her mother was trying to call a silent truce, she knew, but she didn't want any help with her packing. 'It's only a two-star hotel with rubbish reviews. Your grandad left it far too late to find somewhere that still had three vacant rooms in peak season... could well be a sticky carpet kind of place.' She laughed a little but the sound of it clashed horribly with the way Anna felt.

'Nice!' Anna grimaced and pushed the flip-flops into a pocket at the side of her case. Helene folded some of the clothes still strewn across the bed, piling them neatly beside the suitcase.

'You don't want to take this?' She pointed to the make-up collection that Harry had given her, but Anna shook her head.

'It will only annoy Grandad.'

'Does it matter?' Helene asked.

'It matters,' Anna replied curtly. 'Did you know Jacob's getting paid for taking us?'

'Yes.' Helene pushed the uneaten sandwich towards Anna and went to empty the bin full of hair, hiding it from view by tying the top of the bag into a knot.

'Grandad got him his car.' Anna pushed the plate back and ran her fingers over the shortness of her hair. She missed the weight of it, the way it brushed the skin of her arms. *What had she done?*

'I know that too.' Helene spoke with an edge to her voice that Anna had never detected before, and the sound of it confused her.

'Didn't *you* want to drive us? To come to Cornwall?' She stopped what she was packing and waited while Helene fiddled with the bag containing her hair. Her chin was raised and she twisted and retwisted the top of the bag.

'I'm working, aren't I? I've got my new job and I couldn't spare the time. Set your alarm; you've an early start.' She left

EVERY SHADE OF HAPPY

the uneaten sandwich behind and, taking the bag of hair with her, started to open the door to Little Argel.

'But he did *ask* you?' Anna stood up, suddenly realising how desperately complicated the relationship was between her grandfather and her mother.

Helene offered a smile of regret and, just before she shut the door behind herself, Anna heard her say, 'I don't think this is about me.'

12

A Lovely Day for a Drive

ALGERNON

'It's too early.' The child, looking puffy and slightly bedraggled from sleep, came grumbling into the kitchen, placed her cactus on the kitchen table and dropped her bright red suitcase on the floor. Algernon was with Helene, helping to rustle up an early breakfast while Cat, who'd followed the child inside, allowed himself to be scooped up into her arms.

'I feel as if there should be an initiation process,' Helene said. 'Anna this is 6am and 6am this is Anna. Should you need to leave in an emergency, the escape doors are here and here.' She swung her arms forward and to the side as if she were a stewardess at the front of an aeroplane then laughed at her own silliness.

'Funny,' Anna mumbled, finding it not in the slightest bit funny.

'You might think this is unreasonable but you have to set off early because the traffic is awful at this time of year and Jacob will need to drive carefully. Plus, you're probably going to have to stop a million times due to your grandfather's weak bladder.'

Algernon immediately bristled at Helene mentioning his bladder and wondered if, or indeed why, she had taken note of how many times he needed to spend a penny! Even so, he thought, there was no need to make such light of it in the middle of breakfast preparation.

'I'm going to miss you, Catty Cat.' Anna nuzzled her face into the grey fur of Cat and murmured into his ear before she planted a kiss on the tip of it. Next, she turned him round until he lay like a baby in her arms, then she yawned so deeply that Algernon could see inside her gaping mouth. Algernon, however, was far too busy surveying the child's head to comment on her lack of manners.

'Lovely day for a drive!' Helene jabbed him in the back and made a warning face, which he presumed was because she thought he was going to speak out of turn about the shortness of the child's hair. He felt quite disgruntled about it. He may put his foot in many things, but he had no desire to start the day off any worse than the previous day had ended. The cut of the child's hair was a surprise though, despite the fact that Helene had already told him about it last night. However, the way it framed her young, morning-flushed face he decided, was really very lovely.

Helene poured three cups of coffee, one black for herself, one white for him and a sweet latte for the child. She placed them on a small tray, gave him another warning face, then walked off in the direction of the dining room. The child placed Cat on the floor, picked up a cereal packet, a bottle of milk and, rather helpfully, Algernon's bowl of steaming porridge and followed her in. Algernon took up the rear, holding nothing but his pride and his stick.

'Jacob will be knocking on the door at seven so have you got everything ready?' Helene placed the cups on the table before sitting down, waiting expectantly for their answers as if they were children.

'I know how to pack a bag.' Even as he answered, Algernon privately scoured his mind for anything he may have forgotten. He hated the little holes that were in his memory, the gaps in his mind where his moments fell into dark pools of nothing. He hated the panic he felt when sometimes no amount of fishing around in his memory could retrieve the things he knew were once there. He couldn't remember if he'd told Helene how to feed Cat and what day the bins had to be taken out.

His little leather notebook was, these days, the only thing that could put his mind at rest. Taking it from his cardigan pocket he studied it again, confident that his unbendable orderliness, which had always formed the framework of his very being, would see him through. He ran his finger down the recently written list, which did indeed include telling Helene about Cat and the bins, now thankfully marked with an inky tick. He had packed the right clothes, paid Jacob upfront for the petrol, and booked the hotel. As he expected, there was now only one item left unmarked and so, as they were all in the dining room he lifted his walking stick and nudged the child on the leg.

'In that cabinet over there you'll find a little black box.' He pointed to one of the matching mirrored cabinets, partly obscured by a pile of packing boxes, and waited for the child to sleepily but obediently make her way to where he was indicating.

'We'll move all these boxes out of your way when we get our own place,' Helene said, helping the child push their items away so that she could open the cabinet door and retrieve what he wanted.

'You've mentioned,' Algernon replied. The boxes – apparently containing items such as winter clothes, ornaments, mirrors, bathroom toiletries and other such excessive effects – had been taking up a significant section of his dining room since the day after their arrival. They would, he'd been assured at regular intervals, be removed as soon as they found somewhere more permanent to live.

'Here,' Anna said, placing the small box in his hand and returning to her seat to sip at her latte. There in the palm of Algernon's weather-beaten hand was a box he hadn't opened for years and, with the ever-present tremor to his fingers, he lifted up the lid. Taking the item out, he felt the coolness of the metal, the familiar weight of the brass, the essence of time and location and youth all caught in the magnetism of his old compass.

'A compass!' the child declared, leaning over to have a better look.

'A compass,' Algernon repeated, secretly delighted by her interest. He passed it over and saw how she studied it, turning herself this way and that to see how the quivering needle stayed at magnetic north. She handed it back to him and he placed it in the box before sliding it into his pocket. Taking the little pen linked to his notebook with a thin leather strap, he placed an inky tick next to the last item – Compass.

* * *

ANNA

'Drastic!' Jacob commented. He was already waiting outside by his open car boot with his mum and his little brother, who had come to wave them off. He eyed her hair with surprise as she bumped her suitcase down the steps and heaved it into the boot, her chin raised in an effort to look as if she didn't care. Inside, though, his words were stinging and a wave of self-consciousness made her smart. 'I like it,' he added, nodding with approval as she brushed past him to collect her bag for the car. 'I *mean* it.' He caught her arm and held her gaze for a heavy moment while she quizzed the depths of his eyes for evidence of his sincerity. She found it just before he let her go, a sort of visual synchrony that spoke without words. The thrill of her beating heart was drowned out by his shout of, 'Morning, H. Morning, Mr M,' as he sprinted chivalrously up to the house to help her grandfather with his old green suitcase.

'I'll thank you to call us Helene and Mr Maybury.' She heard her grandfather reply testily, and it caused a small smile of amusement to tug at her mouth. 'In the English language,' he continued, 'words and names are typically made up of a series of letters rather than just one. Kindly adhere to that principle, lad.'

'It's Jacob,' said Jacob, grinning mischievously over at Anna as he made his way towards the car and placed the suitcase next to hers, alongside his own small, rumpled rucksack in the boot. 'Bye, Mum.' He gave his mum a hug, complete with a loud kiss on her cheek, then he ruffled his little brother's hair. 'Look after Mum and don't be a pain.' His brother, wearing his astronaut pyjamas, pretended to punch him and

Jacob picked him up and hung him upside down by his feet, grinning at his screams of laughter.

His mother tutted. 'Jacob, stop it! It's the crack of dawn, you'll wake the neighbours.'

Jacob dutifully planted him the right way up. 'Bye, mate,' he said, and Anna liked how he playfully ruffled his brother's hair one last time. She secured Gary into the footwell behind the driver's seat while Helene folded her grandfather into the front passenger seat, then turned to give her a long hug goodbye.

'Good luck doing… whatever it is he's hellbent on doing. And remember, he's old. Make allowances for that OK?' Anna felt herself bristling, still smarting over her mother's collusion in springing all this on her, but as Helene gave her a final squeeze, she relented and submitted to her mother's affection. Helene let go of her then stooped back down to look through the front passenger window. 'Bye, Dad.' She placed a gentle hand on his shoulder and Anna was surprised when he reached his own hand and rested it on hers, holding on to it for a few moments before they both let go, avoiding each other's eye.

'Look after Cat,' he called to her, his voice gruff but softer than usual.

Jacob started the engine and Anna climbed inside and clicked her seatbelt into place, stunned by the tenderness she'd witnessed between her mother and her grandfather. They had just shared a shy kind of love, and it made her feel quite sad that they had to wait for this moment of parting to do so. Her grandfather looked so terribly small in the front seat of the car, as if he'd shrunk even more since she'd met him. His shoulders were so thin compared to Jacob's and his white-haired head was several inches lower in the seat too. He looked so *vulnerable*, as if he, out of all three of them, were now the child. *It's like his body is shrinking away,* she thought, everything apart from his ears which, she noticed for the first time, were huge by comparison.

As they drove away, Anna waved out of the window until she could no longer see her mother, Jacob's mother or his little brother waving side by side at the edge of the road. Helene's blonde hair had now grown long enough to tie in a loose ponytail, which hung over her shoulder, her muscles were getting toned and Anna thought that on the whole, she looked pretty good. Her kiss, the soft imprint of her love, was still where she'd planted it on Anna's forehead, and her words, 'take care of my most precious cargo, Jacob,' still nestled comfortingly in her ears.

The morning sun sent brilliant shards of light bouncing off windows, wet pavements and shiny car bonnets, requiring Jacob to reach for his sunglasses. Anna already had hers on, making everything she could see a bright shade of green, and she slipped off her shoes to make herself comfortable for the journey. She decided to push all her negative feelings aside. She'd seen some beautiful images of Cornwall on her phone and now, in the fresh, albeit green, light of a new day that she was going to be cool with the idea of her grandfather's mad adventure.

All they needed now was some great music and she was sure it was possible that their road trip was going to be OK.

ALGERNON

Algernon fiddled with his little leather book until he found the correct page containing his tick list. Once more he scanned the list to ensure that everything was in order which it most definitely seemed to be: five pairs of socks, six pairs of pants – one extra in case of emergency – five shirts, three jumpers, a jacket, a wash bag and an extra pair of sturdy shoes. He could not, however, shake the thought that something fundamental was missing from his organisation. As a result, an urge suddenly overcame him to have the car turn around and return him home.

'Turn round!' he barked, just as Jacob had tugged on the indicator stick and was already pulling out into the road leading out of town. Jacob, without comment or question, politely did as he'd been asked and, no less than three minutes since their departure, they all found themselves back outside Algernon's house.

'Did you enjoy yourselves?' Helene called from where she was still standing gossiping with Jacob's mother, their mutual amusement clear on their faces. Their humour annoyed Algernon and only made him feel even more rattled than he already was. With the help of Jacob, he shuffled slowly past them. It was all so arduous and embarrassing but it had been so long since he'd made a journey, he absolutely wasn't going to leave without working out what it was he'd left behind. He brought his watch up to his face and peered closely at it. Seven had long since gone and it was already nearly twenty past, yet they were no further forward with the trip. It made him agitated and he muttered crossly to himself: *This will never do.*

Leaving Jacob at the doorstep, he made his way down the hallway and into the sitting room where he stood quite still, sifting through his memory for what on earth it was that he could have forgotten.

As he stood silently in the centre of the room it came upon him with cruel understanding that the item that was missing from the whole adventure was Evie. Suddenly overcome by the reality of going on an adventure without her, Algernon took the little china basket from the mantelpiece and sat down in his armchair opposite the empty chair. Evie had spotted the delicate little ornament in a shop window years ago, its glossy white handle made from the finest interwoven threads of porcelain, the tiny flowers painted with hues of pink and blue. He'd bought it for her when he'd received his pay packet, presenting it to her on a Tuesday after work just as she'd pulled a meat pie out of the oven, her cheeks hot and pink from the heat.

'What is this for?' she'd asked, smiling her big, wide smile for him. 'It's not a special occasion.'

Algernon in his Algernon way had given a simple answer. 'It's because it's Tuesday,' he'd said. He hadn't said, 'Because I love you.' He'd never said that in his life, not to Evie, not to anyone, but despite that she was there, married to him, in the kitchen, making his dinner and growing his child. Never, since the day they'd tied the knot, had he been anywhere without her. He touched each porcelain flower with a gnarly old finger and remembered how radiant she had looked that day. She'd been a little younger than he, blessed with an effervescence that, for their whole married life, had allowed him to live vicariously through her in a way he could never do on his own. He *was* on his own, though, and he'd gone and landed himself with the daunting task of travelling, not just to Cornwall, but back to a time before he'd even met her.

Aware that the carriage clock was ticking its way towards 7.30am and that everyone was waiting for him, he ran the pad of his index finger over the place where it had broken when Cat pushed it off the mantelpiece. The tiny thread-like flaw was barely detectable due to his skill at reparation, but Algernon knew it was there. He felt as if he were about to leave her behind, that he was heading unarmoured into battle without her. *What do I do?* he asked the air in the room. *How do I leave without you?*

'Grandad?' the child called softly from the doorway and when he spun around to look at her, the image of her caught him by surprise. With her shorter hair framing her face he could see in her features that she was even more like Evie than he'd realised. She was wearing shorts, a blue top covered in glitter and her feet were bare. As he held the little china basket in his hands while she stood there he believed that he could hear Evie calling to him and she was saying, *Remember me, not my things. I am not bound in that little china basket, nor am I tethered to my chair.* It was all suddenly so crystal clear that he could hardly get up from his chair quick enough.

Algernon levered himself upright and placed the little basket back where it had always been. 'Give me one moment, child,' he puffed. Making his way upstairs, he removed the box of trinkets and letters from under his bed and with shaking fingers rooted through it until he found what he was looking for. He walked into Helene's bedroom, opened the lid of the tiny box he'd retrieved and kissed the ruby gemstone of Evie's engagement ring.

He could still remember exactly how he'd felt the day he'd bought it for her and how her own smile had shone as bright as the stone. His Air Force friend William had introduced him to his younger sister at a party in London during a weekend leave. 'This is Evie,' he'd said, indicating a girl with curls in her hair wearing a pretty blue and white shirtwaist dress. She'd been sweet sixteen and could jitterbug with the best of them, catching his eye and rendering him smitten from that day on.

Seeing the child just then, it had finally come to him that he wasn't leaving Evie behind at all. She was with him still, living through Helene and her colourful child and he was furious with himself that for all those years he'd denied Evie the chance to show him that, and to experience them for herself. 'It's time I let your mother's love shine again,' he muttered, placing the open box on Helene's pillow.

He made his way downstairs, ran a hand lightly over the back of the empty chair as he passed it and silently followed his granddaughter out of his house.

ANNA

Anna plugged her seatbelt in for the second time that morning and waved goodbye once more to the two mothers and the little brother on the pavement, as they travelled back down the road and round the corner.

When she'd walked into the house to find her grandfather sitting in his chair holding an ornament and not looking for whatever it was he'd gone back in to find, it had taken her off guard. He'd said nothing at all about what he was doing, simply sitting there as if he had all the time in the world. She'd guessed, of course, that it had something to do with her grandma because the room had become all full up with something invisibly painful. 'It's like *Groundhog Day*.' Her mother had laughed as they reappeared from the house and both Jacob and his mother had laughed as well. Anna, on the other hand, felt heavy inside as if she'd just been witness to something she couldn't understand but was now carrying it with her too.

'Right! First thing we need to do is to ensure young Jacob here knows where he's going,' her grandfather announced once they'd successfully driven down the road, round the corner and were on the road heading out of town for the second time. He'd pulled out a map book from his inside pocket and was opening it up, removing a small piece of paper that he'd secured to it with a paper clip. Anna's eyes caught Jacob's in the rear-view mirror as they both simultaneously guessed what her grandfather was doing. On the piece of paper, all written by hand, was a series of road numbers and directions for their journey.

'Oh, it's all right, Mr M...' Jacob started.

'Mr Maybury,' her grandfather interrupted.

'Mr Maybury,' Jacob repeated. 'Anyway, it's all right because I'm using Google Maps. It's already telling me that we need to get onto the A12, so I need to turn left next.'

'What in God's name is a *Google* Map?' Her grandfather sounded unreasonably annoyed that there was such a thing and despite asking the question, he continued to study his own map.

'It's a map that comes up on your phone and it works by GPS satellite... Look.' Jacob reached for his phone, which was propped on a clip on the dashboard, and turned it slightly so that her grandfather might get a better look. He peered over at it and gave a little grunt.

'It doesn't come up on my phone,' he said.

'You don't have a phone, Grandad,' Anna reminded him.

'So that's the smartphone thing again I suppose.' He gave another grunt, louder this time, and Anna noticed that his chin had disappeared from sight into his now hunched shoulders. Jacob pointed helpfully to the screen of his phone where an arrow was clearly visible at the top.

'See that arrow?' Her grandfather squinted at where Jacob was pointing. 'That's how I know I need to turn left. It can basically take you anywhere you want to go.'

Her grandfather stopped pretending to show his interest in Jacob's phone and returned his attention back to his own map for the second time. 'The moon. Can it take me there?' he snapped.

'Well, maybe not the moon, Mr M.'

'Mr Maybury.'

'Mr Maybury,' Jacob repeated again.

'Then it can't take me anywhere, can it? That thing is not the same as a proper map and it won't be as good.' He smoothed over the page of the map with his hand before lifting it up towards his face to get a better look. Then he ran his finger shakily along the road lines until he was pointing at a big blue line that Anna supposed, from where she sat, was the A12.

'Actually, a phone *is* better, Grandad. It can update as the road network changes so you don't need to keep buying new maps, plus it's safer if there's only the driver in the car... *and* it can tell you if there's a traffic jam ahead.' She waited for a response from him, but none came. He hunched his shoulders a little more and brought the map closer to his face.

'That's OK, Mr Maybury, we'll use both,' Jacob said kindly. 'Then if technology fails us we've got the real thing, hey?' Then, very gently, he pushed the map down with his left hand until it was out of the way of his view. 'I… er… need to be able to see my wing mirror though,' he said, just as a sign for the A12 appeared on the road ahead and he pulled the indicator down, preparing to turn left.

ALGERNON

Algernon felt very out of sorts about the fact that his map was deemed surplus to requirements. From what he could see that smart thing didn't even show grid references or contour lines and probably not even magnetic north. If he were honest he would have admitted that he couldn't even see the blooming thing but he wasn't prepared to divulge that. He also felt distinctly embarrassed that he'd blocked the wing mirror with his map, making things difficult for Jacob to see clearly. He still knew how to drive. He still had his driving licence, having declared himself fit enough to continue driving only two years since.

His old blue Ford was still in the garage, still with Evie's gloves in the glove compartment. Although the car was now quite old it was in perfect condition. He'd painted the garage floor with seal paint, put two strips of carpet down, only drove it on a Sunday and went everywhere else on a bike. He'd toyed with the idea of signing the car over to the lad but, when he came to it, Algernon knew he could never consider getting rid of it. It was yet another thing that he struggled to admit was probably beyond him now. In fact, now that he thought about it, he couldn't for the life of him remember when he'd last driven it or where. The car, however, like the house, belonged to both him and Evie and that was the way it would stay until the day he died.

'Put some music on,' the child called from the back of the car and Jacob immediately proceeded to fiddle with the radio tuner, filling the car with a succession of crackles, voices and music until he stopped at a station blasting out a horrible noise. Algernon stared at the lad, wondering what was possessing him to pollute the vehicle with such a racket and when the child called from the back again, 'Turn the volume up,' he slowly and deliberately reached out his hand and turned the radio off.

Relieved at the instant peace that returned to the car he carefully folded his map, taking care not to block Jacob's view again, satisfied that they would be on the A12 for a little while before turning onto the M25. The journey was simple. He still knew it off by heart and in truth they didn't really need the map or the Google whatsit. He settled into his seat and turned his attention to the outside world. A blur was happening through the window, a hazy landscape of greys and greens, all of which Algernon knew was, in reality, much sharper in texture than his old eyes could any longer see.

Before he got a car, he had a motorbike that he'd blasted around the roads at a time when traffic was so much lighter than it was today. He remembered taking Evie on pillion wearing blue slacks, a lavender jacket and with her hair tucked into a cream beret. No helmet back then. Just a pair of goggles and the thrill of air rushing past their faces. Now, however, a huge lorry was in front of them and another behind, and a swirl of traffic in every colour and size was haring in and out of the lanes all around them. He felt as if he were caught in a vortex and pressed his foot hard on the floor of the footwell in a futile attempt to slow the car. The world had become such a hectic place to be… or was it, he mused, just the fact that he was now too old to keep up with the world?

The child reached her arm through the two seats from the back of the car and offered him and Jacob a mint, which they both took, unwrapping the plastic and popping the sweets in their mouths. Algernon sucked on his, resting his head on the head restraint behind him while he tapped his fingers on the folded map on his lap. With a creeping sense of dismay and, disappointingly, only a short way into the journey, his bladder was informing him that his morning coffee had now hit home. He contemplated asking Jacob if that smart thing could tell him where the nearest services were, and how long it might take to get there, but he kept his mouth shut. He'd caused enough of a delay already. *Mind over bladder,* he thought shutting his eyes and tapping his fingers more urgently in the hope of overcoming the situation, at least until they'd made decent headway.

ANNA

Half an hour into their journey Anna saw that her grandfather seemed to be getting quite twitchy. 'Are you OK, Grandad?' she asked, pulling her earphones out and leaning forward to offer them both another mint from the bag. At least, she thought, she had her own music even if no one else, mainly Jacob, was able to appreciate it.

'I'm perfectly fine, thank you,' he answered, reaching into the bag and taking two sweets, one for himself and one for Jacob.

'That's OK then,' Anna replied, eyeing him with uncertainty and sitting back in her seat ready to put her earphones back in.

'I was just wondering…' he began, almost immediately, 'if that thing knows where the next services are, that's all?' He pointed to Jacob's phone and both Jacob and Anna hooked eyes in the rear-view mirror again.

'Do you need to stop for the toilet, Mr Maybury?' Jacob asked delicately. 'We can pull off the dual carriageway at Margaretting in two miles if you do.'

'I *told* you I'm absolutely fine,' he snapped. 'I was just wondering if it could tell one such things, that's all.' His answer was determinedly caustic, and Jacob raised two defeated eyebrows for the benefit of Anna's reflection, having been suitably told. Her grandfather wiped the flat of his hands along his trousers as if his palms were sweaty then adjusted the collar of his shirt before picking his map up again. 'Where are we now then?' he asked, opening it as carefully as he could so as not to obstruct Jacob's view, then peering closely at the print.

'We're still on the A12, Mr Maybury,' Jacob answered.

'I know we're still on the A12 for heaven's sake! I want to know exactly where on the A12?' He studied the map, his head bent over, and Anna could see from where she sat how his ears sprouted an abundance of coarse white hair. He kept looking out of the window, obviously hoping to see a landmark that would enlighten him and being unable to find any was getting ever more agitated. Anna never ceased to be amazed at how much patience Jacob had when it came to her grandfather but then, of course, he was getting paid to have patience. She wondered if he was getting paid hourly, or by the day or maybe a lump sum at the end of the trip and whether he was getting a bonus for putting up with him at all.

'I think that we should stop at Margaretting if it's only in two miles,' her grandfather announced, quietly refolding the map, having run his finger vaguely along several blue lines, seemingly unable to locate Margaretting. Anna felt a twinge of sympathy for him, realising that the print was probably too small, or the car was travelling too quickly for him to take it all in. If he'd only embrace the idea of modern technology, he'd realise it was all so much easier with it than without it.

'Er, we can't now… we've just this second gone past the junction, Mr M, because… well, you said you were fine.' Jacob apologised profusely as if the situation was his own fault and glanced again at Anna, a look of panic in his eyes. 'There should be something else coming up soon. Can you hang on a bit?'

'You *did* say you were fine, Grandad,' Anna defended.

'I *am* fine!' He snapped each word back at her so sharply that it made her shrink back in her seat. 'It's just that I'd be more fine if we could stop… soon. Sooner rather than later shall we say. I need to spend a penny. Ask that smart thing where I can do that?' Anna could see that a flush was staining Jacob's neck and making rosy apples on his cheeks.

'I… I'll leave the road at the next exit but I'm not sure my… er… smartphone has ever been asked where to *spend a penny*,' he said.

'Then it's not that bloody smart is it?' her grandfather snapped again.

'You're going to have to pull over to let him wee in the verge, Jacob,' Anna said, trying to be helpful.

'I am doing no such thing!' her grandfather barked back, and so loudly that she and Jacob *both* shrank into their seats.

'I can't just pull over unless it's an emergency and not even then,' Jacob replied, putting his foot on the accelerator and overtaking two lorries and several cars at speed. A car horn sounded and Jacob breathed a quiet '*shit*' under his breath.

'This is an emergency,' Anna said, looking between him and her grandfather who was now saying nothing at all but was agitatedly spreading his fingers across each thigh.

'Yes, well, peeing on the edge of the road could get him killed,' Jacob said, checking his rear-view mirror and his wing mirrors, pulling from the outside lane and into the left lane.

'That could happen anyway,' Anna said, testily eyeing the sprouting ears and the jutting chin visible in front of her and wondering how she had managed to get roped into this situation.

'We can try here,' Jacob suggested, as he indicated and swerved off the road, his head on a swivel looking for somewhere to stop. 'I need sirens,' he complained. 'My mum would do her nut if she knew I was driving like this.' At the end of the slip road was a mini roundabout and narrow tree-lined lane but no signs for services, or signs for anything other than a blue 'P' sign next to a lay-by at the side of the road. Jacob pulled over, turned the engine off and rushed out to help him from the car.

'Don't be ridiculous! Every man and his dog is here.' Her grandfather barked again as to his horror other vehicles were also parked in the lay-by.

'But I don't know where else to take you, Mr Maybury.' Jacob was properly flustered now and looked pensively up and down the road as if a real toilet might miraculously appear. 'It says P. You know as in *pee...*' He bent down and grinned sheepishly at him through the open door but was met with a stony expression and a gathering of eyebrows.

'I'm not paying you to be a stand-up comedian,' her grandfather said, as Jacob shut the door again and dived back into the driver's seat.

'Help me out of here.' Her grandfather then unbuckled his seatbelt while Anna watched Jacob immediately get back out again and run round to the passenger side once more. It was possibly the funniest thing that had happened to her for months.

ALGERNON

Algernon could hardly bring himself to acknowledge the fact that he was about to relieve himself in public. The fact that a young person was going to have to help him negotiate the rough terrain in order to secure a degree of privacy to do it... *and* that his own granddaughter was in the vicinity was almost more than he could bear. He was almost purple with shame and he knew it because he could feel his pulse throbbing in his neck. 'It's OK, Mr M,' Jacob shouted above the roar of a truck leaving the lay-by, 'I've got you.'

Algernon didn't reply, for no words would come to his throat. He didn't want 'getting', he just wanted the ordeal over and done with and to be on their way with no more reference to it. To his dismay he saw that the trees edging the lay-by were littered with rubbish and tangled with weeds and he wasn't at all sure his shuffling feet and walking stick were man enough for the job without help. He swung his stick in the direction of a clearer patch and allowed Jacob to steer him towards it, praying that the wind wasn't going to change direction mid flow. Thankfully the lad had the wherewithal to discreetly step back a few paces, leaving Algernon to deal with the business end of things alone.

When at last he was back in the car, buckling his seatbelt again, the lad went to the boot of the car where he spent some time fiddling about. 'You all right, Grandad? It was a bit tricky there,' the child called from the back. He wished she hadn't spoken and he certainly wished she wasn't sounding so cheerful about it. Of course it was a bit tricky and of course he wasn't all right – he wasn't a natural exhibitionist in general.

'I don't need an autopsy on it thank you. Let's just get on.' He looked at his watch and felt dismay at how so much of the morning was slipping away. When the lad finally closed the boot and climbed in, starting up the engine, Algernon saw that he was no longer wearing any shoes. 'What's all this?' he said, waving a shaky finger towards the footwell, aghast that Jacob was about to recommence the journey in his stockinged feet.

'I stepped in something, Mr M. You know… something nasty like dog shit.' At that, Algernon leant his weary head back on the head restraint, tried to ignore the child's guffaws in the back, and took a big breath.

'It's Mr *Maybury*.' He sighed.

ANNA

Anna sobered up pretty quickly once they got going again. The atmosphere in the car became horribly lumpy due to her grandfather's ongoing foul mood and the fact that Jacob was concentrating too hard on the task of driving without shoes on to chat much. The car was filling with their combined misgivings and it was causing her anxiety to stir again, sucking the air out of her chest and prickling her skin. She wanted to get out of the car, to fling open the door and run as far as her legs would take her, breathing air that wasn't shared with other anxious people.

This was not an ideal way to spend the first day of her summer holiday. Her mind cast images, visceral and raw, of her friends back home who would be basking in the glory of their first day. Maybe they would walk their dogs together or meet for waffles in town or talk about plans for their holidays abroad. Or maybe they'd visit their relatives... their own grandparents maybe and be greeted with smiles and hugs and squashy warm cheeks to kiss. Her stomach squeezed and her head filled with all the wishes she'd wished that things had turned out differently for herself. *You are home,* her mother had said but *home is where the heart is, isn't it?* she thought. Her heart was in a city far away and she wasn't with it.

She sighed, put her earphones in, turned her music up and absentmindedly picked out church spires and farm animals in the horizon of trees and fields to each side of the motorway. They travelled silently, apart from Jacob getting quite twitchy each time a sign for the services came into view. 'Services coming up,' he announced loudly each time, and each time he was met by total silence until, at last, on the M4 near Reading, her grandfather put his thumb up to indicate that he would like to stop.

It was thankfully an undramatic stop where the only highlight was Jacob washing his shoes with two bottles of mineral water, quite a lot of swearing and a large clump of grass before they all made their way into the services foyer. 'You can stay here. I don't need everybody's help thank you.' Her grandfather unhooked himself from her arm and made towards the loos, stopping to give them both the flat of his hand when they tried to follow him. 'I said you can stay here,' he repeated, beginning to get cross.

'I think you'll find there's more than one bladder in our group, Grandad.' Anna sidled past him and grinned at Jacob as she went by. 'All yours,' she said.

'Coffee for the journey anyone?' Jacob called, when they all congregated back in the foyer. Her grandfather eyed the large paper cups that people were carrying but didn't give Jacob an answer.

'We'll never get to where we're going if he does,' Anna clarified on his behalf, 'but I will... Can you get me a hot chocolate while I take him back to the car?' She tugged on the sleeve of her grandfather's jacket to steer him towards the exit and back to the car park.

'I am not a child,' he complained, allowing himself to be steered all the same.

Neither am I but that doesn't stop you calling me one all the time, Anna thought.

Back in the car and once again immersed in the difficult atmosphere and scent of vanilla, she sipped her hot chocolate, listened to music and thought enviously about what her mother might be doing with her freedom. She was probably striding around the nature reserve with a big smile on her face, looking forward to being home alone to eat what she liked and watch what she wanted on TV. She wondered if her mother was glad that, for a few days, she wouldn't have to live in the shadow of her own father, bending herself to his strict agenda again. She couldn't imagine what it must have been like for her growing up as a teenager in that little house. Had he complained when she invited her friends over, played music, or had parties and sleepovers? They ruffled each other's feathers, that was for sure, and now her grandma wasn't there to keep the peace.

Helene had been devastated when she'd had to go home after so many years but only that morning Anna had witnessed how her mother and her grandfather had held hands with an awkward kind of gentleness. She hoped that this was a good sign. The new job was giving her mother confidence, and it seemed almost as if she'd become ten years younger and several shades happier since leaving Harry. There had been nothing bad about Harry, he just wasn't right for her, or she for him – Anna could see that now. She remembered Harry's warm squeezy hug on the last day and wondered whether he was enjoying his new life too. She hoped he was. He'd sent her a few texts and phoned her a couple of times but he, like everything and everyone she used to know, was also fading away.

Finishing her drink, she closed her eyes and rested her head against the window, allowing the thrum of the car engine to lull her into a restless sleep. She dreamed a lonely dream, trapped in a painting where empty landscapes and dark stormy skies grew thick with oil paint, and where tiny matchstick people were always too far away to reach. When Jacob opened the car door, causing her to half fall out of the car, she woke with a start. 'Wake up, sleepy head, we've stopped for a break. You've been out for hours and we are already past Exeter. Your grandad's hungry… and needs another pee.' He added the last few words in a whisper, while Anna endeavoured to blink away her dream to see her grandfather already standing beside the car breathing a contented lungful of Devon air as he looked towards a tea room and farm shop. 'Arrr West Country produce. Proper job!' he declared in an exaggerated Cornish burr.

Climbing out of the car she looked across a car park where a sign promised Devonshire cream teas and, almost without thinking now, she held her arm out for her grandfather to hold on to.

Entering a café area where a huge array of edible things were deliciously assembled, her grandfather removed a small wallet from the inside pocket of his jacket. 'What do you want?' he asked, as Anna and Jacob peered through the glass counter at the swirls of cream and sponge, cherries, chocolate and cookies, which were waiting for impossible decisions to be made.

'I don't know whether to have the raspberry sponge cake or the cream tea but I think I'm fancying the cream tea more.' Jacob pressed the pad of his finger against the glass where scones were piled high with clotted cream and strawberry jam.

'I'll have anything,' said Anna, reaching for a can of orange fizz to put on her tray.

'Me too then... as long as it's the cream tea!' Jacob reached for a can of orange fizz and put it on the tray next to Anna's while her grandfather stepped forward and removed two ten-pound notes from his wallet.

'Three raspberry sponges, two cans of fizz and a pot of tea for one,' he said.

* * *

ALGERNON

The youngsters looked quite put out when, seated at a table, Algernon told them they could have had anything they wanted... *apart* from a cream tea. 'It's all in the jam and cream,' he said as they took their seats round a table near the window, which overlooked the car park. 'Those scones were already dressed... and they were dressed all upside down. We really should have been allowed to put the toppings on ourselves.' The youngsters looked at him with a total lack of comprehension, but he decided not to elaborate further on the rights and wrongs of Cornish versus Devon cream teas. Instead, he silently promised himself that he would educate them further when they reached their destination.

Pouring his tea into a white china cup he tutted irritably as the liquid turned a weak beige colour. 'God, I hate milky tea!' he complained, lifting the lid off the pot and stirring, but failing miserably at reviving a solitary and unenthusiastic teabag. Their cakes, however, were light and sweet and oozed with the taste of the West Country and, as he ate, disappointing tea aside, he felt the beginnings of a tentative kind of pleasure. He was almost back.

One more toilet stop and a massive traffic jam later they finally reached the outskirts of Newquay where they pulled up outside a tired building that sported a pink neon 'OPEN' sign in the window. Jacob, again, dutifully ran round to the passenger side of the car and helped him out whereupon it took another goodly while for him to unfold himself into an almost upright position. The whole long, arduous journey had really taken it out of him, and pain was now running courses around his body. Despite this, he could feel it, in the breeze around him, the sky above him and the land beneath his feet. After far too long, Cornwall was, once again, wrapping her arms tightly around him, almost suffocating him with her beauty and flooding him with a passion and nostalgia he knew too well. He inhaled deeply, allowing the Cornish air back into his lungs and wondered how he'd ever been able to breathe all this time without it.

'Are you OK, Grandad?' The child, the handle of her red suitcase in one hand, held out her arm with the other, while Jacob carried the remaining cases inside. Algernon let out a measured breath and wondered why everyone should keep assuming he was not OK.

'Stop asking me if I'm all right. Can't a man get his bearings?' He knew he was being waspish, jabbing at her for asking after his welfare, but what she couldn't understand was that if he'd said 'yes' to her question he'd have been lying, yet if he'd said 'no' he'd also have been lying. As he snaked his hand through the child's arm, he thought about resting his hand over hers as a sign of both affection and gratitude, an apology for being so curt. He thought about it, but he didn't do it. Instead, he tapped his stick on the ground and set off to follow Jacob inside. 'Come on, no time for dithering about in the car park,' he barked.

Behind the counter sat a receptionist with her hair scraped back into such a severe bun that it made her look quite surprised. Her lipstick was too bright for Algernon's liking and she didn't look in full control of her lips, as if they might have been recently installed. Her smile was wide though, and she did at least have the decency to finish an apparently hilarious personal phone call in order to greet them. 'Maybury, Maybury and Adams,' he said, tapping his stick officiously on the geometric pattern of the carpet by his feet. 'Three single-occupancy rooms, three nights.'

'Yes I've got you here,' the plump orange lips replied, still smiling widely as she unhooked three sets of keys from behind the counter. 'Breakfast is between seven and ten and the bar is open until midnight.' She pointed to a door on her left where a small bar with optics could be seen, then she pointed to a door on her right where a larger room could be seen containing several plain wooden tables. 'Your rooms are eight, nine and fifteen.' She appeared to be appraising Algernon where he stood, his arm still linked through the child's then she looked at Anna and Jacob. 'There's no lift, and the ground-floor rooms were already taken before your booking. Stairs are down the corridor to the right. Can he… er… can he manage?' Algernon felt his hackles rise. He had, after all, been the founder and organiser of the trip.

'Madam, I'm old, not dead,' he flared, before jutting his chin forward and pushing the child in the direction of the stairs. Putting his foot on the first stair, however, a pain shot from his knee and down his leg, which caused him to stumble. 'Cramp!' he said loudly before hauling himself to the top of the staircase without another sound.

ANNA

The carpet in the foyer was darkened in the centre area where, for possibly many years, a flow of people had walked across, the geometric pattern of it now barely distinguishable in places. Bare hessian backing showed in patches, and over by the bar it did indeed look like a sticky carpet kind of place.

The woodwork was chipped and the paint around the light switches had turned a murky grey, but the receptionist seemed welcoming and their rooms had clean bedding, clean towels and little sachets of tea, coffee and hot chocolate next to a white plastic kettle. As room number fifteen was up a further flight of stairs from numbers eight and nine, Jacob left the other two rooms for Anna and her grandfather and lugged his suitcase up the narrow, winding stairs to what would be his own room for the next three nights.

Following him up the narrow, winding stairs into what might once have been an attic, and feeling rather envious of him having the double bed, Anna laughed out loud when he opened the door to number fifteen. Somehow, a tired-looking double bed had been assembled in a room not much bigger than the bed itself. Then, peering into the en-suite bathroom, Jacob banged his head where the doorframe was ever so slightly smaller than a standard frame. Anna clapped a hand over her mouth and blew raspberries into the palm of it.

'What's funny? It's positively palatial,' Jacob said, as they both stood in front of a tiny shower that was bravely holding its own alongside a smell of damp and a touch of black mould. 'This will do,' he said, turning to pick up his suitcase and plonking it on his bed.

'It's less palatial and more sardine tin, Jacob. You'll never fit in here. I'll swap if you like?' She meant it, coveted it even, but Jacob shook his head and nudged her out of his room.

'He's your grandad, Anna, not mine. I'm just the delivery driver.'

13

The Order of Things

ALGERNON

Algernon was used to order in his life. He created it, planned it and lived by it. Algernon Edward Maybury had learnt the hard way, at the tender age of seven, to live by timetables, strict rules, ringing bells and stinging canes. Out of this solid, unmalleable foundation had risen the man, but the man had been trapped by it. Order and the restriction it brought with it had governed him for the rest of his very long life. Exhausted from the journey, and having ensured everyone was properly fed in the hotel dining area, he closed the door of his room and studied again the agenda he'd prepared several days before.

It had taken him a mightily long time to get it right, the details snagging him with wicked barbs as he'd struggled to put it together. Coming home to his Cornwall had, for his whole life, always been so bittersweet. The glorious surf with its white rolling waves, turquoise coves and crystal-clear rock pools would call to him. The expanse of beaches and craggy rock faces, footpaths and forests that had given him the freedom to roam opened their embrace to him. Yet all the while the calendar would taunt him as each precious day slipped by. It pained him so terribly deeply even now that in each stage of his life he had always had to dutifully leave again for wherever it was he was required to be. As a boy it was school, as a young man it was the war and as a grown man it was to be a husband and father in Evie's home county of Essex.

Despite his accumulating years and ever-dimming memory, he could never forget how, as a boy, at the end of each glorious school holiday the day of leaving, always circled in red on his mother's calendar, would inevitably arrive. How racked with homesickness and rejection he had been on each of those red-circled days. The Austin prepared, the boot loaded, and the awful goodbyes would be said. Each time he set foot back in his homeland his joy would be marred, feeling as he did like a torn limb, ripped from a perfect body to be sent away to boarding school to be a better limb.

No one had ever questioned how they did it, how they honed the boys into brilliant scholars and outstanding sportsmen, how money paid a far higher price than their education demanded. Certainly, no one ever questioned why, when each time he returned home he was a little bit less of himself. How Algernon had yearned to be like his younger sister who waved him off each time as if he were a visitor to her home, her little school, once his little school, just a happy hop and skip away.

He'd spent a long time in his armchair back in the sitting room of his little schoolhouse, pondering his agenda and how best to show everything to the child. The place where he sailed under a silver Cornish moon dipping his fingers in watery stars, wishing he could sail away forever – should that be first? Or the forest where he rode Firefly, wild and free and almost believing he could leave the world behind him if he galloped fast enough – perhaps that should be the first? He had finally created an order for the trip and, checking it once again, he closed the notebook and placed it back on the dressing table of his hotel room, confident for once in his decision-making.

Coming home to Cornwall with Evie had been easier than this, more like a holiday with her by his side. This was different. This trip was about saving his granddaughter. 'You can't save a drowning soul without being prepared to drown while doing it,' he'd thought, but then hadn't he been drowning forever?

ANNA

Fancy a Coke in the bar? Meet you on the landing?

Anna looked at Jacob's text on her phone and was slipping on her boots almost before she got to the end of reading it. Her grandfather had requested an early night and, as a result, they'd all sloped off to their rooms after dinner. 'It's almost a night out, Gary,' she breathed happily, checking her appearance in the dressing table mirror while quickly swapping her top for a floral mesh one. 'Do I look OK?' Gary didn't answer but she believed that he flushed an appreciative shade of green. She applied a slick of lip gloss and selected her warm cardigan. 'In case we go for a walk together.' She grinned at Gary. Finally she picked up her perfume, a delicate little bottle shaped like a bird, which contained the scent of vanilla and happier times. Spraying it liberally on herself – not forgetting a quick spray over Gary – she grabbed her room key then went to meet Jacob on the landing outside her room.

The receptionist, now bar staff, finished serving a pint of beer to a short, round man before filling their glasses with syrupy Coke from a soda gun. The man looked to Anna like a beefsteak tomato, circular and red-faced but his terrier dog was cute and friendly. She knelt down on the carpet to say hello to it, running her fingers through the coarse brown fur as it wagged and licked at her hand. When the receptionist said, 'Watch 'e don't cock his leg up again,' the beefsteak tomato cackled with laughter, causing Anna to spring to her feet and drag Jacob over to a bench seat on the far side of the bar.

'Let's sit over there,' she said, indicating a small sofa in the corner of the room under the soft glow of an old standard lamp. The man they passed, sitting at a table, with his trousers hitched up far too high, and nursing a tumbler containing two large blocks of ice in a measure of whisky, looked joltingly familiar.

'Grandad? I thought you said you were going to have an early night?' She wasn't just surprised but felt a little spurned. Hadn't he thought she and Jacob might want to be included, to join him and sit in the bar too? She knew her disappointment over his exclusive party-for-one was possibly unfair as she and Jacob were doing precisely the same thing, but then, she reasoned, they weren't the ones who'd called for an early night.

'Can't a man change his mind?' her grandfather said, cupping his glass as if he were cradling a thing of great value. Anna sank down in the chair opposite him and Jacob joined them thirty seconds later, plonking a battered box-game of Four in a Row on the table with all the energy of an irrepressible puppy. A trickle of disappointment prickled inside her that, rather than the moonlight walk she'd envisioned, her first evening alone with Jacob was spent losing a board game in a sad little hotel bar that had a very sticky carpet.

In the breakfast room, Jacob emerged from a huge bacon sandwich, releasing a trail of grease that glistened on his chin. 'Six, one,' he gloated. Anna playfully pretended to ignore him and spread some butter on a piece of toast while averting her eyes from the food on her grandfather's plate.

'I haven't had a full Cornish for so long,' her grandfather luxuriated. He used his fork to push a piece of toast through a pool of runny egg before scooping a pile of beans and a wedge of black pudding on top. Anna felt her stomach lurch as the yellow and red juices mixed, trailing off his fork in strands as it travelled from plate to mouth. She even thought she heard his false teeth clack as they lifted and popped back into place as he ate.

'What are we doing today then, Mr Maybury?' Jacob spoke with his mouth full, always, Anna thought, so cheerful, so unbeaten by anything. Although he was getting paid to be there, Anna was actually very glad that he was, for she knew she and her grandfather might have struggled alone without his boundless energy. She hoped that he was also glad to be there.

'Malpas!' Her grandfather wiped a chunk of white bread across his plate and bit into the softness of it, moistened with grease and juices.

'Bless you!' Jacob sniggered. His joke wasn't the least bit funny but her grandfather's comical sideways look of contempt at him was. Anna hid her giggles by biting into a slice of toast that turned out to be disappointingly under-toasted and cold.

'What's Malpas?' she asked.

'*Where's* Malpas,' her grandfather corrected. 'It's a place. A very little place with a lot of green water.'

'Shops?' she asked hopefully.

'No shops,' he replied.

'Beach?' she asked hopefully again.

'No beach. Just a row of houses, a pub and a view.'

'Whoop,' she whispered under her breath and pushed her plate away. Her toast wasn't the only thing that was disappointing about the start of her day.

ALGERNON

'Malpas isn't far from Truro, only about a mile or so.' Algernon popped the last of his breakfast, loaded onto the last corner of bread, into his mouth. Before Helene had started cooking for him, eating had been an almost tiresome thing, a requisite task undertaken purely in order to keep the mechanics of his body going. Now, with his plate empty, although he couldn't smell the food and was pretty sure he couldn't taste more than the salt of the bacon and the sugar in the beans, his memory was doing an excellent job of filling in the gaps of a full Cornish breakfast.

He'd noticed the look of disappointment on the child's face when he told her that there were no shops or beach where they were heading, and he worried that his agenda for the next couple of days wasn't exciting enough for her. She was dressed in the ripped red jeans again and her feet were clad in a silver pair of the chunky boots she was so fond of. Her top barely met her waistband, showing off her belly button, and a pair of yellow sunglasses were balanced on her head. She was out of place in the parts of Algernon's understanding that knew only of tradition and conformity, but he was aware that her quirky appearance shocked him less these days. The splashes of colour she brought everywhere she went were now illuminating his previously dull existence. He could tell, however, that she'd lost weight and he worried about the hollows that had started to appear under each cheekbone.

It's a mission though, not a holiday, he reminded himself.

When they were all fed and watered and ensconced in the car, he clicked his seatbelt into place and, having given Jacob his instructions, he prepared himself for their journey into Truro, a city he'd once known so well. Jacob seemed happy to drive them through the main thoroughfare and was doing a grand job for someone who'd been driving for so little time. A *natural*, Algernon thought contentedly.

As they set off on their journey, his rheumy old eyes darted from left to right, trying to focus on a landscape that played games with his memory. Various city landmarks came into view before they blurred past him again, giving him only seconds to register their detail. *Were they passing the road where Vage Jewellers was, or had once been? The jewellers where he had bought Evie's engagement ring. Was that once the old drapers and was that the bank or that one the hotel?* Buildings holding fast to their age-old architecture still lined the streets but with brand-new faces and brand-new names.

The place had changed. Always *development*, he thought sadly, it offers progress to a modern world yet steals beauty in great handfuls to do so.

When they turned down a road that snaked its way along the shores of Truro River, still tree-lined and still largely recognisable, he felt himself relax. Boats listed drunkenly where the river had withdrawn its tidal embrace and Algernon could just make out the clusters of white seagulls searching for morsels in the exposed silty banks. He felt his pulse quicken as they made their way further along Malpas Road, past old stone and new stone, parked cars and people, children and dogs. It all felt so *busy* this time though, as if a traitor had told the world of God's little secret and now everybody wanted a piece of it.

'HERE!' Algernon tapped the window of the car at the same time as bellowing louder than he'd anticipated he was going to and it made him cough. Jacob dutifully stopped, reversed a short way and began the process of squeezing his car into what was possibly the only remaining space between the many parked cars. To their right was a sign saying 'Malpas Marine', a tiny patch of hardstanding with boats and a jetty. The sight of it rushed Algernon back so many years it almost made him dizzy. 'Get me down there,' he ordered, pointing past the marine to where the green waters of the rivers Truro and Tresillian met.

ANNA

Anna had enjoyed the drive through Truro, feeling at home in amongst the throng of people, the rush of cars and the city buildings that reminded her of home. She always believed it was harder to feel lost in a city and definitely harder to stand out in a crowd. In a city she was one of the glorious diverse and she loved it. Thanks to her grandfather's agenda they were somewhere quiet, parked in a narrow road with nothing but boats, a pub, a few houses and an awful lot of the green water he'd mentioned. This, however, was where he'd chosen to stop and this, it would seem, was where they were going to spend the first morning of their first day. She went round to his side of the car feeling very much that her red jeans, crop top and silver DMs were not part of all this. They were not shorts and deck shoes or striped nautical tops and she felt garishly out of place.

It took them some negotiation and quite a lot of support for her and Jacob to get her grandfather out of the car, down the marine slope and onto the small patch of river beach without incident, but they managed it. 'It's called a confluence,' her grandfather announced, when they eventually came to a stop. 'See there, where the land is? And there and there where the two rivers meet each other?' He waved his stick in the air, staggering backwards in the process, requiring Anna and Jacob to grab at him before he fell. 'That's the River Truro and that's the River Tresillian and way down there...' he pointed his stick somewhere off to the right of where they stood '... is another confluence where the River Truro meets the River Fal as it flows out to sea.'

'Really?' Anna said, feigning a weak kind of interest. She didn't need a geography lesson on her first week out of school. Next he'd be going on about oxbows and erosion and before she'd know it she'd be asleep face down on the beach with total boredom. Pebbles and sand crunched under their feet as, with her grandfather's insistence, the three of them made their way nearer to the water's edge. Directly opposite, where the land bulged like a full belly, trees rose up in a cloudy green mound and a quintessential cottage could be seen peeping through the foliage.

'And here...' her grandfather said, aiming his stick at a point in the river just a few yards from their feet '...is where that photo was taken of me in *River Pisky*.' Anna stared past the boats that hugged the jetty, towards an empty patch of watery green where the July sun dropped sparkles on choppy little waves. It was just like the photograph with the cottage in the background and an expanse of green trees. Only the little sailboat itself was missing. Despite her original apathy, her imagination leapt into life, immediately visualising *River Pisky* in the water in front of her. Silver ripples were circling her hull, her sail was furled and there, clinging to her mast, was a young, tanned boy smiling back at them all.

Small clouds gathered in white puffs against a blue sky and seagulls wheeled in the air, calling out their song of the sea and Anna suddenly felt inexplicably sad. It was as if the passage of time was meshing into one, as if the two Algernons were about to meet each other again. 'See that cottage over there... the pretty one?' Her grandfather broke into her thoughts and nodded his head in the direction of the little cottage opposite.

'Yes,' she said, following his gaze. 'It's the one in the photograph.'

'Yes. It's called Ferryman's Cottage. A long, long, time ago, the ferryman lived there and any passengers waiting to cross the river from this side could ring a big bell to summon him. When I was just a little boy, my friend Bobby Passmore lived in the lane just behind it. We got up to all sorts of pranks together. I wonder whatever happened to him?' Her grandfather stared past the cottage, deep in thought for a moment, then pointed somewhere past the cottage and across the bend in the river towards another cloud of trees. 'And there is the estate where I lived.' Anna and Jacob scanned the countryside where he was pointing but there was nothing to be seen apart from trees and a quilt of fields. Still pointing, her grandfather again fell deep into thought, standing completely still, lost in another time. Then he dropped his arm and gave the merest hint of a chuckle, which Anna could tell was laden with memories and nostalgia.

'I can't imagine what it must have felt like to be this free.' She scanned the view in front of her, calling up the image of *River Pisky*, and sighed at how wonderful it must have been.

'Free?' her grandfather repeated, uttering the word as if he were tasting something sweet on his tongue. 'It felt as if I was part of this land... as if it flowed in my blood and grew in my bones.' There was a shine to her grandfather's eyes as he spoke that Anna had never seen before, like a light was on and a movie was playing. It was one of those movies that made you smile as if your heart were singing one minute, yet made you cry as if your heart were breaking the next. 'Can you feel it?' he asked.

Anna breathed in the scent of the river until it filled her lungs and quite unexpectedly began to feel the draw of the place, the magical beauty and tranquillity of it all. She imagined herself in the little sailboat, letting the wind take her away from all that trapped her in a place she didn't want to be. She nodded her reply.

★ ★ ★

ALGERNON

Algernon was reminded of his own mortal frailty as he adjusted his footing on the stony beach and leant heavily on the child's arm to do so. He could hear the rasp of his own breath as his heart fought to keep up with the general excitement of the morning and it made him cough several times. For a glorious moment, though, when he first stepped foot on the beach, he'd felt like the boy he used to be. Like the boy in his photograph, smiling at them all as lithe and able as the two teenagers either side of him now. His younger self was still here, on the breeze and in the water and in particles of sand beneath his feet, a tangible ghost of the person he'd left behind.

A little later, sitting outside The Heron Inn looking across at the view, the child sucked ice-cold cola through a straw while he sipped from a tall glass of shandy and Jacob embarked on an episode of enthusiastic stirring, having heaped three teaspoons of sugar into a cup of tea. The sound of it was chinking its way through Algernon's hearing aids, metal against china over and over again, making dents in his reverie, stealing his thoughts. Jacob's nose was virtually pressed against the screen of his phone as he did whatever the young people did with those things and Algernon was getting irritated. He was ready to snatch Jacob's spoon and toss it away, but the child, much to his relief, got there first, yanking it out of Jacob's hand and placing it firmly in the saucer.

'How come you never came back here to live?' The child cupped her chin in her hand, as if she were a small child preparing to hear a story and he wasn't at all sure where to start with her question. He had come back to Cornwall of course, from time to time. He'd brought Evie, and Helene when she was young, for holidays or to see family who one by one had all now slipped away. That is all they'd ever been, though: visits that were as cruel because of their briefness as they were sweet. 'By the time I was able to leave school and finally come home, the war had begun and I was called away again, to the Air Force this time,' he said. 'Then during the war, I met your grandma.' He knew the child was really asking him how he'd ended up in a faceless little town in Essex, working for the Corporation for the greater part of his life instead of coming home to this wonderful place. 'I had a *situation*,' he said cryptically.

'*Situation*?' the child quizzed.

'Situation,' Algernon confirmed. 'Your grandma's father – your great-grandfather – offered me an office job in Essex.' He shrugged his shoulders sadly. 'I was in no position to refuse.' It had been so much more than that of course. It had been the end of his dream to fly. He scanned the view from The Heron Inn and although his eyesight was failing, even with his distance glasses on, he knew every inch of this landscape and didn't need the clarity of physical detail to remind him. Thirty-nine interminable years he'd worked for the Corporation instead of coming home to Cornwall. Sometimes, he knew to his shame, on trips back home he'd made Evie cry with his waspish ways, finding it easier to take the coward's way out of his resentment. To take the sting from himself by stinging her instead. She always said she understood, speaking silent words with a simple squeeze of her hand.

The child's chin was still cupped in her hand, waiting for him to elaborate, but he just couldn't find the words for this part of his story. Not yet. Instead, he had an overwhelming desire to climb into one of the boats tied to the jetty near where they sat and sail until midnight, or maybe forever, or maybe even to sail back in time and start all over again. He would do that if it were possible. He would click his fingers right this second and have another go at it because since the arrival of the child in his life a thought had slithered inside his mind like a dark worm... *Did life let me down – or did I let life down?* He looked into the young dark eyes that he had missed out on for nearly sixteen years and already knew the answer.

ANNA

They sat in The Heron pub for so long that orders for lunch had now been made and were on their way. Her grandfather didn't continue their conversation and she decided not to prompt him again as he'd looked so incredibly sad about it. He stared out at the water until an unfortunate waiter had placed their food on the table and dared to assume they were tourists. 'I think I know more history of this whole area than you've had hot dinners,' her grandfather blasted. Then he muttered under his breath so that only dogs and Anna could hear, 'Bloody tourists indeed.'

'Tell us more about the good old days then, Mr M... er, Mr Maybury?' Jacob requested as he picked up his knife and fork. Her grandfather checked his own food over, lifting the short-crust lid off a steak and ale pie with his fork and nodding his approval at the steaming hot filling.

'Yes, Grandad. Tell us more about when you were the boy in the photograph.' Anna hoped that this might prompt more conversation from him than the last question had. She picked at her chips and nibbled at her burger while listening to an uncharacteristically ready account of Smith's Island, of *River Pisky* and *Peanut* moored on the sand, and potatoes with charcoal skins and fluffy centres baked under fires made of sticks.

'Sometimes in the school holidays I'd creep out of the house at night after everyone had gone to bed,' he told them. 'I'd go down to the river and row my boat through inky black water along a watery path lit by the moon. I'd stay out for hours and get back before dawn. No one ever knew.' He'd told her this before but never with such emotion and with such a sparkle in his eye that she could almost believe it were happening to him now.

By the time they'd finished their meal, Anna felt as if she'd actually met the young Algernon in the photograph. She wanted to ask him to stay and to not disappear again behind the frequently grouchy mood and fearsome eyebrows of the old man he'd become.

ALGERNON

It would be the last time he ever travelled along the road to Malpas. The last time he saw the boats moored up on the river edge, or the curl of the land, or the old stone of The Heron Inn or the little cottage that peeped through the trees on the opposite bank. Jacob indicated and pulled out onto a roundabout and headed out of Truro, skirting round the edges of a wonderful city that Algernon would also never visit again. It was a beautiful kind of pain and one he tried hard not to dwell on.

The sun came in flickers and dapples through the car window as Jacob drove past buildings and trees, causing Algernon to shut his eyes against the intermittent glare. He felt so very, very tired. The crack in his concrete heart was spreading, crazing and letting everything out that he'd kept safe all these years, and it was so hard to sort through it in his mind.

'You've been asleep, Grandad. You're going to melt in the car.' He was being nudged on his arm, dragged away from a wonderful dream where he was galloping like the wind on his horse through a Cornish forest. He dug his heels into Firefly's flank to make him go faster but someone was pulling at him causing him to slide from his horse and slip to the forest floor.

'Leave me!' he slurred, his mouth still half asleep, his mind desperately grasping at the fading shreds of the dream. Firefly was turning back, looking for him, scraping at the ground with his hoof, his chestnut coat shining in the dappled shade of the trees, the crack of a gun dropping him to the ground. 'How... *dare*... you,' Algernon spewed, each word coming out in a deep staccato burst while Algernon's own father stepped away into the rapidly fading edges of his dream.

ANNA

Anna and Jacob were sitting cross-legged on the grass verge overlooking the sea where they'd stopped in a car park on the edge of Newquay. Her grandfather had been asleep since they left Truro and they'd decided to let him sleep a little longer. The sea, a grey teal in colour, swelled and rushed into land, bubbling with lacy foam edges as it crashed into shore.

'I wish we could have a go at that.' Anna watched surfers and body boarders braving the waves, endeavouring again and again to meet the challenge of the sea. 'I could probably buy one of those cheap boards. My mum gave me some spending money.' She pointed to the cluster of teenagers in padded life jackets, running barefoot in and out of the water, brightly painted polystyrene boards in their arms.

'We couldn't anyway really,' Jacob rationalised. 'It would mean leaving Mr M on his own for too long. Despite his resurrection in terms of conversation he's physically very frail and I, for one, am not going to be responsible for leaving him alone.' They both turned their heads to check up on her grandfather again and saw that he was still asleep in the car, buckled into his seat, his head lolling towards his chest. The car doors were open but despite the sea breeze, occasionally lifting his wispy white hair, the sun was shining directly onto him.

'He's out cold. Going down memory lane must have exhausted him. Should we wake him up and get him some water or something? He's wearing a jumper – he must be boiling.' Anna squinted at him through her yellow sunglasses and chewed uncertainly on a fingernail. Second-guessing how her grandfather was going to react to anything she did or said was always an impossibly daunting task.

'Let's wake him up anyway. He's been asleep for over an hour and he'll probably thank us from saving him from dehydration.' Jacob unfolded his long legs and stood up while Anna followed, walking round to her grandfather's side of the car. His arthritic hands were balled into fists and his lower lip hung listlessly towards his lap revealing his lower set of dentures.

She tentatively nudged his arm but he didn't stir. 'Grandad, wake up,' she said, nudging his arm harder until he finally moved, sucking on his slack lips to draw them back into place. 'You've been asleep, Grandad, you're going to melt in the car.'

She was about to release the buckle on his seatbelt and help him to his feet but he resisted, pulling his arm away and growling so deeply at her that she had to take a step back. '*How dare you*,' he growled. In those three, short, angry words, all that they'd built up together that morning came tumbling down again.

Hurt to the core, Anna slammed his car door shut again. 'That's him "*thanking*" us for saving him from dehydration.' She glared at Jacob over the top of the car as if it were all his fault then she turned her back on both of them and walked away. 'Let him cook himself. Or better still, let him cremate himself… save someone the job!'

She didn't know why she was so cross, but she just was. They'd had a lovely lunch and now he was having a go at her. She just couldn't understand him. This must have been how her mother had felt when she was growing up at home. She wanted to ring her and tell her she finally understood.

'Come on, Anna, get in, he was half asleep,' Jacob called through the driver's window but she wasn't interested in any of his excuses. She wanted to be left on her own. Her eyes were smarting again and she knew that any minute now she was going to cry.

'You're getting paid to be his chauffeur, so you deal with him,' she called back as Jacob drove along slowly beside her, urging her to get back in the car. She could see through the window that her grandfather was quite obviously wide awake now and was fiddling with his little black book. There was no word of an apology or look of remorse and she was simply not going to get back in the car and just pretend that everything was OK. She marched along the road until, in the end, clearly bored of trying, Jacob drove away.

She did cry of course, walking the streets of Newquay with a snotty nose and swollen eyelids. Had her mother cried when she'd been a teenager? Had she struggled with not being able to understand the complexities of such a man and he, who was in turn unable to understand the complexities of a young girl?

Anna suddenly found herself aching to meet her grandma. To see for herself the person who Helene had found so easy to love by comparison. The back of her neck was burning in the sun and she paddled in the ocean with hot and sore feet, holding her silver boots in her hands, a dribble of tears on her cheeks. She wished her mother had joined them and that she didn't feel so alone on this stupid *mission*. The air smelt of salt and seaweed, sun cream and pasties and all around her it seemed as if everyone was having a good time. Through her yellow sunglasses, the world was a yellow place, bright and sunny and totally the opposite of how she felt inside. With sand between her toes and her jeans still rolled to the knee, she sank down on a bench and watched the world go by.

'I don't think he was actually awake when he got all angry.' Jacob appeared out of nowhere and sat down beside her holding out a can of Coke. Anna jumped a little when he appeared out of the blue and briefly wondered how he'd even found her amongst all the holiday makers swarming everywhere. 'It wasn't you he was having a go at. I think it was someone in his dream.'

'You think?' she said sarcastically, her bitterness rising to the fore again. She hadn't wanted Jacob to seek her out and yet, if she were honest with herself, she hadn't wanted him *not* to seek her out either. She wiped her eyes, feeling suddenly grateful for the company, and reached out to take the can from him.

'I think,' Jacob said firmly. He took a drink from his can, shoulder-bumped her and then burped, making no effort whatsoever to do it quietly. Anna widened her eyes in surprise at the volume of it then gave in to a small giggle, which she pressed between tight lips. A couple close by gave them a disapproving look.

'Where is he now? I thought you didn't want to leave him?' She ignored the couple and looked around as if her grandfather might be lurking close by.

'He's still in the car, getting very hot again. I tried to take him back to the hotel but he wouldn't get out. He got worked up about me leaving you and insisted I drive back to get you. I told you you were a big girl now and that you'd be OK but he's a stubborn old boy. So now I reckon we've got another ten minutes before he passes out in the heat.'

'Maybe I don't give two kahonies if he passes out.' Anna absentmindedly tucked her hair behind her ears and was reminded again of the shortness of it.

'He wants to take us for a cream tea.' Jacob stood up and she looked up at him through her yellow sunglasses, knowing that she couldn't stay sulking forever. 'Apparently we need this in our lives. It's *the* Cornish cream tea and not to be missed.' Jacob held out his hand in an offer to pull her up but she didn't think she could face a cream tea, Cornish or otherwise. Her stomach was already full with her own hurt. 'Come on,' Jacob urged, waggling his fingers at her. 'There's a vicar coming up the path now and I'll do my loudest burp just as she reaches us if you don't get up right this second.' He lifted his can to his mouth and started to pour fizz into his mouth. The vicar with a dog collar, dreadlocks and a very cheerful face looked as if she could handle anything, but even so Anna hurriedly stood up and reluctantly followed him back to the car.

ALGERNON

They drove down country lanes where the trees formed a guard of honour, their green and yellow canopies touching each other, creating a magical living tunnel. The sun splashed golden puddles through little leafy gaps onto the road below and Algernon was again satisfied that his memory of these tree-lined Cornish lanes had held true. The child was very quiet in the back though and he knew that it was his fault.

He'd never got over his father shooting his friend. That his father had decided his old horse should not endure another winter had been understandable. That his father hadn't given him the chance to get back for Firefly's final hours was unpardonable. To not be able to stand by Firefly when the moment came or to look him in the eye so that he was not alone when he fell, had been more than Algernon could bear. Forgiveness for such an act had never found its way into Algernon's heart.

The animal had been his friend since he was seven years old when he'd been given Firefly in order to learn responsibility and horsemanship and to prevent idleness during his school holidays. Algernon, however, was not an idle boy and Firefly had never been a responsibility; he had only ever been a privilege. For Algernon, this beautiful creature had been the one living thing with whom he was able to share the best of times and the worst of times. Whenever he came home either from school or later, on leave from the RAF, Algernon would press his forehead into the massive chestnut neck and breathe words of sweet relief that he was home. Then he and his magnificent friend would take off together, spending hours making their way across fields and through woods and along country lanes until they reached their resting place down by the green waters of the River Fal.

His dream had been so real, so excellent, yet somehow the child had pervaded it, melting its magic into a nightmare. As he sat in the car, nearing their destination, he chastised himself for the fact that, even in his sleep, he'd said the wrong thing.

When a cottage, its old stone walls garlanded with the puffy blooms of rhubarb and custard hued roses, came into view, Jacob turned the car into a small gravel area and parked next to a thick wooden fence. 'I'm not very hungry, Jacob,' the child muttered under her breath, but Algernon's hearing aids picked up on it anyway. Perhaps he'd overthought the fact that she might want to take part in this activity and suddenly the shine came off his idea and tarnished it. He toyed with asking Jacob to return them to the hotel but they were there now and if nothing else, the lad would probably appreciate another meal.

The cottage garden was long and narrow, smattered with tables and chairs each draped in red gingham cloths. Although it took the child a wordless age to get him down the uneven path and settled at the first table they came to, she managed it. 'Three cream teas please,' he said, before the waitress even had time to hand them menus. She looked like a child herself as she cheerfully – and he thought, unnecessarily – giggled at his request, her hair bouncing with curls as she did so. She wouldn't know that he'd visited this very cottage many times before she was even born, in a time when he could walk unaided and upright to a table of his choice.

'Are you on your holidays?' The waitress grinned at them all and, as with the waiter in The Heron pub, Algernon became instantly riled again. Of course he wasn't on his holidays; he was West Country born and bred but before he could answer her, the child answered for him.

'No, we're on a mission,' she said.

'A *secret* mission,' Jacob chipped in, and the waitress, quite understandably, wanted to know more.

'Ooh, a secret mission,' she gushed. 'Any clues?' She held the menus aloft as if that might help her listen better, her eyes eagerly whizzing between each of them.

'Three cream teas, please,' Algernon repeated carefully, then he placed both hands on the table in front of him and drummed his fingers. His intentions as to why they were in Cornwall, secret or otherwise, were not the subject of a flimsy chat.

'Well… I'll just go and get your order then,' she said with an embarrassed flush that Algernon didn't feel at all bad about. When Evie appeared next to him, though, and placed a hand upon his shoulder, he knew he should calm himself down and behave better. *You should be here*, he said in his head. *You should be chatting to these people and saying the right things… making my mission easier.*

Evie stroked his shoulder, then straightened the collar of his shirt as she always used to do. He was sure he could hear her answer, 'If I were here, my darling, there would probably be no mission.'

Algernon stopped drumming the table with his fingers and took a deep breath, knowing that it was perfectly true. He was on a mission and he was alone, and because of that he was wholly responsible for his young granddaughter and for the success of the venture. When the waitress came back with a tray laden with their order, he realised that he hadn't thought to ask for squash or fizz or whatever the youngsters might want to drink instead of tea but having no desire to engage in further conversation with her he took out his big white hanky and blew his nose.

'So…' he began, as she placed everything in front of them: three pretty cups and saucers, china milk jug and sugar bowl, a huge white teapot and finally a three-tier server containing freshly baked scones. 'Anna, Jacob… this is a *Cornish* cream tea. Spread the jam first, that way you can taste the clotted cream better.'

ANNA

It was almost a ceremonial activity, the eating of the cream tea, and despite how upset Anna had felt earlier, she had to admit she was enjoying it. The scones were warm and delicious, the jam packed with strawberries and the cream was like no cream she'd eaten before. 'It's on your nose,' she told Jacob as he emerged from a massive bite.

'Don't care. It's delicious,' he replied, his mouth extremely full, a mix of strawberry red and clotted cream white smeared over his teeth.

'It *is* pretty amazing, Grandad,' Anna said, noticing immediately how light came to his eyes when she said that. He looked so delighted about such a simple thing that she decided, for now, to forgive him. She wanted to eat more, just for him, and she did try, filling her stomach beyond the point of comfort but one bite into the second scone and she was done.

'You eat like a bird.' Her grandfather eyed her plate where nearly a whole scone and several large crumbs were left. It was true, she couldn't deny it – she'd always been a lover of food, the sweeter, greasier, crunchier the better but lately it was like her insides were already full up before she started eating.

'I'll have yours,' Jacob said, reaching over and picking up the pieces of her scone. 'Oh, unless you'd like it, Mr M?'

'Mr Maybury, and no thank you, I have plenty here.' Her grandfather then revealed his bright white dentures as he bit into his second cream-laden scone.

'Did you ever bring H here?' Jacob asked, as he poured more tea into everyone's cups.

'You mean Helene?'

'I do,' Jacob replied evenly.

'I brought her when she was about the same age as young Anna here.' As her grandfather replied, Anna, who was not a fan of tea and had just finished spooning several sugars into her second cup, looked up.

'You took Mum here?' She was surprised by this, but she didn't really know why. She immediately tried to imagine her mother sitting at the little gingham-covered tables when she was only fifteen, natural blonde hair and teenage face, a cup of tea and a scone in front of her. Her mother had never said anything about it. Surely, the ceremonial eating of the Cornish cream tea, which brought such a light to her grandfather's eyes, would have been something worth mentioning?

'Of course I brought her here.' Her grandfather wiped his mouth on his paper napkin before taking a sip of his tea.

'It's like a ritual then?' Jacob said, scraping the last of the cream and the jam out of the pots and licking the spoon.

'Exactly.' Her grandfather nodded at Jacob.

I've just taken part in a family tradition, Anna thought to herself, and having little family to speak of until now, the idea of it felt very special. As if she at last belonged to something.

'Maybe we could come again?' she suggested, hoping that her grandfather would be pleased by her appreciation of the tradition and that the light would shine in his eyes again, but it was not to be. Jacob pushed his last bite of scone into his mouth and wiped his lips with the back of his hand.

'I think not.' Her grandfather pulled out his little black book, the one with the agenda in it, and put a tick against one of the lines. She presumed he'd just ticked the line labelled 'cream tea' and didn't understand why it had to be so final. 'I have other things on my agenda and this one is done now,' he said, in a matter-of-fact way.

Later, when Anna was back in her hotel room on the phone to Helene, she had so many things to say she hardly knew where to start. 'He showed me where he used to sail *River Pisky*, and he told me about his childhood friend Bobby, and about the bell, and the ferryman, and everything.'

'He told you a lot of things.' Helene sounded surprised. The line went quiet for a moment, and Anna wondered what her mother might be thinking. 'I don't think he ever told me about that boat or that he had a friend called Bobby.'

'Didn't he ever tell you about where the two rivers meet?' Anna wondered why her mother didn't know this stuff and why her grandfather might have chosen to share it with her instead. The relationship between her mother and her grandfather seemed even more complex than she'd originally thought.

'I don't think he did.' Helene's voice sounded sad.

'So he didn't tell you the stories of his midnight feasts or about Smith's Island and the baked potatoes?'

'No... no, I don't think he told me that either.' Her response was stilted.

'Or you didn't ask,' Anna said quietly. Another silence came down the phone and Anna waited patiently for her mother to fill it.

'Or I didn't ask,' Helene repeated eventually.

Anna suddenly felt a little like the filling in the middle of a sandwich. The bit that holds two slices of bread together, without which they would have no chance of staying together. How could two lives be so close and yet so far apart, each person understanding so little about the other? It made her feel strangely suffocated. 'We went to the old cottage where rhubarb and custard roses climb the wall. We sat at round tables in a pretty garden and he told me that he took you there for cream tea when you were my age. He said that you were part of the ritual too.' She waited again while Helene gave a soft, reminiscent kind of sigh.

'I didn't tell you that because... well I suppose I didn't think about it being a *thing*. I'd almost forgotten that place but now you say it, I remember that he always said you can't go to Cornwall without having a Cornish cream tea. If it's the same place I'm thinking of, he said that café had always been his favourite place. How lovely that it's still there. I think the whole ritual thing, as you call it, must be more important to him than just an afternoon tea. Maybe it represents the taste of home, or something... like it's the only way he knows how to tell people how much Cornwall meant to him.'

'How come you didn't tell me any of that?' Listening to her mother talk this way, for the first time, about her grandfather caused a worm of irritation to grow in the pit of Anna's belly and she had to let it out. 'When we were first driving to Grandad's house and I asked you about him you had nothing good to say whatsoever. You were so busy telling me how great my grandma was that you never gave Grandad a look-in. Why? Why did you think that was OK not to tell me *anything* nice about him? It made it all so much worse. I thought I was going to live with an ogre.'

'I'm sorry, Anna. I shouldn't have done that.' Helene breathed a rush of apologetic air into the receiver of the phone and it crackled in Anna's ear.

'No, you shouldn't have done that. It wasn't all bad, was it? Life with Grandad?'

The reply when it came, was stilted but raw in its honesty, and Anna was grateful for that. 'No, it wasn't all bad... it wasn't great... but it wasn't all bad. We just clashed a lot because we didn't understand each other I guess. Then, when your grandma died, our love for her tore us apart.' Anna rolled the idea around in her mind and found it catastrophically sad. Perhaps, she thought, it was her grandma who had been the filling in the sandwich back then. 'These last few weeks...' Helene continued '... it's like at long last we're laying our swords down or something. I think I can see him in another light.'

'You can?'

'I'm trying, at least. I think… *hope*… he is seeing me in a different light too. Do you know something rather lovely? He gave me my mum's engagement ring. He put it on my pillow the day you left for Cornwall. I found it there when I went to bed that night. I can hardly believe it. Daft old sod is full of surprises.' Anna remembered how, when she'd gone back to find out what was taking her grandfather so long, he had stared at her and the room had been all full up with something invisible yet painful. Had her grandfather disappeared upstairs to find the ring then? To leave something special behind for her mother? No note, no ceremony, just a quiet waving of a white flag that said more than any of his words could say.

'It's been difficult between him and me, Anna, I can't deny that. But with you he seems different. Perhaps love is easier when it skips a generation.' Anna wanted to tell her then that love, when it skipped a generation, wasn't easy at all. Especially when you were the filling in a sandwich that had taken nearly sixteen years to make. But she didn't want to start another argument.

Helene sighed heavily, causing another rush of crackles in Anna's ear. 'I know there's more to him than I will ever understand. Maybe I never will.'

ALGERNON

Later, in the hotel bar, Algernon nursed a whisky while Anna and Jacob slurped on colas. The heat from his drink was making him feel uninhibited, for once, and even his aches and pains were keeping away for the time being. The young people seemed flabbergasted when he told them about the motorbike he had before he bought his first car. Their reaction was of such incredulity that it was as if they thought he must have been an old man forever.

'It was a Norton!' he said, recalling the weight of the motorbike as he sat astride it, then the further bounce of weight as Evie climbed pillion behind him. Jacob whistled through his teeth.

'That's cool, Mr M.' Algernon felt so tickled that he'd said something *cool* that he forgot to correct the lad over not using his full name.

'Blimey, Grandad,' the child breathed, 'I can't imagine you having one of those. Was it fun?'

'Do you know what? It *was* fun,' he replied, recalling the pure thrill of it and he realised that it was the first time in a long time that he'd used that adjective for anything. He knew he might be losing his short-term memory, of course he did, he could hardly remember what he'd gone into the next room for these days but his recollections from the past were as secure and as accurate as if they had been filmed and stored in mini reels in his head. He could almost feel the exhilaration of speed beneath him and how the wind turned his cheeks icy cold.

'Grandad?' The child touched his arm. 'You were telling us about your motorbike?'

'Oh, I was, wasn't I?' he said, lifting his gaze to the child and realising how it was becoming harder these days not to disappear inside his own head. 'Did you know that when we were married and your mother was on the way, your grandma travelled all the way down here to Cornwall in a sidecar? How it didn't shake them both like a jelly all those miles I'll never know, but she never complained.' He lifted his glass to his mouth but it was empty save for two remaining chips of ice, which he tipped into his mouth and crunched. The drink was loosening him as if it was flowing inside his mind and, although not a big drinker, he wanted the effect to continue. 'I'll have another drink,' he decided out loud. Even though his heart and blood pressure medications fought against the very idea of it, he wanted another one so another he would have.

'I'll get them. Same?' Jacob halted his task of trying to catch a giant stack of beer mats that he'd flipped into the air and pointed at Anna's almost empty glass of Coke.

'Get yourselves some crisps or nuts too, on me. Put it on my room tab. *Carpe diem*, hey?' Algernon had tried to make a joke but it came out more like a whisper of defeat that he had left it so late. He suddenly wished more than anything that he'd always lived for today and for all the thousands of todays he'd had, regardless of what hurdles life had thrown at him.

'Carpy what?' Jacob asked. Both youngsters were frowning at him.

'*Carpe diem*,' he repeated. 'Seize the day. Make the most of everything while you can.'

'Thank you very much. I'll *carpe diem* and get us both a Coke *and* a Twix, then.' Jacob winked at Anna and made his way to the bar.

When the third whisky arrived, he knew it was a bad idea. In an uncustomary fashion for Algernon, however, he gave a mental shrug. His head and his heart wouldn't thank him in the morning but for once he really didn't care. He turned to the youngsters and said, 'Did I ever tell you about my fun flying a Tiger Moth?'

ANNA

Anna and Jacob supported her grandfather to bed at the end of the evening. Three tumblers of whisky and he was as unsteady on his feet as a baby. Anna didn't dare ask him if he was OK, for fear of making him mad, instead she and Jacob propped him up one on either side and manhandled him up the stairs until they got to his room. When he leant forward to put his key in the lock and banged his forehead on the door, both she and Jacob dipped their chins and pressed their laughter into their chests. 'I've got you, Mr Maybury.' Jacob gave a half-suppressed laugh and grabbed her grandfather's shoulders, steadying him as best he could.

'I don't need getting! Stop *getting* me,' her grandfather complained, trying to brush Jacob's helping hands away. Jacob, still giggling as quietly as he could, held his hands up in surrender. Anna guided her grandfather inside his room, placed his room key on the bedside table and hooked his walking stick on the bedstead. Unexpectedly then, with his gnarly old liver-spotted hand, he covered her young hand and patted it affectionately. Anna stared down at his fingers curled around hers, the skin stretched over knuckles and sagging over bone, then she looked up into his face. White bristles speckled his chin and his eyebrows were getting long again, but his faded turquoise eyes were trying to speak to her with a hundred silent words. What it was he was trying to tell her she didn't ever find out, for after an almost imperceptible nod of his head, he indicated for her to step outside his room then he shut the door behind himself.

'Thank God we didn't have to undress him,' Jacob whispered, once the door was shut. 'I don't fancy seeing your grandad in his undercrackers. Can you imagine?' Anna didn't want to imagine anything of the sort.

'Goodnight, Jacob,' she said, shutting her own door behind her, still feeling the touch of her grandfather's hand on hers. She thought back over the evening. By the second glass of whisky, she'd noticed how her grandfather had smiled and, although it was only once, she'd seen how it splashed the faded turquoise of his eyes with the colour of the Newquay sea. It was during the third glass that he'd actually laughed, a reaction so out of character it had caught her off guard and even now, getting ready for bed, she could still see the crinkles at the corner of his eyes. It made her smile to think of him smiling.

Lying on her bed, she imagined the little yellow Tiger Moth aeroplane he told them about doing loop-the-loops in the air above her. She could see him in goggles and a leather cap, drawing huge circles in the sky, high above the boarding school he used to attend. She could hear the engine roaring into the sky then dropping down low, the sound of it causing a glorious disturbance for all who were still trapped inside. What a marvellous moment of thrilling revenge he had taken on the school he had hated so much. How she wished he could have done that above her school during the awful hours she'd sat alone at her desk. Her own grandfather making circles in the sky just for her.

As she drifted off into restless dreams, she contemplated if she was doing the same thing the young Algernon had done in leaving her happy self behind in the city. She pulled the duvet

over her shoulders and yawned deeply, choosing to believe
that it was different for her. She'd lost Harry and her home
and her bedroom with her mural on the wall. She'd lost the
city with its parks and cinemas, waffle houses and swimming
pools and friends who would hug her and welcome her back.
Yes, it was different for her.

ALGERNON

Algernon woke feeling distinctly awful. His bones ached
and his tongue felt huge and dry in his mouth. He lay in bed
searching his mind for what had gone on the night before but
the finer details of it were already escaping him. He groaned
as he remembered having more than his usual single whisky
and felt cross with himself for stepping outside his self-
imposed boundaries. Boundaries that had held him together
and served him well for decades. Running a hand over his face
to press wakefulness into it, he felt a bruise on his forehead
but couldn't think for the life of him how it had come about.

He did, however, remember telling the youngsters stories of
a time when he was young and energetic. Of a time when he
had a motorbike and a pilot's licence, a head of sandy blonde
hair and a fine moustache the 'King of Hollywood', Clark
Gable, would have been proud of. He knew he had enjoyed
an evening of abandonment, slipping back into the past and
finding his true self. As he lay there feeling more than slightly
worse for wear, the realisation dawned that he'd always
been someone who only ever looked backwards instead of
forwards. Now, he thought regretfully, there was no time left
to look forwards; there was only the here and now.

Edging himself out of bed and sliding his legs over the edge to place his feet on the floor, he sat up and reached for his glasses to put them on. There, in front of him was the dressing table mirror and his own reflection staring back at him. The buttons of his pyjama top were misaligned, his feathery hair was sticking up and his mouth curled inwards against his gums... and he was old. He was so damn old.

14

A Concrete Heart

'Today we're going to the village of Tregelly and then on to Lamorran Woods.' Anna's grandfather announced this fact over breakfast the next morning. He didn't look very sparkly – not that he ever did – but his cheeks were paler than usual and she wasn't going to ask him if he was hungover for fear of getting her head bitten off! 'It will be a very long day, so you need to eat well to get some strength.' As he spoke, his red-rimmed, watery eyes rolled pointedly between her and the solitary piece of toast on her plate as if to ask why, when there was so much breakfast on offer, she should eat so little. He and Jacob again had a full Cornish breakfast, and their plates had been piled high with it, but she didn't fancy any of that. Her grandfather pushed the toast rack towards her and she pushed it back. One piece of soft, cold toast was enough.

'Is there anything to do in those places you just mentioned?' she asked, tearing a small bite out of her toast. She hadn't listened closely enough to repeat the place names but was already guessing that, if it was a village and some woods, there was probably going to be a handful of houses and an awful lot of trees. She also guessed that one of those places was where he'd buried the *thing*, partly because today was their last day but also because beside him, on the table, lay a trowel.

He scooped the yolk of his egg onto a corner of toast soaked in bean juice and made no effort to answer her. A gelatinous blob of albumen dangled from his fork before it all went inside his mouth and, despite the fact that she was now sitting next to him rather than in front of him, she caught sight of it and her stomach lurched. 'Grandad?' she repeated, turning her focus away from the sight of it and out of the window where a cobalt sky promised another searingly hot day. 'What are we going to be doing there? Should I bring my bikini? Can we go swimming?' She was dressed for summer, wearing her purple DMs with pink denim shorts and a fuchsia-coloured spaghetti strap top. Her hair was pushed off her face with matching pink sunglasses, and she felt good about the way she looked.

'You're in the pink,' her grandfather quipped.

'Rinki-dink-pink,' Jacob added, putting his knife and fork down on his now empty plate and excusing himself from the table.

'And what is all this?' Her grandfather pointed his food-smeared knife at the skin of her wrist where she'd drawn a bangle of violets. More violets adorned her left shoulder and another violet appeared on a green stalk as if growing from the inside of her boot and up one bare calf. 'You're not going to start getting tattoos all over your skin, are you?' He scowled at the idea of it, the loose bit under his chin wobbling and Anna moved her hand to her lap, shrinking under the spotlight of his scrutiny. She wished very much that he'd mind his own business.

'I may. My body, my choice,' she said, defensively. Today she'd woken up with the feeling that it should be a positive kind of day and had spent a while with her body art pens perfecting her artwork. She wasn't sure if she would ever get a tattoo and was quite happy with her pens, coming up with different ideas and changing her mind whenever she felt like it. One day flowers, next day rainbows or a line from a poem... some days nothing at all. 'Do I need a bikini or not?' she asked, her feeling of positivity rapidly fading.

'No,' her grandfather replied as Jacob returned with three mini boxes of cereal. 'There will be no swimming today, just a forest.'

Anna sighed loudly and slumped back into her seat. 'I get it, it's a *mission* not a *holiday*.'

'I like a bit of a forest,' Jacob said, as he happily mixed coco pops with cornflakes and shreddies all in the same bowl and attacked it as if he hadn't already had a whole fry-up.

'I like a bit of a *beach*,' Anna echoed moodily. Who came to Cornwall and didn't go for a swim?

ALGERNON

They all three stood outside his old village school in Tregelly, the sun beating down on their heads. The stone walls and peaked roofs looked no different to how they'd looked when he was a boy. 'I climbed on that school roof once to retrieve a ball someone kicked up there. I was seven years old.' They all looked upwards to the roof and he was sure they were wondering how such a small child could get up that high. He himself was wondering the exact same thing as now he could hardly even tilt his head back that far to look without his neck complaining.

He remembered shinning up the side of the building with his skinny little legs and arms while excited children called out below, a delicious sense of fear at being caught rising in his belly. He remembered his ultimate success as he threw the ball down to his classmates, which had made him a playground hero and how just two days later he was in a very different school. A school that ensured that children arrived but men were made and which, in the name of religion, tore you apart and put you poorly back together.

He wished, as he stood there now, that he could have kept that little boy safe. That he could go back and tell him to look forwards, never backwards. Evie had always tried to tell him that but he hadn't managed it. How he wished he had. The only thing he could do now was to teach the child the same lesson and hope that she listened.

ANNA

'And here is where I grew up.' Her grandfather pointed to a wide five-bar gate that spanned the lane where they all stood. The village of Tregelly was small, dominated by a church and peppered with very old houses where red-bricked chimneys stood tall over slate roofs and lattice windows. It was all so perfectly perfect, with box hedges and hanging baskets and not a single shop in sight. The five-bar gate was edged by two huge stone gate pillars and was signposted 'Private'. On the other side was nothing except green and trees and a very long road.

'There's nothing here. It's just a road.' Anna looked along it to check she wasn't missing anything. 'I thought you lived in a housing estate?' She frowned at her grandfather and was really very confused, but then Jacob nudged her.

'I think he means *estate*, like Downton Abbey kind of estate. He's not… he's not *royalty* or anything, is he? Should we be curtsying?'

'He's right, it's not a *housing* estate it's an "estate in *land*".' Her grandfather waved a swollen-knuckled finger towards the end of the lane. 'And this isn't a road, it's a drive. A long way down there is Penwithiel mansion now owned by the Treherne family. My father was estate steward there. It was a position of responsibility and came with a big house in the grounds with access to the stables and all the land. It was where I lived. It was my home.'

Anna quickly typed Penwithiel Mansion into her phone and the images that came to the screen made her jaw drop down to her chest. It was a real-life, massive mansion and *her* grandfather had lived there. So far in her fifteen years she'd lived with her mum in a high-rise flat, a maisonette, a house that belonged to Harry and now a shed at the bottom of a garden – and her grandfather had once lived in a palace! She showed Jacob her phone and his eyebrows disappeared into his hairline as he whistled through his teeth. 'Shit,' he hissed. 'We should definitely be curtsying.'

'I used to ride Firefly down this very lane that you're standing in now,' her grandfather said. 'A big chestnut beauty.' He staggered on his feet again and both she and Jacob launched themselves at him to stop him from falling. As they did so,

Anna thought she saw the corners of his eyes glistening. He stared ahead of him, his jaw jutting determinedly forward and she guessed that, in his head, he was imagining riding his chestnut horse again. He was so caught up in the moment that she thought she could also sense the beat of hooves on the ground and feel the air stirring as he rode past them all, the coat of his horse shining in the sun, the colour of new pennies. She knew then that he'd loved this place where he'd been happy and wondered if perhaps her situation wasn't so different after all.

She thought about her friends back home and the city life that was so important to her and how sad and angry in equal measures she'd felt since she'd moved away. She thought about how she'd felt when she walked into her new school that day, her hair giving a bright blue 'up yours' statement to the world, her frustration at life a blaze of fury in her chest. She, however, had been able to go back to her mother each and every day, back to Little Argel and her own belongings – unlike her grandfather who'd had to count the weeks until he could return again. There would have been no escape from bullying for him, no one to hug him, hand him tissues and kiss the top of his head as her mother had done for her.

'I'm bloody starving.' Jacob's loud voice cut through the air and both Anna and her grandfather startled at the sound of it.

'Shut up, Jacob,' she said, throwing him a look but too late; her grandfather was pulling at her arm and the moment was ruined.

'Come on,' he said, 'I can't stand for much longer anyway; my legs are hurting and I very much need to sit down.'

'Pen-whateveritis, grows fruit now and the garden and

shop are open to the public. Shall we go?' Anna walked in time with the slow pace of her grandfather and looked at her phone hoping desperately to be allowed to go to at least one shop on the trip. The money her mother had given her was beginning to burn a hole in her pocket.

'It's pronounced Pen-with-i-el and no, I don't want to go there... I don't want to go back. I don't want to be a visitor... or a tourist!' They passed a big bush with flowers on it and her grandfather stopped to admire it. 'The gardens at home were so beautiful. Did you know that?' Anna, of course, didn't know that, and she wasn't going to know that if he wouldn't let them go there. 'Your grandma, she loved the gardens when she came to visit. She loved walking amongst these...' Anna waited, his words trailing into an elongated pause as he struggled to remember what sort of bush he was looking at '... the, oh what are they called? Evie?' He was sounding cross with himself but when he called out her grandma's name Anna looked across at Jacob and they both frowned. *Evie?* she mouthed.

'I'm... I'm *Anna*, Grandad,' Anna said carefully.

'Rhododendrons,' he said suddenly, pulling his eyebrows into a furious knot. 'Camellia... she loved too. And I know full well that you're Anna, it's just that Evie always knew the names for plants much better than I ever did. Magnolias! That's another one.'

'So, are you sure you don't want to go then... see the beautiful gardens... go to the shop?' Anna crossed her fingers behind her back. It was hardly a high street but one shop was better than no shop.

'I told you I don't want to go to the gardens again,' he snapped. 'I don't want or need anything in the shop and as for the café, they only do cream tea and we did cream tea yesterday.'

'I could eat another cream tea,' Jacob said, pressing the remote control for the car with a bleep and opening the doors to let a blast of hot air out.

ALGERNON

They left Penwithiel and, as with Malpas, he knew it would be for the very last time. He tried not to dwell on that fact as they drove down lanes and past old houses, to where the forest grew thickly either side of the river. Algernon put another tick in his little leather notebook and looked back out of the window where gnarly old trees danced with younger trees, braided with vines and bramble, their branches entwined. It was now time to tackle the last item on his list. The reason he'd undertaken this mission in the first place.

In the gaps between the dense rabble of bark and leaf the sun fell in dazzling pools and droplets, raining light through the canopy to the forest floor below. He could feel his heart quicken the closer he got and he ran a hand over the trowel balanced on his lap. Had his memory and his instructions served him well? Would he be able to find the exact spot? He felt the shape of his compass through the material of his jacket pocket and patted it assuredly. Despite the fact that the smartphone apparently knew everything, he steadfastly held his map in his hands, neatly folded to the page where Sett Bridge could be found spanning the River Fal on the edge of Lamorran Woods. He ran his finger over the map, trying to follow the proximity of where Jacob's car might now be driving, tracing it over black swirling contour lines, grey roads and green patches and down towards the blue of the river.

A sharp bend in a tiny road, which brought them out of the dappled shade into a carpet of lime green, told Algernon all he needed to know. 'We're here!' he announced loudly. Jacob checked in his rear-view mirror then jammed his foot on the brake, turning the car into a sliver of bare dirt track on the side of the road. 'Not *here*... there...' Algernon indicated with frustration to a spot further down the road and Jacob manoeuvred the car along to the next inlet. Here an even smaller sliver of dirt was available and spiteful hawthorn scratched the paintwork of his car, making him cringe at the screech of it. 'No! Not here... further down... there's a bridge, can't you see?' As he turned to Jacob he caught sight of him and the child sharing looks with each other in the rear-view mirror and it rattled him somewhat. 'I know exactly where we need to park and it's on the other side of the bridge, so don't think I don't know.' He grumpily shrugged his neck into his shoulders but a sharp pain plus the rapid beating of his heart forced him to immediately sit upright again to expand his chest.

The old bridge, as always, was just as he knew it would be. The river continued to rush in a gurgle of white through the arches of the ancient stone, falling into calm on the other side. It still flowed in crooked twists and turns as far as the eye could see, ending in ribbons of silver on the horizon. Algernon knew every inch of every inlet and boulder of this place. He knew how the forest to either side of the river rose high with beech and hornbeam and oak until it sloped into the misty distance.

'This is Lamorran Woods.' He brushed his hand in the

direction of a dense forest of trees. 'And this is Sett Bridge.' He pointed to the old bridge they had just driven over. 'And this is the young River Fal. This... all of it... was my haven when I was a boy.' He sat silently absorbing the moment, the windows of the car open, the cool breeze fanning against his face. Cow parsley and red campion speckled the roadside, peeping between tufts of grass and busy hedgerow and, to his intense disappointment, he realised he needed another pee!

ANNA

Anna waited patiently while her grandfather's weak bladder was dealt with. He emerged, eventually, from a gap in the trees, sunlight glistening where he'd splashed his shoes, Jacob close by to grab him if he stumbled. Jacob indicated for her to get out of the car and she obediently unbuckled her seatbelt, put her phone in her pocket and pushed her sunglasses onto her head, stepping out into the heavy scent of earth and river water.

Getting out from the car she expected to see something amazing. It was his *favourite* place after all. His favourite place in all the world, more favourite than the rivers where he'd sailed and the grounds of Penwithiel, apparently. For Anna it seemed to be a place where there was just water, an old bridge and another load of trees and, although she tried to find what it was about Sett Bridge that made it so wonderful, she was at a loss. She yawned and took a photo sending it to her friends with the message 'nature' and an emoji rolling its eyes next to it.

Jacob sucked in his chest, breathing warm air into his

lungs and tipping his face towards the sun as if he could see something lovely about the place that she couldn't. 'We should have brought a picnic,' he said, looking at the soft grassy bank over the other side of the river.

'I used to bring picnics here when I was your age.' Her grandfather stared in the same direction as Jacob and nodded his head at the same patch of grass. 'Firefly would drink from the river and get fat on rich grass while I lay in the sun eating pasties. Cook made the most wonderful pasties.'

'But what did you *do* here?' Anna just couldn't see what made it so great – no shops, no swimming and not an ice-cream hut in sight – certainly not enough to keep anyone entertained for *hours*. Her grandfather turned then and looked directly at her, appraising her with his turquoise eyes as if she were the mad one for not seeing it.

'What did I *do* here? This ground right here…' he banged at the earth with his stick and swept the hand that clutched the trowel around in the air '… is where the forest meets the river and the river carves her path through the land and all of it is still unspoilt, linked together by hundreds of years of history embedded in the age-old rocks of the bridge. What did I do? I allowed myself to simply *be*… that's what I did.'

Allowed himself? Anna turned his uncharacteristically poetical words over and over in her head, trying to make sense of them. When he wasn't in *River Pisky* he was with his horse just *being*. This was the other thing he did as soon as he came home from school… when he wasn't sailing he was here. These places, the river and the forest, she realised, must have been his retreat – his safe place. 'Is it… is it like Little Argel?' she asked cautiously, knowing that this seemingly simple question had a multitude of layers to it if she were right. He looked her directly in the eye and nodded. She realised then that even before they met, her grandfather had understood what it meant for her to need somewhere to go when life took hold of you and ruthlessly shook you to pieces.

'Just like Little Argel,' he confirmed, then he made his way carefully over to where another five-bar gate blocked their path. For a while, Anna stood looking at his hunched frame as he tried to negotiate the uneven ground. She saw a very old man who often drifted away or forgot what he was saying, whose hair was whisper-thin and skin waxy and crushed, and yet, when he'd looked into her eyes just then, she knew now that he was so much more than that. 'First we need to negotiate this,' he said, ignoring a sign saying 'private' and pointing with his trowel to where the latch was padlocked shut. Anna went over to join him and experienced a moment of defeat when all she could see was a gate and an awful lot of spiky-looking hedgerow.

'Rules are made to be broken,' said Jacob decisively as he stepped over to one of the gate posts and started to trample aside the foliage growing around it. He pulled and steadied while Anna pushed and guided but getting her grandfather through the narrow gap to the other side of the gate was a painful task. Hawthorn sliced red lines into the skin on their arms and then her grandfather became hooked on an unwieldy bramble that wrapped its way round his trouser leg, catching thorns in the cloth. Once they were on the other side of the gate though, standing side by side and staring at a number of trees, her grandfather handed Anna the trowel and called the numbers 'six and six' out loud.

'Twelve,' Jacob answered with an expression that attempted to say he was amusing if not smart.

'Idiot,' her grandfather muttered, clearly not impressed. He delved into the pocket of his jacket and pulled out the little brass compass, then opened the lid and examined it. 'We have to take fourteen paces north-east, which will take us past six trees, then eleven paces north-west past another six trees.' He pointed his stick in the directions they needed to take while Anna wondered how he was going to pace anything when he could barely lift his feet off the ground. 'Help me,' he urged, waving a hand at Jacob to support him over the rough ground as he handed the compass over to Anna. 'Hold it in the flat of your hand,' he instructed.

'I... er, have never used a compass,' Anna admitted, trying to make sense of the many numbers engraved on the dial.

'Perhaps you have an *app* on the smartphone,' her grandfather muttered, his sarcasm entirely intentional.

'Actually, Mr M, there is a compass app,' Jacob chipped in. 'Do you want me to show you?'

Anna shot Jacob a furious look, and he fell silent. She glanced at her grandfather's face and the look of disappointment she found there was quite heart-breaking.

'Really?' he muttered.

'No, not really, Grandad,' Anna lied, holding the compass with renewed interest. 'Jacob's just being annoying.' With her grandfather's help she turned the dial until north-east was under a directional arrow and the quivering needle settled on magnetic north, then set off, making fourteen large strides. She counted each tree she came to. 'One, two, three, four, five, six!' Next, she turned slightly to her left and made eleven further large strides in a north-westerly direction, counting a further six trees. Finishing the final stride, having counted the trees as she went, she stopped where, not one, but several trees were heavily wrapped in vine. The ground beneath them was a mass of weeds and moss and as she studied the area she realised that even if they knew which tree to start at, it was going to be impossible to dig up all that forest growth with a tiny trowel. She held her arms up in defeat to the others. *Pointless,* she mouthed to Jacob.

When her grandfather finally gasped his way to a standstill next to her, he stared at the ground, a look of such intense dismay on his face that Anna wanted to cry for him.

ALGERNON

'Did you count six and six?' Algernon's breath was coming in rapid puffs and a horrible feeling of agitation whipped up a storm in his gut. There were a lot of trees and to make things worse they were all covered by vine and some trees had fallen while others had been cut down over the years.

'Yes I did, Grandad, and I did north-east, north-west like you said.' The child looked back along the path they'd all taken and, although she sounded positive, she looked extremely uncertain. 'I *think* this one here is the sixth one... but it could be this one... or even this one.' She pointed to a hornbeam and Algernon muttered under his breath, blowing his nose on his big white hanky, his hands trembling more than normal.

'That's a hornbeam, *Carpinus betulus*. We're looking for a beech, *Fagus... Fagus...* something or other. It's all changed since I was here last.' He felt unsure of the area he was now standing in, unsure even of details he knew he could once recall without thinking. He hadn't intended on remembering where he'd buried it. He'd always intended on forgetting about it, but being one to look backwards rather than one to look forwards, he'd been unable to. A feeling of stupidity rose like bile into his throat. He'd dragged everyone here and for what? 'You held the compass correctly?' he asked, snatching it off the child and making sure they were facing the right way.

'Yes, Grandad, I held the compass correctly – north-east, north-west, like you said.'

Algernon dismally surveyed the forest around him and stepped forward to examine the two trees in front of him. 'It's under a beech so there's no point looking at the hornbeam or the oaks,' he snapped.

'I don't know what a beech looks like,' the child defended.

'Do *you* know what a beech looks like?' He addressed the lad who looked just as blank as the child. 'Can *either* of you identify *any* species of tree?' They both simultaneously shrugged as if it were of no real concern to them.

'I know what a conker tree looks like and I know that a sycamore has seeds which are like helicopters... but other than that I've never had the need to be honest.' The child turned to Jacob who was attempting to juggle three pinecones he'd gathered.

'Me neither,' he said. 'But you can get an app for your phone that tells you all that stuff if you do have the need.'

'Of course.' Algernon sighed inwardly and pushed away his desire to swear openly about the bloody smartphone and its bloody apps. 'That is a beech and so is that.' He waved his stick in the direction of the two trees close by. 'Pointed oval leaves with wavy margins.' He was annoyed with himself and his legs were beginning to hurt, his back was aching and he still didn't feel quite right from the evening before. The child, perhaps sensing his increasing fatigue, came and took his arm while Jacob made his way over to the two trees he'd just pointed at and picked off a leaf.

'Pointed oval with wavy margins,' he announced, grinning at both of them.

'Do either of the trees have the eye?' Algernon asked.

'An eye?' The child looked confused again and so did Jacob and he suddenly couldn't remember if he'd mentioned the eye or not. He thought he had but obviously he hadn't... or maybe the youngsters hadn't been listening. He could see it though, in his mind. The freshly dug earth at his feet, a lump shaped just like a huge eye in the bark of the beech next to it. He fought for the correct name but it wouldn't come.

'One of those things in the trunk, a disfiguration... a bump... an eye... oh you *know*?' But both the youngsters looked blankly at him and he realised that if they barely knew what tree was which they probably wouldn't know the answer to this question either. His frustration mounted as they waited patiently for him to remember what he was trying to say. 'It's one of those,' he said, pointing to a tree further away where two donut-shaped mounds were visible on a tree whose trunk had split into three.

'Knots!' the youngsters enlightened him, speaking at the same time, and both looking very pleased with themselves that they, at least, knew that much. Algernon, however, was not pleased. He was positively fed up that not only had the word been elusive but so was the particular knot he remembered.

'The tree I buried it under had a large knot in it, shaped like an eye about this big.' He gestured with his hands as to how big it had been but everything where they stood was covered in vine choking the bark from sight.

'Um... they all look a bit like eyes,' Jacob added unhelpfully, spinning slowly round and surveying all the trees around him. 'The only tree I can see with a knot that looks more like an eye than all the other eyes is this one.' He stepped over to a tree a little further behind the two that they were standing by and leant in towards it. 'Pointed oval leaf, wavy edge,' he declared again, holding another plucked leaf in his hand and waving it at them. He then tugged at a clump of vine that broke away in his hands to reveal a large knot shaped like an eye. He cupped both hands beneath it as if he were holding it on a platter. 'Observe a beech tree... with an *eye*!' he said, proudly.

'That's it!' Algernon cried, flapping his hands at the child to start digging with the trowel. 'Somewhere about here,' he tapped the ground with his stick. 'Under the watchful eye of the tree.'

ANNA

The ground, under layers of dead bracken and dropped leaves, was unexpectedly quite soft, coming up in easy mounds as she dug the trowel into the earth. It didn't take long before she was unable to push the trowel any further, the blade of it banging against something hard and she could hardly wait to unearth whatever it was. Dropping the trowel, she knelt on the ground and scooped and brushed at dirt until the corner of a box was clearly visible, her heart beginning to race. 'I... I need to sit down.' Anna looked up to see that the colour had slipped entirely away from her grandfather's face and that he was now leaning heavily on his stick as if he were about to collapse.

'Wait here, Mr M,' Jacob called, as he frantically looked around for a makeshift seat and he disappeared into the trees, twigs and bracken crackling under his feet and he returned very quickly, dragging a large storm-damaged branch behind him, shedding alarmed beetles in his wake. Anna brushed the forest dirt from her bare knees and helped to lower her grandfather down on it, worried at how precarious he looked.

'Is it because I'm digging for the *thing*?' Anna asked, wondering if the excitement was getting to him.

'No, it's because of three bloody whiskies,' he grumbled, pushing his eyebrows together in frustration. 'My blood pressure and heart rate can't deal with keeping the rest of my body upright for more than ten minutes.' His hands, speckled brown with age, shook as he rubbed his eyes and smoothed back his hair before leaning forwards to grasp each of his bony knees for support. 'Carry on,' he ordered, nodding his head in the direction of the hole in the ground. 'We can't stay here all day!'

Anna obligingly went back to her task and thought how sad it was that the very last time the box had been touched was by his young and unspeckled hands. The anticipation of what it was he'd buried all that time ago was almost too much to bear. Pulling it out she physically shivered and brushed away the insects that scurried in all directions as she placed it next to her grandfather's feet. The box had been fashioned from a mixture of wood and metal but was now dark and rotten and jammed shut with time and rust. It took her some effort to prise the lid open with the blade of the trowel but when at last it came apart, they all leant forwards to get a closer look.

Whatever it was, the thing was dark and, like the box, was rotting. 'It's all right – it won't bite.' Her grandfather sounded strange, as if his voice had gone up a few notes and she warily delved her hand into the mass and pulled it out.

'What *is* it?' she said, gingerly lifting what looked like a strap. As she held it aloft, more straps came with it, rotting and delicate and with rusty buckles attached.

'They're the reins of my horse. Firefly.' Anna, who had been studying the straps, looked up at her grandfather and saw that his eyes were full of sorrow. Jacob became suddenly extremely interested in the various plant life of the British woodland and, with a rare sensitivity, lolloped off to study a crop of mushrooms.

'He was special, then, Grandad.' Anna kicked herself for saying something so flipping obvious. *Of course he was special if they had come all this way to dig up his reins.*

'Oh yes. He was very special. He asked nothing of me and yet gave me everything in return.' He took his big white hanky from his pocket and wiped a dewdrop from his nose, then suddenly clasped the old reins in both fists.

'Tell me about him?' Anna croaked the words out, hoping it was OK to ask, her throat dry with held breath.

ALGERNON

Firefly snorted warm air through his nostrils, his huge soft lips only inches from Algernon's face. 'I'm back, old fella,' Algernon whispered, rubbing his hand over the huge jawbone of his friend before resting his forehead against the warm chestnut neck allowing Firefly's strength to flow into his own veins. He told his horse everything. He talked of the shadows that haunted him at school, spilled the secrets the Brothers had sworn him to keep, vented his fury and released his pain, all the while telling him everything that he couldn't share with anyone else.

Algernon's boots clattered on the stable floor as he took a brush and groomed his horse until the coat lay flat and glossy, talking to him all the while. He took a blanket and placed it on Firefly's back, positioning it forward over his withers and sliding it back into place, nudging him to keep still. 'Patience,' he crooned as he lifted the saddle and put it gently in place, tightening the girth and checking everything carefully. 'Nearly boy, nearly.' Then he reached for Firefly's black, leather reins and slipped them on, fastening the buckles and leading him outside into the frosty air. Sparkles of ice glistened on the stable doors and the brick walls surrounding the yard, a blue light still clinging to the early morning air. 'Ready?' he said, smiling as Firefly rotated a listening ear.

Algernon placed a booted foot in the stirrup, lifted himself into the saddle and clicked his cheek with his tongue. He was home! Back on Cornish soil, the crisp air filling his lungs, his horse responding to his every move as they took off through the gardens, through the scent of eucalyptus and winter-flowering viburnum and out through the tall stone gate posts of the Penwithiel estate. The wind lifted his fair hair off his face as, hatless, he gripped the reins and whooped his joy out loud. They cantered across winter-hard fields where the early morning sun cast long shadows of themselves on the crisp grass. They walked down lanes and past winter bare trees, to the sound of hooves on tarmac, redwings and starlings busy with the start of their day.

Finally, they made their way through the woods, crackling

bracken beneath them, dodging branches above them and coming only to a halt where Sett Bridge spanned its ancient arches across the River Fal. Spent, Algernon dismounted his horse, his feet landing hard upon the earth and, still holding the reins, he reached to pat the sleek chestnut coat.

'How amazing, Grandad,' the child breathed when he finished trying to explain. She was still sitting at his feet and the log was beginning to dig into his backside, making him fidget. 'So how did his reins end up here?'

He stroked the reins in his hand and tried to find a way to start. The last time he'd held them was the day he'd gone into Firefly's empty stable at Penwithiel and taken them from their hook. He'd placed them inside an old croquet box, grabbed a spade and marched his agony across the estate gardens. He'd taken the memory of his magnificent friend, along with all the dreams for his own future, striding angrily across fields, down lanes, through the woods and over to Sett Bridge. Finally, where the tall grass had rustled in the wind and the river had rushed through the ancient arches of the bridge, he lay on his back, under a cloudy sky, with the weight of all his sorrows in a box on his chest. It was then, and only then, that Algernon had cried.

Now, while the child waited patiently, he moved his feet into a better position and adjusted his bottom on the log. 'As you know, I hated school. More than hated it. I was miserable.' He looked the child directly in the eye, knowing that they shared something fundamental together. 'Then, when school was far behind me and I became a young man, there were three things that I was absolutely sure of. One, that I loved your grandma. Two, that we were going to live together in Cornwall. And three, that I was going to be in the RAF until the day I retired.

I loved all these things, you see. They were all part of me and who I was… in here.' He tapped his chest firmly in the place above his heart. 'I loved flying so much. The roar of the engines, the importance of the dignitaries I transported, the exhilaration of it all. I visited many countries, flew over vast deserts and huge mountain ranges, high above clouds or low across water. It was… it was…' He raised his eyes upwards into the canopy of trees, searching a perfect square of blue sky for the perfect word.

'It was happiness,' the child said simply.

'Yes it was. It was happiness indeed. And then… suddenly it was over.' Algernon grasped the reins even tighter and moistened his lips with his tongue, feeling his chin wobble and his eyes water.

'But why was it over, Grandad? Was it the *situation*?' It took him a moment to realise that the child was referring to the conversation he'd had with her back at the Heron pub in Malpas, and he squeezed his eyes shut. He could hear the grinding of metal and the breaking of wood, recall the searing pain in his shoulders, his back and arms and how everything had gone black.

'Yes.' He gave a trembling sigh. 'It was the *situation*. It was 1947. I was travelling in an Air Force truck in Cairo. Then the truck I was in crashed with a bus. One minute the high-spirited chat of the air crew and the promise of a cold beer, the next minute the hushed voices of nurses and the medicinal scent of an Egyptian hospital.' He breathed in deeply as if he could still smell the awful tang in the air, and shuddered. 'I was unconscious for days. When I eventually opened my eyes I saw my mother by my hospital bed,' He'd woken to find her sitting on a chair by his side, writing a letter to Evie and remembered thinking how surreal it was that even as he lay there broken and bandaged, she was wearing her vibrant lipstick and her earlobes still wobbled with the weight of her best pearl earrings.

'What had you done to yourself?' The child ran her eyes over him as if looking for injuries she hadn't noticed before. He remembered being told by his surgeon that a huge section of wood from the bus had gone right through both shoulders like a grotesque sort of coat hanger.

'Damage. That's what I'd done. A lot of damage, which affected my back and shoulders, arms and hands.' He stretched his fingers out and they both looked down at them. 'You wouldn't really know now, would you?' The child shook her head. 'It was months before I could be flown home to Cornwall, to Penwithiel, to recuperate. I thought if I worked hard at all my exercises I'd be tickety-boo again in no time. The groundsmen at Penwithiel took me under their wing and taught me carpentry skills to help with my recovery. For months I measured and sawed, bevelled and dovetailed, whittled and sanded until my arms and hands grew stronger. That's how I learnt to love making things like Evie's garden bench.' He shifted his position again, feeling a terrible numbness begin to creep through his buttock which then headed down his left leg.

'But *why* was it all over then, Grandad? Why when you were tickety-boo again couldn't you fly anymore?'

Algernon felt touched at her clear investment in his story. 'I never was tickety-boo again.' He pulled a downward smile, remembering how the letter informing him of his medical discharge from the RAF wounded him far more than the accident ever would. 'Damaged goods,' he added quietly. The

EVERY SHADE OF HAPPY

child reached for the reins and lightly touched them with her fingertips.

'And Firefly?'

Algernon's hands shook and the discomfort of sitting on the log for so long was beginning to get too much for him. He couldn't give up now though; he'd come too far. 'My father had Firefly shot while I was still in hospital in Egypt. Mother told me it was because he was old and it wasn't fair for him to endure another cold winter at his age. Because I wouldn't have been in a fit state to ride him or even walk him before the winter set in. Father apparently thought it would be better for me if it happened before I got home.' Algernon managed to make it sound so clinical, so matter-of-fact, but then the last words got caught in his throat and they cracked with the agony of it until the child's eyes, along with his own, glistened with unshed tears. 'It wasn't better for me, though. Father should have waited. *I* should have been the one to stand by Firefly and look him in the eye so that my friend didn't have to go alone. I let my friend down... after all those years of him being there for me.' They looked at each other, he and the child, and a single tear plopped from her eye.

He took a breath, then another, fighting for air and the right things to say. 'These...' he said, tapping the reins '... were a symbol of everything I'd lost. Not just my childhood but my future... my *me*. Do you see? I buried *myself*.'

ANNA

Anna sat on the forest floor with twigs and bracken digging into her skin but she could hardly feel it with everything she was hearing. She ran the back of her hand across her cheek where her tear had fallen and tried to hold all the other tears back. The reins that she'd dug up were a symbol not just of everything that her grandfather had tried to forget but everything that he'd let eat away at him all his life. It was a very sad story and she really didn't know what to say. 'You could have had Cornwall though, couldn't you, Grandad?' She swallowed loudly. 'When you married Grandma... you could have stayed here?' Her heart nearly cracked in two as he shook his head, looking so terribly sad, and she reached out to cup his gnarly old knuckles in the softness of her palm.

'I couldn't have that either, I'm afraid. I'd only ever trained as a pilot so I wasn't in a position to pick and choose jobs. Your grandma and I were soon to be married but I knew I couldn't support her. She wrote to me when I was recovering with news of a little schoolhouse that was for sale near her parents' home in Essex and that her father had managed to secure me an office job, and well, I couldn't say no. I wanted to support my Evie and to make her happy, and that was the only way.'

'Then you must have loved her very much,' Anna said.

ALGERNON

That was true, of course. Although he'd never been able to say the words out loud to Evie, he *had* loved her very much. No longer able to offer her much and give her the life she deserved, he'd packed his bags and moved away from Cornwall forever. That first day, however, when he'd walked into the buildings of the Corporation and sat at his desk, he had known without a doubt what a bird must feel like to have its wings clipped. He felt the touch of the child's fingers on his and wanted so much to get this moment right for her. Not just for her, but for Evie and Helene too. 'Can you understand what I'm trying to say, when I say I buried myself?' he asked.

'I... I think so,' she replied tentatively.

'Your mother, she can ride any storm... rising to the challenge of whatever life throws at her and your grandma was the same... both entirely marvellous. You, young Anna, are more like me.' He turned to her, pushing his glasses further up his nose to put his vision in focus, wondering if he'd just suggested that she was *not* entirely marvellous. 'What I mean is that life has already thrown some hurdles in your path and that you had to leave your home and your friends. I know you're having a tough time at your new school but when you're all grown up you can take any path you like. And if you take a wrong one, pick another. You're at the very beginning of your life, so don't do what I did and get all bitter over the hurdles in your way. Jump them – and jump them high. Do you hear?'

'I hear, Grandad.'

The child was still cupping her hand in his, her skin smooth, her fingernails pearly pink, a bracelet of flowers drawn around her wrist. To him, she looked like a wild and colourful flower herself in her rinki-dink-pink clothes, vibrant against the green forest floor and he knew then that even though he could never say it out loud, he loved her.

★ ★ ★

ANNA

Anna took the reins from her grandfather. *So that's what this whole trip is about*, she realised. *It's about me.* She flattened the reins into the box and fought to press the lid back on, stalling for time over what to say. Everything they had gone through over the last few days had been all for her and her insides were aching with the knowledge of it. She stood up, dirt and leaves stuck to her knees, and picked up the box that held the symbol of all that had stopped him embracing the rest of his life. 'I understand now, Grandad,' she said, looking down at his tired old face.

'Then get me up off this thing before you have to bury me too.' He held tight to his stick and reached an arm up for support while she put the box back down and called Jacob over. He'd given up with the mushrooms and had been sitting on a branch up a tree playing a game on his phone, leaving them to their moment together. Between them both they managed to get her grandfather upright but having sat on the log for so long, he'd virtually seized up.

'What should I do with the box?' she asked, picking it back up off the ground and holding it towards him once he was steady.

'You decide,' he said, turning back towards the car and waving a dismissive hand behind him.

Anna was appalled. She gave a look of anguish as Jacob and her grandfather walked away and she called after them, 'I can't decide that. It's too big a decision to make on my own.' Her anxiety flared, as she battled with the right move. Should she put them back in the ground where they'd been for decades or to take them back to the car? 'What do you want me to do?' she called, clasping the box, a bug creeping out from under it and scuttling across her hand.

ALGERNON

'You come back here one day, you hear?' His voice deep and gravelly and laced with uncleared phlegm, Algernon begged the child to heed him. He turned to look at her once they were all seated in the car but she looked back with dark and solemn eyes. 'Come back here... bring me... and Evie with you.' The child continued to study him, her brow now furrowing into deep lines above her eyes.

'Um... Grandma is... no longer with us, Grandad,' she said, nervously tucking a stray lock of hair behind her ear, a crimson flush creeping up her neck. 'She's... well she's...'

'She's in my wardrobe, that's where she is. In a pretty purple box. We had an agreement. We live in Essex but we rest in Cornwall. It's all in my will. I want you and Helene to have a part in it. So, once I've been flambéed and I'm also inside a box, you can shake us up together and bring us both here.'

'Oh.' The child spoke so quietly that his hearing aids struggled to pick up the sound of it. She had nothing more to offer than a feeble interjection and it really wasn't good enough.

'You hear?' he rasped.

'I hear,' she replied.

'Launch us off Sett Bridge into the Fal,' he added, making his voice as soft as he could muster. 'But be sure to assess the direction of the wind first.' He offered an uncustomary wink and feeling an unfamiliar tickle of amusement growing from deep inside himself, he chuckled quietly. 'Don't want us blowing back over you.' His ever painful shoulders jiggled up and down as his laughter found its way out. The lad laughed too and then the child joined in until they were all laughing out loud together as if they were never going to stop.

Endorphins fired off everywhere and paradoxically Algernon found he was experiencing one of the most marvellous moments he'd had in a long, long time. The notion that his very last action on earth could be so ludicrously comical really tickled him. In fact, as he choked with laughter and coughed at the same time he wondered if he were in danger of being finished off right there and then!

15

A Little Bit of Lovely

ANNA

Anna's head was buzzing with everything that had happened the day before. Knowing that the long journey, the strict agenda and the sticky carpet hotel had all been for her was quite something to take on board. In all the difficult weeks since they first came to her grandfather's house he'd understood all along that life had dumped a roadblock in her way and that instead of finding a way round it she'd let it stop her in her tracks. He was telling her that life had given her lemons and she hadn't made lemonade. Her mother, on the other hand, had not only made lemonade but she'd added ice and a slice and a double shot of gin. She knew that her grandfather understood that about his daughter too, and hoped that Helene knew he saw that in her.

Sitting in front of the dressing table mirror, having almost finished packing her bag for the journey back to Essex, she tied her hair into two stubby bunches. Her brown eyes stared back at her, no make-up, no mascara, no winged eyeliner... no blue hair. What she did have, however, was Firefly's reins.

She'd agonised for ages over what her grandfather expected her to do with them, dithering in the forest whilst holding them in the muddy and rotting box. Then it had hit her. He didn't expect anything. He wanted her to do whatever she wanted to do with them. Life, he was saying, was her choice.

The box was in the boot of Jacob's car, probably infesting it with beetles or things with too many legs, but she was going to take it home and decide what to do with it later. She didn't want to bury it again. It didn't feel right to leave her grandfather's heart in the forest as if it were something that should be forgotten. It was strange to think that a pile of rotting leather had such a story behind it and that the story belonged to her own grandfather. She cast her mind back to the journey from Harry's to her grandfather's house that very first day. How she'd asked her mother to tell her more about her grandfather and yet she could think of very little to say. It was sad that she knew so little about his motorbike or his horse, his boat or the fact that he'd once flown in loop-the-loops in a little yellow aeroplane.

His words were hitting home. She dreaded following the same path he had, being difficult to get to know or talk to. Was it already happening with the people in her new school? Was it because she wasn't letting them in? Would someone one day say that Anna Maybury was an old lady who let life get in her way and had nothing to say about herself?

When Jacob knocked on her door three minutes later on his way to breakfast she impulsively leapt up and opened the door, pulling him roughly into the room by his T-shirt. 'Am I difficult?' she asked, shutting the door firmly behind him.

'No, you're very easy-going and perfectly normal,' he replied, straightening the crease she'd made in his T-shirt.

'I mean, am I like my grandfather?' Her feet were planted slightly apart, her hands on her hips and she challenged him to say the right thing, whatever the right thing was.

'Um... sometimes?' he replied hesitantly, wary of what the right thing to say should be and whether he was going to get a punch for saying it wrong.

'Really?' Anna's hands dropped wearily to her sides, her dismay obvious in the raised pitch of her tone. 'So am I sometimes closed off and grouchy?' The room went silent as Jacob spent too long thinking about her question, balancing his room key on the tips of his fingers then flicking it into the air and catching it again between his thumb and forefinger. He was about to do it again when she snatched it from him and clasped it in her fist. '*Am I?*' she insisted.

'No not at all,' he answered cheerily, shaking his head in a jokily mocking way. 'But burning my letter and giving me the middle finger when we first met could have probably benefited from a different approach.' He raised an eyebrow then held his hand out for his room key but she didn't give it back.

'I didn't know who you were back then. I thought you were someone from school giving me a hard time.'

'I *was* someone from school but I *wasn't* giving you a hard time because, guess what...? Not everyone is out to get you.' Jacob sighed and then jiggled about with frustration like a small boy. 'Why are we doing this now? It's breakfast and my stomach is rumbling.'

'I'm not like him, Jacob,' she said, quietly.

'OK, then you're not like him. Can we eat now?' He lunged at her for his room key, wrestling her onto the bed and prising her fingers away from it, his breath just a caress away from her cheek. She laughed out loud but as his hair tangled with her hair and his chest beat against hers, she wished the moment would last.

'Got it!' he cried, leaping back off the bed and pulling her up by her hand until she was standing in front of him, her cheek still warm from his breath. 'You're not like him you know,' he said gently, reaching for the handle of her door, his eyes looking into hers, his hand still holding her hand. A lovely kind of quietness grew between them, during which she dared to hope that Jacob might be feeling something for her in the same way she was for him. Then he grinned suddenly and flung the door open. 'Fewer wrinkles... more teeth!' he called, as he ran down the stairs for breakfast.

ALGERNON

Algernon had never been impulsive in later life but today he felt like doing something *fun*. 'You're lucky,' the receptionist said, checking her reflection in a pocket mirror. 'They've had a group booking delay their visit by one day, otherwise you'd never have got in at this time of year. You have to be out by eleven tomorrow morning though.' The receptionist had managed to find three rooms at The Idle Rocks hotel overlooking the sea in St Mawes and Algernon could not be more delighted. A fuzzy feeling appeared in the pit of his stomach when he thought about telling the youngsters of his change of plan.

'One day is perfect, thank you.' Algernon gave her a polite nod of his head then shuffled his way slowly to the breakfast room puffing with a mixture of exhaustion and something akin to excitement. 'We're just having cereal, no full Cornish this morning,' he told them, getting in quickly before the youngsters could order from the receptionist, now waitress, who had come to take their order. 'We need to be off nice and promptly because I've decided we're not driving home today... we're staying one extra night in St Mawes.' He was still wiped out from his adventures over the last three days but even so, he sat back in his seat entirely satisfied with himself, pretending not to notice their surprised expressions. 'It's not far and I think you'll both rather like it,' he said.

ANNA

'From the belly and out through your throat.' Jacob was endeavouring to teach Anna how to produce a burp with the impressive resonance of his own ability but, despite all his efforts, she was incapable of matching it. They'd just finished swimming in the sea, their hair drying in salty strands as they sat on their towels on the beach. Anna's grandfather sat in the shade nearby, a large blue cotton hat with St Mawes embroidered across the front covered most of his head, hurriedly bought in a souvenir shop in order to offer him some protection from the glare of the sun.

'This place is so beautiful.' Anna wedged her can of lemonade between two stones and turned her attention from Jacob's lesson on gas expulsion to the view of St Mawes bay instead. Soft coastal colours of teals and yellows cupped the water like a salty bowl full with billowing sails and bobbing boats, and the air was heavy with the scent of seaweed. 'I didn't know a place could smell as lovely as this.' She breathed in through her nose so deeply she could almost feel the salty air filling her capillaries. She took a photo and sent it to her old friends, *Wish you were here* written across the screen.

'Isn't it a shame we only have one day here?' Jacob said wistfully, tipping his head back and letting the sun turn his cheeks and forehead an unhealthy shade of pink.

'No,' Anna replied, watching three little Mirror dinghies with bright red sails all turn about at the same time. 'You mean, isn't it great that we have a *whole* day here? We are enjoying a little bit of lovely.'

'Anna Maybury, what's happened to you? You don't mean to say you *like* it here, do you? It's not a city!' He poked her in the ribs and she squealed, pushing his hand away and flicking a piece of dried seaweed at him. He was right, though: this place was not the city where she'd always felt at home. It didn't vibrate with engines and voices or smell of car fumes and fast food. It didn't rise out of the ground with office blocks soaring into the sky. It had something else. A quiet kind of something... a beauty that was making her heart beat with a different rhythm.

'My grandad said that this place was his own father's, my *great*-grandad's, most favourite place in all the world. I think I can see why.' She looked over at her grandad who raised a hand in their direction, then, satisfied he was OK, she allowed her gaze to return to where a family were hunting for sea treasures in the glinting water. The sun beat down on her skin and she absentmindedly dug her toes into the shingle to find the cool layer beneath. 'It's strange to think that members of my family would have come here and looked at this same view. Up until a few months ago I didn't even have a family.' She picked up a creamy white clam shell and brushed the sand off it before placing it on Jacob's back. 'Or that my own grandad might have searched for shells like this when he was a little boy, right where we're sitting now.' She glanced over again at her grandad and saw how his spine curved, how huge his hat seemed on his head and that he still had his shoes and socks on. 'It's a shame we couldn't get him to paddle in the water. I think he'd have enjoyed it.'

Jacob closed his eyes, a warm sleepiness seeming to overcome him and he yawned loudly. 'I think he's absolutely knackered. I don't think we understand how difficult everything is getting for him now.'

'To think he's spent half his lifetime wishing he was somewhere else. That's a bit crap, isn't it?' Anna picked out another shell and dug her finger into the shiny pink centre of it to clean out the sand.

'Pretty much,' he said, taking the shiny pink shell from Anna and placing it on her arm near to where the flowers were still visible on her wrist.

'That's what I've been doing, isn't it?' She licked her finger and traced a clear line in the dried salt water on her skin, while seagulls flew above them living their best lives on ozone and stolen chips, laughing to each other across the sky. 'That's a bit crap too.' she repeated.

'Pretty much,' Jacob confirmed. 'And I bet you've been thinking about your old friends this whole trip, haven't you? Thinking about what they were doing instead of what you were doing?'

'I miss them,' she admitted.

'But I bet they never tried to teach you how to burp, hey? And I bet they can't juggle?' He placed his hand lightly on hers and she felt a jolt in her stomach. She braved curling her fingers around his and to her joyful astonishment he did the same. They lay like that for a while, sharing silent thoughts with their eyes, and previously hidden feelings with their smiles. Jacob glanced over at her grandfather, who was looking out at the horizon, then he planted a soft and salty kiss on her lips.

For Anna, it was a moment that threatened to burst out of her insides. It was a moment that tasted like the sea of a beautiful bay and smelt of ozone and coconut sun cream. It was a moment that sounded like calling gulls and lapping waves. It was a moment coloured by teals and yellows, and red and white billowing sails. It was a moment that, along with her grandfather and her great-grandfather before him, told her that St Mawes might have just become her favourite place in all the world, too.

'Come on,' Jacob said, pulling her reluctantly up from the beach by the hand that was still in his. 'I think he's given us long enough.' He handed Anna her dress and she slipped it on over her bikini. 'Butterflies are attracted to bright clothes like this aren't they?' He tugged at the orange polka-dot fabric of her dress where the halter-neck tie hung down her back. 'Perhaps a yellow butterfly will land on you and sprinkle you with the happiness dust from its wings.'

Anna stood on the sand and allowed herself one more minute to take everything in. 'Perhaps it already has,' she said.

ALGERNON

The hotel was really very smart, which went an awfully long way to help Algernon swallow the price of their rooms.

Coastal and rustic, it looked over the waters of St Mawes harbour affording a heart-stopping view of Percuil River yawning into the English Channel and around the headland towards St Anthony Head. All three of them sat at a table on the hotel balcony, each wearing a pair of the child's coloured sunglasses while they waited for their supper to arrive. 'Yellow for you, Grandad,' she insisted, handing him a cheap pair of sunglasses with round yellow lenses. 'Rose-coloured specs for you, Jacob, and blue for me of course.' She seemed very pleased when they agreed to put them on, and asked the waiter to take a photo of them together.

'Could you take that to the shop and get it developed when we get home, please? I'd like to have it as a proper photograph to keep.' Algernon studied the image on the screen of her smartphone while the child laughed a little as if he might have said something funny.

'I don't need to get it developed but I'll get it printed for you, Grandad,' she said, lifting her phone to her face and smiling at it as if she were taking her own photograph. Evie appeared then, glowing yellow through his glasses and she sat down amongst them all and patted his hand. 'You did well, my darling,' she said, and the remembered scent of her perfume filled his nose. As the image of Evie faded he could see through her to where a ferry was chugging its way back from St Anthony Head for the last time that day. 'Yes, I think I did,' he replied quietly.

'You think you did what, Grandad?' The child put her drink down and waited for him to clarify what he meant but he wasn't about to divulge the fact that he often spoke to someone who wasn't there. 'I said, I think I'm glad we came here for an extra night.' He sipped at a whisky, pledging to stick to just the one this time.

'Oh yes, it's lovely – it really is.' The child's cheeks shone with a summer glow that helped erase the hollows beneath them while the breeze played games with her hair, sending it into a pretty nut-brown whirl around her shoulders.

'There's so much more to see of course.' Evie had all but disappeared from beside him but for once he believed he was coping valiantly on his own. 'I would have liked to have shown you smugglers' coves and hidden beaches, the statue of King Arthur and...' he gave the merest hint of a laugh '...the treacle mines.'

'*Treacle* mines?' Anna and Jacob repeated, both at the same time.

'Look inside the smartphone if you want to know more. There might be an app.' Then he reached out and covered the child's phone with his hand. 'Or better still, come back and find out for yourselves.'

'Or we could stay another night?' The child looked so eager that he was quite taken aback. She hadn't looked so positive about anything since he'd met her and he felt quite bucked over her enthusiasm for his homeland. For the first time in his life, however, he really didn't have it in him to stay.

'Not at these blooming prices,' he sniffed, as a waiter arrived at their table bringing a supper of fresh Cornish catch of the day. What he really meant was that he needed his own bed, the comfortable place where he and Evie had slept for so many years, the firmness of his own mattress supporting his back before it gave up completely. He was so very tired and so very ready to go home. 'Home,' he muttered, aware of the fact that at long last he could think of his little schoolhouse in Essex as *home*.

ANNA

When her grandfather didn't appear at the table for breakfast, Anna and Jacob were confused. 'He's *always* at breakfast before us... even at home.' Anna looked around the tables and out towards the foyer of the hotel.

'Tea or coffee? Or we have a very nice selection of breakfast juices?' A waiter came to their table, smiling at them through green-rimmed glasses. He indicated at a colourful array of fruit and vegetables on a stand nearby.

'What's the green stuff?' Anna asked, frowning at carrots and beetroots and green things mixed in with apples, oranges, grapes and a whole host of other fruit.

'It's spinach... or there's also kale,' the waiter said. 'Very healthy. You can take a little basket and fill it with anything you like and we'll take the basket to the kitchen and make it into fresh juice.' Just as she spoke another waiter came past their table carrying a large glass full to the brim with something green.

'I'll stick to regular orange juice I think,' said Jacob, looking a little green himself at the idea of vegetables squeezed into sludge for breakfast.

'We're waiting for my grandad,' Anna said, looking around the dining area again. She picked up her phone and checked the time on it.

'You can help yourself to anything on the display while you wait,' the waiter smiled.

'Thank you, I will,' said Jacob, immediately standing to make his way over to the display of food, taking a plate from a pile of china on his way. He returned to the table with an obscene number of pastries and a glass of cold milk to find Anna fidgeting in her chair.

'Something's not right. He's always up early... *like always.*' Her insides were doing little flips and she didn't really know why. 'This is our last morning and I don't know about him but it's the best hotel I've ever stayed in so I can't believe he isn't here to enjoy it.' She looked around her to prove her point. Large seaside-related ornaments adorned nooks and crannies, colourful chairs and wicker baskets brightened up corners and bright pictures hung on the wall. The scent of ozone and salt filled the air and, until twenty minutes ago, she'd been loving every minute of it.

'Go and knock on his door then,' Jacob said, tucking into a large bite of apricot Danish while buttering a croissant at the same time. 'Leave me here, I'll be fine. I've never stayed anywhere like this before so I'm happy just eating my way through the whole display.' Anna did as he said but ten minutes later she was back at the table where Jacob was now sipping at a large glass of something pink. 'I tell you what... these baskets are great! I thought I'd give it a go so I filled it full of strawberries, apples and bananas and something else... can't remember, not *kale* obviously.' He pulled a face as if kale was something that could kill him and he held his glass towards her. 'And then I got this back! It's delicious!'

'He's not in his room. I knocked for ages, but he's not there. Do you think he's gone for a walk?' She sat back down at the table and felt a little sick over the amount of food Jacob had helped himself to. How anyone could eat so much and still be thin defeated her.

'Or he *is* in there but not coming to the door?' Jacob was about to take another gulp of his pink drink but caught her eye over the rim of it when he realised what he'd just said. He put the glass down where they both stared at each other for a moment before scooting their chairs back at the same time and rushing from the table. Slaloming around the other tables they ran past people and ornaments, colourful chairs and bright pictures, past shells and books and up the stairs two at a time.

'Mr M?' Jacob knocked on the door and Anna did the same.

'Grandad?' Her voice was getting louder and their knocking on the door was getting more urgent but still there was no sound from inside.

'Can I help you?' A member of staff with a trolley of clean towels came to a halt in the hallway.

'My grandfather's in there... at least I think he's in there. He's late for breakfast and we have to be out by eleven and he's never late and he wouldn't be late anyway... not while we're here in this lovely hotel and...' The member of staff gently held his hand in the air towards Anna encouraging her to stop her torrent to let him speak.

'I'll try phoning his room number and I'll go and find the manager. Wait here, don't worry.' He disappeared around the corner and Anna could hear him running down the stairs so fast it was as if he believed that there might indeed be a need to worry. Two minutes later they heard a phone ring inside her grandfather's room. As it continued to ring, Anna started to feel really sick and despite what the member of staff said, she *was* worrying. She was worrying a lot.

'Something's happened – I know it has.' She pressed the flats of her hands and her forehead against his room door and felt her anxiety igniting in the pit of her stomach and growing rapidly until it became white-hot panic inside her. 'What are we going to do if he's not well... or even if he's...?' She stared into Jacob's concerned face and for once he had nothing to say. After an agonising wait, the member of staff reappeared with the manager, who held a key in her hand and asked a series of time-wasting security questions before she finally conceded to open the door. They all simultaneously poked their heads inside.

He was there, lying on the bed, face to the ceiling, completely still. Anna felt panic rush so fast through her body that she thought she might throw it all up onto the carpet. 'Shit!' Jacob hissed, as he stepped aside to let Anna past.

'Shit!' Anna repeated, as she passed Jacob.

'Shit!' the member of staff said, as the manager walked past him and into the room.

Her grandfather was so thin. So much smaller than she thought, almost lost in the striped counterpane of the huge hotel bed. His hair, in white wispy spikes, blended into the stark white of his pillow but the tufts that grew from his ears and his nose seemed more obvious now. His mouth, partially open, was all crinkled around the edges where his teeth should be. The room, painted in coastal blues and creams, smelt of clean laundry and old skin.

Anna rushed over to him while the manager sent the member of staff to call for an ambulance and Jacob hovered uselessly on the periphery, hopping about and unable to keep still.

'Grandad?' Anna put her hands on his shoulder, feeling the bones of him beneath her touch. Her face was wet from crying. Silver stubble was pushing through the grey skin on his face, sinking into the hollows of his cheeks, and Anna's words were lost as she sunk to her knees and leant towards him. 'Grandad,' she sobbed. 'You didn't say goodbye.'

ALGERNON

When Algernon woke to find several people in his room and the child's face looming over his, he nearly jumped out of his skin. 'Good Lord!' he grumbled, trying to sit up. His back, however, wouldn't allow him to move in a hurry and his mouth hadn't woken up yet so instead he flailed hopelessly under his duvet until he could free his arms. The child screamed and landed on her bottom at the side of his bed and he couldn't for the life of him think what she was doing in his room.

'We were worried about you.' The child looked up at him from where she was still sitting on the floor but, although he could see her mouth moving, he couldn't catch much of what she was saying.

'What?' He cupped his hand over his ear, curling it towards her, but then Jacob came forward and scooped his hearing aids off the dressing table and handed them over.

'That's why he couldn't hear us banging his door or hear the phone ringing,' he said, as Algernon put the first hearing aid in.

'What's that about a phone ringing? I didn't hear a phone!' Algernon popped the second hearing aid into place.

'I was saying, that's why you didn't hear the staff ringing the phone by your bed, Mr M... because you didn't have your hearing aids in.'

'It's Mr Maybury,' Algernon corrected, levering himself up against his pillows and slipping his glasses on, putting the room back into focus. In addition to the youngsters he realised there was also a strange woman standing at the bottom of his bed. 'Madam!' he announced. 'I am not a spectator sport!' As he spoke he saw another chap at his open door and began to feel rather riled. 'What are you all doing in here for heaven's sake?' he complained. 'Can't a man have a lie-in once in a while without waking to the Band of the Coldstream Guards?'

'I'll leave you to it, then.' The woman hurriedly pushed the chap at the door aside to let her pass. 'False alarm,' she said briskly, before she quietly shut the door behind them.

'I... *we*... thought you were... you know?' The child looked as if she'd been crying but he couldn't for the life of him think what had gone on to cause such a stir.

'We thought you were deceased,' Jacob said helpfully.

'Well, I'm not... as far as I can tell.' He lisped the words out through his toothless gums then patted his knees under his duvet pretending to check that he was still there.

'You didn't come down for breakfast so we got worried...' The child barely got to the end of her sentence when Algernon checked the time on his watch and whipped back his bed covers.

'Get out of my room,' he ordered, sliding his legs over the side of the bed causing his pyjama trousers to ride up most uncomfortably. Ignoring all his aches and pains that were always worse in the morning, he staggered across the floor to the bathroom. 'Out!' he ordered again, as the youngsters scurried to leave his room. 'Let me get dressed, it's my last chance for a full Cornish and I'm bloody well not going to miss it.'

16

A Different Kind of Summer

ANNA

It was a different kind of summer. The days slipped by, long and leisurely and often devoid of anything much to do. Anna's mother went off to the nature reserve most days, increasing her hours with any overtime offered, returning home in the evening, often to something Anna had cooked. Her grandfather seemed delighted that his granddaughter had discovered a talent she never knew she had, making him meals that were plain and simple, just how he liked them. Lunch was often spent in the garden, eating sandwiches or soup as they sat on the bench with Cat at their feet, all three of them watching bumblebees and butterflies going about their day.

Anna and her grandfather didn't converse a lot. He did his crossword or read a book while she quietly drew or painted pictures. Occasionally they downed tools when he thought of something to tell her and more than occasionally he thought of something he'd already told her. Anna never let on. She enjoyed their time together and was getting used to the moments when the cantankerous side of him slipped out.

When he bruised her with his clumsiness she did her best to remember that it was about him and not about her. Anna was just content having a grandfather in her life.

Since the trip to Cornwall, life at the little schoolhouse had become much more harmonious. Upon their return they had all hugged each other. The kind of hug that lets you know without a doubt that you are well and truly loved. Jacob fell straight into a summer job at a sports shop and Helene continued to thrive in her outdoors job. Anna noticed how, even though her mother's fingernails were often caked in mud when she came home, she never took Evie's engagement ring off her finger. She understood, now, how important it was that Helene could carry a special part of her own mother with her everywhere she went.

Firefly's reins were now in Little Argel, being supervised by Gary, and her grandfather never mentioned them again. She still didn't know what she was going to do with them but for now they were still tucked in the old, less-beetle-ridden box, quietly reminding her that life and how she tackled it was her choice.

When Jacob clattered his way onto the roof of Little Argel bringing a half-eaten packet of biscuits and a carton of grapes, Anna felt her stomach flip at the sound of it. She was wearing her brown and white cow-print shorts with a yellow crop top and was reading a book on how to draw portraits. She'd also spent ages curling her hair until it whirled around her head in spirals, pushed away from her face with a band of blue ribbon. She hoped she looked nice. 'School starts next week,' he announced, as he dropped down onto her bed.

Anna moved over so that he could get comfortable but felt her stomach tightening into a knot at the thought of school.

'One more week and I'll be grey again.' She gloomily picked out a single grape from the bunch Jacob was already tucking into but, as she spoke, he stopped eating and went quiet. After an uncomfortably long time appraising her he suddenly jumped down from the bed and opened the cupboard doors underneath.

'Get in,' he ordered, in a mock stern voice. 'Get inside and I'll shut the doors behind you.' Anna pulled a face but Jacob simply pointed inside the cupboard. 'Bear with me,' he insisted.

'But I've got all my clothes in there,' Anna complained, thinking that he'd gone completely mad.

'Then take them out before you get inside,' he insisted again. '*Trust* me.'

Dubiously, Anna climbed over the frame of her bed and opening the cupboard doors she pulled all her clothes out onto the floor before climbing inside and letting him shut the door behind her. From the pitch-dark she could hear the wrapper of the biscuit packet crackling just before she heard the sound of crunching as he ate one. 'I'm trusting you here, Jacob... this had better be good,' she called.

'Are you still Anna?' he asked, his voice muffled not just by the biscuits, but by the cupboard and the mattress above her head.

'You *know* I'm still Anna,' she replied, her eyes adjusting to the darkness as she picked out slivers of light coming through the edges of the cupboard doors.

'But how do *I* know you're still Anna?' he asked. 'I can't see you can I?'

'Because you've just witnessed me get in the bloody cupboard!' she replied.

'True, but I can't see you now and yet I still happen to know that I like you. That you're funny... and kind... and have an amazing talent for art. And I know all these things about you regardless of whether you're wearing an orange polka-dot dress or a bright green onesie, regardless of whether you're shut in a cupboard in a garden shed... or wearing a grey uniform.' He waited a moment for his words to sink in. 'It's still you on the inside, isn't it?'

Jacob then opened the doors and climbed inside the cupboard with her as she tried to unravel the meaning behind what he was clumsily trying to tell her. He reached for her hand then and held it, waiting patiently until she finally spoke. She told him how she'd felt leaving home at Harry's, leaving all her friends and her security; how difficult it had been to show her true personality in the new school. She told him how amazing it was that her grandfather had taken her halfway across the country to save her and how much better everything was now... yet she was still petrified of going back to school.

When she finished, a quiet lull settled over Little Argel and as it drew out into a long silence, she immediately began to worry that she'd shared too much. She opened her mouth to apologise for her own failings when Jacob drew in a deep breath.

'My dad was ill,' he announced, squeezing her warm hand in his. 'He died when I was twelve.' Anna felt her whole body freeze. Jacob had never mentioned his dad. She'd just assumed he wasn't on the scene like her own father and now she felt completely awful, blinkered and self-centred. He was always so carefree, so funny and so *there for her* and yet all the time he'd been keeping this... this *huge* thing to himself.

'I'm so sorry Jacob,' she apologised lamely. 'Here I am bleating on about myself and I... well I always thought you never had a care in the world... like you'd got your shit together, and yet all this time...'

'I suppose I have got my shit together. He was my hero, and when you watch your hero being defeated by the one thing that is bigger than he is, I suppose you grow up pretty fast. But the last thing he said before he went was "Guys! Death? It's simply what happens when you've finished living. Live your best life and it will all be worth it." He was a great guy. For his sake, I don't ever want to stop living my best life.'

Silence fell heavily on the air, and Anna's respect for him grew until it filled her right up to the brim. This boy who had entered her life through the skylight of her shed and had brought her so much happiness, had been hiding a broken heart all along. She leant her cheek against his shoulder with tears in her eyes. 'I want you to feel the same way about life as I do,' he whispered.

'Your dad sounds awesome,' she croaked.

'Yes, he was,' Jacob said simply. They sat quietly like that for a good while, holding hands in the cupboard under her bed, until he suddenly moved, making her jump. He delved into his pocket and handed her a cinema leaflet that had been folded into four and was quite crumpled. 'So, it's your birthday soon and I thought I'd treat you to the cinema. If you'd like that of course?' He handed her the leaflet and she unfolded it, noticing a slight blush to his cheeks. She wondered why they didn't just look on their phones to see what they'd like to watch when she saw that a page torn from an exercise book was taped to the inside. On it there was handwriting – black ink and sketchy, high dots over the i's:

Anna Maybury,
I hereby invite you to the cinema on the eve of your sixteenth birthday. Onesies are obligatory. Please apologise to Gary that there is no ticket for him as this is my way of asking you on a date.
Yours in all seriousness (sort of)
Jacob, Number 5

'Thank you.' She breathed her gratitude, going purple with pleasure. She didn't quite know what to say after everything that had already been said, but already Jacob was scooting his long body out from under the cupboard and pulling her onto her feet.

'It's pumpkin time,' he said, showing her on his phone that it was 5.30pm and time for her to make supper. He hauled himself up through the skylight, and then stopped to look down at her from above. Tapping his hand against his heart, he called down, 'Anna Maybury. It's called life! You have a talent and you have something to give.' Then he left, leaving her with her beating heart, her clothes on the floor, crumbs, a biscuit wrapper, and a lot to think about.

It was a warm but cloudy Sunday afternoon and Helene was inside ironing a pile of laundry, when Anna appeared out of Little Argel carrying her pens. Her grandfather was sitting on his garden bench watching birds swoop down onto his bird table, having just sprinkled leftover cake and a handful of peanuts for them, while Cat feigned interest in a daring wren that hopped too close.

'Um… Grandad?' she began, her voice hesitantly sing-songy even to her own ears. He looked up at her from under one eyebrow and waited for her to spit it out. After a few more seconds of expectant silence, she said, 'Can I draw on your feet?'

ALGERNON

Algernon had been quite content to sit in the garden on his newly varnished garden bench admiring how well the plants were coming along after being neglected for so long. Faced with the uncustomary question as to whether he would let the child decorate his feet had, however, thrown him into a bit of a fidget. 'It's not something I've ever been asked before,' he said, keeping his feet, which were perfectly comfortable inside his socks and shoes, planted firmly on the ground. It wasn't an idea that thrilled him, if he was honest with himself, but the child looked so young and so hopeful that he heard himself answering, 'Perhaps just the one foot.'

Life for Algernon had taken an upturn. Having his daughter and his granddaughter in his life meant that, for the first time since Evie had left, he had something to get up for in the mornings. The fact that Helene wore Evie's engagement ring without ever taking it off told him he had most definitely done the right thing by giving it to her. The little jar containing sprigs of wild tansy and cornflower on his bedside table, accompanied by a bar of his favourite chocolate and a handwritten label saying, *Thank You, Dad x*, when he arrived home from Cornwall, meant everything that words couldn't say. A delicate kind of peace had settled in the little schoolhouse, a waving of the white flag between him and Helene, and although he wouldn't say that life was always a walk in the park, or that he didn't seek his own company once in a while, in general things were going rather well.

With his agreement, the child knelt on the ground and waited for him to disrobe his foot, which he did with a degree of difficulty, as always. When, at last, his shoe was removed and his sock was peeled off, the child let out an audible gasp. 'Grandad, what happened to your toes?' Algernon looked down and saw that the end of his foot was, indeed, a bit of a mess. Blood had stained the skin around his toenails and he remembered with embarrassment that he'd tried to cut his own toenails only that morning and made a right old hash of it. He could hardly see his toes, let alone reach them anymore. He shrugged his neck into his shoulders and harrumphed loudly, wishing that the child hadn't asked him to partake in such a ridiculous activity.

'But I could have helped you, Grandad... or Mum would have done.' The child looked horrified and it only served to make him feel worse.

'Mum?' She was hollering for her mother now and that wouldn't do either. He wanted her to stop drawing attention to his failings. He wanted to put his sock and shoe back on and go back to watching the garden birds. 'Wait there,' the child said, springing up from the ground and disappearing into the house. She returned, to his dismay, with Helene, some cleansing wipes and a packet of plasters.

'What have you been up to, Dad?' Helene asked, kneeling on the ground by his feet and beginning to wipe them clean.

'You've missed the nail on half of these and clipped your skin instead.' Algernon was aware of that fact... *now*... and it only made his feeling of incompetence worse.

He didn't say thank you to Helene for helping him, or for her being so gentle. He didn't say anything while she wrapped a sticking plaster around two of his toes and tidied everything away to go and finish the ironing before putting the dinner on. He couldn't find the words to say how pleased he was that his daughter and his granddaughter were back in his life... but he thought they knew regardless.

ANNA

When the plasters were on and her grandfather was comfortable, Anna picked up her pens, ready to begin. 'You agreed,' she reminded him, as he fumbled crossly to get his sock back on. She moved his sock and shoe just out of his reach until he admitted grumbling defeat and read a book while she busied herself with her pens.

Kneeling by her grandfather's feet, drawing careful curves and tiny circles on his skin, she felt a thrill go through her at how good her drawing was beginning to look. If she kept her eyes away from either his plasters or the hair coming out of the knuckle of his big toe, she could almost believe what she'd painted was real. *Thank you, Grandad and Jacob from number five, I'm going to get my shit together from now on,* she said to herself. *I have a talent. I am Anna Maybury, and I have something to give.*

'Nearly finished, Grandad,' she said eventually, tucking a lock of still-curly hair behind her ear and putting the final touches of yellow and burnt umber hues on her drawing. 'There! I'm going to take a photo of it and send it to my friends. See?' She laughed and the sound of it tinkled in the air. 'My friends get to see a picture of your feet after all!'

Her grandfather looked down at his foot and screwed up his eyes in order to get a clearer focus. Gradually, with pleasant surprise, his eyebrows rose upwards into the furrows on his brow and she sat back on her heels, both of them surveying the perfectly beautiful wings she'd created.

'Oh,' he remarked, 'what sort is that then?'

'It's just a yellow butterfly, Grandad, but the colour yellow means happiness.' She breathed out a long and contented sigh and smiling, looked up at him. 'I call it the happiness butterfly.'

ALGERNON

A late evening sun cast an orange glow through the window of Algernon's sitting room, lighting a strip of gold on the chair opposite. Wasps and flies, drowsy with the end of summer, buzzed in and out of the kitchen and Helene had been busy batting at them with a swat before coming into the room with two cold drinks for them both. 'Bloody flies,' she moaned as she sat on the chair opposite, her hair and her skin lighting up within the golden strip. The ruby ring on her finger sparkled in the glare, reminding him that all this time Helene had needed Evie just as much as he had. How happy Evie would be with them both if she were here now.

With that in mind, he decided it wasn't fair on Helene for him to feel that she were squishing the place where Evie had sat by his side all these years and knew that it was time to buy a fourth armchair. He'd seen a recliner that he was sure Helene would like, cosy and comfortable, perfect after a long day in the great outdoors. He'd buy it as a present for her... a surprise.

'I've found a flat, Dad,' she said, as she handed him his drink and, as he took it, his world seemed to tumble around him. Crestfallen, he picked up his leather notebook and crossed *buy new recliner* off his list of things to do. 'It's not too far away and Anna will still go to the same school of course – she'd never forgive me if she was too far from Jacob. It's small but it has two bedrooms and we can at last get all our things out of your dining room. I've put down the deposit on the rental agreement and everything.' She was beaming. Full of accomplishment and pride and desperately seeking his approval. 'I've done it, Dad. I've finally grown up and got a proper job. Better late than never, but I've done it.'

'You have, haven't you?' He sipped at his drink, having replied with what he knew was an insufficient remark for something so hard-earned. He'd known it was coming of course, that the family he'd chased away all those years ago should want to leave again. *But were they really leaving so soon?* He wished he could tell her he was pleased for her and that he'd always known she was made of great stuff. Instead, he raised his glass to her in a gesture akin to a toast and, desperate to know how much precious time he had left with his daughter and his granddaughter, gave a rueful smile. 'Congratulations, when do you move out?'

Helene looked wounded, tutting her tongue on the roof of her mouth as she got up from Evie's chair. 'You asked me that last time. You're obviously keen. The answer is... as soon as

I can. The current tenants are buying a house and hope to exchange by the end of the month. Relax,' she said, as she made to leave the room, 'we'll be gone before you know it.'

'I didn't mean it like that,' he choked, placing his glass on the table beside him as Helene halted in the doorway. He put his head in his hands and cursed himself for being such a fool. For pushing her away all those years ago and now seemingly pushing her away once more.

'Then how did you mean it, Dad?' He looked up to see her shoot him an accusatory glare, her chin tilted with years of hurt. She was the daughter who'd climbed on his lap when she was still in pigtails. The girl who had grown from toddler to adult before him. The girl he'd judged too harshly on so many occasions. The girl he'd blasted out of his house for his stupid old-fashioned views.

'I meant... you don't have to leave. This is your home. You could stay.' The golden light slipped slowly off the chair and onto the carpet as the sinking sun squeezed its last drops over the rooftops outside. 'I *want* you to stay.' There! It was out at last, his feelings, buzzing in the air like the annoying wasps and flies in the kitchen and neither of them quite knew what to do next. They stared at each other, chins tilted, their lips quivering, both standing on the same rickety bridge that spanned the gulf between them. His heart bumped hard behind his sternum as he watched how a look of such sadness grew upon her face.

'Is it me you want to stay, or Anna?' she asked quietly.

The skin of Helene's knuckles bloomed white as her fingers grasped so tightly around her glass he thought she may be in danger of cracking it. He was taken aback by her question. As floored as if she had pushed him to the ground. He recalled how Helene had once said, *If you knew her you would love her.* He had of course, come to know the child. To delight in her colourful ways. To know that his life was enriched by her in a way he never thought possible. Helene was part of himself... part of Evie. The child was part of all of them. He cleared his throat and coughed, blowing his nose on his big white hanky, his emotion catching all that he wanted to say and holding it back in his throat. He was full to the brim with light and colour and family and it was all thanks to his wonderful daughter coming back into his life and bringing her magical child. Where once there had been shadows and bitterness his concrete heart was, at last, healing. It was all he could do to croakily repeat, 'Stay.'

Helene, still hovering in the doorway, allowed a splash of tears to spring from her turquoise eyes and she wiped them away. 'It... it's too late, Dad,' she said softly. 'It's too late in the day to change things. We need our own space, and I'm sure you do too.'

'As you wish.' Algernon pushed his hanky back into his trouser pocket, nodded courteously then picked up his newspaper and pretended to read it until she left. *I know now that it's never too late in the day,* he thought, but in his Algernon way, the words never came.

ANNA

The first few days of year eleven, as it turned out, were the best days that Anna had experienced since arriving at the new school.

Like one of the stepping stones leading to Little Argel,

the art studio at school manifested itself as a patch of solid ground. A miraculous bolthole through which she could escape between lessons when her anxiety became too much. As study was becoming more intense for the GCSEs she'd been told by her teacher that, as her art was outstanding, she – along with some others – were allowed to spend their lunch breaks working on their art pieces. The atmosphere in the art studio was a wonderful combination of peace and industry and became the one place in the whole school day where her anxiety lay dormant. She'd been experimenting with mixed media, spending hours making bold charcoal marks, carefully blended shapes and sweeps of acrylic paint. The result was a large charcoal portrait of an African lady wearing a glorious multicoloured head wrap in teal and gold acrylic and it was very nearly finished.

'It's really very good,' her teacher said, 'you've captured her wonderful bone structure perfectly and that head wrap is so realistic.' Miss Angelico had an easy way about her, as if she could glide through life casting petals of positivity everywhere she went – and for Anna, her approval was everything.

'It's amazing,' breathed the girl who worked next to her, leaning in to get a better look. 'You can see the sheen of the silk and everything.' Three girls who all sat together working on pottery sculptures then left their seats and came over to see what was so amazing.

'That really is good,' they agreed in unison. Yet as they crowded round her, Anna could feel her anxiety stir, swelling inside her, making her breath come in short puffs and the palms of her hands tingle with sweat. This was her safe place and they were invading it. She put down her paintbrush and wiped her damp hands on her skirt, unsure how to react but as they returned to their seats her new mantra filled her head. *I'm Anna Maybury, I have a talent and I have something to give.*

As loud as she could manage, she uttered her 'thank you'. Had they heard her? Did they know she was trying to show genuine appreciation of their praise rather than be the girl who was unapproachable? Then, and she wasn't sure how she came about doing it, she scooted her chair back and forced herself to move. She would return the favour. She would go and look at the work the others were doing. 'I like yours as well,' she said, where the three girls were working on their pottery, 'And yours,' she said to the boys.

She felt her heart pound with her bravery as she made her way back to her chair, passing the first girl who'd said that her work was amazing. Propped on an easel was a delicate painting of a tree, the branches of which formed a mystical face. The girl's style was unusual but it was lovely, almost illustrative. 'I really like yours. It's different and I like different,' she said, aware that she had said more words in one lunchtime than she had said in all the time she'd been at that school. Picking up her brush and dipping it once more into the glossy teal-coloured paint, she waited for her nausea to go away.

The girl paused in her work, her pen hovering over delicate inky leaves that dropped from her mystical tree. 'And I liked your blue hair,' she said. 'I thought it was awesome.'

On the eve of her sixteenth birthday, Jacob rocked up to her grandad's front door wearing a tuxedo onesie. 'I didn't think you were serious about the onesie.' She giggled.

'I'm absolutely serious,' he replied, stepping into the house and ushering her back towards Little Argel to put on her own onesie. When she emerged, fully clad in green and yellow, they stood side by side in the sitting room with her mother laughing hysterically and her grandfather's jaw dropping so low she thought he was in danger of losing his teeth.

On her actual birthday, Jacob bought her a funny little cuddly bear that looked like a bean. She called it Bean. He then joined her, her mother and her grandfather for delivery pizza. To say she was thrilled that the evening of her sixteenth birthday was spent doing something so simple was an understatement. Her heart was full. She and Jacob squashed together on her armchair, while the four of them all watched a film together, ate pizza and drank Coke. As she watched her grandfather lift a slice of pizza from its box, the cheese making long yellow strings that dangled off his chin and caught in his moustache, her full heart burst with joy. *This is my family,* she thought.

'These are from both of us – me and your grandfather,' Helene declared, as Anna unwrapped bright paper from a big box at the end of the evening. Inside she found a pair of DMs, black but decorated in a vibrant splash paint design. She took them out and hugged them tight. 'They're perfect,' she gushed, putting them on there and then and parading round the sitting room for everyone to see.

'They're clown boots,' her grandfather moaned, yet when she caught his eye, he was smiling.

The other box was an artist's set. A beautiful wooden case with paints, brushes, charcoals, pastels and pencils of all colours that must have cost them a fortune. *I'm Anna Maybury, I have a talent and I have something to give.* She repeated her mantra silently in her head that evening and again every time she saw the beautiful artist's box where she had placed it on the shelf in Little Argel. She may have to wear a grey uniform on the outside but her toenails were painted blue and on the inside she was still a riot of colour. She had a talent for art and she, Anna Maybury, was now determined to let that shine.

17

Touching the Moon

ANNA

Anna lay in bed, staring through the skylight into a starry night for hours. Her mother had found a flat and they were going to have to move into it in just a few weeks' time. It didn't, however, have a skylight in the ceiling of her bedroom, or have Jacob next door climbing down through it bringing sweets or treats with him. It didn't hold the scent of wood and varnish in its walls or have lavender and white roses just outside the door. It didn't have a wonky bed for her to sleep in or stepping stones that meandered their way to a grandfather she'd come to love.

So it was very late when she finally got out of bed, the security light blazing over the garden as she padded across the damp grass in her bare feet. Letting herself into the house, her heart was beating with trepidation and marvellous daring in equal thumps. The house was in silence, other than the ticking of her grandfather's clock on the mantelpiece as she tiptoed across the floor using the torch of her phone to light the way. Everything about the place was pleasantly familiar now, the three armchairs, the huge sash window, the quirky features of the old school, even the fusty smell. The fourth stair as she made her way upstairs creaked, causing her to stop in her tracks and hold her breath while Cat, who'd followed her inside from Little Argel, rubbed his sides in a figure-of-eight around the newel post.

'Grandad?' Anna tapped her grandfather's arm, trying not to look into the hollow of his gaping mouth as he slept. Long, drawn-out snores came down his nose and a loud snort suddenly caught him in the back of the throat, breaking the rhythm of his breathing. Next to his bed was the photo frame she'd given him weeks ago, the blue ribbon tied into a perfect bow around the edge of it. Next to that was the photo of him with her and Jacob in St Mawes, all three of them wearing her coloured sunglasses and posing for the camera. Beside that was another photo of her grandfather standing next to her grandma and, on the shelf above his bed, eight photo frames containing various pictures of her mother sat proudly side by side.

Anna shone the torch of her phone at them, thinking how beautiful her mother had been when she was young. Still beautiful, Anna supposed. For someone who apparently didn't have much of a relationship with his daughter though, his photograph collection was telling a very different story.

'Grandad?' Anna repeated, whispering loudly so as not to wake her mother in the room next door. She tapped his arm repeatedly but apart from smacking his lips together before they fell open again he didn't wake. Her torch lit up his hearing aids, which were on his chest of drawers, making her realise that he couldn't hear her and it was only when she shone the torch of her phone directly in his face that he

EVERY SHADE OF HAPPY

opened his eyes, mumbled something incoherent and then jumped out of his skin.

'Bloody hell, what's going on?' he exclaimed, as he pulled an arm out of the covers to shield his eyes. Anna lit up her own face with her torch and shushed him with a finger pressed to her lips, then handed him his hearing aids and waited for him to gather himself.

'It's only me, Grandad. There's something we've got to do,' she whispered.

ALGERNON

He could see that her lips were moving thanks to the light from her torch but he couldn't hear a thing. The child put his hearing aids into his hand and he fumbled to put them on, trying to gather his senses and shake groggy sleep from his head. Next, she handed him his glasses so that he could see properly. His heart was complaining with the effort of waking up and he was imagining fire and flood at the very least.

'It's only me, Grandad. There's something we've got to do.' She tugged at the arm of his maroon cotton pyjamas then reached behind the door for his old brocade dressing gown, urging him to get out of bed.

It took her a goodly while to get him down the stairs, having helped him into his dressing gown and wrestled his feet into his slippers but she pulled a bit of a face when he sent her back upstairs to get his teeth. What with his ears, his eyes and his teeth, she didn't realise that he virtually had to rebuild his whole head before he could get going. Then, when she reappeared bringing them still in the glass, he had to sit on his armchair for a moment to reclaim his wits. Embarking on a midnight adventure at his age was proving to be a challenging thing.

'What are you up to?' he asked again as she steered him through the kitchen but the child only pressed her finger to her lips and shushed him.

Standing side by side in Little Argel, having negotiated the stepping stones under the blinding glare of the security light, she patted her bed as if she might expect him to climb into it. 'We're going sailing, Grandad,' she said, turning off the main light to Little Argel and leaving only a string of fairy lights above them.

'Sailing!' he cried, unable to quite believe what he was hearing.

'Sailing,' she confirmed, with a huge smile across her face.

Algernon looked with stupefaction between his granddaughter and the bed that she expected him to climb onto and his jaw hung open. He wondered if she was mad for suggesting such a thing or whether he was mad for getting up in the middle of the night in the first place. 'I'm a thousand years old, child. I'm never going to get up there let alone negotiate the frame.' He assessed the height of the cupboards that held *River Pisky* and although it was only waist height, without a stepladder, for him, it might as well have been Mount Everest. His hips no longer fully rotated and he'd left his stick inside, so a dandy pole-vaulting manoeuvre was out of the question.

The child, however, moved her cactus and several, thankfully, unlit candles from a little stool she was using as a table, then she slid it over the floor towards the bed.

'You have to,' she insisted. 'It's a full moon... it's in exactly the right place to view through the skylight. And hardly any clouds... it's perfect.'

Algernon stared at the stool and then at the bed, craning his neck back as far as it would go. Above them the moon, completely round in a clear sky, hung directly over Little Argel and shone a bright pool of light onto the child's duvet. He considered the task ahead for a little longer while steadying himself against the wall of Little Argel.

'You can *do* it, Grandad,' the child urged. 'If you once climbed up onto the roof of your village school then I *know* you can do this!' Remembering that once upon a time he used to be the most adventurous of boys, Algernon inched his way towards the bed and began to climb.

ANNA

It wasn't easy getting her grandfather over the wonky frame of her bed, and getting him settled into a reasonably comfortable position, when his arthritis prevented him from bending... but she did it. He made a lot of huffing and puffing noises and she was pretty sure he blew off but coughed at the same time to cover the sound of it. Bodily failings aside though, he made it... and in one piece.

The moon was perfectly round and beautifully silver, queen over a star-speckled sky and Anna sighed with delight. 'Imagine, Grandad, that water is all around us and that we've tied *River Pisky* to a green buoy that's bobbing about on little waves.' She pointed towards Gary who, being green and round, made for a perfect mooring.

'Cats don't like water,' her grandfather said, as Cat, who'd jumped up to join them, tried to get in on the action. Anna gently nudged Cat to the side and put her large mirror on the bed where hers and her grandfather's legs met in the middle. She angled it so that it perfectly reflected the moon before reaching for a pot of her special silver glitter make-up, which she then sprinkled onto their hands. The glitter shone as if light from the moon was reflecting in water on their skin and the effect, complete with the fairy lights above was perfect.

'Dip your fingers in the water, Grandad,' she said, touching the mirror with her own fingertips and leaving a trail of glitter in their wake. 'See how the light from the moon is glistening on our wet hands? It's as if we are actually touching it.'

He watched her carefully as if trying to remember what it was like to pretend, then he ran his hand thoughtfully over his white moustache and issuing a glittery chuckle he placed his own fingertips on the mirror.

ALGERNON

'You've had an amazing life, Grandad,' the child said, as she continued to trail her fingers through the pretend water of her mirror.

'That was a long time ago, I'm just a crusty old fool now,' he replied. He was still trailing his silvery fingers into the pretend water alongside hers, feeling so enthralled by this madcap idea of his granddaughter's that he was struggling to hold tight to his self-control.

'You're old but I don't think you're crusty... not now I don't. How many other people's grandads would get up in the middle of the night to do this?' She giggled, and her young laughter filled his heart. She was right, it really was rather wonderful that fast approaching a telegram from the Queen he should, once again, be going on such a midnight adventure as this. His shoulders shuddered with the joy of it and he tipped his head back and laughed with her until the pain in his whole upper torso forced him to stop. This child, as imaginative and magical as ever a child could be, was his very own granddaughter and the knowledge of that filled his heart to the brim.

She tucked a lock of hair behind her ears leaving a spray of glitter behind then she smiled at him, a wide and beautiful smile that lit up her entire face and tilted the tip of her nose. 'You're very like your grandma,' he began.

'I thought you said I was like you?' she replied.

'I meant you were in danger of living your life in the past like I have, of letting life's hurdles block your way. What I mean is that you have a way about you that is very like your grandma. You shine... and so did she.'

'Tell me about her, Grandad,' the child asked, the light of the moon shining blue upon her cheeks and he so wished that Evie was here to meet her granddaughter in person.

'She would have loved you. She was kind, funny, impulsive and caring... and she passed all those qualities on to Helene. So if you want to know what your grandma was like, look at your mum and you'll find her.'

'Really?' the child asked.

'Really,' he confirmed. 'They both made everything seem so easy, motherhood, life, *living*.' Algernon privately winced at how he himself had got these things so wrong, so upside down and inside out. 'I found it so difficult when Helene first told your grandma and I that she was pregnant with you,' he confessed.

'I know,' the child said quietly.

'I don't think either of us handled it well,' he said, thinking that in truth he'd been an old-fashioned fool over the whole thing.

'It was a long time ago,' she said kindly.

'I wish I could turn the clock back.' He reached a hand out and gently touched the child's sparkling hand. 'You've made an old fool very happy.' She curled her hand round until it rested in his and gave him her biggest smile.

'Look forward not back Grandad. That's what you told me in Cornwall isn't it? What was that word... *carpe* something?'

'*Carpe diem.* Seize the day. Ha! You're right. Here we are on an adventure and I'm spoiling it.' He gave a sharp laugh. 'So, where were we?'

'We're floating in a river with the silver moon at our fingertips,' Anna reminded him.

'Of course,' he said. 'So, what can we hear?' He let go of her hand, cupping his ear and pretending to listen in to the night.

The child cocked her head, happy that he was playing her game. 'We can hear the water against the hull?' she suggested.

'We can indeed. I used to think of it as river music. The gentle lap of the water on the hull... slap... slap... slap and the tinkle of halyards from the moored boats nearby, rattling against masts in the breeze. And listen!' The child cupped her own hand to her ear. 'We can hear the calling of seagulls at night. Can you hear it? Screeching, cackling and calling. A whole vocabulary of bird call!'

'At night? Don't they sleep?' she asked.

'Not always. There are different theories as to why seagulls call at night but one of the theories is that when young chicks are learning to fly the adults call out to them.'

'Like they're calling them back?' she said.

'No, I think it's because they're encouraging them to fly,' he said.

'I like that.' The child rested her head against her pillow and yawned so deeply that he caught it from her and yawned too. Then, in sleepy silence, they shut their eyes and listened to the music of the river and the wisdom of seagulls, until, together, with Cat, they slept, by the light of a full moon, in what was once a boat and was now a bed, moored to a cactus.

ANNA

The next morning at breakfast Helene put down her half-eaten toast, finished her mouthful and said, 'So, come on, why are you both glittering? It's everywhere!' She was wearing a befuddled expression but her grandfather gave nothing away, apart from the glitter that still clung to his moustache and one of his ears. He simply scooped porridge into his mouth, his tongue poking out to lick off a stray lump.

'I have no idea what you're talking about,' he said vacantly, scooping another spoonful into his mouth. Anna's joy over their magical adventure slid all the way down to her bare feet and through the floor. Could he really not remember how she'd got him up in the middle of the night and heaved him over the frame of her bed, how they had floated in the river and touched the moon? How she had to manoeuvre him back over the frame when he was half asleep and get him into the house and back up his stairs. How she'd had to wait for him to use the bathroom because he was so unsteady on his feet, tinkling into the pan for what seemed like an age. How when she made sure he was tucked up in bed he'd forgotten to take his teeth out and how she'd cringed when he'd taken them out and given them to her to put in the bathroom. How when she dropped them on the floor they'd both giggled relentlessly afterwards.

'There's even glitter on Cat,' Helene said, bemused, as Cat sashayed into the dining room and flopped on the floor, stretching his limbs out on the carpet.

'What glitter?' her grandfather said, bending to look at Cat and frowning even deeper grooves into his forehead than he already had. Anna's heart was doing flips inside her chest as she ached with the knowledge that their adventure had been all for nothing. 'So there is!' her grandfather declared, having finished his investigation of Cat. Then he picked up his cup of coffee and shakily raised it to his lips. Looking at Anna over the rim he then winked a turquoise wink, sparkling with the glint of a Cornish sea under a summer sun.

ALGERNON

When Evie sat down in the chair opposite, she seemed so real, so physical, that Algernon struggled not to get up from his own chair and go over to her. 'I always think you're in my head,' he said out loud, 'because you're there one minute and then you're gone again. I hate it when you do that.' Evie simply smiled at him in the way that Evie always smiled at him.

'But I'm here now,' she said.

'That you are,' he said. He reached across to swap his distance glasses for his reading glasses and to get his little leather notebook. He glanced at the infernal ticking carriage clock and saw that it was already 5.20pm. There wasn't much time before supper or before Cat came in to remind him about it. 'I forget too many things these days,' he said to Evie, pausing for a moment and trying to remember what it was he wanted to make a note of. 'I need to write everything down before it slips away.' He thought for another moment longer then scribbled something else down on his list. When he finished he reread what he'd written before resting his head on the back of the armchair.

'It's been quite a summer,' he said.

'It has that,' Evie agreed.

'I think I put things in order,' he said.

'You most definitely did,' Evie agreed.

ANNA

When they found him, he was sitting in his chair with the little leather notebook on his lap, open on a page where he'd written several notes in pencil. Anna's mother gently moved the notebook and placed it on his table where he kept his crossword and pen. 'He's definitely gone, Anna,' she said gently. Anna sunk down on the new armchair and covered her face with her hands while Cat circled around her before jumping onto the arm of her chair, hungry for his supper, nudging her with the top of his head.

'We didn't get to say goodbye,' she sobbed, pressing the

palms of her hands hard against her eyes until she could see swirling lights behind her eyelids. She gasped for air and leant forward in her armchair, her pain crushing her insides until she thought she couldn't breathe, then she knelt down by his armchair and held his hand, his gnarly old fingers cold against hers.

Later, when her grandfather had been taken away and they were alone in the sitting room of his little schoolhouse, Helene sunk down in his empty armchair. 'Oh, Dad,' she sighed, running her hands over the arms of his chair, stroking its tartan upholstery as if he were part of it. 'You know, he never liked this thing?' she said, taking the carriage clock from the mantelpiece and removing the batteries. 'Hated it in fact. Nearly forty years he was in the Corporation. He must have thought he wasn't worth more to them than a bloody clock.' She placed it back down and reached across to where Anna was sitting and squeezed her hand tightly. 'It's funny, I never sit in that new armchair of yours. I always sit in my mum's chair. I like it. It makes me feel as if I'm close to her again, as if her chair is part of her somehow... and now I'm doing it with Dad's chair.' She looked up at Anna, who still had fat tears running down her face. 'I think, though, that we crossed the bridge between us in the end, your grandfather and I.' Anna didn't reply, for no words would come to her lips.

They sat together like that for some time, the evening bringing a quiet darkness into the room, Cat at their feet licking his paws, the carriage clock silenced at last, and at some point, when they could hardly see each other through the dark, Anna uncurled herself from the armchair and put the light on. Then she crept into the kitchen to make Helene a cup of tea and herself an instant chocolate, gulping down great hiccups of pain again while her grandfather's old kettle boiled.

'Look, he's made a list.' Helene was holding his little leather notebook in her hands when Anna returned to the sitting room with their drinks. 'He must have been planning to tell me all this at some point. Listen to this.' Even though Anna's eyes were swollen from crying she could tell that Helene was surprised by what she'd found in the notebook and sat down to hear her grandfather's last words. 'One,' she began, 'tell Helene to do whatever she wants with the house. Sell it or keep it, never be a slave to it.' Helene sniffed and blew her nose loudly into a crumpled tissue then wiped the back of her hand across her eyes. 'Oh, Anna, he's given me the house. It's mine... *ours*. And... oh listen to this... *two*, tell Helene about selling all the grassland and the monies from that.'

She slowly lowered the notebook and looked at Anna, her jaw hanging down in shock. 'Anna, the grassland was *huge*. It belonged to the house when it was still a school but I never knew my mum and dad owned it. He must have been the one to sell it to builders... to build all those new houses... like Jacob's.' They looked at each other in shock and uttered, '*development*' both at the same time.

'But Grandad hated development.' Anna was confused. 'He would *never* have done that.'

'Well, he did because listen... *number three*... tell Helene about the *Trust Fund* set up from some of the proceeds of the sale, in the name of Anna Evelyn Maybury.' She placed the book down on her lap then and gasped, and her mouth twisted into knots as she began to cry. 'I visited him when you were just a little thing strapped into the child seat in the back of my car, and the grasslands were there then. He stood on his doorstep just looking over at my car where you were, and didn't make any attempt to see you. He must have sold the land directly afterwards. He did care after all. He did it for you, Anna… he did it for both of us. Oh, Dad.'

Anna's heart was doing flips in her chest. For all those years her grandad had been thinking of them both and making plans for their future. How complicated the relationship had been between her mother and her grandfather, how fragile the love they shared, neither of them perfect and neither of them blameless. Yet, she realised then that if Derek had never turned Harry's head and they had never come to the little schoolhouse, that fragile love would have been lost forever. She knew now that if you managed to jump the hurdles that life threw at you, you may find better things on the other side.

They sat for hours together like two owls in the night, trying to take everything on board, unable to bring themselves to end the last day that would ever start with Algernon Edward Maybury still alive. Helene stayed sitting in his chair absentmindedly stroking the fabric of it, and Anna felt as if her mother was sitting on the ghost of him. She imagined him complaining about it, having a right old go as he squeezed his way past her. *We will take you back to Cornwall, Grandad,* she promised him silently. *To the place where the ancient bridge spans the River Fal. We will put you together again with Evie, along with the ashes of the reins belonging to a horse called Firefly. We will check the direction of the wind and shake you both free.*

It was Helene who eventually tore the silence into two. 'We

don't have to rent that little flat I found now,' she said. 'We can do what we want.' Anna saw how she continued to stroke the fabric of her grandfather's chair. She could see how totally exhausted her mother was, ravaged by the events of the day combined with regret for all the lost moments with her father. A lot had happened since she'd painted the mural of the moon and the bright red kite in her bedroom back at Harry's. Although the string of the kite she'd imagined letting go of all those months ago still bobbed about, its string trailing loose, it was closer now, as if she could reach out and pluck it from the air.

Choices they had never thought possible were open to them. She closed her eyes for a moment and imagined herself doing what she had wanted to do for so many months: walking into her old school wearing blue ribbons in her hair and being folded back into the embrace of all her old friends. For a moment she hugged the familiarity of her old life. Then, in her mind's eye, she released it all, like Chinese lanterns floating the golden flames of her memories into the sky.

She thought of how happy her mother was now. She thought of how much she loved living next door to Jacob, of how much she loved Little Argel and her sailboat bed. She thought of her art teacher Miss Angelico, and of her new friend at school who she now ate her lunch with. She thought of the quirky little schoolhouse with the beautiful garden and the wisteria that tumbled over the great big windows. This little schoolhouse was the place where broken hearts had been mended. It was the place where fragile love had found a way to grow. She imagined her grandfather now standing beside his chair, reaching for her grandma's hand and giving her a silent nod of approval to stop dwelling in the past.

'I think Grandad would tell us to raise the anchor and start sailing,' she offered.

'What does that mean?' Helene asked with a questioning look.

Anna sighed contentedly as she ran her hand along Cat's soft grey fur. 'It means, I think we're home.'

18

A Keepsake

ANNA

Anna and Helene sat on the bare mattress of her grandfather's bed. The bed had been stripped several days ago, the linen washed, dried and folded carefully before being put in a charity bag along with the embroidered floral counterpane. The old brown wardrobe at the end of the room had both doors open, the rail still with her grandfather's and her grandma's clothes hanging neatly, their shoes in boxes on the wardrobe floor. A navy-blue wide-brimmed hat was on the top shelf, dust gathering in silk flowers stitched to the band. Her grandfather's ties were hanging on a rack on the wardrobe door. The green tie with the red spots was there, the one he'd worn on the first day of their arrival.

On his bedside table was the blue ribbon that had secured the wrapping paper of the 'swapsies' gift she'd once given him. He had tied it in a bow and kept it. Without a doubt, even though he had never voiced it, he had loved her. She tucked the ribbon into the front pocket of her purple dungarees and pressed it next to her heart. Alongside where the ribbon had been was the photograph of him with her and Jacob taken by the waiter at the hotel in St Mawes. She'd had it printed, enlarged and framed for him. Printed in black and white with the coloured sunglasses they had each been wearing digitally enhanced. Blue for Anna, pink for Jacob and yellow for her grandfather. In the photograph he was smiling. A smile as wide as the one of him taken decades ago in *River Pisky*. He had, Anna was certain, found happiness again. She kissed the pad of her finger and pressed it against his photograph.

Between where they sat was an old hatbox that Helene had found under the bed. Inside the box there were letters. Lots of letters, photographs and trinkets and all sorts of things that her grandparents must have kept for years. Helene pulled out a clump of envelopes held together with a band. 'There are so many,' she said, giving another clump to Anna. 'Letters from your grandma to your grandad. Letters from your grandad to your grandma. Letters from Grandad's parents to him and letters from Grandma's parents to her. They've kept them all… and look here…' Helene held up an open letter, scribed in impossibly cursive handwriting. 'This looks like one he must have written to his parents from boarding school… it's dated 1931!'

'Did they even have pen and paper back then?' Anna joked.

'Funny,' Helene replied. Then she opened a large manila envelope and pulled out some handmade cards and Anna noticed how a tear suddenly bulged and glistened in the corner of her mother's eyes. 'Oh, look. My Father's Day cards to him. He has kept every single one.' She pressed them to her chest and the tear released itself and slid down her cheek. Anna reached her hand out and placed it on Helene's knee. 'It's fine. I'm fine,' she said, wiping at the tearstain as another fell from the other eye. 'There's so much in here. Decades of memories. It's as if your grandma and grandad left something of themselves behind for me... for *us* and it's... it's wonderful, that's what it is.'

Anna dipped her hand into the box, realising that everything in there had a story behind it, like her bed in Little Argel. Everything had once belonged to lives and a time she knew little about and yet held the echoes of her own amazing family. She ran the pad of her finger over a silver medal that had a dancer on it, an old coin and a brooch with the brightest of feathers caught behind a dome of glass.

'I think we should make two very large hot chocolates and start going through these things,' Helene said, sniffing back the threat of more tears. 'I didn't understand my dad while he was alive but now, maybe thanks to these letters, I can get to know him better.'

'I know that he could gallop a horse and sail a boat, and that he rode a motorbike with Grandma on the back,' Anna said, studying a little gold locket on a chain. 'And I know that he wanted to fly forever instead of being tied to a desk.' She pulled at a tiny catch on the locket to reveal two tiny photographs of people she didn't know.

'I'm glad he opened up to you before it was too late,' Helene said. 'He tried to tell us he loved us in his own way, didn't he?'

Anna nodded, hoping that wherever her grandfather was he might know that she had loved him too and that she had tried to tell him that the night she took him sailing to the moon in Little Argel. She missed him so much and wished with all her heart she could have one more day with him. 'Could I have something of his please... from the box? A keepsake.' She picked more things up carefully before putting them back in their place – another brooch, a delicate watch, a thimble souvenir of St Michael Penkivel in Cornwall.

'Take your pick,' Helene answered, examining the little photographs in the locket that Anna had found.

'I like this. What is it?' Anna held out an embroidered badge that fitted snugly into the palm of her hand. 'It's like the wings of a bird but in the shape of Grandad's moustache.' Helene reached out and took it, smiling fondly at it.

'Gosh I recognise this. It's strange that you picked it out because I'm sure that out of everything here he'd want you to have it.'

'But what is it?' Anna took it back and held it again in the palm of her hand while Helene quickly rifled through a pile of old photographs in the box until she found what she was looking for. She held it up for Anna to see. There, in a black and white photograph was her grandfather, taken at a time before life stole his dreams. He was wearing a Royal Air Force uniform, a peaked cap over his sandy blonde hair and was smiling broadly beneath his carefully trimmed moustache. On the left breast of his uniform was the very same badge she was holding.

'Oh,' Anna breathed, as she ran the pad of her finger over the stitched silken embroidery. 'It's his wings.'

Acknowledgements

The idea to write this story began as an ode to my late father so that I could better understand the kind of man he was when he was alive. As a result, it became very much a family affair. My sister Pam Pugh (nee Shrimpton) supported me every step of the way, through endless phone calls and her amazing attention to detail, until at last 'Anna' and 'Algernon' found a story of their own. My sister and I shared hundreds of memories over the months and never in our lifetime have we laughed and cried so much together. Thank you, Pam, from the bottom of my heart.

Thank you to my lovely agent Broo Doherty for your enthusiasm and tireless support and for pushing this book under the nose of the wonderfully dynamic Thorne Ryan, without whom it would not have landed with the amazing team at Aria Fiction. Thank you to Rachel Faulkner-Willcocks and everyone at Aria for all being fabulous.

I would also like to thank my cousin Guy Shrimpton for coming with me on exciting adventures in Cornwall to visit our family haunts and to share snippets of the lives of our fathers Peter Shrimpton and Paul Shrimpton, and of their brother, our Uncle Stephen (Terry) Shrimpton. Thank you, Uncle Terry, for emailing me to share your wonderful memories of growing up in Cornwall.

Thank you to my brother-in-law Rip Pugh for reaching inside and sharing your memories of boarding school.

Thank you to David, my very patient husband for listening quietly when I wanted to talk bookish blurb and to Geraldine Davey for enthusiastically joining in when I wanted to talk bookish blurb.

Finally, a heartfelt thank you to my daughter Rebecca Katelyn for finding a way through the difficult process of changing schools, for emerging with grace, and for being the most colourful person I know.

Author's Note

The inspiration to write this book came to me on a beautifully sunny day in 2020. My sister and I were sitting in the garden of her home beginning the task of looking through the large box we'd found in our parents' house after their passing. In the box we found a treasure trove of letters, photographs and postcards spanning several decades, all from various family members no longer with us. Having the most marvellous time, we laughed, sighed and drank coffee as we unearthed a host of fabulous memories. Amongst everything, we came across a pile of letters tied with ribbon that our father had sent to our mother over 70 years ago. One of these envelopes, however, was plumper than the others. Inside, dated 1947, was an 8 page, double-sided, handwritten letter headed Nairobi, Kenya. I can honestly say that the contents of it quite literally took our breath away. We put down our coffees, held the sheets of thin, time worn paper in our hands and together we cried.

The father we knew had been a man of few words. He'd been difficult to understand and would close down easily when asked to talk of his life. We knew that he was raised in

Cornwall, that he was educated in a strict Catholic boarding school, that he loved our mother and that he used to be a pilot in the RAF but beyond that he gave very little away. On that sunny day in 2020, the letter my sister and I found told of a very different man from the one we thought he'd been.

This letter was scribed from the heart. A heart that was big, deep, and full with passion for life. The letter was written, not by someone who had little to say but by someone who was capable of sharing his dreams and aspirations.

Through the looped and inky writing he wrote of his life in the RAF. He described his love for flying, of the roar of engines in endless skies, and of the rivers, mountains and deserts of Africa. We read how our father had danced in the mountains of Africa and, in his own words, he'd *had a wizard time*. We read how he wanted to tell our mother *what a glorious trip I have had so far and there is more to come*.

Sadly, there was no more to come.

After writing this letter, and before he made it home to Cornwall, the military truck he was travelling on in Egypt was involved in a crash. Suffice to say, that although our father survived the terrible injuries he endured, he was unable to stay in the RAF. He never flew again. We realise now that he had carried the emotional, along with the physical, scars of losing his dreams, for the rest of his life.

And so, the inspiration, or even perhaps the need, to understand my father better through my writing began and 'Algernon' was born.

I have included a few of the pages and extracts from this letter that particularly struck me, and which fed into the creation of Algernon.

The inspiration for 'Anna' came from my daughter.

At fifteen years old she had to endure moving house and changing schools due to my husband's work commitments. At a horribly vulnerable age for such a move she sadly struggled at school and I had to watch my artistic, vibrant, and so very colourful, daughter begin to fade. I wanted so much to give her a safe space, to give her a best friend and for her to find her true value in life. Having coped with this period of loneliness and anxiety she bravely triumphed, ultimately spreading her beautiful butterfly wings to become the confident and amazing person she is today.

In the writing of *Every Shade of Happy*, I have taken the essence of two people – one at the end of his life and one at the beginning of hers – and I have introduced them to each other.

Together Anna and Algernon teach each other how to put the colour back into their lonely lives.

Phyllida Shrimpton
January 2022

1

Nairobi
Kenya.
13·4·47.

My Dear Shirley,
"2000 Miles into Africa" by 'Shrimp'.
On Tuesday 4 March I flew
an Anson up to Cairo and landed there
in spite of a lot of bad weather and very
low cloud. Then I went over to the otherside
of the airdrome and thoroughly inspected
the Anson I was supposed to fly to Nairobi.
Whilst inspecting this aircraft
I met w/c Delap who was to fly the other
aircraft which was also going. We took our
respective aircraft into the air for half an
hour to see how they behaved, and
returned with the hopes of them lasting
for the journey.
We then went with our
crews to Head Quarters for briefing where
I learnt that I was to be responsible for
the flight as the 'Wenco' had had no

experience in Route Flying in Africa

Seven thirty on the
morning of the fifth saw us both airborne
and heading Southwards towards a horizon
of rocks and sand. Gradually the Nile
dissappeared on our right leaving two
small aircraft suspended between a
canopy of blue and a floor of rusty
golden desert, scarred by the beds of
dried up water coursed and crumbling
hills.

On and On with a
feeling of great detatchment, as if
there were no one else in the universe,
and the other aircraft on our left
was non existant. Nothing of interest
below, no life no trees no fields,
until at last the meandering course
of the Nile brought that mighty river
once again into sight.

Gradually our two

'mike' I said to the 'Winco' you take starboard
I'll take port, over the air came a verry hurried
comment from Malakal flying control who thought
we were going to beat up the drome. However
after we had shown the boat what the
top of our aircraft was like we went on
and landed.

The next morning the Winco
could not get his aircraft started so I took
off and spent a verry happy ¼ hour really
beating up the drome, I had a wizard
time. When the other aircraft was
eventually airborne we set course for Juba.
This time I flew at about 500 feet over the
land which was becoming more densely
vegitated. We saw a few giraffe, and
just before reaching Juba we saw about
fifty Elephants.

At Juba we stopped for the
night at another excellent hotel. We had
a swim and a game of tennis, and then

13

Now I am writing for the Wellington which is going to take me to Aden on Friday via Mogadisu. But what a glorious trip I have had so far and there is more to come. So it any or wonder that this poor mortal does not want to leave this air force.

I know that when I get home, which I hope to be by the last few days in april, I shall have a lot of talking to do to you, about all the places I have been too.

Well Darling I think that I have written enough for today, any-way I think that my arm will refuse to work before long. Please overlook any spelling mistakes as I have no one to correct my errors.

Yours with love
Peter

About the Author

PHYLLIDA SHRIMPTON obtained a postgraduate degree in Human Resource Management, a career choice which was almost as disastrous as her cooking. Thankfully her love of books and writing led her to a new career as an author. Her young adult novel *Sunflowers in February* won the Red Book Award for YA Fiction in 2019. Having lived in London, The Netherlands and the Cotswolds with her husband, daughter, giant Saint Bernard and grumpy old terrier, she now lives on the Essex Coast in a place she likes to describe as being where the river meets the sea. *Every Shade of Happy* is her first adult novel.